CRITICAL CONDITIONS

CRITICAL
CONDITIONS

STEPHEN
WHITE

A DUTTON BOOK

DUTTON
Published by the Penguin Group
Penguin Putnam Inc., 375 Hudson Street, New York, New York 10014, U.S.A.
Penguin Books Ltd, 27 Wrights Lane, London W8 5TZ, England
Penguin Books Australia Ltd, Ringwood, Victoria, Australia
Penguin Books Canada Ltd, 10 Alcorn Avenue, Toronto, Ontario, Canada M4V 3B2
Penguin Books (N.Z.) Ltd, 182–190 Wairau Road, Auckland 10, New Zealand

Penguin Books Ltd, Registered Offices: Harmondsworth, Middlesex, England

First published by Dutton, an imprint of Dutton Signet, a member of Penguin Putnam Inc.

First Printing, March, 1998
10 9 8 7 6 5 4 3 2 1

 REGISTERED TRADEMARK—MARCA REGISTRADA

LIBRARY OF CONGRESS CATALOGING-IN-PUBLICATION DATA
White, Stephen Walsh.
    Critical conditions / Stephen White.
        p.   cm.
    ISBN 0-525-94270-X (acid-free paper)
    I. Title.
  PS3573.H47477C7   1998
813'.54—dc21   97-34056
                                                                    CIP

Printed in the United States of America
Set in Goudy

PUBLISHER'S NOTE

This book is printed on acid-free paper. ∞

to Al Silverman
one was a privilege, six is an honor

The law,
in its majestic equality,
forbids the rich
as well as the poor
to sleep under bridges,
to beg in the streets,
and to steal bread.

—Anatole France

Freedom's just another word
for nothing left to lose.

—Kris Kristofferson
"Me and Bobby McGee"

I hold the hands of people I never touch.

I provide comfort to people I never embrace.

I watch people walk into brick walls, the same ones over and over again, and I coax them to turn around and try to walk in a different direction.

People rarely see me gladly. As a rule, I catch the residue of their despair. I see people who are broken, and people who only think they are broken. I see people who have had their faces rubbed in their failures. I see weak people wanting anesthesia and strong people who wonder what they have done to make such an enemy of fate. I am often the final pit stop people take before they crawl across the finish line that is marked: I give up.

Some people beg me to help.

Some people dare me to help.

Sometimes the beggars and dare-ers look the same. Absolutely the same. I'm supposed to know how to tell them apart.

Some people who visit me need scar tissue to cover their wounds. Some people who visit me need their wounds opened further, explored for signs of infection and contamination. I make those calls, too.

Some days I'm invigorated by it all. Some days I'm numbed.

Always, I'm humbled by the role of helper.

And, occasionally, I'm ambushed.

One

Diane Estevez poked her head into my office at twelve-thirty. "You free for lunch?" she asked.

I try not to schedule appointments on Friday afternoon and had nothing on my calendar until three o'clock, when I had to pick up Lauren at the District Attorney's office to drive her to DIA for a flight to Washington. Her mother had just been hospitalized with a suspected heart attack, and my wife was heading home to be with her family.

I answered Diane, "Yes, as a matter of fact, lunch sounds great. We haven't done that for a while."

"I have one call to make, then I'm ready. How about Jax? Is Jax okay?"

"Jax is good."

Diane went to make her call, and I locked away a couple of charts that were on my desk. She and I share an old Victorian house that we had renovated to house our clinical psychology practices. At the time we made the financial leap of faith required to invest in the building, we both had thriving fee-for-service practices that paid the bills and rewarded us handsomely for our labor. Over the last few years, though, changes in health care financing had altered the landscape for most health care providers, us included.

Diane and I had adopted different strategies to confront the revolution in the way health care was provided and paid for. She went into the psychological evaluation business with a vengeance, while I retreated into the narrow oasis of doing only fee-for-service psychotherapy. The commonality between us was that neither of us belonged to any managed care rosters of certified or approved providers if that membership required that we either reduce our fee or agree in advance to limit the care we might provide to our patients.

In the managed-care revolution, we were saboteurs. Fortunately, it was a luxury we could each afford. She had a wealthy husband. I had a working wife and a lot of experience living on lean income.

Jax Fish House, where Diane wanted to have lunch, was on the west end of Pearl Street in Boulder, only a couple of blocks away from our offices on Walnut. She arrived first and settled onto the chair I would have chosen if she had offered me the choice, which she never did.

She snapped open her napkin and draped it over her lap. "So, you ready? 'Cause this is what's going on—I got a call from John Trent today. You know Trent?"

I thought I had heard the name. "He's a psychologist, right? I think I may have met him at the IDC luncheon you dragged me to. But I don't really know him." IDC is the Interdisciplinary Committee on Child Custody, a group of mental health professionals, lawyers, and judges intent on making the process of determining child custody more humane. To me, the committee's task felt, at best, Sisyphisian, at worst, quixotic. Diane was an officer and a recruiter for the organization. I was one of her recruiting failures.

"Yeah, he's the one. John's kind of new in town, what, eight months, a year, something like that? Maybe not that long. He's from the Midwest somewhere, Kansas maybe, he's been trying to get established. He does gatekeeping out at Prairie View Hospital, does custody evals, and some forensic work at the jail. Anyway, I'm indirectly involved with a custody case with him, nothing special, really, a run-of-the-mill Boulder divorce." She watched me fumble with the bread on the table. "You paying attention here? I'm not just talking for exercise, you know. The details are important."

"Every word, Diane. I'm hearing every word."

"Okay. This is what it is, then, the custody eval? My psychotherapy patient is the husband-slash-father. He's a decent guy with some character flaws that I certainly wouldn't put up with for a weekend, but then I wouldn't have married him, would I? Still, he has a heart the size of Bill Gates's wallet and some parental instincts that you just can't train. Okay?"

I nodded and kept eye contact. I really wanted to open my menu. I didn't dare.

"The wife-slash-mother isn't in treatment with anyone, but I suspect she's a narcissistic personality disorder who sucks Absolut when her kids aren't around. She's been investigated twice by Social Services—once for psychological abuse after she threw a tantrum at her daughter's school, once for neglect after she stranded her kids with a babysitter while she slept off a binge."

"I'm with you so far."

"My patient—the father—files for divorce awhile back and asks for custody of the kids. Girl, seven, girl, four. Court assigns the custody eval to John Trent and a social worker named Dani Wu who he's teamed up with to do evals. I know Dani from IDC. She's good people. She's good with kids, I like her work."

Our waiter dropped by. "Hello," he said, "welcome to Jax. May I bring you something to drink?"

Before my lips had parted, Diane said, "Iced tea? Alan, that okay with you?" Lifting her eyes to the waiter, she said, "Make it two, no no no, don't leave. Alan, you like specials?"

"Generally I do, but—" I held up the menu forlornly.

She faced the waiter. "Good. We'll have two specials. And some bread, please, and thank you." She sipped at her water and turned back to me. "If that was rude, and I'm relatively certain it was, forgive me, but I have to get back for a two o'clock and sometimes waiters disappear for so long in this town that I start looking for their pictures on milk cartons."

She wanted me to smile, so I did. When I didn't get a chance to be with Diane for a while, I really missed her.

"So back to John Trent. From my point of view, custody determination is a no-brainer. Both my patient and his wife are flawed, but if my patient has a common cold, his once-beloved has Ebola. My patient has warned me from the start that it wasn't going to be easy. His wife's father, it turns out, is connected big-time, like with gold-plated Monster Cable. He's some super Republican muckety-muck from La Junta, you know, is friends with George and Barbara, golfs with Gerald in Beaver Creek, advises Newt about PR, is on Colin's Christmas card list. You get my drift?"

"Yes." I also got my iced tea. I squeezed a lemon into it and stirred in a packet of sugar. I liked the sweetener that came in either the blue packet or the pink packet but I could never remember which one I liked, so I used sugar unless Lauren was around to remind me whether I preferred the pink or the blue.

"That's not all my patient is up against. Not only is his wife's father connected, it turns out her sister is married to some entrepreneur gazillionaire."

"I'm with you."

"Good. So the custody eval starts a month ago. John Trent seems like he knows what he's doing with it. He gets the appropriate releases and does a heads-up interview with my patient. Dani Wu sees the kids. Trent calls me once to ask my opinions and find out how the treatment is going. Between the lines he's letting me know everything is going to come out like I think it's going to come out. Kids will live with my patient, with liberal visitation for Mom."

"But."

"Yeah. 'But.' But earlier this week Trent calls again and says there are some new developments he's checking out and that I shouldn't jump to any conclusions about his recommendations, and he implies that now he's leaning toward Mom."

"And?"

"And nothing. That's it. What do you think?"

"About what?"

"About the possibility that Trent's been compromised by all these power animals that the wife is related to?"

"Sounds far-fetched, Diane. For now I would just take him at his word. See what he has. Maybe the eval revealed some things you don't know."

Diane sat back on her chair and lifted her iced tea for the first time. After scoffing at my suggestion that there were things she didn't know, she said, "Heck, I buy lunch for my favorite conspiracy theorist and this is all I get. I was hoping for a little more Oliver Stone–type intrigue from you."

"Sorry. Seriously, how much leverage do political types have with people like us, Diane? What can they do? Anyway, you're talking about interfering with a judicial procedure. The consequences would be devastating if that ever got out. The politicians are much more vulnerable in this situation than John Trent is."

The specials arrived. Halibut in a chunky tomato broth with capers and chilis. I tasted it. It was delicious. I said, "You're lucky this is good."

She felt all around her on the bench and looked on the floor beside her chair. "And you're lucky I didn't order any wine. I think I forgot to bring my purse. You're buying. You've heard about Trent's kid?"

Diane usually forgot her purse. I knew I was buying. I said, "No. What about his kid?"

"Diagnosed with some terrible heart virus. Apparently it's destroying her heart muscle. She's real sick. It's been on the news because of some insurance problems."

"What kind of insurance problems?"

"One of the usual kinds. The insurers say the treatment the doctors want is experimental and the policy doesn't cover it."

I sighed at the familiar refrain. "That's awful. How old is his kid?"

"Just a baby. Two and a half, I think."

"Where's she being treated? Children's?"

"Yeah."

"How bad is it?"

"Bad. Apparently, once the heart muscle is infected, the condition is often terminal."

"God. What about a heart transplant? The insurance will pay for that, won't they?"

"A cardiologist friend of mine—you know Harriet Lowenstein?—says the problem is the virus. They don't know how to kill it. If they go ahead and plop in a new heart, it might get infected just like the old one."

My food was getting cold. I was losing my appetite.

Diane continued eating between sentences. "John Trent is married to that investigative reporter who's new on Channel 7. You know that at least, don't you?"

"I don't watch much television news these days. It stopped being fun last fall. And you know better than anyone that I'm not included in the local gossip circles. If you haven't told me something interesting, then I probably don't know anything about it."

The mention of the events of the previous autumn caused a temporary hush between us. Diane's husband, Raoul, had been an important part of all that. We didn't mention it often now.

She dipped a crust of bread in some broth and left it on the lip of her plate. "Well, Trent's wife—Brenda—is one of those investigative types, specializes in uncovering graft in government and business and industry.

Her first big thing had to do with plastic recyclers. She apparently had them shaking in their recycled vinyl boots over kickbacks that were being shoveled to some local politicians."

"Oh, I did hear about that, maybe from Lauren. One of the district attorneys involved asked Boulder County to supply a special prosecutor, I think. Didn't some politicians have to resign?"

"Two mayors and a city manager that I know of. One of the mayors, I think from Thornton or Northglenn, even tried to kill himself. His wife walked into their garage, found him hanging from the rafters next to their Buick, and had herself a heart attack on the spot. Turns out the mayor wasn't actually dead. He was just hanging there asphyxiating watching his wife have a coronary."

Hearing that story, I should have totally lost my appetite. I did. "Did the guy live?"

"Not exactly the word I would choose to use, but he did survive."

"What about the wife?"

"Noop."

I used a sip of iced tea to cover my distaste with the story. "I bet Trent's wife makes some enemies doing that kind of work."

Diane shrugged. "Probably no more than a custody evaluator, though."

"Touché. I guess you get used to it."

"Have to be thick-skinned, like me. It's part of the territory. She and John moved here for her career. He gave up a good practice for her. I have to remember that about him, give him some rope. It's another sign that John Trent must be a progressive thinker."

My ex-wife had been a producer at one of the Denver TV stations and I was well aware of the musical-chairs nature of local news markets. If John Trent and his wife had really moved to Denver from Kansas, she was moving from a small market to a much larger one. The pressure would be on.

I said, "I don't know about that, Diane. But he must be a pretty devastated daddy. Are you worried that the situation with his daughter may be interfering with his judgment about the custody eval?"

"I've thought about it, but, you know, you and I have both gone through tough times and managed to get our work done. I'll give John Trent the benefit of the doubt, too."

"This is worse than anything you or I have gone through, don't kid yourself. A sick baby? That's as bad as it gets."

"You're probably right, but I'm not just blowing smoke about this political angle. Everybody can be goosed. I don't trust what I'm seeing with this case. Custody-wise, it's open-and-shut."

One of Diane's few faults was a tendency toward transient clinical myopia. "You always think you know best. You don't know that it's open-and-shut; you're only seeing one side of it. He's doing the eval, he's talked to everybody, and you haven't. Maybe he discovered something. Raoul knows all those people, doesn't he? The people you're concerned about, the conservative money crowd? What does he say?"

"He says leave him out of it."

"Your husband is a wise man, Diane. I think I'll take his advice. Why don't you leave me out of it, too?"

"You're both wimps, you know that?"

"I won't speak for Raoul, Diane, but I certainly am."

Her tone didn't change noticeably as she asked, "How's Lauren doing?"

Diane's voice had changed fractionally, just enough to let me know she was asking about my wife's battle with multiple sclerosis. I said, "Better than last fall, not as good as last summer."

"Any progress?"

"Slow. Too slow for her taste."

"How's the new medicine working?"

"Too soon to tell. But it makes her pretty sick."

"How are you doing with it?"

"Better than last fall, not as good as last summer."

Diane looked away. She said, "I can see how hard it is for you."

I said, "Thanks. Lauren's off to Washington this afternoon." I looked at my watch. "Couple of hours. It looks like her mother may have had an MI last night."

"Oh, my. How is she?"

"Stable, apparently. She's in coronary care. All the kids are rushing home."

"Lauren doing okay? She doesn't need this kind of stress, does she?"

"No, she doesn't need the stress. What can you do? Things are worse for John Trent, right?"

Two

Adrenaline affects my friend Adrienne in the same paradoxical way that Ritalin affects hyperactive kids. It seems to calm her down.

On Saturday morning, as I was pushing my bicycle through the front door after doing ninety hard minutes on the hilly roads of eastern Boulder County, the phone rang. I was tempted to let the machine catch the call; I wanted to get out of my sweaty Lycra, I needed fluids, and I was desperate for a shower. But I answered anyway, hoping it might be Lauren with some news about her mother.

Adrienne said, "Hey, Alan, how you doing? It's me." The casualness of her greeting alerted me that something might be up; as often as not she didn't even bother to say hello when she phoned. "Hey, you doing anything? You busy right now? I have someone I think you should see."

I paused a second as I greeted my dog, Emily, who was pushing her flank against me forcefully, as though I were a sheep she was planning to herd to a different pasture. My pause was also intended to allow Adrienne an opportunity to explain what she wanted. When she didn't, I said, "I just got in from a ride. Where are you, at your house? What's up?"

Adrienne, a urologist, and her young son, Jonas, were our only nearby neighbors. They lived just up the hill from Lauren and me, in a renovated farmhouse that sat on a rise across the gravel and dirt lane.

"No, I'm at the hospital. Been playing Zorro with bladder cancer in the OR since seven. Just when I finished up the operation, Marty Klein found me and asked me to consult on an ER case, an adolescent female overdose. You know Marty, don't you?"

"Yeah, I know—"

"I'm still here doing the consult, and I think you should see her, too—the kid."

"Isn't there a psychiatrist on call for that?" Although I did occasional psychological liaison work at the hospital, I didn't routinely consult in the hospital ER, probably hadn't seen a case there in two years.

Impatience crept into Adrienne's voice. "I didn't say I think *somebody* should see her, Alan. I said I think *you* should see her. Can you hear the difference?" She paused. "Anyway, Levitt's on call."

Whenever Adrienne had an impulse to assail the mental health profession—not an infrequent urge on her part—Natt Levitt, M.D., was her incompetent-practice poster child. His name at the top of the ER on-call roster helped explain why I was being drafted to see the adolescent overdose.

I asked, "What's the kid's condition?"

"She's critical. Her vitals are . . . her vitals are shit. Consciousness is waxing and waning. Her kidney function is way whacked, and she has gross hematuria, which is why Marty wanted me on board. She's on her way to the ICU soon."

The severity of the girl's condition was unnerving. Adolescent suicidal behavior is a crapshoot. Sometimes it's manipulative and benign, sometimes it's lethal as hell. Sometimes the kid screws up and actually kills herself when she doesn't really intend to.

I asked, "Why does she have blood in her urine? She take aspirin?"

"Don't know what she took. But ultrasound indicates a perinephric hematoma. We'll confirm with CT."

"Which means what in English?"

"She has a mild renal contusion, a little rip in her kidney. So she's bleeding into her bladder."

"What can cause that?"

"Fifty different things. Little traumas. Falling out of bed, tripping over a cat. Punch in the gut."

"Any idea about the precipitant? What does the family have to say? Did she just break up with someone? Problem at school? What?"

"We don't know anything. Family isn't here. Police say a frantic kid—called herself a girlfriend—found the patient unresponsive, called 911. The friend left the front door of the house open for the ambulance, but she wasn't there when the paramedics arrived. The kid's parents are nowhere to be found. The police are trying to find everybody involved. But we're pretty much in the dark."

"Has she been oriented enough to say anything since she was brought in?"

"Not to me. Marty said she asked about her sister. Twice, I think he said. She said, 'Is she all right?' Something like that."

"And her sister's not around?"

"No, I haven't seen anybody with her, you know, visiting."

"Has anyone checked the house for the sister? This could have been some kind of suicide pact."

"I hadn't thought of that. The police went over to the house after the ambulance picked her up. I'll phone and make sure that they looked around real well."

"The kid hasn't spoken to you, Ren?"

"No, since I've been down here she's been in the ozone."

"Is she going to make it?"

"She's just a girl, Alan. She damn well better make it."

"What did she take?"

"Like I said, we don't know; it's polydrug, probably a cocktail. She responded to Narcan, so some narcotics for sure, and it looks like three, four, five other drugs, maybe more. There was a lot of stuff in the house. We'll be sorting out the toxicology for a while."

"Why—"

"Because I think you're the right one to see her. That's why."

"That's not what I was about to ask." It actually was, but I wasn't about to admit it. "What about the attending? You said it's Marty Klein? Is he okay with me seeing his patient? He's the one who'll have to absorb the flack when Natt Levitt finds out he wasn't called first."

"Done. Marty doesn't like Natt any more than I do. Does anybody like Natt? What keeps him around? I don't get it. Since when is having a medical license supposed to provide as much security as having tenure? But Natt's not your problem, he's mine. The order is written."

"Well—"

Adrienne laughed. "Most of the time I'm irresistible, aren't I?"

Adrienne was a true friend. And she asked few favors, professionally or otherwise. "Yes, Ren, you are." I glanced at my watch. "I have to shower first. I'll try and be there by eleven."

"I'm sure she'll be in the ICU by then. Look for us upstairs. And Alan, one more thing."

"Yes."

"I don't think it's too likely you'll get reimbursed on this."

So what else is new. "No insurance?"

"Worse, I'm afraid. We're not totally sure of her identity, but if she's who we think she is, admission records for a previous ER visit for a finger laceration show that, back then at least, she was MedExcel. Are you a provider?"

"I was. MedExcel and I didn't see eye to eye."

"What do you mean?"

"Slight difference in philosophy. They wanted to run the treatment and I sort of thought that was my role. I wanted to be paid and they thought that was pushy of me. Little conflicts like that."

Her tone was mildly admonishing as she said, "You're just too sensitive for the current managed care environment. There are worse companies than MedExcel, let me tell you."

"I don't want to know about them."

"But you'll see her anyway?"

"Sure, I'll send you the bill, Ren. You're rich."

She found my threat amusing, "Go right ahead. If you think insurance companies are hard to deal with, wait till you try to get a dime out of me."

I took a quick shower and thought about Lauren. She was, I guessed, sitting by her mother's bedside in a hospital in eastern Washington. Had she been home, I think she might have said something to caution me about what I was doing.

I ate a banana and some toast and peanut butter, and poured a cup of coffee for the road. Emily's dish had plenty of fresh water.

I have found every intensive care unit I have ever visited to be an eerie place. Almost by definition, ICUs are hallowed temples of tragedy or triumph. The final results of the labors there are binary, either a zero or a one. The practitioners are either heroes or they are failures. The mood in the space, in the area that exists between the linoleum tiles and the ceiling tiles, is subdued, as though the players—the doctors, the nurses, the therapists—don't even pause to acknowledge the immense stakes that are always on the table.

I greeted the ward clerk in the Community Hospital ICU, identified myself, and asked where I could find the new transfer from the ER. Without looking up from a duty roster, he asked, "Which one?"

"Adolescent OD. Female. Don't have a name. I'm Dr. Gregory, for a psych consult."

He raised his head and gestured toward the far corner and said, "Ms. Doe. She's in bed four." As I walked past him he said, "Good luck." In the vernacular, I assumed he meant that for her more than me. A dividing curtain was partially pulled in front of the bed in the distance, so from the nursing station I couldn't see much more than the footrail.

I asked, "Is her chart here?"

"No, her nurse has it out there."

On the far side of the bed a stocky woman with red hair wearing a brilliant chartreuse top was adjusting the controls on an infusion pump. I wondered where Adrienne was.

I turned back to the ward clerk and asked, "Is Dr. Arvin here?"

"Is he the attending?"

"No. She's the urologist."

"The little one?"

"Yes."

"She's over there, I think, with the patient. Was a few minutes ago, at least. I haven't seen her come back out, but I was in the john for a minute."

A glass wall separated the nursing station from the eight ICU beds. The moment I was through the glass door into the unit I was confronted with the familiar but disconcerting smells and sounds of last-chance medicine. My breathing grew more shallow.

I found Adrienne behind the drawn curtain. She was sitting on the edge of a chair, her eyes fixed on the monitor above the bed. The indicator for number of respirations per minute read a sharp red "09."

Way too low.

She was holding her new patient's limp hand.

Adrienne didn't turn, but she knew I was there. She said, "I didn't tell you before on the phone but, downstairs? She was in Cardiac Three. When they brought her in that's where they took her. And that's where I saw her. So this one's special to me. Okay?"

Adrienne had become a widow in Cardiac 3, the number three cardiac treatment room of the Emergency Room. Peter—her husband, my friend—died in Cardiac 3 after a brutal knife attack.

I said, "Okay," and touched Adrienne on the shoulder. With her free hand, she felt for my fingers.

Staring at the bright red numbers on the monitor, I stated the obvious as I gestured at the pale figure on the bed. "She'll be on a ventilator soon, won't she?"

Adrienne nodded gravely. "Her gag reflex is gone; she's stopped controlling her airway. They're setting up for the vent right now."

On masking tape at the endrail of the bed someone had written, DOE, M. in bold capital letters.

M. Doe was a tall girl. In unconsciousness, she seemed to stretch out over the length of the hospital bed. Monitor wires snaked from the upper end of her torso, which was immodestly covered by a pastel hospital gown that had seen about fifty too many washings before it had been pulled over her thin frame.

"Do you mind covering her up a little better please, Ren?" I asked.

The nurse turned and said, "I'll do it."

I thanked her and introduced myself. She smiled at me with a patronizing face that said, "We have a lot of work to do before you're going to do any good."

An automated blood pressure cuff began to inflate on the girl's upper arm, a drain gurgled, and the infusion pump measured another dose of fluid into her IV tubing. A nice little ICU symphony.

Adrienne said, "Don't you think she's lovely? I think she's really pretty."

My first thought was that in these circumstances, no one was lovely. But I said, "Yes, she is," trying to imagine what M. Doe looked like twenty-four hours earlier, and what events, what pain, had brought her here.

The child moaned and rolled her head to the side. She coughed once, a tiny cough, an infant's cough, before her eyes opened slowly and froze on me. Her eyes were puzzlingly clear, the same luminescent purple as my ex-wife's. And like Merideth's always had, this girl's eyes pierced me instantly in a way that compromised my balance.

"Hello," I said, moving forward half a step.

She blinked once before her eyes closed again.

Adrienne said, "She's done that a few times so far. Don't be fooled, it doesn't mean anything."

"Is she responsive to pain?"

"Was earlier, now only minimally to deep pressure. But I haven't played any Barry Manilow CDs yet. That might get a scream out of her."

I smiled.

Behind us we heard the squeak and drone of rubber wheels on linoleum. I turned and saw Marty Klein accompanied by a scrub-suited doc whom I didn't know. Behind them, a respiratory therapist was pushing a ventilator and a treatment cart our way. I said, "Hello, Marty."

He nodded. In other circumstances, I knew we would end up talking about bicycles, my passion, and golf, his. Not this time. He said, "Hi, Alan, thanks for coming, sorry she's not too talkative. We're here to get her on the vent. Step out a minute, please. Okay?"

"Of course." I had no desire to watch what he was about to do. None.

Adrienne asked, "Marty, do you need me?"

"No, Adrienne. We're fine. I'll have somebody call you with the kidney functions as soon as they show any change."

"You have my home phone?"

"It's on the chart, right?"

"Yes. I want to talk with the parents, too. When you find them."

"I'll find you, don't worry. Get out of here. Go play catch with your son or something," he said as he pulled the curtain farther around the bed.

I began to follow Adrienne away from the bed when I remembered why I was there. "Just a sec," I said. I walked back and reached inside the curtain and grabbed the chart and flipped a few pages. Beside me, Adrienne had begun pacing. I think Marty's admonition about spending time with Jonas had some special meaning as this young girl hovered near death with her parents nowhere to be found.

"You have a pen?"

She gave me one. I used it to sign onto the case and then scribbled a brief progress note that reported an apparent overdose, an unconscious patient, absent family, and no progress. On the order sheet, I wrote, "When patient attains consciousness: Suicide precautions should be in place, including 1:1 staffing × 24 hrs." I also left instructions that I be called immediately when the parents were located or the patient became oriented.

Adrienne glanced at my notes. "You're ordering a full-time one-to-one? Nursing staff's gonna love that. And MedExcel? Yeah, they'll be thrilled. They're going to reimburse on this, mmm-hmmmm, sure. Probably cutting that check as we speak."

"She may not be done trying to kill herself, Ren."

"I know that. I'm just giving you a hard time. With Lauren out of town, somebody needs to, right? You heard from her?"

"Not this morning, no."

"You'll let me know?"

"Of course, thanks."

I turned back to the admissions data. The data field was mostly blank. But the first line read, "Doe, Merritt."

Out loud, I said, "Her name is Merritt."

Three

Adrienne had a peds patient she wanted to check on before she left the hospital. I said good-bye to her at the elevator, told her I'd be available all day, and headed home. Before I leashed Emily up for a walk I put a fresh battery in my pager. I had a patient in my outpatient practice who had a newfound love for single-edge razor blades and another patient who had been paging me to pay phone numbers on weekends just to check on me and reassure himself that I was a responsive and caring human being. Although he never said a word when I returned the calls, I could tell from our sessions that he knew I knew who he was.

And now I also had Merritt Doe lying unconscious at Community Hospital awaiting whatever magic I could provide that would help her view the world as a place in which she might wish to continue to maintain residence.

All in all, more than enough reasons for a fresh battery in my pager.

Emily and I were only ten minutes from the house when the call came in to my beeper. I had Lauren's cell phone with me. I punched in the number from my pager screen and the call was answered by the distinctive lilting voice of the ward clerk from the ICU. As instructed, he was alerting me that although Merritt wasn't awake, her parents had been located. They were with their other child, another daughter, who was hospitalized in Denver at The Children's Hospital. One of them would come to Boulder immediately.

I thanked him.

The ward clerk wasn't done. In a breathless rush, he said, "You know who I bet this is, don't you? I think it's that little Chaney Trent, that little girl from the news. *That's* who Merritt's sister is. I bet that's why she tried to kill herself. She must be soooo distraught about her little sister."

I looked at my watch, silently added an hour for Merritt's mother or father to get to Boulder from Denver, and told the ward clerk when to expect me at the ICU. "Make sure whichever parent shows up waits for me, okay? No matter what, I need to speak with one of them."

"Absolutely," he said, still energized by his suspicion that he was on the very periphery of notoriety.

Since the shootings that Lauren and I had been involved in the previous October, I had stopped watching the local news. Too many people I knew and cared about were on too often those days, almost always presented in ways that made me sad or angry. Usually angry. Sometimes I would watch Headline News or wait and tune in to the local network affiliates at twenty minutes after the hour just in time to catch the weather and sports, but mostly I relied on out-of-town newspapers to fulfill my anemic craving for current events. With the newspaper, it was easy to skip articles I didn't want to read, and the editors of the Denver dailies and USA Today didn't seem to give a crap what happened in Boulder, Colorado.

I hadn't exactly missed the whole to-do that had been going on about the little girl, Chaney, and her illness, but I hadn't focused on the names. To me, it was just another public tragedy. Lately they seemed to be falling like raindrops, and I had my fill in my own life and my friends' lives and my patients' lives and all I wanted was an umbrella to shelter me until the storm passed. I wanted, first, to pull Lauren in out of the rain with me.

What I knew, all I knew, from glancing over a few stories in the local paper was that there was a TV reporter mommy from the Boulder area who had a sick little girl who was being denied treatment with some experimental protocol that had a low double-digit chance to save her life. The denial was coming from her cost-conscious insurance company. The mom/reporter's name hadn't stuck in my head, nor had the little girl's last name. The child's first name had stuck, though, like a yellow sticky note.

Chaney.

I figured she had been named Chaney in order that she be memorable, and now she was. For all the ink the father received, I would have guessed that the sick child was a member of a single-parent family.

I didn't recall Merritt's name ever being mentioned in anything I had read about the sick little girl. But then again, I admit that I hadn't paid a whole lot of attention.

It would have been better if I had.

*   *   *

I had some time before I needed to return to the hospital to meet up with Merritt's mom or dad. I preferred to be armed with information rather than saddled with ignorance, so I called Diane Estevez, who does gossip as effectively as CNN does news.

"Diane, hi, it's Alan. Can you fill me in some more on this sick little girl in Denver, the one who's been in the news all the time lately? It looks like I may be getting peripherally involved."

"Wow, no kidding. Hold on, let me get comfortable. God, you're so out of touch sometimes. You really don't know the story? Really?"

"Really. But I want to know more about the situation you alluded to at lunch. John Trent's kid."

"Of course. But first, dear, you have to dish. How are you involved?"

I considered how much I could share with Diane. "Adrienne called me from the ER at Community this morning to see a patient. The two cases, the ER and the sick little girl, may be related; that's all I can tell you."

"What do you mean, 'may be'? You don't know who your patient is?"

"My patient is unconscious. Let's just leave it that there's reason to believe that the case may be linked to the kid on the news. Come on—"

"Do you know your patient's name? Is it Trent?"

"Please. Let's not play twenty questions."

She made an unpleasant noise before she said, "This is John's first marriage. I'm pretty sure of that. I can check with someone if you need me to. But maybe his wife brought a kid along with her. Remember, she's that reporter for Channel 7, Brenda, a, um, Strait. Yeah, Brenda Strait, that's her name. She calls her news reports The Strait Edge." Diane mounted her best on-air voice imitation and said, "This is Brenda Strait at Woeful Recycling in Arapahoe County, and this is The Strait Edge."

Strait. "Tell me about the sick kid, Diane."

"She's a cutie, Alan. Breaks your heart to see her. Like I told you at lunch, she has some rare cardiac condition. I think it's called, don't quote me on this, viral myocarditis. It's an awful thing. I mean, she has a runny nose and, poof, a month later she has a terrible heart disease that may kill her. The news reports say there's a program in Vancouver that's doing some experimental things with some drugs from Japan to try and arrest the virus, but the chances of success are still pretty low. The kid's docs believe the only real hope for her is a team in Seattle that has been using the same drugs as the Vancouver people, but for kids with problems as critical as Chaney's, they follow the drugs with a heart transplant. But the kid's insurance company won't approve the funds for it."

"This is all from the news?"

"You expect me to rely on single sources for my information? I'm insulted, Alan. This is from Dani Wu. Confirmed by the news. But my sources are reliable."

"You said it's an insurance company? Which one?"

"Excuse my vernacular—it's actually a managed care company. I think it's—"

"MedExcel."

"Right. How did you know?"

"Lucky guess. Usual suspects. Is MedExcel on solid ground in refusing to pay for the procedure?"

"Sounds like it. Everybody agrees it's an experimental approach the Washington hospital is doing. The drugs they use to kill the virus aren't approved by the FDA for anything but investigative use."

"How critical is Chaney's condition right now?"

"The news reports make it sound grim. Dani—she works with John Trent a lot, she should know—says it's bad, the baby's heart muscle is mush, that John's in Denver whenever he's not working, day and night. Mom is carrying the ball publicly, trying to raise sympathy to keep pressure on MedExcel, without further alienating them. Tough act, huh? I think the parents are still hoping for a last minute change of heart, so to speak. Me, I think the strategy is naive."

"Sounds naive to me. I think I'd just call Jon Younger and take my chances with MedExcel at the courthouse." Jon Younger is a lawyer friend of mine.

"Me, too."

"How much does it cost? The procedure that they won't approve?"

"I think I heard the Seattle hospital wants almost four hundred thousand dollars in cash to walk in the door."

"And what kind of success have they had?"

"Remember, it's rare and experimental. Even the Seattle center says so. They've only done a handful of cases and they've saved a couple, three maybe."

"That's hopeful, given the prognosis otherwise, right?"

"It definitely beats the alternative."

"What's Brenda Strait like?"

"I only know her from the news. She's pretty in a hard way. Acts like one of those eighties women who thought they had to be way too serious to get along in a man's world. Remember them? But her hair's a little too big and she wears clothes that are a half-size too small for her, you know, like Oprah does. And if you ask me, she should wear a little less makeup and a lot more sunscreen."

Diane was never far from an opinion. "And her work? How is it?"

"I admire her work. She pisses people off. Uncovers graft. Makes politicians look silly. Exposes consumer fraud. That's her beat." The media voice came back. "She is Brenda Strait and she gives us The Strait Edge."

I did recognize her. I think I'd seen Brenda Strait on a billboard or the side of a bus.

I arrived back at the hospital before she did. When I walked in, the same ICU ward clerk I'd met earlier was having a whispered conversation with, I'm guessing, his boyfriend. It was something about someone getting home too late last night. I dug for Merritt's chart and flipped through Merritt's spartan record to discover that her last name had been changed from "Doe" to "Strait," that she was just shy of fifteen and a half years old, and, as of twelve minutes before, she was still unconscious. It was absurd of me to read the chart to find out her level of responsiveness; it was akin to tuning in the Weather Channel instead of glancing out a window to discover that it was raining. I knew it was absurd, but it allowed me a transition to the clinical tenor of intensive care, a distance I needed.

I replaced the chart and started toward Merritt. From ten steps away I could hear her ventilator. My ears told me it was the only one operating in the unit. The puffing sound it made was much too mundane to be so essential to life.

The red-haired nurse stood at the next bed. Her arms were above her head as she hung some fresh IV fluids on a person so bandaged up I could determine neither age nor gender. She looked at me, mouthed a silent, "Hi. Motorcycle."

I nodded and pulled a chair up beside Merritt. Without thinking, I reached for her hand. She was warm. I was a little startled, unconsciously expecting Merritt's body temperature to have taken on the chill of the circumstances.

Merritt's hand was large, as large as my own, and her fingers were thin and beautifully proportioned. The nails were painted carefully with a bright red polish, though the nail on her ring finger was broken badly, exposing some of the tender skin below. The break must have hurt.

Her hand wasn't limp; she had tone. But her fingers didn't respond with any pressure to my touch. I said, "Hello, Merritt, I'm Alan Gregory, Dr. Gregory, and I sure hope that I can help you."

Behind me, across the room, I heard a loud, "I'm her mother, that's who I am. Where? Where? Over there? Is that her? Is that my baby?" and saw the face from the side of the bus rushing across the ICU. I released Merritt's hand and stood.

The nurse stepped between Brenda Strait and her daughter, Merritt.

"Excuse me, please, ma'am, you are . . . ?"

"I'm her mother, damn it, get out of my way." Brenda stepped sideways to maneuver around the nurse, who anticipated the deke and managed to outflank her.

"Hello, I'm Susan, I'm Merritt's nurse. Have you talked with the doctor yet?"

"No, we played phone tag the whole way over here." Brenda's voice broke. "Please get out of my way. May I see my daughter? Oh, God, Merritt. Oh, my baby."

Susan, the nurse, grabbed Brenda Strait's hand and led her to the bedside opposite me. Although Brenda was incapable of hearing anything but the puffing and exhaling of the machine that was breathing to keep her daughter alive, Susan adopted a compassionate tone and began to patiently explain Merritt's condition.

"Ma'am, as you can see, your daughter is on a ventilator to help her breathe. She is still unconscious from her ingestion but her vital signs have begun to . . ."

"Is she okay? She's not okay, is she? Where's her doctor?" She noticed me standing across the bed as she leaned close to her daughter. Her arms were hovering but not touching, the machinery of survival an effective barrier to a mother's touch. She didn't look at me as she said in a voice that was half-demanding, half-pleading, "Are you her doctor? She's going to be fine, right? I can't lose two girls. Please tell me she'll be fine. Please, please."

"I'm Dr. Alan Gregory, I'm a clinical psychologist. I was called in by her—"

"Oh, God, where's her *doctor*? What did she do? Oh, Merritt, what the hell did you do? Oh, God." She took a deep breath. "I promised myself I'd be calm. I need to be calm." Another deep breath. "Can she hear me? Merritt, darling, can you hear me? It's your mom. I'm here, oh, sweetie, I'm here."

"Mrs. Strait, I'm Dr. Klein. Marty Klein." I turned and saw Marty holding out his hand. "Why don't you take a few minutes to be with your daughter and then we'll talk. Alan, you'll join us, please?"

I guided Brenda Strait into a small conference room off the ICU and listened to Marty while I observed his defeated audience of one.

Brenda Strait's frantic entrance had deteriorated into a semicatatonic hand-wringing that was as full of pathos as anything I had recently observed. Occasionally Brenda interrupted Marty's recitation to ask a question, as often as not confusing her younger daughter's symptoms with her older daughter's symptoms, the lines of despair having blurred and blended in mother's horror.

Twice, after requesting a clarification about something Marty was explaining, she said, "Excuse me, I haven't slept much. Did I already ask that?"

Her eyes were red and the tissues wadded in her hands would have needed to be sea sponges to manage to contain all her tears and sniffles.

Marty was patient, twice ignoring beckons from his beeper, but he was not able to ignore the urgency of a STAT overhead page. He took Brenda Strait's hand in both of his and excused himself reluctantly, promising to answer all her questions another time, before rushing back to the ER.

Brenda, hollow-eyed, watched Marty's hustled exit and then turned back in my direction, viewing me as disdainfully as she would have scanned the leftovers at a buffet.

"You're a psychologist, right? Right? Well, why did she do this?" she demanded. Her tone was mocking and condescending. I wasn't sure whether it was intended to belittle me and my profession—and by implication, her husband and his—or her daughter, and the inconsiderateness of her suicide attempt.

Maybe she wanted me to bite on the hook of her anger. I couldn't be sure. But I didn't bite. I said, "I'm at more of a loss than you are, I'm afraid. I was hoping you and I could begin to puzzle that out together."

She fidgeted. I think she would have preferred being provoked.

From the aroma building in the enclosed room, I hazarded a guess about her agitation. "Would you like to walk outside, Ms. Strait, for a cigarette maybe?"

"I quit three weeks ago. Chaney, you know? I could never get away from the hospital room for a smoke. You can still smell it on me, can't you? I chewed half a pack of gum on the drive over here. I need to get to the dry cleaners. Maybe buy a new wardrobe."

I said, "I know. It's hard to quit."

"My husband's a psychologist. Did you know that?"

"No, I didn't." Until verified, I still considered Diane's information to be gossip.

"His name is John Trent. You know him?"

"We may have met once. I've heard of him. He hasn't been in town very long, has he?"

"Maybe it's better that you don't know him."

"Better how?"

"Better for Merritt. It'll be easier for her to trust you. I'm guessing."

"Is trust an issue between Merritt and her father?"

"Stepfather. Oh, God, please don't do this shrink-wrap shit with me. I get enough of this from John." Her intensity accelerated; she was almost spitting words now. "What do you want to know? What could you possibly need to know that isn't already apparent? This is obviously about Chaney, right? And about me ignoring Merritt. Right? What else could it be about? Well? What else am I going to be punished for? Tell me that. Go ahead, what else have I done wrong?"

I learned a few things.

Take away the burden of the stresses caused by the fact that her younger daughter was at death's door, and that her older daughter had just joined her there, I suspected that Brenda Strait was a decent woman.

Smart and incisive, and with a reservoir of wit that could carry her through the onslaught of most stresses.

Not these two stresses. But most.

The family move to Colorado had been accomplished despite Merritt's objections. "My God, I understand that," Brenda said. "She was fourteen years old. When we moved, we took her away from her friends, her school, her security. I would've hated my parents for that, too. I understand her being angry, okay. I thought I did, anyway. But at some point she has to get over it, right?" She sighed, swallowed. "I'm not being fair to Merritt, I should be fair. The truth is that Merritt was doing better before Chaney got sick. She was starting to adjust. She was being a trooper. That's what John said.

"But Chaney, that, God, that's done us all in. All except John. He's been a rock for that baby, for all of us. Maybe except for Merritt. Before Chaney got sick, John was Merritt's buddy at home. They'd be out on the driveway shooting baskets at all hours. The neighbors used to complain. Police even came by once and suggested that eleven was a little late for playing horse." She smiled meekly at the memory. "I work a lot, odd hours, and John filled in with Merritt, with both girls. He's good with them. But now he's been in Denver so much, too. Maybe Merritt's angry about that—about John being gone. Maybe she feels deserted, left alone. Like we don't care about her. I've thought about that, I'm not insensitive.

"When we moved, we left Merritt's dad, my ex, back in Wichita, too. She misses him. Who could possibly be a more receptive audience to bitch about your mother to than her ex-husband? So there's that, too, not seeing her dad. It's a lot, huh . . . ?

"School? You probably want to know about school. She does well. She did better in Wichita. John says to give her time to adjust. So we don't pressure her about grades. She's an A and B student getting B's and a few C's. She plays on the basketball team. She's tall and thin like her dad. Gosh, you've never seen her standing up, have you? Basketball's been good for her . . .

"Friends? Boyfriends? Kids don't really date these days like we used to. They go out in packs, don't have to deal as much with the pairing-off pressure. Not a bad adaptation—do you remember high school?" Brenda's shoulders shuddered in response to some distasteful memory. "Awful. She hasn't had to be part of all that. Merritt's popular, she's funny, she's pretty.

She has two best friends. One in Wichita, Toni, and another girl who's here in town, named Madison. They hang out together . . ."

I asked, "Have you and John talked about this . . . this suicide attempt?"

Brenda exhaled as though she were intent on deflating. "I'm not ready to call it that. So far, I can barely say 'overdose.' But, yes, we talked before I left Denver."

"I'd like to call him."

"Fine, I'm sure he wants to talk with you, too. Chaney's in Room 406. He spends nights there, too. One of us always tries to be with her."

"You looked like you were about to say something else?"

Her shoulders sagged. "I thought things were going to get better. For all of us. I'd been getting death threats for a while. I did a story that re-sulted in somebody dying. Maybe you heard about it. Afterwards, I got some nasty phone calls and then some threats. They stopped a few weeks ago. The threats. I told myself everything was going to get better."

"Do you know who the threats were from?"

"No. I did a recycling story that had some major, I don't know, ramifi-cations. A mayor tried to kill himself. His wife had a heart attack. It's about that. Someone slashed my tires at work. Broke my car window and threw a dead cat on my seat. The police don't know."

"But the harassment stopped?"

"Yes. It stopped."

I moved on. "Your first husband, Merritt's father? Where is he? Wichita?"

"Right now, he's in the Persian Gulf on an oil platform; when he goes abroad, he's over there for weeks, months even, at a time. You know—the Middle East? I'll call him. If you need to talk with him, I'll have him call you."

"Please."

"He's more of an uncle to her than a father. Do you know how it started?"

How what started? I shook my head. "No."

"Sniffles. Chaney had a runny nose, just like a hundred other little colds. That's how it started. Sniffles. And now this."

Brenda was a talker. All in all, I didn't do much more than provide a few prompts. Still, before Brenda Strait returned to her daughter's bedside, she had dumped a lot of her anger at my feet. She had made a transition from feeling victimized by fate to feeling able to once again be a mother. The anger wasn't over, but the pressure was off for a few minutes, or a few hours. I felt confident that for some brief time, Brenda would be able to view her daughter's struggle to survive with love, not just with fury.

I also learned a few things that I hoped I might be able to use to help Merritt when she recovered consciousness.

Four

Late Sunday night, Marty Klein ordered Merritt off the ventilator.

The only break I had in my outpatient schedule on Monday was at lunch, so I wasn't able to get over to the hospital to see her until shortly before noon. She had already been moved from the ICU to a private room.

Her hair had been washed and fell in long tawny waves past her shoulders. She looked fresh and young. Although her purple eyes danced at the activity as I knocked at her open door and entered the room, the whites of her eyes were still milky and dull. Her gaze seemed suspicious. I had spent a couple of hours with her already, yet I had no reason to believe she had any idea who I was.

Approaching the meeting with her, I had anticipated that she would appear defeated and full of ennui or embarrassment, but instead she looked to me to be defiant, the head of her bed up high, her posture erect and proud. The TV was on, tuned to local midday news. Not Channel 7. The only evidence of how close she had come to death was the infusion pump still sighing intermittently beside her bed.

The defiant posture concerned me. I had an instinctual fear, a healthy one, I thought, of entering into a power struggle with an adolescent, but especially with an adolescent who had already demonstrated that suicide was a viable part of her arsenal of weapons.

On the far side of the room, between Merritt's bed and the window, a bored nurse sat on a chair reading a paperback book about angels. She was the staff member who was responsible for accomplishing the 1:1 I had ordered two days earlier. Suicide precautions should have dictated that she sit between Merritt's bed and the door to provide a feeble impediment to an escape, but I didn't say anything about it.

I walked to the foot of the bed and said, "Hello, Merritt, I'm Dr.

Gregory," then to the nurse, "Why don't you take ten? I can give you a little break. I'll stay with her until you're back. Thanks."

Merritt studied me but didn't return my greeting. Her already parted
lips moved a tiny bit. They were pale, almost the same color as her complexion. A small wound had scabbed over in one corner of her mouth. I
figured it was treatment trauma. The tip of her tongue searched out the
rough surface of the scab.

The nurse left her book on the windowsill, said, "Doctor," and hustled out of the room before I had a chance to withdraw my offer.

I took a step closer to the foot of her bed to be certain I was at least
part of Merritt's peripheral vision. "I'm a clinical psychologist, Merritt. You
may not remember me—I don't see how you could—but I've been by to
see you each day since you were brought into the hospital. I was hoping we
could talk about what happened."

No reply.

"May I sit?"

She shrugged her shoulders, touched her hair.

Merritt had a narrow chin and cheekbones still flush with the fleshi-
ness of youth. In a year or two, maybe less, the roundness would give way
to sharp definition and no one would dream of calling her a kid again. Pale
freckles trickled down her face as though fine sand had spilled from the
corners of her eyes.

She held her shoulders back against the pillow and brushed something off the lettering of her T-shirt with her left hand. In large letters, inside a burgundy oval, it read ROXY. My contemporary IQ was low and I
didn't know what ROXY referred to. I guessed rock 'n' roll.

Merritt was wearing no makeup, and I was left to wonder whether
that was typical for her.

I pulled a chair up and sat a few feet from the bed and waited for her
to begin. Her expression was composed, even assured, although her eyes
danced in a way that seemed bashful. For a long time, at least a minute, I
felt she was arranging her thoughts, preparing how to deal with this
stranger who was intruding on her most intimate and sanguine moments,
and offering to help.

But she didn't speak.

I wondered what her silence meant. Had the ventilator left her throat too raw? I prodded. "We've been really worried about you. I'm sure you know that."

Her lips parted even farther and she licked the lower one and probed the wound in the corner of her mouth once more before squeezing her lips tight. I wondered momentarily if she was being gamey, but her eyes betrayed caution now, not defiance, and if I was reading the signals correctly, some shyness.

I waited two minutes or more for Merritt to find the trailhead that would allow her to begin with me. I listened to a long commercial break about antiperspirants, used cars, and a movie of the week.

Merritt didn't speak. Her lips parted again, but she didn't speak.

Gently, she scratched her face and ran her fingers through her long hair, leaving it carefully arranged over one clavicle. She picked again at that annoying something on the x of ROXY, and then she examined her fingernails.

I noticed that the red polish I had seen in the ICU had been removed and that the broken nail had been filed smooth.

Each time the story changed on the news she looked up briefly at the tube, then away. I wondered if she was waiting for some update about her sister or whether she was just using the program as a distraction so she didn't have to deal with me. Perhaps both.

"You tried to kill yourself. And came incredibly close to completing the process."

Maybe a deeper than usual exhale, not quite a sigh. When she inhaled deeply her breasts took on definition and her shoulder bones were pronounced and sharp.

No words.

"You almost died."

She smoothed an eyebrow with her index finger and I heard Adrienne's voice in my head saying, "I think she's really pretty." I reminded myself to keep in mind that for many young women beauty was burden as well as blessing, and I tried to stay focused.

But Adrienne was right. Merritt was lovely.

I didn't know what to do next. I hadn't been prepared for her silence. It made the determination of suicidal risk a little awkward.

A nurse, a different nurse, entered the room after a perfunctory knock. With much too bright a smile, she said, "I'm here to pull that IV, babe. Good news, you don't need it anymore."

Merritt looked at me, terrified, as the woman set her tray down on the bedside table and pulled on latex gloves. Merritt's eyes screamed, "Do something." I was sure she was about to break her silence in order to mount a protest or to scream, or something. But all she did was bite her bottom lip while the nurse began to peel away the tape that was covering the catheter in her wrist. When the tape was removed and the thin catheter that snaked into a vein on her arm was exposed, Merritt turned her eyes away, reached out with her free hand, and squeezed mine with poignant desperation.

The nurse said, "Here goes, babe, this won't hurt a bit, promise." She laughed as though she didn't expect to be believed. Two seconds later she pressed a gauze dressing over the site and, in a smooth motion, slid the catheter free from Merritt's arm. I was acutely aware of Merritt's terror, could feel her tremors of fear. I was also touched by her desperate use of me for comfort.

The nurse eased a cotton ball and a Band-Aid over the IV site. Merritt watched. The nurse said, "All done, now that wasn't so bad, was it?" Merritt stared at the bandage, then lifted that hand and spread her fingers in front of her open mouth. It didn't seem to me that she was even aware that she was still holding my hand.

When, finally, she looked back down and saw our hands intertwined, she tensed, looked once at my face, and hesitated before removing her hand from mine. She pulled free with great deliberation, allowing her fingers to graze along the skin on the soft part of my palm.

I said, "I'm glad that's over, Merritt. I bet you are, too. I get the feeling you're not very fond of needles."

She opened her eyes wide and nodded. I wanted to hear her cry or laugh or giggle as the tension melted away, but she didn't.

So I waited, hoping the brief intimacy we'd shared would shake something loose between us. Something verbal. But Merritt composed herself quickly and returned her attention to the noon news.

I needed to let her know where things stood before I left. "Merritt?" I waited until she looked my way. "One of my jobs is to help everyone—you, your doctors, your parents—decide how likely you are to try to kill yourself again. It will be difficult for me to do that if you don't talk with me."

She swallowed.

The nurse doing the 1:1 poked her head back in the door. "You need me yet?"

"Uh, no, not yet. Do you mind waiting at the nursing station? I'll be out in a few minutes. I do have some questions for you."

She mumbled, "I bet you do," as she closed the door.

Merritt raised her chin a little and focused again on the news. A cute story about a cat in a tree and a swarm of bees and engine company six.

I was absolutely certain by then that Merritt wasn't anxious about not talking. Given the clarity of her reaction to the removal of the IV, had she been suffering a neurological impairment that precluded her being able to speak, she should be terrified by the disability.

I asked, "Do you feel able to talk? Physically able?"

She didn't respond. She wasn't going to help me. I had to consider the unlikely possibility that Merritt's silence was hysterical, not volitional, and that her lack of apparent anxiety was actually *"la belle indifférence."* If the right constellation of previous experience, serious trauma, and secondary gain came together, Merritt could be suffering from a hysterical inability to speak that would have no physiological basis.

The odds were extremely low that her silence was hysterical, maybe one in ten thousand. I had seen conversion symptoms only twice in my career.

In a soft voice, I said, "This is important. I need to let you know how things are going to work between you and me. You'll talk to me, I figure, when you're ready. Or you won't. That's okay, and it's up to you. Until you decide to talk, though, I'm going to have to make a decision about your risk of attempting suicide again. Regardless of how you feel about not having died a couple of days ago—and I'm not making any assumptions that you're thrilled about that—we, all of your doctors, are going to do everything we can to keep you alive so we can try and help you with whatever was going on that made you think eating all those drugs was a good idea.

"In the meantime, if you continue to improve medically as quickly as you've been improving since last night, and I certainly hope that you do, your medical doctors will be ready to discharge you from the hospital and send you home soon.

"That's where I come into the equation. If I judge you to be at risk of further suicidal behavior, or if I'm unable to determine the level of risk of further suicidal behavior because you won't talk with me, you won't actually go home at all. You'll be transferred from here to a psychiatric hospital so that we can take whatever steps we need to take in order to protect you until the risk of you hurting yourself diminishes."

She had lowered her eyes from the TV screen and focused them on the bandage on her wrist. I thought her parted lips were quivering, just a little.

"Do you understand what I'm saying, Merritt?"

She moved her eyes up slowly until they met mine. They opened wide and brightened. Her focus had narrowed to include only me. Her upper body seemed to deflate. Her lips tightened into narrow pink lines. I read her expression to say, "You wouldn't really do that to me, would you?" But this was someone accustomed to the dictates of authority. This was a kid who still attended when her parents spoke. This was a good kid.

I played the best card I had in my hand. "And before I go I want to tell you how terribly sorry I am about what's been going on with your sister, Merritt. It's very sad, and scary, and it must be difficult for you."

Her eyes filled with tears. She wiped them instantly with the fingers of the hand that hadn't been tethered to the infusion pump.

I waited, hoping that I had catalyzed something. She crossed her arms over her chest in an X and rested her chin on one wrist. She seemed incredibly sad.

"I've spoken briefly with your mother to get some history and I'm hoping to meet with her or your stepfather sometime later today or tomorrow. I'm planning on talking with your father as well."

I watched for a reaction but couldn't find one. I reached into my wallet and withdrew one of my business cards, scribbling my home phone number on the back, something I'm usually reluctant to do with patients. I said, "Call me anytime, for anything. I'll be back to see you again soon."

I asked the nurse who was doing the 1:1 to stand outside Merritt's room with me while we talked. I didn't feel comfortable leaving Merritt unobserved.

The nurse was a plain woman who wore nursing whites. She seemed like the old-school type who had suffered philosophical angst over the fact that nurses were no longer required to wear little white caps attached by bobby pins.

She didn't wait for me to query her. "I don't know if you've read them, but I put everything in my notes. I'm a comprehensive note taker. Some of these new nurses just like to put down the numbers and do the checklists, but I write notes. Real notes. And like I said in my notes, not a word from that child. Not one. She's pointed at a few things she wanted me to get for her, but no, she won't talk, and no, if you're wondering, she won't write anything down, either. And she's not upset about it. I think she's decided not to talk, that's what I think. She just flips around on that clicker looking for news on the TV. I saw how interested she was in the TV news, so I brought her the newspaper up from the cafeteria after my morning break. She tore through it like I had delivered the Bible and she knew she'd better study it because it was almost her time to meet the Lord. I've never seen a young person care so much about the TV news. With the killing and the raping, to be honest, I'm not sure it's a healthy pastime."

"Has she spoken to anyone on the phone?"

"No. Won't touch it. Acts like it's gonna bite."

"Any visitors?"

"Her mother was here early, then she went to Denver to see the other child, you know, Chaney, the sick little girl from the news. My dear Jesus, I'm afraid I'm going to spend half my time praying to the Lord for this family. What troubles, oh my, what troubles."

"Just the mother came, not the father?"

"That's right. Some other man came to see her, though, an uncle or something. She seemed surprised to see him. But he only stayed a few minutes. I mean, what's the point, the baby won't talk."

"She didn't speak to either of them?"

"Not a word that I could tell. Do you know why I get the call to come in when there's one of these suicide watches? I worked ten years at the state hospital in Pueblo"—she pronounced it Pee-eb-lo—"then did ten more years with teenagers at Fort Logan, you know, the state hospital. So I know crazy when I see it. But this girl's not crazy. Want to know what I think?"

"Please." I knew I was going to hear her opinion whether I really wanted to or not.

"That child's in bed with some demon, some evil, evil force— mm-mmm—and she's decided that if she talks, that demon is going to raise his ugly head and have his way with her. That's what I think."

Through the small window in the door to her room I could see Merritt's face. Her eyes were glued to the tube. She was still embracing herself, her arms crossed over her chest, no one else available to do it.

"That's an interesting thought," I glanced at the nurse's name tag, and added, "Ms. Hayes. I'll keep it in mind. Thanks for your help. I'm grateful that someone with your experience is available for this. I'll be back later, this evening, probably around the dinner hour. If there's any change in the meantime, please give me a call, especially if she begins to speak to anyone. I'd like to know that immediately."

I gave the nurse my business card and watched her rejoin her patient. I returned to the nursing station, fished around for Merritt's chart, and paged through it, looking for a recent note from neurology. The neurologist had seen Merritt only an hour before I had. Her note was the last one on the record.

Merritt's neurological exam had been normal during rounds this morning. I wasn't surprised by the news. I added my chart note to the long list of progress reports and renewed the order for the suicide precautions and the one-to-one monitoring.

Behind me, I heard, "She's gotcha, doesn't she? We real doctors did our part, *boychik*. She's alive. Now you have to do your part, and keep her that way."

I swiveled on the chair. "Hi, Adrienne. How you doing?"

"I'm doing."

"You know she won't talk?"

"I know."

I tapped the chart. "No medical reason?"

She said, "Sorry. That would be convenient for you, wouldn't it? I'm sure her throat's a little raw from the ventilator, but no, most patients can't wait to chatter after that hose comes out of their throat."

"If she won't talk, I can't judge how dangerous she is, Ren. If you're ready to discharge, I'm going to have to transfer her to a psych hospital."

"I know. Maybe it's what she wants. Poor kid's been home alone a lot since her sister got sick. Maybe she just needs some TLC."

I smiled. "I have an idea. If that's all she needs, why don't you take her home, Ren? She could babysit for Jonas. That would be great."

"You get her better, Alan, and I'll not only grant you a one-year moratorium on making fun of your profession, I'll also gladly foster-child this one forever. There's something really, really good inside Merritt Strait, I feel it." Adrienne pressed hard on her own chest. "It took some of our best work to keep her alive over the weekend and, you know what, it makes every miserable day of my residency worthwhile to see her skin pink and her kidney functions almost normal."

"Are you ready to discharge?"

"We'll watch her for another day or two. But soon she'll be ready to go."

"I may need you to go to bat for me with MedExcel, Ren. Marty called this morning and told me they've already complained about the expense of the one-to-one nursing. They want it d/c'd. You know they're going to scream if I try to transfer her to a psych unit."

"I'll talk to Marty. We'll work something out with MedExcel or the hospital or something. Order whatever's necessary, Doctor. Not to worry."

Five

The Rangers were in town to play the Avalanche and Sam Purdy was psyched. The plan was for him to come by my house around six and drive us to Denver to the hockey game.

He paged me at five-thirty, just as I was finishing with my last patient of the day. The number he left on the screen of my beeper was unfamiliar.

I picked up the phone and punched in the number. Sam answered gruffly after four rings. "Sam, is that you? It's Alan. What's up?"

"Change in plans, I'm afraid. Can you drive tonight? I'm at a crime scene without my car. I think it would save time if you just picked me up. I'm out east, not too far from your house."

"You have the tickets with you?"

"Right next to my heart."

"No problem, I'll pick you up. Give me directions."

He did.

All the rules had seemed to change in my relationship with Sam Purdy after he had exercised his cop discretion and chosen not to believe me after I confessed to him that I thought I had shot someone last October.

Before that night we had enjoyed a friendship, but it was an odd hybrid of being buddies and being adversaries. We'd tried to enhance the relationship before; we bicycled together for a while, but that faded away from mutual neglect, and our friendship continued to languish within the bloody boundary lines where his police interests and my psychological acumen overlapped. We occasionally had breakfast together, sometimes spoke on the phone for no reason other than to stay in touch, and made vague plans about getting together that we rarely followed through on. Not once had Lauren and I rendezvoused socially with Sam and his wife, Sherry.

But over the last winter things had evolved, and Sam and I started meeting away from work. The first couple of invitations were from me, generated, I think, by my persistent anxiety that he would change his mind about ignoring my confession and end up busting me for some capital offense related to that gun going off. Right from the start, though, the incident the previous October seemed dead for Sam. I tried to make sense of how something so monumental for me seemed so inconsequential to him. I finally decided that by behaving the way I did that night in October I had passed some initiation ritual that was meaningful for Sam in a way that I might never understand. Maybe by caring enough to do what I did that night, I had crossed a line, joined some unnamed fraternity, earned some invisible stripe, and to Sam, I was now good enough to be a member of the club.

What club? I don't know.

Those first few meetings we met late, after nine at night, after Sam had tucked his son, Simon, into bed. Sherry was a morning person, and was usually in bed shortly after Simon. What Sam normally did during those late-evening hours with his family asleep, I don't know, but he seemed grateful for the opportunity to get together with me.

For a month or so we struggled to find the right place to meet. We tried the brewpubs, Walnut and Oasis, and played some pool. We tried some coffeehouses. We met in a few of Boulder's bars—the West End, the Boulderado, even one memorable evening at Potter's. But nothing felt right until Sam decided that maybe I would be a suitable companion to accompany him to hockey games and invited me to Denver to watch the Colorado Avalanche.

Sam had three season tickets in the second row of the second deck in the southeast corner of the arena. One for him, one for Sherry, one for Simon. On a cop's salary, the tickets were a big investment. On school nights, Sherry wouldn't let Sam take Simon along, so Sam was left to fend for himself on weeknight games.

Sam had been raised in northern Minnesota and had played hockey all his life. The arrival of a National Hockey League team in Denver brought him joy that was hard for me to understand until he took it upon himself to begin to teach me about offensive defensemen and blue lines and two-line passes and clearing zones and delayed offsides and the importance of finishing checks.

During those late-winter games, I was a hockey student. He instructed me about nuance without ever taking his eyes from the ice.

And during the twenty-minute breaks between periods, Sam and I stopped being buddies and started becoming friends.

During the first game we attended together, in the break between the second and third periods, Sam started talking about a case he was doing, some guy who was using legal tricks to get some incriminating evidence dismissed against him.

"He's a damn rapist, Alan. Just slime. We suspect him in two other assaults. We have fingerprints, we have semen, we have him cold. I don't care what his lawyer does; this guy is not going to walk." He tried to flag down a popcorn vendor, who ignored him. "See, justice isn't the same as law, Alan. It isn't about cops or prosecutors or judges or legal procedure or any of that shit. Justice is about doing the right thing, about making sure, absolutely sure, that the right thing happens. Sometimes unlawful things result in justice. Cops know that. Civilians don't get it."

For some reason he pointed at the Zambonis preparing the ice for the third period. "Hockey players know about justice; basketball players don't. Basketball players want the referees to provide justice; hockey players don't rely on the cops. See, justice is reluctant; it's not really a natural state of affairs. The natural state of affairs is survival of the fittest. But justice isn't about that. Justice is about the weak surviving, too. It can be unnatural. And because it's not natural, it often needs a shove."

"Are we talking about last fall, Sam?"

"What? That? I don't know, I don't know. The right thing happened, didn't it? Could be."

The crime scene he was working the day of the Rangers game was in an upscale residential neighborhood in east Boulder, north of where I lived. The chief trial deputy in Lauren's office, Mitchell Crest, lived in a more modest corner of the same subdivision. Lauren and I had been to his house once for a seder.

I said, "Sam, depending on traffic, I can be there in fifteen, twenty minutes."

"I may need a little more time than that to finish up. But I really want to be at the game when they drop the puck. I was dying to see the warmups, but I'm afraid there's no way now. This is the Rangers, you know.

We're talking Sandstrom and Gretzky. I'll hustle to pull this together. When you get here, check in with one of the patrol guys."

"Whatever."

As I drove across town I wondered, of course, about the crime scene. Sam was a senior detective and he investigated mostly felonies, crimes against persons. Given the socioeconomics of the neighborhood, I was guessing that a domestic situation had ended way out of hand, or a burglary had gone sour after a homeowner discovered an intruder in his house.

The home where Sam directed me was on a cul-de-sac that backed up to greenbelt. Only three immense houses shared the little horseshoe-shaped street. When I arrived, though, it seemed as if the three families were sharing their quiet road with most of the law enforcement community of the City of Boulder. I was forced to park over half a block away on the closest cross street before I meandered over to try to track down Sam.

I joined a throng of neighborhood gawkers at a deep perimeter marked off at the end of the cul-de-sac by crime scene tape. Microwave trucks from the Denver TV stations were already setting up nearby for live remotes. As I approached the perimeter, I tried to be certain none of the news cameras were pointing my way.

Judging from the activity level that was apparent, the crime, whatever it was, was serious and had taken place in the middle of the three houses. The stately front door of the mansion faced the mountains; its backyard would welcome tomorrow's sunrise.

My first goal was to find a Boulder cop walking the perimeter with a clipboard. There would be no getting inside the tape to find Sam unless I found whomever had been assigned to control access to the scene.

A uniformed patrol officer in his late twenties spotted me heading his way at the same time I recognized that he was the likely gatekeeper. He raised his chin a centimeter or two, and I thought he looked like he was preparing to repel me from the scene with gusto.

I smiled in an ingratiating manner and said, "Hello, Officer. I'm Dr. Gregory; I'm looking for Detective Purdy, Sam Purdy. I would be very grateful if you get him word that I've arrived. He's expecting me."

"Just a sec." He glanced down at the board and found something with his index finger. "Are you Dr. Alan Gregory, by any chance?"

"Yes, I am."

"May I see some ID please, sir?"

I dug my psychologist's license from my wallet. I could have used my driver's license for identification, but never in my professional life had I a reason or opportunity to show someone my psychologist's license, so I thought I would take advantage of this one.

He examined the flimsy little paper card as though he'd never seen one before, which I was sure was the case.

Finally he checked his watch and said, "Come on inside. He's waiting for you."

I said, "Thanks," and ducked under the crime-scene tape. I turned back to him and asked, "What's going on over there? What happened?"

"I thought you knew. Some doctor ate his gun. Let's go. I'll escort you over."

I had spent a brief but memorable period of time as a paid consultant to the Boulder County Coroner a few years back. My supervisor then had been a man named Scott Truscott. His was the first face I recognized as the officer walked me up a wide herringboned brick driveway.

"Scott? It's Alan Gregory. How are you?"

He looked up, and he looked surprised. "Alan? Hi. They call you in on this?" He had been standing near one of the three garage doors. He took a few long strides my way, down the driveway. The officer left us, returning to his post on the perimeter.

I shook my head. "No. Sam Purdy and I are going to the Avs game tonight. I'm just picking him up here. You've been inside already?"

"Yeah. I'm done for now. The coroner is going to have his hands full for a while, though, with this post. You're really going to see Gretzky and Sandstrom tonight? Damn, wish I had tickets for this one."

Scott wanted to talk hockey, while I was getting more curious about the size of the response to this crime scene. I figured a quarter of the investigative resources of the police department were on this block. "So, you've been here a while? This is just about wrapped up?"

"This? Body was discovered right after lunch, I think. Lost some time getting a warrant. But this isn't wrapped up. No. Not by a long shot. I have a feeling this one'll have legs."

"The cop at the perimeter said it was a doctor. Is it a physician? What, suicide?"

Scott picked at an uneven cuticle on the index finger of his left hand

and then examined the other nine for flaws. He seemed to be making a judgment about the nature of my curiosity. He said, "Yes. Yes. No."

I looked for a smile. There wasn't one. "No? It's not suicide?"

"I'm not even close to being prepared to recommend a determination of manner to the coroner, Alan. But it doesn't look like any gunshot suicide I've ever seen. The scene is upside-down and backwards. My gut says it'll take a lot of investigating and a lot of interviews and a lot of forensics to sort this out."

I was surprised. Scott Truscott was a seasoned medical investigator and read the vagaries of death scenarios better than I read MMPI results. I said, "Really? The cop at the perimeter said he ate his gun. He made it sound, well, straightforward."

Scott was not known for talking out of school, and he was apparently done sharing his secrets with me about this death. He shrugged. "It may have looked that way when the first officers arrived, but it doesn't look that way now." He shook his head and glanced at his watch. "Remember JonBenet? Things aren't always as they seem. Listen, I have to run. I'm sure Sam Purdy will tell you more than I will."

Scott took two steps toward his coroner's van before he stopped and turned. "You wouldn't know of anyone who has any other tickets available, would you? I mean, for the Rangers game tonight?"

"We're using Sam's tickets, Scott, not mine. I don't know. I'll ask him if he has any extras. Can he reach you on your pager?"

"Yes. Absolutely."

I figured Sam had the unused ticket for the third seat with him in his pocket. I didn't know whether he wanted Scott Truscott to sit in that seat. Sam seemed to like to use it as a coat rack and as a place to hold his food.

As I made my way from the driveway to the front porch I ran into Mitchell Crest, the chief trial deputy of the DA's office, Lauren's colleague. "Hi, Mitchell. Stop here on your way home?"

He wasn't as surprised to see me as Scott Truscott, but I didn't feel he was pleased, either. "Hello, Alan. I wish. What are you doing here? How did you get inside the tape?"

"Everyone keeps asking me that. I'm just running a taxi service, looking for Sam Purdy. He and I have plans in Denver tonight."

Mitchell nodded as if he didn't really believe me. Lauren did the same thing sometimes. I suspected there were advance seminars on the technique in law school.

"I just saw him in there. I don't think he's quite done inside."

"I'll wait, I guess. Who's the dead doctor?" I was afraid it was someone I knew.

He furrowed his brow, snapped his finger. "Edward Robilio. Dr. Edward Robilio."

I shrugged. I had never heard the name. "I don't know him. Does he practice here in town?"

"I only knew him as Ed from the homeowners' association. He's the past president, ran the meetings like a parliamentarian from the Weimar Republic. He had this obsessive thing about wanting to revoke the covenant that prohibits parking an RV on your own property in the neighborhood. He owns this cream-and-peach-colored Holiday Rambler that's the size of a Greyhound bus. But yes, he's a physician, although I don't think he practices anymore. He's a businessman of some kind. Something to do with health insurance."

"I'm sorry if I was flippant, Mitchell. I didn't know you knew him."

"It's all right. We were acquaintances, not friends. I actively supported keeping the RV parking ban. Ed took that personally, figured it made me a jerk."

"What exactly is a Holiday Rambler? That's an RV, like a Winnebago?"

Mitchell smiled. "Not exactly. Hearing you say that would probably make Ed turn over in his grave, if he was in one yet. Apparently, Ford is to Mercedes-Benz as Winnebago is to Holiday Rambler."

"I don't see one around anywhere. I take it your position on the parking ban prevailed?"

"Yes, we won. Dr. Robilio was forced to move his pride and joy up to his ranch in the mountains."

I tilted my head toward the house. "So, was this a suicide?"

"Suicide? You thinking maybe he was that distraught about the parking ban? Hardly. It looks like he's dead by gunshot. But there's no weapon on the scene. You can try real hard, but it's difficult to make that look like suicide. Maybe not impossible, but certainly difficult."

"What are you guessing? That the killer screwed around with the scene?"

"Let's just say the scene is complicated."

"But the shot was in the man's mouth?"

He eyed me. "Yes, it was. Close, anyway. How did you know about that?"

I didn't want to point a finger at the patrolman with the clipboard. "Somebody at the perimeter said that the deceased ate his gun."

Mitchell seemed to be thinking of how to respond. Finally he said, "It may be true, about him eating his gun. If it is, though, it looks like it was a case of force-feeding. Who knows, maybe he literally ate it and we'll get it back on autopsy. That would be a first." He stuffed his hands in his pockets. "That's not funny. Sorry. Keep all this to yourself. If any of those reporters stop you, and they will, just 'no comment' them, okay?"

"I know the drill, Mitchell."

Right then the wind shifted, or someone opened a window somewhere in the house, creating a crosswind or something. But I was almost bowled over by a blast of air so fetid and distinctive that I had no trouble recognizing its source.

Mitchell smelled it, too. He smiled at my reaction. "Dr. Robilio's been dead awhile. Smell wasn't bad until they started moving him around. Lauren's lucky she's out of town. When rich doctors die by gunshot, prosecutors on the felony team don't tend to get too much sleep. Say hi to her for me. Her mother's doing . . . ?"

"Her mom's stable. Thanks for asking."

"And Lauren's feeling okay, I hope?"

"Yes, Mitchell. She's well—fine." Lauren would despise the fact that everyone asked about her health as though she were an invalid. She would hate it. I wouldn't tell her.

Six

I declined Mitchell's offer to take me inside to Sam.

Maybe five minutes later, he found me where I had parked my butt on a lacquered teak bench behind an entryway pillar about the diameter of a giant sequoia. The bench was flanked by large cement statues that looked like artichokes.

"I heard you were here, Alan. Been waiting for you to come inside and act nosy."

"This is more pleasant. It's a nice evening, I can smell the lilacs. The alternative aroma where you've been hanging out isn't so pleasant."

"Vic is ripe now, I'll give you that. Friday's mail was picked up, Saturday's paper was still on the driveway, so it looks like he's been fermenting since Friday afternoon or Friday night. Though I think I'm getting immune to the smell. It's the bugs that make my skin crawl and he doesn't have any. Why is that, do you think?"

"You mean, why aren't there any flies on his body?"

"No, I mean, why do I hate bugs on dead people?"

I shrugged. Analysis of Sam's necro-insect phobia could wait for another time. I was glad I was outside.

"The smell could have been much worse—air conditioner was on when his wife found him around noon. She'd been gone all weekend. If the air had been off, whoa, I don't even want to think about it."

"I talked to Scott Truscott and Mitch Crest already. Sounds like quite a puzzle inside."

"They filled you in?"

"You know Scott. He was discreet. Mitch told me a little more."

"It is a confusing scene. But my part is done for tonight. I'm just a dwarf on this one, fortunately. Malloy is playing the role of Snow White for now. But I bet the sergeant, maybe even the chief, will be on it like white on rice."

"Which dwarf are you, Sam?"

He smiled. "Sherry says that depending on my mood, I'm all the dwarfs, all seven of them. Though she thinks there should be nine in all, that Snow White should add Farty and Horny to the menagerie."

"Do you have to go write this up before the game?"

"No, I'll do that after." He looked at his watch. "We still have a little time before we have to hit the road. Do me a favor before we go. Take a look inside. Tell me if anything strikes you."

"Sam . . . I really don't want—"

"Don't whine, Alan. Be flattered by my faith in you. Come on. I just want an initial impression. I can impress my sergeant by showing him what a humanist I am, involving the mental health profession and all."

"Sam, you always say you just want me to have a look. Then there's always something else. And then before I know it, I'm knee deep in police shit."

He ignored my protest and held out a hand to help me up from the bench. "Sometimes there's shit. Not today, though. A lot of blood and some dried urine, but no shit."

I admit to being overwhelmed by proximate murder. I don't easily find my bearings. The stimuli seem to rush at me from five different directions at once. Smells, sounds, and new things to see, all blend together in a cacophony that I don't filter against well.

I don't do so well at cocktail parties, either.

I barely noticed the details of the fancy house we were in before Sam's voice intruded. "Hey, hey, try not to touch that banister. The CSI's cleared a path for us but they'll be lifting latents all night. This place is big. You want gloves?"

"No. I'm fine, I'll be fine," I said, stuffing my hands in my pockets as I followed him downstairs. The foot of the stairs faced some large sliding glass doors, a big yard, a pool, and a lot of prairie.

"Over here."

Across the big room, two crime scene techs were packing up their gear outside a door that opened into a wood-paneled room. Numbered evidence tents were scattered across the entire basement. A colleague was dusting the glass on the sliding doors. Another was on her hands and knees just outside the doors doing something my quick glance couldn't decipher.

Sam stood next to the doorway across the room. "This way. Go ahead, go inside. Go, go. It's harder if you hesitate. Dive in, go."

To my profound relief, the body of Dr. Edward Robilio had already been bagged. The dark plastic sack was on the floor, parallel to the front of a clubby brown leather sofa. Unfortunately, the smell of Dr. Robilio's decomposition had not been successfully bagged along with him.

"What do you want, Sam?" I made a point of breathing through my mouth.

"That's him, as I'm sure you've surmised. Lucy said the patrol guys are already calling him Dead Ed. It's a good one, I think it's going to stick. Funny how cops do that, the nickname thing. Probably a distancing mechanism, don't you think? What do I want from you? Don't really know. Sometimes you surprise me. Whatever strikes you is what I want."

Dead Ed?

I treaded carefully across the room, which was about fourteen feet square. I avoided the evidence markers and danced around the most obvious stains on the carpet. Below the room's solitary window sat a chair that matched the sofa. The chair was badly stained with long swipes of dark pigment that I assumed was blood.

"He was sitting there, I take it?"

Sam said, "Yep, at one point he was. It's going to go downtown later tonight. Soon. The chair, I mean."

"Has anything been removed? Was the room this neat when he was found?"

"I'll show you pictures later if you want. We took a few little things as evidence already. Address book. Checkbook. Mail. Answering machine. But it was a neat place, just like the rest of the house. Wife may have cleaned something up when she found him, though she says she didn't. She says that a housekeeper comes three times a week, but not on weekends."

"You don't believe her, the wife?"

"When people are dead and smelly and full of bullet holes, I don't believe hardly anybody. Call it a character flaw. Don't worry, I'm working on it."

"No note?"

"If there was, the wife has it. And the handgun that goes with it."

"Are you thinking murder?"

"I'm thinking."

A thin palmtop computer sat beside the phone on the pristine desktop. It was open, the screen exposed. "What's on the computer? Anything? Was he working on something?" The palmtop was a tiny Compaq, the same model Lauren used to keep track of her schedule.

He shrugged. "Don't know yet. We're getting an addendum to the search warrant to cover it. We'll have it examined by our computer guys. They've been called."

I noticed the flashing light above the lilliputian keyboard. "Do you know that it's turned on already? It's in hibernation mode. That light there, the green one, it indicates that it's hibernating. That means that it was left on and when he stopped using it, it went to sleep after a while to protect the batteries."

"Lucy has a laptop. I think she uses it to manage her money. She said the same thing when she was in here. But she hit the keyboard and nothing happened. She said that hitting the keys should have brought anything back up that the guy was working on. She said that he must not have had any software running."

That didn't make any sense. "Generally, that's true. Lauren has a machine just like this, Sam. After a while it goes into a deeper sleep. You actually have to hit the on button to get back to where you were. Give me a pair of gloves, I'll show you how to do it."

Sam called to someone in the next room. "Do you have that addendum to the warrant yet?"

A deep voice replied, "Yeah, five minutes ago."

Sam pulled gloves from inside his coat. I pulled the powdery latex onto my right hand and touched the tiny off/on button. The palmtop emitted a static-laced whir and the screen came slowly alive.

Sam stepped forward and bent toward the screen. "Amazing little thing, isn't it?" He leaned back again, doing the dance of farsightedness. He reached inside his coat pocket and pulled out some half-glasses, which he perched on the end of his substantial nose.

"When did you start wearing glasses?"

"I don't wear glasses. I got these at Kmart."

"They look like glasses."

"They're from Kmart, they don't count. It doesn't count if you don't go to an eye doctor."

Sam had apparently already worked out the details of his denial. I realized that he hadn't answered my question. Nothing new about that.

Over his shoulder, I read a few words on the computer screen and said, "Wow. What do you know?" The screen was half-covered with single-spaced type. I fought an impulse to scan; instead I forced myself to read the words carefully.

Sam said, "That looks like a damn suicide note. This doesn't make any sense."

It did look like a suicide note. "I wonder if he wrote it himself."

"What, you think he'd need some help? You suspecting a ghostwriter, or you think that Dr. Kevorkian was here? Too bad, far as I know, they can't do handwriting analysis on a word processor."

"It's not made out to his wife. That's odd."

"Why?"

"Who else was going to find him?"

"Maid? Who knows?"

"Maybe there are latents on the keys, Sam."

"Maybe," he said dismissively. "That'd be too easy." He stared hard at the screen, then scanned the room as though a fresh look was going to tell him something. "Shit. There shouldn't be a damn suicide note here."

I said, "Let me see something. May I?"

"As long as you don't erase anything."

I touched one of the function keys to check the battery status of the tiny computer. "The battery is almost dead, Sam. You want me to save this screen to disc so you don't risk losing it?"

"If the battery dies, we'll lose that note, what's on that screen?"

"Yes, unless it's already been saved."

"Has it?"

"I don't see a file name assigned to it. It needs a file name to be saved. So I'd guess that it hasn't been saved. I can search for previous files named 'suicide note' if you would like."

He ignored my offer. "How much time does the battery have left? What does it say?"

"The meter isn't that precise." I pointed at the little icon. "It currently shows virtually no reserve. If it functions the same way Lauren's does, that could mean two minutes or two hours."

Sam turned and yelled over his shoulder, "Is Harker still here?"

A bored voice replied, "Gone, ten minutes ago."

"Then somebody call and get Macready down here to pick up this computer. Now, not later."

Someone said something back to Sam in a quiet voice that I couldn't quite hear.

Sam could. He barked, "I don't care about her dentist. Call her back. I want her here an hour ago. Second best is right now. We've apparently got some evidence that's disappearing into cyberspace."

He turned to me and said, "You really know what you're doing? You won't screw this up for me if I tell you to go ahead?"

I nodded. "I promise that I do know what I'm doing. But all I can tell you is that I'll try not to screw things up. That's not a promise. What's your badge number, Sam?"

He told me. I used the touchscreen and the keyboard and saved the note on the screen to disc using Sam's badge number as a file name.

We waited for Macready, the department's computer guru, to show up and claim the computer. When she arrived, Sam told her what we had done, never mentioning me. He talked as though he knew exactly what he was doing, as though he were describing the act of pushing down a lever to make toast, an act he had done a thousand times.

Macready didn't look old enough to drink, let alone wear a badge. She resembled a contestant I had seen recently on *Singled Out*. The woman had picked a real geek for a date, and they'd had to go bowling.

She collected the little machine and said, "No problem. I'll get a printout and a report to you tomorrow."

Sam said, "Not me. Route it to Malloy. Hope your teeth feel better soon."

As we walked toward my car to drive to Denver, I told Sam that I thought Scott Truscott would really appreciate Sam's extra seat to the game.

Sam seemed to be considering it. "He'd owe me one, wouldn't he? Big time."

"Yeah, I'm sure he would. He sounded desperate for a ticket."

A shiver seemed to work slowly up Sam's spine. He said, "It's tempting, the leverage. But hockey's sacred to me. I don't mix home and work, and I don't mix hockey and work. I don't think I can do it."

An hour later we settled into our seats in Denver to watch Gretzky and Sandstrom and Sakic and Forsberg do their things.

Simon Purdy's seat sat empty next to Sam.

The Avalanche opened badly; they lost a player for a game misconduct in the first five minutes. Sam wasn't upset by the penalty, explaining that the player had been defending his goalie. "It was a necessary hit. The guy had been screwing around in Roy's crease from the moment they dropped the puck, and he wasn't getting the message. This is only one game. But the guy whose face ended up in the glass will remember the lesson when the stitches come out. And he'll remember about justice the next time he sees the Avs. And, most important, he'll remember when the playoffs come in a couple of weeks.

"Keep that in mind, Alan. In hockey, you're always thinking about the playoffs. The rest is just setting the table."

Seven

Sam wasn't exactly grumpy during the game. But he was preoccupied. Mostly, though, he wasn't content. I counted on Sam's underlying contentedness, even when he was irritated or pressured. His demeanor was a constant, like the color of his eyes or the contours of his immense shoulders.

Shortly after Sam and I had started going to hockey games, Lauren had asked, "What do you guys talk about? Just sports, or what?" I knew that it was sometimes Lauren's style to begin meaningful conversations with a distancing move. Years ago, my interpretation of her style had been wrong; I'd decided since that the tendency had little to do with her discomfort with intimacy. Rather, she was protecting some transferential image she had of me, allowing me room to pretend that nothing meaningful was actually occurring during the conversation. It was a simple relationship sleight-of-hand to try and keep *me* from running.

She asked the question about Sam and me and hockey as she turned her back to begin clearing dishes from the dinner table.

Instinctively, I thought I knew where she was heading. I said, "Well, we do talk a lot of hockey. Sam's a hockey evangelist and I don't think he's going to stop preaching until I'm converted and can recite every name on the Stanley Cup since 1950. But we talk about other stuff, too."

"That would be hard? The Stanley Cup name thing?"

"If you're not Canadian or from Minnesota, yes, it would be hard."

"Like, what else do you talk about?"

"Cop stuff. Life. You know."

"No, I don't know. Hanging out at sporting events isn't exactly your style. It's forty-five minutes to McNichols, the games seem to last forever, it's forty-five minutes back home. You guys go to two games a week sometimes. You're spending a lot of time together. Does he talk about his family, do you talk about us? What goes on?"

I presumed that she wasn't interested in just the facts. "You know how Sam used to seem content all the time? I mean gruff and prickly, but content?"

She thought about it a moment, said, "Yeah."

"It's different now. I'm not sure what it is, but I think he's working up to telling me about it, whatever it is. Something has knocked Sam off balance. We're still dancing around it."

"Different how?"

"The contentedness, the joy, is gone. He's brooding about something."

"Something with Sherry?"

"Maybe. He doesn't talk much about her."

"Do you ask?"

"I don't pry."

"Simon?"

"He seems thrilled with Simon. Simon's great. Soccer, peewee hockey; Simon even has Sam out rollerblading, if you can believe that."

She tried on the image. "I think I'd like to see that."

"Me too."

"Work? Is it work?"

"No, I don't think so. If I had to guess, I'd say family, or maybe something existential, some life-change thing. I'm not sure yet."

"Does it have to do with last fall? With the shootings and everything?"

"That's what I thought at first, but no, I don't think so. He doesn't seem to dwell on that much. I really don't think that what's bothering him is anything he's talking about."

"Well, then, it must be something he's not talking about. What is he avoiding?"

I'm the psychologist. It should've been my line.

I said, "That's a good question, sweets. But I'm not sure. Maybe it's Sherry, maybe it's his marriage. I'm patient. He'll talk when he's ready."

She pulled a stool up to the sink so she could sit, and started washing dishes. With her back turned, she said, "You avoided my question before. Do you and Sam talk about us, about you and me?"

I had avoided it once and I was tempted to ask her to repeat the question and blame it on the running water. I didn't. I said, "Yes, sweets, we do."

She nodded.

"You want to know about what?"

"You'd tell me?"

"Of course."

She edged closer to the front of the stool so she could more easily reach the sink. "I'm not sure that I want to know. I'll let you know when I do."

Our eyes never met during the entire interchange.

My mother always said don't ask questions that you don't want to know the answer to. Prosecutors, like Lauren, always say don't ask a question that you don't already know the answer to. My assessment was that this time Lauren's discretion adhered to both rules.

What she wasn't prepared to hear again was that her illness had changed us. I thought she wanted to know if I was confiding in Sam about it. But what was more compelling to her was her need to hold onto the luxury of pretending that her ascetic style of coping with multiple sclerosis was working like flawless software, and that our marriage remained blissfully uncontaminated by the toxic neurological residue of her stripped myelin.

Gretzky had scored during the early penalty but the Avalanche were up three to one when the second period ended. Peter Forsberg had a hat trick already. Sam said he liked Forsberg's toughness much more than his puck handling and then stood and asked me if I wanted anything. He meant at the concession stands.

I replied, "Yes, Sam, there is something I want. I want to know what's bugging you lately."

"Case today is screwy." He didn't miss a beat before replying and pronounced his answer in a convincing fashion, as though he were really upset about work.

I said, "Yes, it sounds like it is. But it's not your case and that's not it anyway. Screwy cases consume you, they don't bum you out. Anyway, whatever has been going on with you has been going on quite a while. Much longer than Dr. Edward Robilio has been Dead Ed. What is it, Sam?"

He looked at me as though he were actually going to answer. Instead, he shook his head a little and said, "I have to piss," stood up, and disappeared down the tunnel that was next to his seat.

Ten minutes later he returned and handed me a soft pretzel covered with hard grains of some product that was masquerading as cheese. I said, "Thanks." The scent of the faux Parmesan flashed me back to the aroma of Mike Toohey puking on my desk in the seventh grade. I held the wax paper at arm's length and started breathing through my mouth.

He asked, "Don't you ever have work things that get you going? Make you goofy?"

"Sure. All the time. Right now I have a new patient in the hospital, a kid, who's, I don't know, on my mind a lot."

He said, "See? Some of it's like that. And okay, some of it's Sherry. What's going on. Some of it's her family. I'm not used to crap like this." He filled his mouth with pretzel and chewed for a while. "My family in Minnesota is normal. People talk to each other, they help each other out. I don't know about family grudges and holding stuff in. And I'm not handling it well with Sherry and her damn family and their squabbles. There're apparently all kinds of goofy rules that get applied by these people and I don't seem to know any of them."

I waited a few heartbeats to see if he was planning to continue on his own before I asked, "What is it? What's going on with Sherry and her family?"

He drained his beer. "Sherry has one sister. Older, by a few years. The sister moved to town eight, nine months ago. Boulder. The two sisters, they don't get along, haven't as long as I've known Sherry. Sherry won't give her sister the time of day because of this thing that happened years ago, and Sherry says she's furious at her sister because of how she treats their parents. All of this was bad enough for me when the sister lived out of state, but Sherry has been—well, what Sherry has been is a first-class bitch since her sister and her family moved to Colorado."

He looked over. I don't know if he was checking for boredom on my part, or what, but he apparently approved of what he saw. He continued.

"See, okay, this has been hard for Sherry. Her sister and her don't talk at all, not a word."

He paused. I said, "That's funny. This new patient who's on my mind? She's not talking either."

Sam was focusing on his story. "The sister is this big-time TV reporter. You watch Channel 7, the news? Brenda Strait? Seen her? That's Sherry's sister. Brenda Strait, you know, the Strait Edge? It drives Sherry crazy—it's her maiden name, Strait. Sherry wants to pretend her sister doesn't even exist and then she drives around and sees Brenda on billboards and on the sides of buses all over town. In our house, we can't watch any programs on Channel 7 so that Sherry doesn't have to run the risk of seeing some promo pushing her sister's latest exposé. I don't think she's told anyone that her sister is Brenda Strait. It's been eating her alive since Brenda's family moved to Boulder."

At the mention of Brenda Strait, I was busy catching my breath, sucking air through my mouth, visualizing dominos falling over, trying to peer far enough into the future to see where the last one was going to tumble.

Sam saw my near-apoplexy. As much for diversion as for compassion, I said, "I bet I know where you're going, Sam. The little girl, Chaney. The one who's been on the news all the time. She's your niece, isn't she? It must be awful, her being so sick."

"Yeah." He stared up at the rafters, then back down at the Zambonis. "Chaney's my niece. You know me, Alan. I want to help. And I barely know her, Chaney. But it's tearing me up. Brenda gives me the cold shoulder when I try to help. And John, I don't know him that well. He's her second husband. If I call, Brenda's cold, tells me they're doing fine, considering. I take food over, you know, for the family. Like I was a neighbor, but I'm family. I'm not somebody she works with or something. So I give it to the older daughter. Brenda and John are never home since this started, they're always working or at the hospital. So I give it to the older kid, who I know a little better. I mean, I've known her longer, at least. I think she likes me, anyway. And . . ."

Sam paused and swallowed nothing. The new, more recent injury was more tender and raw and more difficult for him to talk about.

I didn't know what to say. I tried, "That must be rough for you, too."

The platitude failed to distract him. Sam exhaled in a quick burst and spun on me. His reaction to my feeble comment would not have been more intense had I warned him that his chair was on fire.

I tried to look compassionate and concerned. There were no mirrors anywhere around, but I feared that I ended up looking merely sheepish.

Sam seemed to be replaying the last two minutes of conversation in his head. And he didn't need a road map to see what was going on. He said, "Oh, shit. I can't believe this. The patient who's not talking? You're the one—oh, shit. No."

I said, "Sam, until right this minute, I didn't know she was your niece. Honest. If I had known, I probably wouldn't have agreed to take on the case. I would have asked someone else do it."

Sam tilted his head back and stared at the catwalks criss-crossing high above the arena. "Oh, God. Oh, hell. This is too much."

Bruce Springsteen stopped singing mid-lyric and the players moved to center ice. The crowd hushed. The referee dropped the puck to start the third period. A Ranger one-timer from the blue line brought a loud buzz.

I tried to continue the conversation.

Sam said, "Later, after the game."

After the game, we talked hockey, not family. The game ended with the home team up six to four. Too much scoring for Sam, who prized defense above all hockey skills. He had been a defenseman when he played in the Minnesota youth leagues as a kid.

"And I wasn't one of these 'offensive defensemen,' either. The only time I scored was when somebody on the other team screwed up. But people didn't score much on me, either. I look back on it sometimes and believe being a defenseman was good practice for what I do now. It's like being a cop."

We were walking to my car in the east lot at McNichols Arena. I liked to beat the traffic. Sam saw the postgame jam as part of the hockey experience.

He continued, "Except, what's different is, in hockey, it's all over in three hours. I like that better. Sometimes the cop stuff seems to drag on forever."

He hadn't mentioned his two nieces or Dead Ed Robilio since the third period had started. I valued my well-being too much to be the first one to broach the subject of his extended family. I figured he would get around to it.

He didn't.

Almost an hour later we were back in Boulder. I turned into the lot on the south side of the police station where the cops park their personal vehicles and asked him where he had left his car.

"I'm not going home yet. I have to do the paperwork on Dead Ed before I go home."

"Oh, I forgot."

He smirked, "It seems to be one of your prerogatives. Forgetting."

I killed the engine. "You're way off base, Sam. I didn't know Merritt was your niece."

During a loud exhale he asked, "You talked to Brenda and John?"

"I'm on the case, Sam. Okay? I'm trying."

"Brenda tell you about the other shit? The threats? The vandalism? All the trouble she causes?"

"Why don't you pretend I don't know. That's not your case, is it?"

He shook his head. "God, no. Mostly being handled by Denver. We provided some protection for a while, some extra patrols."

"It has to do with a story she did?"

"Yeah. Recycling contracts. She exposed some kickbacks and bribes and some mayor tried to kill himself, gorked himself out instead. His wife found him with a rope around his neck and then she had a coronary and died."

"Yeah, I heard. Did they ever identify a suspect in the harassment?"

"Not that I know of. The guy was good at what he was doing. No wits, damn little physical evidence. Everybody figured it was because of the story. They were looking at personal connections, you know, irate relatives, and they were looking at the politicians who got swept up by her story."

"Is the vandalism still going on?" I asked.

"Apparently it's stopped."

"At least there's that."

"Yeah, I guess that's something. Small favors. So Brenda didn't mention Sherry or me?"

"Let's just say that I didn't know she was your niece. But you know I can't tell you what anyone said to me. That this is a member of your family doesn't change any of those rules. I'm sorry."

He opened his mouth as though he were going to say something, but just cleaned his molars with his tongue. I got the message clearly.

Sam said, "Well, I can say whatever I damn well please. John's in

Denver all the time at the hospital. Probably why you haven't seen him. If it were Simon who was sick I know I wouldn't leave his side for a second. Like I said, I don't know him well, but I think John's all right."

I wasn't sure where Sam was heading. It sounded as if he wanted his impressions of his sister-in-law's family to be part of the mix I was considering in treating Merritt. If I was right, he was inviting me to descend a slippery slope.

"This is going to be awkward for us, Sam. I'm deep into this already. I mean with Merritt. Maybe too deep to get out cleanly, without doing some damage to her. For Merritt's sake, you and I are going to have to find a way to sort all this out. One thing for sure is that I'm going to have to tell Merritt that you and I are friends. She has a right to know that we know each other."

He shoved his lower lip under his mustache the way he does sometimes and curled his big hands into fists the size of pumpkins. He turned to face me. "I only plan to say this once. You ready?"

"Yes, I'm ready."

"Don't even consider getting holier than thou about this situation, Alan. And don't even think of sermonizing to me about your work. I'm not a player in this, so don't consider me. This is about helping Merritt. She's a kid who deserves the best. If you are indeed the best person to be helping her right now, I can live with my role as fucked uncle. If you are not the best person to be helping her right now, God help you, you'll need it."

He took a deep breath and held it. My own breathing was shallow.

"So, from this moment forward, I'm going to assume that my niece is getting the best goddamn psychological care available on the face of this planet. Does that sit well with you, my assuming that?"

"Yes."

"Good. Because if you jeopardize that care in any way, if you put Merritt at any risk by bailing out on her because of some misguided sense of propriety or because you decide some of your precious professional ethics are being threatened, well, God help you."

"Sam—"

"Shut up. See, I know you better than you think, Alan. I've watched you in crisis. When things get hot, at first you're a jumble of conflicting emotions, a damn philosopher in a foxhole. Dangerous shit, that. I also know that when things go from hot to flaming, you are able to do things that make me proud you're my friend. Looking back, more than once, you've shown me you can take the heat.

"Don't worry about me. I'm not going to pressure you to tell me Merritt's secrets or to tell me what makes Brenda and John tick. All I'm going to do is to make sure you know that we, this family, are fast descending into a hell I could never imagine. And that makes this situation as hot as it gets. All I ask of you is that you make me proud one more time, buddy. That's all."

With an effort that seemed monumental, he lifted himself out of the car and closed the door gently.

Eight

I left Sam at the police station, drove home, and checked my voice mail. John Trent had left a "returning your call" message at my office number.

Given the difficulty I'd had reaching Merritt's stepfather, I'd toyed with the idea of leaving him a message and extending the professional courtesy of providing him my home phone number, but decided that such an offer was premature.

In the meantime, our telephone tag continued.

I replayed the message he'd left, listening for nuance. "Dr. Gregory, John Trent returning your call. I'll be in Denver tonight and most of tomorrow. Call anytime until, say, midnight or after seven tomorrow. Thanks. I should be at the same number you used the last time."

John's tone on the recording was calm and level. I wondered whether, despite my clinical training and experience, I could muster such an even tone in the face of the multiple stresses that John Trent was suffering.

But before I returned the call, I knew that Emily required some attention and some exercise. We headed outside and I threw a tennis ball as far down the lane as I could. Emily sprang after it, tracked it well, and pounced on it. She swooped it up, shook it a couple of times to be certain it was dead, dropped it exactly where she was, and ran back to me. With Bouviers, there was no telling if she planned to stop her galloping advance before she plowed into my knees, so I had to jump out of her way to avoid a collision that could easily sever both my ACLs.

I threw a second tennis ball. She repeated the chase-it-and-kill-it-and-leave-it-where-it-dies scenario. I knew from frustrating experience that this game was the Bouvier des Flandres version of fetch. It was reasonable fun for the dog, I supposed, but required an unusually healthy supply of tennis balls. After repeating the scheme with half a dozen more balls, Emily was panting, I was bored, and I had only a few minutes left to reach John Trent before midnight. I'd collect the tennis balls sometime tomorrow.

I grabbed a bottle of raspberry lemonade from the kitchen and took the portable phone with me into the living room. I hit the shuffle button on the CD player and wondered what disc would come up.

I was guessing that I was going to get some Basia that Lauren liked, but the music that filled the room was a Jimmy Buffet album that I didn't remember loading into the changer. Must have been Lauren's, too. It made me smile.

John Trent answered on the first ring and said hello absently, as though he were picking up the phone at home.

There was an accent there, something I couldn't quite place, something that had been tempered by time, certainly, and effort, maybe.

"Hello. May I speak with John Trent, please."

"Speaking."

"This is Alan Gregory."

"Dr. Gregory—finally—thanks for calling back. I'm sorry I've been so difficult to reach."

It wasn't often that a fellow psychologist called me "Doctor," and I was puzzled by the formality. "It happens, we're both busy." Over the years, I'd struggled to find ways to use small talk to grease my entrance into people's misery. It never worked. Better to move directly to the meat. I said, "As I'm sure you know, I was called in to evaluate your older daughter after her ingestion, and—"

"Stepdaughter, for the record. I'm prouder than proud to call her my daughter, but technically, I'm just Merritt's stepfather. She's a great kid, isn't she? God, I feel so bad about this."

"I've hardly had a chance to get to know her, but that's what everyone says, that she's a special young woman. May I call you John?"

"Please, of course. My hands have been really full with Chaney since the weekend. She's had to have a couple of difficult imaging procedures. Her doctors are quite concerned about her blood gases and her lung function. I feel terrible that I haven't even made it back to Boulder for Merritt. Brenda and I thought that, well, since Brenda's her mom, she should be the one to see Merritt first. One of us stays in Denver with Chaney all the time."

I had anticipated some defensiveness from John about the impossible decisions he had to make to juggle his concern for his two daughters. I wasn't disappointed.

"My sympathy goes to you and your whole family about Chaney. I can't imagine the stress you're under. You don't have any easy choices now, do you?"

"No, Dr. Gregory, I don't. The only thing more painful than being with Chaney right now is not being able to be with Merritt." John's voice remained level, but it took on a hollow ring, as though he had cupped the microphone close to his mouth with an open hand.

I wasn't sure how far to carry my compassion about the family's complicated circumstances. I reminded myself that my focus, and my patient, was Merritt. "Merritt's ingestion was almost fatal, John. I'm sure you can understand that I'm very worried about her state of mind, especially about any continued suicidal ideation, and I would be grateful for any insight you might have about her mood prior to the weekend, or for her motivation for taking all those drugs."

"You know I'm a psychologist too, don't you?"

"Yes, my partner, Diane Estevez, has mentioned your name, and Brenda reminded me as well when she and I met."

"Psychologists' kids aren't supposed to do this sort of thing, right? That's what you're thinking?" He paused and processed his own words. "Whatever, that's what I'm thinking."

I wondered whether I was hearing guilt or a prelude to something else. "I don't think we're immune, if that's what you mean."

"I'm talking about what I missed. I didn't see it coming. I've gone over the past few weeks in my mind, every last detail of every last second I spent with Merritt or talked with her over the past month and, darn it, I didn't see it coming. Not a hint. I'm not pretending I'm in perfect touch with her lately—I'm here with Chaney almost all the time I'm not working. My practice isn't that busy and it's more flexible than Brenda's job. I usually sleep here and I have the cafeteria menu memorized. That's not an excuse—it's a choice Brenda and I made—but Merritt's been left out in the cold ever since Chaney became so ill. There's no need to sugarcoat it. We've done what we can do, but she's been the forgotten kid."

"There was no one you could call on to help with her? With Merritt?" I was fishing now for some admission about Sam and Sherry, but hoped only the lure I was using, and not the line, was apparent.

"We're new in town."

"No family?"

He paused before he said, "Unfortunately, none close enough to help with this."

If I didn't already know about Sherry and Sam, I would have been left to believe that John Trent's use of the word "close" was a geographical reference, not an emotional one. I noted the obfuscation.

I said, "That's too bad."

"Believe me, I'm not callous to Merritt's needs. Far from it, I've been worried about her and I've tried to pay attention to what's going on with her and I've tried to stay in touch with her but these last few weeks have been . . . can you hold just a second?"

The line was quiet for a moment. John came back on and said, "This will take a minute or two. Please wait. I'm very sorry."

I could hear a distant beeping and a female voice entering into a conversation with John. Finally he said, "Good, that's great, thanks, Terry."

He came back on the phone. "Chaney had a kink in her IV line. We took care of it. Where were we?"

"Merritt's isolation."

"That's it. But she wasn't isolated, not in a depressed sense. I was watching for it. She was doing okay with all this. I mean, she was desperately worried about her sister, and she missed our family time together, but she was handling it. I thought she was, anyway. She was staying in touch with her friends, her schoolwork was getting done, she called her father whenever he was available, which isn't often. He's in the Persian Gulf somewhere on an oil platform.

"No matter how bad things have been, we've made a point of having at least one dinner together a week. Brenda and Merritt and I, away from the hospital somewhere. She likes the chicken dinner on Sunday nights at this place close by called the Aubergine Cafe. It's right by Channel 7. We've gone there a few times. And Merritt has been appropriate, in terms of mood and affect. I thought she had been, anyway. I don't know, maybe I'm just trying to rationalize the fact that I missed it, how depressed she really was, is. But she hasn't been withdrawn, she hasn't changed the way she relates to me. Her appetite seemed fine. She eats, sometimes a lot, sometimes not. Her schoolwork had slipped a little, but she was getting it done. And she was still playing basketball whenever she could.

"You should see her play. God, is she graceful. She has this fallaway jump shot that you can't stop. She kills me with it. We play a lot of one-on-one."

"I'd love to see her play." I'd love to see her do anything but be in the hospital.

"What's remarkable about her game is her patience. She doesn't take bad shots, doesn't make bad passes. When she gets a little stronger under-neath, a little more comfortable with her size, watch out. One game this year against Fairview she was up against this big girl, I mean big. The girl was manhandling Merritt on defense and Merritt wouldn't take bad shots. She just moved the ball around and found her open teammates. She ended up with eleven assists from the forward position. Twelve points and eleven assists, a double-double. Her game is all patience and good judgment.

"Do you know that Ceal Barry, the CU women's coach, has come by to see her play twice already? Merritt's that good; she's really good."

"It sounds like it." I was hoping my platitude would bring him back. It did.

"I can twist it every which way, I can put it under any microscope I can find, but I just didn't see it. I love that girl, Dr. Gregory, and I didn't see it coming. That's the bottom line."

I wanted to keep him focused on Merritt. "You didn't mention much about her friends, John. Just that she stayed in touch."

"No," he said. He seemed distracted.

"Any changes there?"

It was at least ten seconds before he spoke again. "Chaney is so rest-less on these drugs they're giving her. She doesn't really sleep."

"Do you need to attend to her?"

"No, no, I think that I've taken care of it for now. Umm, Merritt and her friends? That's where we were?"

"Yes."

"She has one close girlfriend, Madison, the one who found her after the overdose. They hang out other places mostly, not at our house. I don't know Madison well, but she's not like the kids that Merritt usually gravi-tates to. Madison's boy crazy and nonathletic and she smokes and has a tat-too. You know. But I don't know her well. I'm sure Brenda has her phone number, though, and who knows, maybe Madison knows something. You know what it's like with teenage girls and best friends."

I thought, *Only in theory.* "Nothing else?"

"I wish. I can't think of anything."

"Do you mind providing me some general history, John? Whatever you can tell me about Merritt since you became involved with the family."

John knew precisely what I wanted from him and after absorbing my empathy and my dispensation over whatever were his sins of omission with his stepdaughter, he settled in to providing me with a history of his involvement with Brenda and Merritt, the birth of Chaney, the family move to Colorado, and their adjustment to a new home. He related their history with the dispassionate accuracy of a mental health professional who had heard it done a few hundred times before.

He did, however, leave out any mention of Sherry and Sam Purdy.

He offered nothing that piqued my interest in regard to the genesis of the suicide attempt. No red flags. No yellow flags. Nothing.

Either this sincere guy had totally missed whatever it was that had been troubling Merritt, or this family was hiding something from me.

I didn't know which was true.

Nine

Other than bumbling through another session with a still mute Merritt Strait at Community Hospital, the next day developed in a way that felt almost normal.

I had been home from work for less than an hour when the phone rang. The thought of what to do about another dinner alone had been perplexing me for a good five minutes. I was deciding between throwing together some sesame noodles or making a big bowl of popcorn. Popcorn was winning. I answered the phone with eager anticipation, expecting to hear Lauren's sweet voice in my ear. But the voice I heard was bold and defined.

"Dr. Gregory? Brenda Strait."

I was disappointed and I was defensive. I was always defensive when a patient, or someone related to a patient, phoned me at home. It left me feeling as though I were in the witness protection program and somebody with a grudge had managed to track me down.

I wanted to snap, "How did you get this number?" but restrained myself, quickly remembering that I had left it on the back of the business card I'd given to Merritt. I said, "Hello, Brenda," as evenly as I could.

Her manner was crisp, and she anticipated my aversion to being disturbed after work. "I tried your office number and got voice mail. I know how much Trent hates getting calls like this at home, so I apologize for bothering you. But this can't wait until morning. When I'm not working on a story I'm usually not this intrusive. Please trust me that this is important. I'm at home. I'd like you to come over here right away. Before you say no, let me assure you that it's about Merritt and her welfare and I'm afraid it's terribly important."

I pressed Brenda for the reason I was being beckoned, but she wouldn't say.

"I don't want you to hear it from me. I want you to see it yourself."

"See what?"

"Soon. I don't think you'll like what you find here, Dr. Gregory. But you won't regret coming over."

For no particular reason, I believed her.

The family home was in Wonderland Hills, a subdivision in northwest Boulder, and a good trek from where I lived. I fed the dog and threw ice cubes into her water dish before I left. I didn't want to waste the time it would take to make popcorn, so I grabbed a handful of almonds and a bottle of lemonade and jumped into my car. The drive across town ate up most of twenty minutes. Boulder's traffic was beginning to drive me crazy.

The Trent/Strait household occupied a two-story cedar and shake affair that, with the exception of the distinctive basketball hoop in the driveway, and the key and free throw line that had been painted meticulously on the concrete in canary yellow paint, looked just like a third of the other houses on the block.

The yard showed signs of recent neglect, not surprising given the circumstances in the family. Newspapers that had been tossed up the walk littered the base of the low privet hedge that led to the front door.

I parked my car on the street. I was halfway up the path when the garage door began to slide in its tracks. Brenda called, "Dr. Gregory? Over here. Why don't you come in this way?"

Brenda was dressed for work. I couldn't tell whether she was coming home from the station or going to the station. I made a mental note to check out one of her reports on Channel 7. Her hair was just so and her makeup was fresh and applied without sufficient restraint. Her avocado business suit was tight across her bosom and hips. She had kicked off her shoes and was standing on the concrete pad in her hose.

"Hi, Brenda."

"Thanks for coming. Maybe calling you wasn't the smartest thing in the world, but I didn't know what else to do. Maybe I should have called Trent first, but he's with Chaney and I didn't want him to leave her. And for this he would have left her. Follow me, this way."

She walked me through a kitchen that looked like a museum of takeout containers from Boulder's franchise restaurants, down a short hallway, and upstairs to a wide landing. Outside a closed door, she stopped, took a deep breath, and said, "Here's what happened, what, an hour ago, is that all it was? This is Merritt's room, and I was snooping. I admit it. Merritt can't stand it when Trent or I go in her room. We respect that. Usually, anyway, we respect that. But today I was snooping. I was looking for a diary, although I'm embarrassed to admit I don't even know if she really keeps one. This whole suicide thing doesn't add up to me. Yes, Merritt's upset about her sister. Yes, Merritt's been neglected lately. Yes, she has plenty of reason to be depressed. But suicide? Sorry, I figure there has to be something more. My best guess was that there's a boy someplace that I don't know about. I called her friend, Madison, to ask her but she hasn't returned any of my calls since . . . you know. And Merritt still won't say a damn word to me, or anybody else for that matter. Has she started talking with you?"

I shook my head.

"Didn't think so. So I make the fateful decision that I'll snoop a little, see if she has love notes from Troy or doodles about Todd or whomever. It's a long shot; she's not that into boys, but . . . who knows, maybe I might get lucky and find a diary she's been keeping with a long explanation for why she did this."

Brenda still hadn't opened the door.

"But you found something else instead?"

She turned the knob.

Facing me on the far wall were basketball posters. Grant Hill. Antonio McDyess. Sheryl Swoopes. The biggest poster on the wall was of the victorious USA women's Olympic basketball team.

To break the ice, I said, "She really likes basketball, doesn't she?"

Brenda wasn't above a sarcastic retort. "Pretty perceptive of you, Doctor. Yes, basketball is her passion. She plays forward for Boulder High. It's been good for her, helps her feel okay about being so tall."

Maybe if I walked into the bedrooms of a hundred different adolescent girls I would have a better idea of what to expect. But I haven't, and I didn't. This bedroom seemed normal enough. A four-poster double bed with a Battenburg lace comforter and a few stuffed animals seemed to be the room's solitary altar to femininity. A tiny bedside table held a clock radio and a stack of vigorously thumbed copies of *Seventeen* and *Sports Illustrated* and a paperback horror novel by John Saul that looked like it had been read more than once.

On the wall between the bedposts was an elegantly framed poster of the Nike "If you let me play" advertisement. It made me smile.

Behind where I was standing, the double closet doors were plastered haphazardly with rock 'n' roll memorabilia and posters. Merritt seemed to be into Beatles-era oldies, Phish, and Alanis Morrisette. A pile of CDs the size of a loaf of bread was stacked next to a boom box that sat on top of a cherry trunk under the room's only window.

Merritt kept her space neat. A pair of leggings had been swung over a club chair, but everything else was put away in drawers or on shelves.

"Is she always this tidy?"

"She wasn't back in Kansas. This compulsive phase started when we moved here. We haven't had to bug her about her room since she took over this space."

"Impressive," I said, while I wondered what else Merritt had been doing to cope with the stresses she'd experienced after the family move to Boulder. "You know, Brenda, I'm at a real disadvantage right now. I don't know what I'm supposed to be seeing. Is there something out of place, or something missing? What am I supposed to notice?"

"I'm sorry. Let me get back to my story. I'm snooping, remember? It's what I do for a living. I snoop, and I'm thorough. I don't just check the top drawer of the desk and shrug my shoulders. I check everywhere. I'm methodical. I started in her closet, felt down her clothes, looked inside her shoes, opened every box. Then I moved to her desk and examined every piece of paper in every drawer. I felt inside her jewelry box. I turned her daypack inside out and flipped through every book in her bookcase. Nothing."

I wanted to get on with it. I told myself to be patient. She was explaining something in the way she was telling this story.

"I felt inside her pillows and beneath her mattress and then I looked under her bed. She has three plastic boxes that slide under the bed. You know, for storage? She keeps her sweaters in them during the summer. She really begged me for them. It's all part of this new compulsive phase. Everything has to be in its place."

Brenda dropped to her knees and reached behind the plaid dust ruffle. She fished around for a moment and then slid a plastic storage case onto the carpet. The case was clear plastic with an opaque blue lid. It measured about eighteen inches by three feet.

"I didn't know what to expect, I mean, I don't know what she keeps in these things when they don't have sweaters in them." She flicked open the lid. "Well, imagine my surprise when I discover that what she keeps in them is bloody basketball clothes."

Brenda changed positions, tucking her knees below her and pulling down her skirt.

I lowered myself to a crouch and leaned forward to examine the case.

A gray practice uniform with Boulder High School's insignia, underwear, a sports bra, socks, and some black and white Nike basketball shoes were thrown in a jumble into the storage case. Rusty bloodstains were on everything. In some places the stains ran amber, almost red. The aroma was metallic.

"I touched them. It's still a bit tacky in places. The blood, it's pretty recent, I think."

I tried to make sense of what I was seeing, of the clothes and the blood. "Brenda, I don't remember ever seeing anything in the hospital chart. Had Merritt been cut someplace?" I recalled images of Merritt in the ICU and wondered if I could have failed to notice linear slashes on her slender wrists.

"No. She's not injured. I helped bathe her in the hospital when she was still unconscious. She's not cut anywhere, I'm sure of it. I suppose it could be menstrual blood, but I don't even want to think about how that might have gotten all over her clothes. There's only a few streaks of blood on her panties, so it doesn't really make sense that it's from her period."

"Is it just clothes in there, in the case? Nothing else?"

"I think so, clothes and shoes. I didn't take everything out. After it registered what I was seeing, I shoved it back under the bed and called you. What should we do? Should we pack it all up and take it to the hospital and confront her with it? See if that will make her talk?"

"Let's think this through, Brenda. Right now, I'm not sure what to do. I guess we need to know if it's her blood. Does she get in fights?"

"No. Merritt's the family peacekeeper. She believes in unilateral disarmament. I think it's part of her rebellion against me and my assertiveness."

"She hasn't mentioned any problems with friends lately, nothing at school?"

"No."

"Has she shown any interest in cults, ritual—"

"No, absolutely not."

The amount of blood screamed serious injury. "Does she carry a knife?"

"Not that I know of. I didn't find one in her backpack. I suppose that's where she would keep one."

An honest answer. Many parents, maybe most, would have stead-fastly denied their daughter carried a weapon. Brenda was apparently will-ing to acknowledge that every adolescent guards some secrets and has some private places that may be as dark as an executioner's heart.

"Wait," I said, "Adrienne—the urologist in the ER? She found blood in Merritt's urine, right?"

"Her urine was pink, that's all. Dr. Arvin said it could be nothing more than a basketball injury. Not serious enough for this." She waved her hand at the bloody clothing.

"Is there blood anywhere else in the house? In the yard? Any sign that things were cleaned up? I guess I'm wondering where this happened."

"I haven't noticed anything. But I don't think I've been in the yard since March. Since Chaney first got sick. That's Trent's domain, the yard."

"Well, if some of the blood is really not dry, this certainly may be re-lated to whatever caused her to try to kill herself."

"I know that. I have no idea how long they've been here. Putting wet clothes in this case is like sealing them in a plastic bag." Brenda suddenly sounded despairing. She stood. I felt as though she had expected some breathtaking insight from me and I was letting her down.

I, too, raised myself from my crouch. "Is this where she was found? After the suicide attempt?"

"No, the EMTs told the doctors she was in the bathroom. It's next door, through there. Chaney and Merritt share that bath." She crossed her arms and raised her chin before she continued. "Let's think about what all this could mean. It could be animal blood, right? There's that possibility. Or it could be something she found, like from a medical laboratory or a blood bank? That seems unlikely, though. She's smart enough not to touch that. Or it could be intestinal blood, she could have been vomiting blood, right? That's possible, too. I can check with Dr. Klein on that. He'll know if she was bleeding internally, although he never mentioned anything to me, which is odd. It's worth asking, though . . ."

She paused as she watched me bend back over the open storage case. The sole of the left Nike was turned up. I wanted to look at the tread.

Brenda asked, "What? What are you looking at?"

"I want to see if there's blood on the bottom of the shoes."

"Why?"

"I'm still wondering whether she wore them home bloody or whether this—whatever this is—happened here."

"And?"

"It looks like there's blood dried inside the treads, but not on the surface."

"So this happened someplace else?"

"That would be my guess, but I'm no expert."

"What difference does that make?"

"I'm not sure."

I stepped toward a closed door across the room. "Is this the bathroom, Brenda? The one where she was found?"

"Yes."

I pushed open the door. The bathroom had a vanity on either end with connecting doors that separated off a communal section with a tub and toilet. I didn't see any evidence of dried blood. Certainly not evidence of the amount of blood that was on Merritt's clothing.

Only one used towel was hanging in the center section of the bathroom. Chaney hadn't been sharing the bathroom with her big sister lately. I visually checked the dark green towel for blood, but couldn't be sure of what I was seeing.

I said, "She had to bathe. I mean, to get that much blood off before she took the pills, she had to bathe."

Brenda replied, "Yes, I'm sure she did. There would be residue on the tile or in the drain, wouldn't there? Can't they do chemical tests for that?"

"They can," I said, considering how much O.J. had changed our society. "Where was she when the paramedics came?"

"Right there, on the floor, between the bathtub and the toilet."

I continued to look around the narrow bathroom as though discovering evidence that Merritt had showered away the blood would tell me something new and important. If I were covered in blood, what would I do first? I decided that I would wash my hands.

I lifted the bar of soap from beside the sink. The creamy muck below was tinted pink.

"Brenda? Look, she washed up in here."

Brenda said, "So? She obviously washed up somewhere. It figures that it would be here."

"You're right, it doesn't mean anything." I put the bar of soap back in place and, to dry my hand, chose a towel from a neat stack on top of the vanity.

Beneath the top towel was a small handgun.

Ten

"Brenda? Brenda?"

In the bathroom mirror I watched her. Her lips parted and she backed slowly away from me, feeling for the cool tile of the wall, edging her sculpted nails into the grout lines, putting distance between herself and the reality of the gun. Her complexion had paled to the same color as the off-white ceramic tile. I tried to imagine what it would be like to discover a handgun in your child's bedroom and saw the answer in Brenda's face: shock and horror and disbelief.

"Brenda, come on, let's get out of here, go find a place to sit down."

I took her hand and led her back through Merritt's room to the landing at the top of the stairs, where a pair of ladderback chairs flanked an elaborately painted hunt table. Meekly, she lowered herself to one of the chairs.

"Brenda, I'm so sorry. This must be yet another terrible shock for you." Silently, I rebuked myself for how lame my words seemed, how they always seemed to sound in the face of the harsh winds of tragedy.

She moved her lips as though she wanted to speak, but no sound emerged; all she managed to do was shrug her shoulders in resignation, look plaintively back toward Merritt's room, and start to cry.

I realized as I stood helpless that the house was growing dark. I flicked on a hall light and the brightness seemed to nudge Brenda from her stupor.

She spoke so suddenly and so rapidly, she startled me. I had trouble changing gears to keep up with her torrent of questions. "Why does she have a gun? Why does Merritt need a gun? Is she in some kind of trouble? Why is it in the bathroom? Why would it be there?"

My impulse was to say something perfectly inane like, "Kids today, who knows?" but caught myself enough to offer a less offensive platitude instead. I said, "I'm sure there's an explanation."

"She's my baby, my little girl." Her words were slower now. After weeks of dealing with Chaney's illness, she was so accustomed to the shock of trauma that it now energized her only briefly.

"Brenda, the gun in there? Does it belong to you and John? Do you recognize it?"

"No, no, no. God, no. We don't own any guns. With the baby in the house, oh God, no. I wouldn't think of it. Trent wouldn't have it."

I've been told I'm slow sometimes. But it wasn't until that moment that the events of the previous thirty-six hours joined my current consciousness and I realized that Dead Ed Robilio had spilled a lot of blood recently and that no murder weapon had been discovered at his home. Although a connection between Merritt and Dr. Edward Robilio seemed remote, I feared the worst. Boulder, Colorado, just didn't have too many pools of unexplained blood, bloody basketball uniforms, or bathrooms with mysterious handguns.

"Brenda, I want to go see something. Please wait for me here, okay? I'll be right back."

She nodded through her shock. If I had said I was going to be gone a minute to pick up some keys I'd left on Jupiter, she would have nodded at that, too.

I found my way back to the bathroom and turned on all the lights and bent close to examine the weapon, still resting on the towel. I was pretty sure the gun was coated with a not insignificant amount of dried blood. The caked, rusty tint covered not only the grip but also the blunt barrel.

I flicked the bathroom lights back off and returned to Brenda at the top of the stairs. I didn't think she had moved a centimeter.

Brenda asked, "What? Did you find something?" Naive hope infused her tone, as though she expected me to come back with news that the weapon was really a toy and that Merritt was playing a cruel joke.

"Yes, I did. I went to see if there was any blood on the gun."

"Is there?"

"Yes. There's blood on the gun."

"Oh, God," she said, the vigor returning to her cadence. "What should I do? I can't handle this now. I just can't. I can't handle any more anything. And I have to go to work. I can't miss any more work. I just can't. And then I'm spending the night with Chaney. It's my night with Chaney. And Trent? Oh, God, poor Trent. What did she do? Merritt, damn it, what did you do?" The words spilled out smoothly, like a child down a slide.

Brenda cried again and then her muscles tensed as she tried to contain the pressure of her agony. Tendons appeared to burst through the smooth surface of her skin and I thought her neck was so taut and constricted she wouldn't possibly be able to breathe.

"Brenda, look at me." I used my softest voice but tried to imbue it with determination and authority. Lauren had once told me when I used it with her that it was one of my sexiest tones. I never understood that.

Brenda raised her eyes to mine.

"This isn't just a family problem anymore. I think what you need to do right now is call your husband and tell him what it is that we found."

"You're right, I need to tell Trent about this. I do, right? Don't I?"

"Yes, you need to talk to your husband. Then you need to call the TV station and tell your boss you won't be in tonight. I can do that for you if you would like; I'll just explain that it's something about your daughter. I'm sure they'll understand."

"I'm supposed to tape tonight. It's a story I've been working on. But I can't do that now, no. Yes, would you call them for me?"

"Of course." I wanted her to face me. Her eyes were fixed on the stairs, as though salvation were coming from that direction. "Please look at me, Brenda. After we do those other things, I think we need to phone the police."

"The police? Call the police? You think Merritt's done something wrong, don't you? Something with that gun in there?"

"Yes. I guess I do think that's possible."

"And you think, what, that she feels terrible about whatever it was and that's why she tried to kill herself?"

"It's a simple explanation. It may not ultimately be correct, but it's a reasonable place to start."

"You want me to call the cops on my own daughter?"

"Well," I said, steeling myself for her reaction, "actually, I'm thinking we should call your brother-in-law and ask him for some advice. He'll know what to do."

"What?" Her face was as incredulous as if I had suggested she call the White House and ask the First Lady for counsel on how to handle Merritt. *What would you do if you found a bloody gun in Chelsea's bedroom?*

"I said I think you should call Sam."

"You know my brother-in-law? You know about—? You know Sam and Sherry?"

In my face she probably saw a mixture of acknowledgment and confusion.

"How do you know Sherry and Sam? Are you friends with them? Goddamn it, you should have told me."

"I know Sam, not Sherry. We're friends. It started off as a police thing a few years ago, but since then we've become friends. I barely know Sherry."

Brenda made a series of funny little popping sounds, rapidly expelling air from between her closed lips. I wondered if it helped her think.

"But he told you about . . . that Merritt was his niece, that I'm his sister-in-law, that—you know?"

"No, no one told me. Sam and I stumbled over the connection last night. We went to a hockey game together, and he started telling me about some personal things, some family things. Chaney's situation came up—"

"And you pieced the rest together?"

"Yes. We both did."

"And he told you about the . . . division between my sister and me?"

"He told me there was a problem, but he didn't go into any details about it."

"But you know enough to understand that calling my brother-in-law for help isn't the most uncomplicated choice that I could make right now?"

"Yes, Brenda, I realize that. But if I were in your shoes—and I admit that it's hard for me to imagine what your shoes must be like right now—with what we found, I would certainly want Sam to be the first one to look in Merritt's bathroom and in that box under her bed. If it's not Sam, it's going to be some faceless cop who doesn't care about Merritt. Sam cares. I don't know how well you know him, Brenda, but I really trust him to know what to do, and to do what's right."

Brenda ignored my vote of confidence in Sam. She asked, "Do the police have to know? Do they?" Her voice rose with challenge.

"What do you—?"

"Do they have to be notified? I mean, let's think about this carefully. Is it a crime to have bloody clothes under your bed? Is it a crime to have a gun in your own bathroom? Why do we have to call the police at all? I don't see any crimes anywhere. Do you?"

"Are you saying you don't want the police to know about the bloody clothes and the gun?"

"I'm not sure what I'm saying. What's the crime here? What do the police need to know? My family is suffering about all we can suffer right now. Actually, I would have said that this morning, but I never imagined . . . you know, I don't think I want to invite any more misery on my girls or on Trent. What if I don't call the police? What if I just throw everything away, get rid of the gun? I'm not obligated to talk to the police."

"Brenda, do you really mean what you're saying? Do you realize what the implications would be? You would be destroying evidence."

Her denial was becoming more palatable to her the more she discussed it. "Evidence of what? Why not? You can't say anything to anyone. You're a therapist. What if I just clean everything up, find someplace to dump it? Life goes on with no increase in the misery quotient."

I wasn't about to volunteer to be Brenda's accomplice. "I'm Merritt's therapist, Brenda. Not yours. And I would have to think about it some more, but I doubt that our conversations here, today, are covered by therapeutic privilege. I'll be as clear as I can be right now. I strongly recommend calling Sam. Merritt could be in much more serious trouble than you and I imagined earlier."

Her eyes looked betrayed. "You'll call Sam even if I don't?"

I shrugged. "First, I'll take a few minutes to consider everything that's happened tonight a little more rationally, but yes, in the end I think I might. The point is that you should call him."

She seemed to be considering what I said I might do while I was having second thoughts about whether I would actually do it. She nodded twice, assuring herself of something or reminding herself of something.

"I'm . . . a little out of touch," she said, managing a self-conscious smile. "With the news, I mean. I've had a few little things on my mind distracting me the last few days. I've paid no attention to the rest of the world. Is there . . . has there been something that happened recently, a crime, something specific, that you're worried Merritt might be involved in? A shooting? I guess I'm asking if there's been a shooting. Something I should know about, but don't."

I found it ironic that Brenda, a reporter, was out of touch with the news. I had hoped to not have to go into yesterday's crime scene with her. "Yes, Brenda, there was a shooting. The victim was found yesterday. It's in today's papers."

"I haven't seen today's papers. I've been with Chaney. The shooting was in Boulder?"

"Yes."

"Yesterday? Then the timing is wrong. She's been in the hospital since—I've lost track of days—since Saturday, right? I mean, the shooting couldn't have happened before Merritt took the drugs, could it?"

I thought about the decomposing body of Dead Ed and the air-conditioned study and Sam's comment about how much more noxious the smell could have been. "I don't know that the coroner has determined time of death. But the police were thinking sometime Friday. Close enough that it's impossible to rule out Merritt."

"No arrests yet?" Her voice seemed to be coming out of a long tunnel.

"Not that I've heard about."

"Who was it? Who was shot?"

"A doctor across town was shot in his own home."

Her face flushed. "Do you know his name?"

"Yes, I do. His name is Edward Robilio."

She looked like she'd been slapped. "Oh, my God." She covered her mouth in her hands. "No! Did you say Dr. Robilio? It can't be. No, it can't be." Her lips pulsed as she expelled another long series of tiny puffs of air.

I misjudged Brenda's shock over the victim's identity. "I'm sorry, I didn't know you knew him."

She pulled one hand from in front of her face and waved me off, as if we were playing charades and I wasn't even close to guessing what her pantomime was supposed to mean.

She said, "Dr. Robilio is dead?"

"Yes."

"You're sure?"

"Yes."

"Murdered?"

"It appears so."

"Dear God in heaven, I don't believe it. Merritt, Merritt, Merritt. Oh my dear baby, what did you do?"

"Brenda, what do you mean? Do you know Dr. Robilio? Does Merritt?"

She shook her head and waved her hand as though she could erase the words she had spoken from midair. "Nothing. No, I don't know him. Merritt doesn't either. I didn't mean anything. Nothing."

I pressed her to no avail.

With the mention of Dr. Robilio's name, Brenda stopped protesting and didn't continue to question the wisdom of including Sam in whatever it was that was evolving under her roof. She did make it clear that she wasn't looking forward to dealing with the repercussions that would rock through the family once Sam became involved.

I placed the call. We moved downstairs to the living room to await Sam's arrival.

Eleven

Sam arrived no more than ten minutes after I phoned him. He greeted Brenda meekly, awkwardly, from just inside the front door. He didn't seem to know what to do with his hands.

Her comfort level with him was much higher. She had regained some of her composure and stood up from the sofa and kissed him politely on the cheek before retreating to her cocoon and pulling a big pillow to her abdomen.

He eyed me suspiciously. I expected he still wasn't quite comfortable with the level of intimate involvement I was having with his family.

I said, "Thanks for coming so quickly, Sam."

He dismissed me by saying, "Yeah." He turned his attention back to his sister-in-law. "What's up that you need a cop, Brenda? Alan said it's about the girls." Sam didn't relate to Brenda what I'd said to him on the phone, that I was afraid Merritt was wrapped up in whatever terrible events had transpired at Edward Robilio's house.

Sam was wearing his cowboy boots, a pair of jeans, and a flannel shirt the size of a patio umbrella. He had rushed over from home, not from the office. I wondered how, or if, he had explained this errand to Sherry.

Brenda just stared at her brother-in-law, and didn't seem to know how to respond to his question about why she had wanted him to come over. She looked to me, suggesting it had been my idea.

Which it had. Intent on diffusing the awkwardness and latent antagonism, I piped in, "What she needs, Sam, is . . . family who just happens to be a cop."

He kept his eyes on Brenda. He said, "Why? What's this about? I've been trying to help for weeks. Why are you willing to let me in now, Brenda? What's changed?"

Brenda said, "Sam, I'm sorry you've been caught up by . . . me and Sherry. But this is about Merritt. I'm afraid," she pointed at me with her chin, "*he's* afraid that she's in trouble. I want your advice, okay? Alan, would you take him upstairs and show him what we found up there? I don't think I can go through all that again."

I said, "Of course. Sam?"

He hesitated before he followed me up the stairs. When we reached the landing, I began to explain about the call I had received from Brenda earlier in the evening urging me to come right over, and then I recounted Brenda's story about rifling through Merritt's things, hoping to find an explanation for her suicide attempt.

"What did she find? A note?"

"Worse. See for yourself."

We moved into Merritt's room. Sam paused at the door and his shoulders sagged. He gazed upon the cozy space as an uncle would, not as a cop would. His eyes were warm and hovered on the basketball tribute wall with silent approval. For him, it was a poignant introduction, another significant step or two into his niece's life.

He said, "Have to get this girl some hockey posters, what do you think?"

I said, "That would be nice, Sam. Maybe Forsberg, or Ricci, the girls seem to go for them."

"Yeah. I'll get her a Forsberg. Maybe I can get it signed. I know some people."

He hadn't turned toward the storage case. "Anyway, when Brenda looked under the bed . . . Sam, do you have gloves with you? Latex gloves?"

"No." His voice betrayed his increasing concern. "Do I need them? There's some in the car."

"You decide." I pointed at the plastic storage case on the floor by the bed. "Those are Merritt's things in there. A basketball uniform she uses for practice. Her shoes."

He lowered himself gracefully and squinted at the contents of the box. He pulled a pen from his shirt pocket and moved a couple of garments with the blunt end.

In one long exhale, he said, "And this is blood. Lots . . . and lots and lots of blood."

"Brenda says some of it was still tacky earlier. She fished around in there before I came over."

"This thing was where?"

"Under the bed, with the lid closed."

"You know that for sure, or is that what Brenda says?"

"It's what Brenda says."

Over the years I've learned that when he ponders things, Sam's breathing grows shallow, and I sometimes find myself straining to see the smallest movement of his chest or back to be certain he is still inhaling. I didn't see a quake in his muscles before he spoke again half a minute later.

"If you and Brenda thought this was Merritt's blood all over these clothes, you wouldn't have called me, would you? There wouldn't have been a reason to call me. Kids bleed all the time, and ninety-nine point nine percent of the time it's not a crime."

Sam was thinking out loud and seemed to be reaching a conclusion that he had been summoned here more as cop than as uncle. His question about the blood had been rhetorical. But I was anxious, so I answered anyway.

"Merritt's not cut anywhere. Brenda helped sponge-bathe her in the hospital when she was still unconscious. She says she doesn't remember seeing even a scratch."

He swallowed. "Menstrual blood?"

I shrugged but he wasn't looking at me. "Possible, but not likely. Brenda says the underwear that's in that pile has only a couple of small streaks of blood on it. Take a look yourself."

He exhaled deeply. "No . . . thanks, I'll pass. I think I'll leave it to someone else to examine my niece's underwear for evidence of someone else's blood. Jeez. What does Brenda want me to do? Get the blood tested?"

"Calling you was my idea, Sam. I had to talk Brenda into it. And it wasn't just because of the clothes, but also because we found a gun."

"Oh, hell, this is great, you found a gun, too?" His voice betrayed resignation now, no longer curiosity.

"After the suicide attempt, the friend who came over and found Merritt found her in the bathroom." I pointed to the open doorway across the bedroom. "I went in there to see if there were signs of blood there. I was figuring that there was so much blood on Merritt that she had to have washed up somewhere because she wasn't bloody when she was brought into the ER. I lifted the bar of soap on the vanity, and sure enough, there's pink scum underneath it. When I took a towel to dry my hands, I saw a gun sitting on top of the next towel in the pile. I knew then we had to call you. We didn't touch it."

Sam eased me out of the way with a swipe of his forearm and leaned close to the chunky handgun. "It's a Smith and Wesson. And it's caked with dried blood, right? Is that how you have it?"

I didn't know about the Smith and Wesson part. "Yeah, that's how it looks to me."

"Is the gun John's?"

"Brenda says it's not, they don't keep any guns in the house."

Sam's mind took bits and flakes of information and turned them into criminal theories with the artistic skill a mosaic artist uses to assemble tiles.

"Well, they have a gun in the house now. Except I'd bet a pitcher of beer that the serial number on this one is going to tell me that where it really belongs is over in Dead Ed Robilio's house. What on earth is Merritt mixed up with? Do you know what kinds of kids she's been hanging around with? You don't know the answer to that, do you?"

Sam was asking me if Merritt was talking to me, her psychologist, about Dead Ed or guns or bloody clothes. He knew I shouldn't answer. He didn't expect that to matter. This was family.

"Let's just say this is news to me. My guess now, Sam, is that I'm beginning to understand the reason she's not talking to anyone. This . . . this discovery is an important step. Maybe it'll shake her out of her silence."

"Alan, if that gun is the one missing from Dead Ed's house, and if the blood all over those clothes is Dead Ed's blood, Merritt's going to receive enough of a jolt either to shake her out of any stupor, or to jar her into total catatonia."

"You're right, there's no telling."

"You know, Malloy doesn't have shit on Dead Ed. They don't know what to do about that suicide note. If it's murder, they don't even have a suspect. There's two dozen people working on it and the investigation is wide open. And now it looks like I'm going to hand them my niece on a silver platter."

"Maybe we're wrong. How long will it take to analyze things? The blood and the gun?"

"The serial number on the weapon? I just need to make a call. The ballistics should be straightforward. We have the slugs from Dead Ed's house. Everett could do the match in his sleep. Given the hour, he may have to. The blood? The lab guys will know something tentative by morning, maybe later tonight if they're motivated. And I have a funny feeling they're going to get motivated."

"DNA?"

"Takes weeks, even months."

"Why don't you make the call about the serial number? The suspense isn't doing anyone any good."

"Yeah." He started to walk out of the room. Took a few seconds to assess Merritt's space. "Neat room. Neat kid. This doesn't add up."

"No, it doesn't, I agree."

I am not someone naive about teenagers, and never really expect adolescent lives to line up in patterns that approach orderliness, but at that moment Sam was an uncle, not a cop, and was seeking solace from me, not counsel.

In my outpatient practice I was treating a sweet nineteen-year-old girl with an eating disorder. Over the past week she had begun talking about having molested her young male cousin over a two-year period when she was younger. I didn't believe her at first. Believing that such a sweet, fragile kid was a child molester was like discovering that Mother Teresa masqueraded as a hooker.

I had been thinking about that girl a lot lately. And I had been thinking about Merritt a lot lately. But I didn't tell Sam. He wanted to believe that Merritt was a good kid and that she hadn't killed Dead Ed. For now, that was probably best.

He stopped at the landing at the head of the stairs. "I don't know if they're going to listen to my advice. Brenda and John. So I want you to make sure that if this serial number comes back a match that the first call they make is to Cozier Maitlin. They're under too much pressure, they're not thinking straight. I don't want them doing anything to jeopardize this kid. Maitlin will know what to do. Cozier Maitlin. You got it?"

"I understand what you're saying, Sam."

He turned his back on me before he said, "I'm not offering advice here."

"I know, Sam. Cozy's a good choice. I know what's at stake."

"No, you don't. You don't have a clue."

Twelve

Cozier Maitlin arrived in his black BMW before the Boulder Police Department reinforcements showed up en masse. I met him on the driveway and quickly underscored the complications of his new client's situation.

Cozy towered over me. Briefly, a few months back, Cozy Maitlin had been my lawyer—and Lauren's—and I'd spent quite a few hours getting to know him. I'd never become accustomed to his full head advantage over me. I stand a touch over six-one, yet with Cozy I always felt like a point guard trying to drive the lane against a towering center.

He relished his size when he was trying to be intimidating, and he was capable of intimidating with aplomb. After my presentation of a synopsis of the night's events he was visibly upset with my actions and he didn't mince words letting me know it. "Given what you suspected was going on you should have called me first, right away, not Sam Purdy—"

"He's family, Cozy. He's—"

"I don't care. Sam's a cop, and because he was invited into this house that means I don't have much of a reason not to grant a waiver so that any cop who wants to can come into this house, which means the police don't need to harass a judge for a warrant for permission to poke around inside. They would have gotten in anyway, but now we've lost the advantage of being able to appear cooperative."

"Brenda and I did cooperate. We called the police right away."

He seemed to be considering whether to lecture me in more depth as he looked toward the front door. "Where is she? The mother? Is she inside? I hope she's not chatting with Sam, or anyone else for that matter."

"I don't think so. Sam's been deferential to her and no one else is here yet. Although she's a little shocky, she's bright, and she understands what's going on. She's inside, in the living room. I suggested she not talk to anyone before you arrived and spoke with her. Sam heard me and told her it was good advice."

His tone softened. "Bravo. At least you learned something from our adventures last fall. Sam Purdy said that, really—told her not to talk? That's hard to believe."

"Merritt's his niece, Cozy, and the family situation is messy. He's worried about her welfare. Although my guess is that he doesn't want anyone to know it, he insisted that I convince Brenda to call you."

"I have to digest all this a little. But I don't trust it. In my experience most cops are cops first and uncles second." He started toward the front door, and his voice dropped and softened. "How's Lauren?"

"Adjusting, Cozy. She's visiting her family right now; her mother is ill. But Lauren's doing okay, considering. Thanks." I rapped the front door sharply and pushed it open. "You're still seeing Adrienne?" I knew he was, but thought I'd see how he would respond. And I was still struggling with what to say when people asked me about Lauren.

Cozy hesitated before going in. "Yes, I am still seeing the little doctor. Being with her is a constant surprise. Every time—I mean every time—it's like parachuting in the dark. You never know what the hell you're going to find. It's fun, it's disconcerting." He stepped in. "Why don't you show me what you discovered and introduce me to my client's mother?"

We walked into the narrow foyer, and turned to face the living room. I said, "Cozier Maitlin, this is Brenda Strait. Brenda, Cozier Maitlin, the attorney we discussed."

I was tired. It hadn't occurred to me that Cozy would know her from the news, but apparently he watched Channel 7 and he recognized her immediately.

With a hint of rebuke in his voice that was directed at me, he said, "Alan—Dr. Gregory—only told me your first name when he phoned. I didn't realize who you were, or the extent of the stress you've been under already. You are the little girl's mom as well, aren't you? The one who is so sick."

"Yes, I'm Chaney's mom. Would it have mattered, Mr. Maitlin, had you known who I was?"

"No. But I like to be prepared, Ms. Strait. In every situation. That's all. I'm terribly sorry for your daughter's illness and for the problems with the insurance company. And, well, for this new . . . complication."

I found it curious that Brenda had calmed so considerably. It appeared she was taking Maitlin's measure. "Do you have children, Mr. Maitlin?"

"No, I don't. My ex-wife has twins. I'm very close to them. I can't imagine what you're going through."

"You know, I can't either," said Brenda.

Cozy continued, "I would like to look around a little before we talk some more. I hope that's acceptable. Would you mind terribly telling anyone who might arrive eager to speak with you that I have advised you to speak only with me for the time being?"

"That's fine, Mr. Maitlin."

"Well, then, Alan?"

I had been wondering where Sam was. Cozy and I found him upstairs in Merritt's room, his hands in his pockets, taking in every minute detail of her bedroom.

"Sam," I said, "Cozy Maitlin's here."

He didn't bother to say hello or turn to face us. He said, "Hold your breath, Counselor. I was invited in."

"Hello, Sam. No need to be so defensive. What have you found?"

Sam finally faced us. It seemed to take him at least five little steps to turn 180 degrees. He stuck his tongue in his cheek. I couldn't tell whether he was planning to be cooperative or whether he was planning to be obstreperous. I wouldn't have taken bets. He said, "Alan told you about the bloody clothes? There they are. Please don't touch them." He pointed at the storage case that was open on the floor. "And the weapon is in the bathroom, through there. Ditto about touching."

In the distance I heard the sounds of vehicles arriving and the muffled thumps of door slams.

Sam did, too. "That'll be the department."

"What took so long?"

"Warrant. This case won't be mine, you know. I wasn't catching tonight, and with the family complications and everything, this will go to someone else."

I said, "Of course. Do you know who?"

"No. But we'll find out soon enough. Depending on how the blood types out, they may just fold this into the Dead Ed investigation."

I asked, "Did you get a call back on the serial number, Sam?"

Cozy was crouched over the bloody clothes. He raised his head from a serious examination of the contents of the storage box and waited with me to hear Sam's reply and for an elucidation of Sam's reference to Dead Ed.

I was certain Cozy already had a few dozen questions of his own. His restraint surprised me.

Downstairs, the front door opened and I heard a voice say, "Police officers," and Brenda Strait reply, "Come in. I'm Brenda Strait."

And this is the Strait Edge.

Sam, Cozy, and I were still in Merritt's bedroom. Sam gazed toward the bathroom for a few seconds, nodded twice, and said, "I have to go bring them up to speed. You two shouldn't be in here alone, you know? You actually shouldn't be here at all. My sergeant's going to string me up for not sealing this room." He made sure my eyes found his before he took a step.

He wanted me to acknowledge that his message had been received. I nodded.

Cozy stopped him. He said, "Detective?"

"Yeah?"

"Thanks for the referral."

Sam snorted, "Don't mention it, Mr. Maitlin. I mean that literally: Don't mention it. And don't make me regret I made it."

Sam was already down the stairs when I said, "Sam was telling me that the serial number is a match, Cozy. The gun belongs to the guy Sam was talking about before—Dead Ed. You read about it? He was shot over the weekend. Edward Robilio. He's a doctor."

Cozy responded impatiently, "Yes, yes, I know who he is. But calling Edward Robilio a doctor is like calling Bill Gates a programmer. If this kid—I'm sorry, what's her name, Merrill?"

"Merritt."

"If she is involved in that shooting, and it certainly sounds like Sam thinks she is, I need to get someone over to the hospital right away and make sure she doesn't say anything to anybody. This is quickly going to become complex."

"Why?"

"Because of Edward Robilio. He founded MedExcel ten, eleven years ago. It's become a major regional health care provider. Exclude Kaiser, and he's probably the biggest player in the state in managed health care. He stands to make tens of millions of dollars when his company is sold."

"I didn't know he was so prominent. I'd heard he was in the insurance business, but I don't usually pay attention to such things."

"Lawyers do."

"Well, I don't think you have to worry about Merritt talking, Cozy. Not her, not now."

"You said she's recovering, right? If she's awake, she can talk. She's awake?"

"Yes, she's awake. But you don't have to worry about her talking."

"Why not?"

"Cozy, just accept you don't have to worry about it, okay?"

Half-jokingly he asked, "Is she mute?"

I looked away.

He said, "She's mute? Not talking at all, that kind of mute?"

"I think I can tell you that at least physically, she is able to talk."

"But she's not talking? She's volitionally silent?"

I was as mum as my patient.

Cozy said, "Totally silent?" Then he frowned. "Gosh, what a gift. Finally, the client of my dreams."

Cozy and I drove across town in my Land Cruiser. He asked questions. I answered or deflected.

He waited in the hall while I walked into Merritt's hospital room. She was dressed in yellow leggings, white socks, and a T-shirt. This T-shirt said XPLOSION. She had raised the head of the bed past forty-five degrees and was staring at the nine o'clock news on the tube. Channel 2. A pile of newspapers carpeted the sheets near her feet.

I excused the nurse who was providing one-to-one. She seemed thrilled at the chance to get out of the room.

"Merritt, hello. I'm sorry to stop by without calling. May I sit?"

Because it was to my advantage, I took her shrug to mean "yes" and lowered myself into the vinyl-covered chair where the nurse had been sitting. The chair felt too good; I was exhausted.

Before I could speak again, Merritt startled me by standing up.

I had never seen her vertical. I popped back out of the chair as though I were performing in a final exam for a Ph.D. in etiquette. She stood, confused, about three feet away from me. She and I both realized that I was blocking her path.

This would have been a great time for her to talk, maybe say something like, "Get out of my way." Anything to break the ice. Instead, she pointed at the door that led to her bathroom and I realized that she thought I had stood up to keep her from running.

I blushed and stepped aside so she could pass. She disappeared into the bathroom and closed the door.

Merritt was tall. As she passed by me I realized that although she was only a couple of inches shorter than me, as long as her legs were, they were still way too short for the rest of her body. She had broad swimmer's shoulders and small, defined breasts, but her hips and buttocks had just started to round. I was reminded of watching puppies grow into their paws, and decided that if Merritt were to grow into that extended torso, she would top out at six-two, easy.

The toilet flushed and water splashed into the sink. Merritt stepped back out of the bathroom and chanced a quick glance my way. She shuffled a step forward as I took one more back. Behind her I could see Cozy Maitlin pointing at his new client's back and then at his watch.

She settled onto the bed. I pulled forward on the chair.

"Merritt, there's something I need to tell you. It's very important. Could you please turn off the television for a minute?"

I immediately recognized that I had shocked her unnecessarily. I watched panic roll into her eyes and settle into her expression. She was expecting bad news about her sister.

Her lips, parted at rest, closed into a tight line. She swallowed.

I waited one second and said, "No, it's not about your sister."

She raised her chin and seemed to force a deep exhale. Her shoulders dropped. But she still didn't relax. I wished right then that I'd paid more attention when people talked about body language during graduate school.

"The TV? Please."

She pecked a button that muted the sound but left the picture intact. It was a concession on her part and it was good enough.

"Your mother called me to your house tonight, a couple of hours ago. Your stepdad is in Denver with your sister and she didn't want to upset them. She wanted me to come over because . . . she found a plastic storage case under your bed—the one with the bloody clothes and shoes in it—and she didn't know what to do. She wanted someone else to see it."

I almost laughed at the exasperated face that Merritt made in response to my grave announcement.

I was left to guess what it meant and I guessed that she was aggravated that her mother had been snooping in her room. The discovery of the bloody clothes was secondary or irrelevant to her.

"There's more, Merritt. After I got there, I went into your bathroom looking for more blood. I discovered the gun that was in the pile of towels by the sink."

She opened her mouth and wrinkled up her nose, which was tiny and upturned, the end barely the size of the knuckle on my pinky, and made a quizzical cluck from the back of her throat as if to say, "What? You found what?"

I noted her surprise. "Your mom and I talked about what to do. Your Uncle Sam came over—your mom called him."

Her mouth opened farther and her eyes were as wide as I'd yet seen them.

I said, "It was my idea, calling Sam—your uncle."

She rolled her eyes. *Duh.*

"Sam took a look at your room, at the clothes, and at the gun. He made a couple of calls to some forensic people at the police department. The serial number on the gun in the bathroom matches one that is missing from the scene of a murder that took place late last week in Boulder. Now everyone is afraid that you might be implicated somehow."

Merritt's face grew sad. I was perplexed as she tried to force a small grin, but when she did the corners of her mouth turned down instead. It was the closest thing I'd seen to a smile from her.

"The police are at your house right now, examining the bloody clothes and the gun, and . . . looking around for other evidence. Your Uncle Sam and your mother and I all thought that . . . because of what was found, that you might be in trouble and that you might be needing a lawyer. The one who Sam wanted for you, the best one in town, is here with me, out in the hall, and he would very much like to meet you. His name is Cozier Maitlin. I'm sure it would be fine with him if you call him Cozy."

Merritt leaned forward a little so that she could see the tall man standing in the corridor. She looked at him warily, as she might examine the newest kid who had arrived in class. With the index finger of her left hand she pushed the button that lowered the bed flat and slowly reclined from his view. As soon as the bed came to rest at horizontal, she rolled away from me as well, facing the window and the wall. I could see the small quivers of stifled cries rumbling through the long, lean muscles on her back.

"Merritt, we all want to help you any way we can."

I thought I heard a sob. "I'm going to invite Mr. Maitlin in unless you tell me not to. He's hoping you will talk to him about all this. He'll need your assistance, Merritt, to make sense of everything."

She didn't protest. I stood and walked to the door and said, "Come on in, Cozy."

Maitlin walked in and walked over to the bed. I said, "Merritt Strait, this is Cozier Maitlin."

Cozy dropped to a squat beside the bed and lowered his voice to an octave level I had never heard from him before. "Hello, Merritt, I'm an attorney. It appears that you may be in some serious trouble with the police whether you have done anything or not. And I would like to help."

Merritt replied with a sob.

"Alan, Dr. Gregory, warned me that you haven't been saying much the last few days. But this is serious. I hope you'll reconsider, at least with me."

Cozy and I both watched her for signs that she was even hearing him. If Merritt was reconsidering anything, it wasn't readily apparent to me.

"Okay. As ironic as this may sound, one of the things I was going to advise you is that it's important that you not speak to anyone but your lawyer and your doctors. It's very likely that the police will pay you a visit tonight. Unless you object, I will notify them now, right away, that you have chosen not to answer their questions. Fortunately, it appears that concurring with my advice about staying silent will be easy for you.

"The next thing I need to let you know is about the possibility that you will either be arrested or detained for questioning in the death of a man named Edward Robilio. He's a doctor."

He waited for her to react to the name of the deceased. She didn't. The name either didn't mean anything to her, or she already knew it.

"Should that occur, I hope that the police will provide me with the courtesy of some advance warning so that I can arrange for someone to accompany you through the process of being booked, but they are not required to do so.

"With your doctors' consent, you may be removed temporarily from the hospital by the police. You must remember the entire time that you have the right to remain silent. And, as I've made clear, I would prefer that you exercise that right. Would you like me to tell you what to expect in the event that you are forced to go through this alone?"

Merritt was as still as a statue.

Her silence in response to questions provided the questioner an awful lot of latitude. Cozy told her what was likely to happen. He asked, "Is it all right with you if Dr. Gregory and I discuss your situation?"

She surprised me by nodding, then reached down with one long arm and tugged the scratchy hospital sheets and thin hospital blanket up past her waist.

I said, "Merritt, your mother will be here soon. As soon as she is done with the police, I imagine. She is very worried about you. Would you like me to stay until she arrives?" I knew I should give her a default option. "I'm going to take no response from you to mean yes, that you would like me to stay with you."

Without facing us or otherwise moving, she shook her head in two long arcs.

I was being dismissed. Without considering the consequences, I reached out and touched her lightly on the biceps of her left arm. I said, "Good night, I'll be back to see you tomorrow."

Cozy said, "Good night, Merritt. We'll do everything we can for you."

Back in the hall outside her room, I motioned for the nurse to come over. She did. I stood near Merritt's door in a position where I could see every move the immobile adolescent might make.

The nurse said, "Yes?"

"Some things have happened that have left this situation much worse than it was an hour ago. Her suicidal risk is sky-high right now. I'm not trying to be insulting by saying this, but doing one-to-ones can be pretty dull duty sometimes. Please don't take your job lightly tonight. That girl's life may depend on it."

The nurse swallowed. I was telling her that the plane she was flying had just gone from autopilot cruise control to engine-out emergency mode.

She said, "This isn't the best environment for a suicidal kid. Maybe she shouldn't be here, Doctor."

"You're absolutely right, she shouldn't be here. But right now she is. My next task tonight is to arrange a quick transfer to a psych hospital. But I'm sure you know how these things go. It may take a while to pull that off, to get approvals and to find her a bed."

The nurse said, "You'll fill in the staff nurses so they can back me up?"

I said, "Of course." She resumed her post.

Cozy said, "How do you read it?"

"I don't."

"What do you mean? I thought reading people was your thing."

"Cozy, she's been upset for days. She's more upset now, that's obvious. But about what? Her sister? The bloody clothes? The gun? The fact that her mother was snooping in her room? The fact that she may be arrested tonight for murder? Maybe about whatever it was that caused her to take all those pills in the first place. We still don't even know what that is. Or maybe it's the fact that her parents haven't been here to hold her hand during much of this. If you can discern any of that from her silence, please tell me, 'cause I don't know the answers to any of those questions."

"I'm just a lawyer, Alan, but assuming the evidence lines up the way it appears it is going to line up, it seems to me that the timing would indicate that her suicide attempt was likely precipitated by her distress over whatever her involvement was in the shooting of Edward Robilio, don't you agree?"

I couldn't shake the succession of images I had of watching Merritt react when I told her about finding the clothes and the gun. "You weren't in there with me at first, Cozy. Merritt seemed more upset about the gun than about the blood. And if I was reading her right, she seemed most upset that someone had been snooping in her room at all."

He considered my words. "Sorry, all that seems trivial to me. I'm not convinced that was it. Maybe you just read it wrong. Lord knows I misread the twins all the time, and they usually don't shut up, ever."

"I'm not jumping to conclusions, either. Right now, though, I need to get her transferred to a locked unit someplace for her own safety."

"To a psychiatric hospital?"

"Yes. A psychiatric hospital. What's your best guess, will she be arrested tonight?"

"Are you asking about timing, or about the police department's intent?"

"Timing, I guess."

"Given what the authorities already have, I'd say she'll be taken into custody, oh, tomorrow sometime. In the interim, if they have as much probable cause as I'm afraid they do, I would imagine that you're going to see a female officer's butt on a chair in this hallway within an hour. Just to keep an eye on things, you know?"

"I know."

"What's her family situation? Brenda's husband is her stepfather? Is that what you said earlier? Where's her real dad?"

"The family has only been in town a short while, maybe six months. Brenda's husband, John Trent, is Merritt's stepfather. He's a psychologist, but I don't know him. I've only talked with him over the phone so far. He's spending almost all of his free time with Chaney, the other daughter, at The Children's Hospital in Denver. Merritt's biological father is currently on an oil rig in the Persian Gulf. I spoke with him briefly already. He'll come see Merritt if she wants him to."

"Are they close? Father and daughter?"

"Brenda says the relationship is fine, friendly. Said he's more like an uncle to her. Merritt, as you know, isn't saying."

"Is he successful at what he does?"

"Presumably, but I don't know. He's an oil-rig worker. Why?"

"Defending Merritt is going to get expensive fast, that's why. I'm hoping someone who loves this kid has some resources to pay me."

At that moment I was thinking it was no accident that managed care arrived first on the doorstep of the medical profession, and not the legal one.

Thirteen

"Do you mind taking a cab back to your car, Cozy? I have some calls to make before I leave here tonight. I need to find an adolescent female bed somewhere for Merritt. And I have to fill out the paperwork to place her on a seventy-two-hour hold."

"No. I don't mind. I'll get a ride." He paused. "You don't have her on a hold already?"

"No. So far the admission has been voluntary. Her docs have stretched out the medical side of her hospital stay hoping she would start talking. She hasn't. But that means she hasn't complained about being here much, either."

He raised his eyebrows at my explanation. I was assuming that now that Merritt was his client, he wasn't sure he wanted her silence to be viewed as tacit agreement to anything. "Will finding a bed for her be difficult?"

"You never know. There aren't that many acute adolescent beds available anymore. I'm going to have to run a gauntlet with her insurance company over approvals, too. But that won't be until the morning."

"If our suppositions are correct, the state will be paying for this admission, I'm afraid. Insurance approvals will be unnecessary."

"I hope you're wrong about that, Cozy. But you're probably right. The truth is that I don't want to see her at Fort Logan. I want her in a private hospital, so I'm going to try to get her a psychiatric bed before she's taken into custody. If we can get that established, maybe the court will be more reluctant to order her moved."

"If she goes to Fort Logan, would you be allowed to continue as her doctor?"

"Probably only as a consultant. Someone on staff would take the case."

"An employee of the state?"

"Yes, an employee of the state. That person could be excellent, could be less than excellent."

"That's not good. I like your alternative better. But, as I said before, I don't think you have more than eighteen hours or so to pull it off. Good luck."

Before he left the hospital, Cozier Maitlin displayed his considerable charm and distributed his business cards to anyone willing to stick out a hand for one at the nursing station. I watched the craftiness from a distance. Although I couldn't hear him, I figured he was busy weaving a legal safety net for Merritt, counting that the good will of the nurses and aides would cause them to call him if they noticed anything unusual happening with the police. From experience, I knew that Cozy didn't miss much where his clients were concerned.

I sat down and wrote an obtuse chart note about the heightened suicide risk and filled out the paperwork for placing Merritt on a seventy-two-hour hold-and-treat. The hold allowed me to hospitalize Merritt against her will for three days because I judged her to be gravely impaired or a significant danger to herself or others. In most instances, after those seventy-two hours expired, I would need to consider other options. In this case, in fewer than twenty-four hours, I feared that the Boulder Police Department would be holding Merritt against her will for reasons much more sinister than mine.

As soon as I finished the paperwork I started calling around looking for available adolescent female psychiatric beds.

Sam Purdy was sitting on the hood of my Land Cruiser when I finally made my way down to the hospital parking lot.

He didn't seem to expend a single calorie of energy as he eyed my long approach across the mostly empty lot. I said, "Hey, Sam."

"I was hoping you would come down pretty soon. I was about to page you. How is she?"

"Hard to say, she's still not talking. These latest developments don't help the situation, I'm afraid. She seems even more entrenched than before."

"Is Brenda up there with her?"

"Not yet. Wait, look, there she is now." Across the parking lot,

Brenda Strait was walking deliberately, with long strides, toward the hospital entrance, her hands in the pockets of a long gabardine trench coat. Her head was down.

"I didn't want to run into her in Merritt's room; that's why I'm down here. It would be too goofy for the kid, I think, given the water that's already passed under the bridge in this nutty family."

"Yeah, I understand. Maybe it's best for now. Merritt actually seemed incredulous when I told her that her mom had called you for help."

"The kid is sharp. Maitlin's on the case, right? That's okay with her?"

"Who knows what's okay with her? But he's definitely on the case. He's working already, putting things in place. He's good, Sam."

"I know he is. That's why we called him."

"Merritt's going to be arrested, Sam? That's for sure?"

He stared at me, not even comfortable with the words I was speaking. His voice suddenly rusty, he said, "Let's get in the car."

I unlocked the doors and we climbed in.

"Merritt's . . . up shit creek. The gun in her bathroom is registered to Dead Ed. It's missing two rounds. Everybody is assuming the blood on her clothes is Dead Ed's blood. You can't know this," he paused to be certain I understood, "but we collected, oh, I don't know, about a dozen good latents from Ed's house that we haven't been able to match to anyone. If any of those belong to Merritt, well, I don't have to paint you a picture."

"When will it all be clear?"

"The forensic team will get some of it packaged overnight. The prints and advanced blood work will take longer. Since Merritt doesn't drive yet, I don't think they will have any file print comparisons for her. While they dot all the i's, someone will watch her hospital room. Is there a cop there yet?"

"No, not yet. Will there be?"

"Soon, I think. She's in a relatively secure place. She's not a flight risk. But she's a kid, and that's always a wild card. We can keep an eye on her as long as she's in the hospital, so there's no real hurry. The profile on this will be stratospheric, given the fallout from the JonBenet case, given who Dead Ed was, given that Brenda's a celebrity, and given that Chaney is so sick and so damn cute. Everyone in the department is going to make damn sure the process looks perfectly deliberate and thoughtful. But I wouldn't be surprised if the DA signs off on the evidence sometime tomorrow, with some fanfare. Then, if I'm reading things right, Merritt will be booked."

"God, Sam, I'm sorry for what everyone is going through. There's enough tragedy here for ten families for an entire lifetime."

"And it's only starting. The worst news could be yet to come for both of these kids. And now I have to go home and tell Sherry."

I glanced over. He was opening and closing his right fist. "You want to tell me about that part? About what happened with Sherry and Brenda?"

"No, not now. Some other time."

I didn't press. "Who's investigating this—Merritt's situation? In the department?"

"The Dead Ed team. It's part of that case. Maybe it's the whole Dead Ed case."

"Whew," I said. "That means Malloy?" Scott Malloy was the detective who, the previous autumn, had arrested my wife for attempted murder and directed a search of my house. I had a lot of feelings about him, not all of them enthusiastic.

"I know you're not crazy about him, but I'm glad it's Malloy, Alan. It could be worse. He'll work it up fair. He's still trying to make amends for what happened with Lauren. And he has kids. I think that will help. It should be somebody who has kids."

"What about motive, Sam? Does anyone have a clue why Merritt would do this?"

"You know, nobody's there yet, as far as I know. That will come last. At first, I wondered about burglary. Sometimes these adolescent girls get into goofy stuff, especially when they're together. But I checked their house real carefully for signs of stashed valuables. I didn't find anything. Maybe she has a partner in crime who has all the stuff stashed. If that's the case, it'll surface. Scum always does."

I asked, "Have you talked to Brenda to get names of Merritt's friends?"

"Yeah, already did that." He readjusted the ventilation vents, which weren't blowing any air.

I said, "I'm going to see one of them tomorrow. A girlfriend named Madison."

"Is this part of therapy? Or can you tell me what you find out?"

"I think I can tell you what I find out."

"Good. What's this button do?" He pointed at the dashboard.

"Rear speakers."

"My car doesn't have any. Merritt's been under a lot of pressure lately. The whole family has. You know that. Doesn't excuse anything, but still."

I said, "Yeah, I know, still. Did Brenda call John while you were at the house?"

"She said she did. She went into the bedroom to do it, though. I didn't hear anything."

"I have to talk with him some more. It looks like I may have to go to Denver to do it."

"John's all right."

I said, "What about the suicide note we found on that little computer? What about that?"

"What about it?"

"If Dead Ed killed himself, there's no crime. Merritt's clean."

"Alan, use your head. There are two gunshots in the victim, not one. No weapon was found on the scene. There's enough evidence—even for an L.A. jury—in my niece's bedroom. The note is easy enough to fake."

"I didn't memorize it, Sam. But it seemed authentic enough to me. I mean, a fifteen-year-old faking that?"

"Maybe, why not? She's bright."

"Were her prints on the computer?"

"We don't have good comps, remember."

"Were anyone's prints but his on the computer?"

He didn't answer me, but his eyes said, "No."

"Wouldn't her prints be on the keyboard? If all those other prints you guys collected were hers, wouldn't hers be on the keyboard, too?"

He placed the pad of a thumb under each of his nostrils and forced air into his nose, clearing his ears. "I know. I know," he said. "It's screwy. I told you that from the beginning. It's goofy."

"Sam, anything else seem not right to you tonight? I mean, did anything strike you as particularly odd?"

"Other than finding my niece's clothes covered with somebody else's blood and a gun in her bathroom? No, nothing else seemed odd at all."

"Brenda didn't seem strange?"

"Come on, Alan. Everything involving this family and Brenda and Sherry is strange."

"Sam, would there have been any reason for Brenda to know Ed Robilio?"

"I'm the last one to ask. I don't know who they know in town. Sherry has never even seen the inside of her sister's house. But given Brenda's line of work, she could know just about anybody, couldn't she?"

"I guess."

"Where are these questions coming from? You know something I should know?"

"I'm not sure where I'm coming from. When I first saw the gun in the bathroom tonight, I immediately thought about picking you up for the Rangers game yesterday and going into that house and seeing . . . the dead doctor. I ran off at the mouth a little about that with Brenda—" I could tell he was about to reprimand me. "Don't, Sam. And I told her that there was an unsolved shooting that had just been discovered in town and told her who the victim was, and I got the impression, when I said that his name was Edward Robilio, that she knew him."

"She didn't say?"

"Not exactly, no. Actually, when I asked if she knew him, she denied it."

Sam said, "But maybe she knew of him? You know, from her work. Maybe she was investigating him or one of his companies for one of her little features?"

"Cozy just told me who he was. He has more than one company?"

"One major one, that's MedExcel; I'm sure you've heard of that one. A couple of smaller related things that he started recently."

"I'll ask her about it, but I don't think she's going to tell me the truth."

Sam nodded. "If Sherry were here, she would be agreeing with that. She thinks that Brenda knows as much about honesty as Simon knows about nuclear physics."

Finally, I had an inkling of what the feud was about. Brenda's lack of honesty was part of Sherry's indictment of her sister. I changed the subject in order to feel Sam out about my plans for the next day.

"I put Merritt on a seventy-two-hour hold tonight. I'm trying to find an adolescent bed in a psychiatric hospital for her. Will the police object to that, to moving her to a psychiatric hospital?"

He was fiddling with the glove box knob. "Probably, but you never know. They may argue that they handle suicide watches better than the hospitals do. If I were you, I would have a judge-proof argument ready, in writing, in case they challenge you. Where are you thinking of putting her?"

"Maybe Centennial Peaks, but I called already and the charge nurse on the evening shift thinks they're full, though they may have a female bed—maybe—coming free by the weekend. There's that new place in Niwot, but I don't have privileges out there and they're getting mixed reviews from people I know, anyway. I'll call them first thing tomorrow."

Sam said, "Wait a second. What about Denver? At Children's? You worked there once, right?"

"Yes."

"It would sure make things easier for John and Brenda, having both kids at the same hospital, don't you think?"

I hadn't considered the advantages of transferring Merritt to The Children's Hospital, probably because it would mean a round-trip daily commute to Denver for me to see her for treatment.

"It's a long way to go, Sam."

"That's my point. Save Brenda and John a ton of commuting. You still okay with the people at Children's, haven't burned any bridges?"

"Yes, I still have privileges there."

"Well?"

"I'll think about it. You want Merritt out of Boulder for some reason?"

"Why would I want that?"

He had that look on his face, so I let it drop. "I don't want her at Fort Logan, Sam. I'll warn you now that no matter where she ends up being admitted, I'm going to try my best to get an ambulance transfer completed before the DA gets all his ducks in a row. I'm thinking it's going to be easier to get a transfer accomplished before the courts and the cops are formally involved."

He didn't actually smile, but his mouth widened. "You're thinking clearly now."

"Can I take you somewhere, Sam? I'm about ready to go home."

"No, I want to hang around until Merritt's protection shows up.

Maybe stop in and see her before I go. It's important to show her we're behind her, right?"

"Absolutely. You're a good uncle, Sam Purdy. She's lucky to have
you."

"I don't know about that. What she needs right now, I'm afraid, is
magic. And I'm no magician."

"Try and convince Lauren and me of that." Sam's police magic had
saved my butt and my wife's butt more than once.

He opened the car door and stepped out. "Think seriously about
Children's. Think of it mostly in terms of what's best for Merritt. And re-
member a couple of things. First, sometimes friends lose sleep for friends.
And second, I'll pay gas, even for this bus."

"You know that's not necessary."

"Good, because I was kidding. I do want to know what that friend of
Merritt's says tomorrow."

I was halfway home when I guessed at Merritt's motive for killing
Dead Ed.

For the first time, I had serious doubts about her innocence.

Fourteen

I drove the rest of the way home thinking about Sam's proposal to hospitalize Merritt in Denver. There would certainly be advantages for John and Brenda, and God knew they could use any break I could offer them. I also suspected that Sam's idea had something to do with Sherry and Brenda that he wasn't talking about.

Emily was thrilled to see me. I'd left her in her dog run while I was gone and when I opened the gate she ran free like an escaped felon. I offered a quick walk down the lane and promised her a meal and a bowl of ice water upon our return. She seemed to think the plan was great, but then, Emily usually thought I was pretty brilliant.

It was one of my favorite things about her.

Lauren had called while I'd been out discovering that Merritt was likely to be arrested for murder.

Bee-eep.

"Hi, hon, it's me. You there? . . . Thought you would be home. Is there a hockey game tonight? I can't keep up. Things are fine here, all things considered. Mom's doing the same. I miss you. I hope you miss me. Give Emily a big hug for me and call me tomorrow. I'm going to bed early. I love you. I mean that. I do."

Lauren usually went to bed early these days. Since the serious exacerbation of her multiple sclerosis that had taken place last autumn, her accommodation to her illness had gone through a major metamorphosis.

Since she had disclosed her illness to me when we were dating, I'd always marveled at her adaptiveness, at how invisible she was able to make her disease appear—or, I guess, disappear. Sure, there were times when I knew she was anchored in place by fatigue or absolutely distracted by some ephemeral pain or unexplainable weakness, but most of the time Lauren managed to appear to live a life unencumbered by her illness. That I knew it wasn't true only managed to make the illusion seem even more magical.

But no more.

The blindness that had struck her last fall persisted to some degree for weeks, and the residual effects were still apparent. Her vision, once so acute and a source of pride, was now compromised by gaps and holes and acuity problems that vexed her daily. She made a silent, unexplained transition from reading the newspaper to watching television in order to absorb current events, and the pile of novels by her bed wasn't getting smaller anymore. She hinted twice that the nineteen-inch TV in our bedroom wasn't really big enough for the room, was it?

The new one I purchased is twenty-seven inches. Much less optimistic than her, I pressed for a thirty-two-inch model. Denial, I think, caused her to insist on the smaller one.

Pain that once struck her occasionally was now a daily siege of heavy afternoon artillery, wreaking constant, wearying, aching damage on the bones and muscles of her legs and hips, sometimes on her hands and shoulders.

When I asked, she complained that her legs were often "heavy" now, and the once daily walks we took with Emily, our dog, on the dirt lanes near our home at sunset were now the exception and not the rule.

She didn't return to work until February 1, and was only now beginning to adopt a caseload in the DA's office that approached half-time. I could see in her face that she wasn't sure she could really do it anymore, but she wasn't ready, yet, to talk about not really doing it anymore.

Alone, I saw all these changes, and alone, I'm sure she did, too.

We rarely mentioned this new evolution of our relationship. I was giving her room to believe that her denial had some validity—that her stubborn belief that all things MS-related would soon pass would again be borne out.

The reality was going to be different this time, I suspected. Although MS is not contagious to other individuals, and I knew I would never catch it from her, I had begun to believe it was a communicable disease within families, and within relationships, and that our relationship was going to need to find a way to adjust to having been freshly stricken.

* * *

All these thoughts went through my head while I walked Emily and fed her and before I picked up the phone and punched in the number for The Children's Hospital in Denver.

If I could pull it off, I decided, I was going to try to get Merritt transferred from Boulder to Denver in the middle of the night. I feared that if I procrastinated, by noon tomorrow Merritt might be on her way first to the Boulder Police Department and then to the state hospital at Fort Logan, out of my care, and out of my influence.

It was simple to discover that there were two female beds available at Children's. I asked the charge nurse to hold one for me and started planning the moves I would need to make to get Merritt to Denver. I knew, to pull this scenario off on time, that I was going to need to be as quick on my feet as Tommy Tune.

Adrienne loved conspiracy, and I had no doubt that I could count on her. When I filled her in on the latest developments, she was irate at the stupidity of the police for even considering arresting Merritt for murder, and she made it clear she would love to interfere with their march to her patient's door. She volunteered to take care of getting Marty Klein's approval for the transfer and would ensure that the discharge and transfer orders were written and ready.

"What about the ambulance?"

Over the phone line I heard her snap her fingers.

"What about MedExcel and approvals?"

"This is the middle of the night, right?"

"That's the plan."

"Merritt is a high suicide risk?"

"Couldn't be higher."

"Sounds like an emergency transfer to me. I'll certify that it's a life-threatening situation and they'll pay for the transfer and probably one in-patient day while they figure out how to save themselves any additional money. After that you'll have to fight with them through the business office at Children's to determine length of stay."

"One day at a time is all I'm asking for now. I can live with that. The state will probably be paying Merritt's bills after tomorrow, that is if they let us keep her at Children's at all. And there are no guarantees about that."

"What about her parents? What do they say about all this? Do they want her at Children's?"

"I haven't asked. That's the last call I have to make. I assume that they'll be agreeable. At least if Merritt goes to the inpatient unit at Children's, they will have both their kids in one building. Let's assume they concur, what do you say we set this up for four-thirty tomorrow morning? We get the paperwork in order and wheel Merritt out of her room in a wheelchair, make it look routine. Do the transfer to the ambulance stretcher down in the ER. There's probably a cop outside her door already, and I don't want the cop to get suspicious about what we're doing until it's too late to stop the transfer."

"Why the dead of night?"

"Sooner the better. Cozy thinks she could be arrested any minute, although he doesn't expect it until tomorrow. And the nurses at Children's don't really want her to arrive at shift change. Is four-thirty okay with you? I said I would try and be accommodating."

"I've synchronized my watch."

Before I phoned Brenda, I also needed to line up a psychiatrist to sponsor the admission at Children's. Given the political ramifications of the case, I wanted that psychiatrist to be one who wouldn't be put off by the media and law enforcement pressure that was sure to follow the revelations about Merritt's arrest.

Joel Franks, the psychiatrist, who was the assistant director of the inpatient unit at Children's, had been a resident of the same hospital in Denver where I had been a clinical psychology intern. Joel and I weren't friends then, and we weren't now, but we had managed to maintain contact over the years through an occasional admission I made to Children's, or at an occasional party at the home of a mutual friend. Although I would never have awarded him psychiatry "best-of-show," I considered him a good example of his breed. My impression was that he viewed me in about the same fashion.

But I knew Joel liked the spotlight. During our training year, I loved attending his case presentations and once skipped a lunch date with a beautiful medical student to see him perform at Grand Rounds. He pushed the podium aside and worked the staid crowd like a stand-up comic with an IQ of 190.

I guessed he would bite at the chance to have Merritt Strait on his unit.

I called him at home, apologized for the lateness of the hour, and explained my dilemma.

He seemed hesitant, as he should have. I dangled details that I'd withheld. First Chaney, then the pending murder charge against Merritt, and finally the elective mutism.

He bit.

As I suspected, Brenda Strait adored the idea of transferring Merritt to Denver and said she would call John and get right back to me.

After less than a minute, the phone rang. Brenda said, "John thinks it's a great idea as long as you stay involved."

"I'm planning to, Brenda."

"Then let's do it, Dr. Gregory."

I had intentionally waited until last to call Cozier Maitlin and ask for his assistance. It wasn't necessary for Cozy to cooperate in this plan, but I thought his presence at the hospital during the transfer might be insurance should we require help distracting the cops.

To say he wasn't thrilled by the hour of the night that I expected him to be in place at the hospital was an understatement.

My head was on the pillow by midnight. Three and a half hours later I was in the shower.

The plan went forward with minimal drama. Everyone did what was expected of them.

I met Brenda Strait in the hospital lobby and together we proceeded upstairs to wake Merritt and inform her of what was happening. She cried at the news and hugged her mother, and then calmly assisted in getting her few personal things together.

The police officer in the hall was suspicious of all the middle-of-the-night activity, but not savvy enough about hospital procedure to actually guess what we were doing behind the closed door to Merritt's room.

The nursing staff helped move Merritt from her bed to a wheelchair for the trip downstairs. As soon as the door to Merritt's room reopened, the officer demanded to be told what was going on. The nurse shrugged and said, "Doctor's orders; we're taking her downstairs for something."

The cop said, "My orders are to stay with her."

The nurse said, "My orders don't say anything at all about your orders. You can come on down with us if that's what you want."

Brenda and I trailed behind. The elevator was crowded and tense.

The ambulance crew was ready and waiting to implement the transfer to Denver, and the cop looked back and forth between them and Merritt before she finally discerned that something was seriously amiss.

"Wait, I'm sorry, what are you doing? You can't take her from here. My orders are to—"

This was Cozy's cue to hit his mark. His timing was, as always, perfect. He stepped onto the scene from the doorway to a small office nearby and said, "Excuse me, Officer, have I missed something? I'm an attorney and this young lady is my client. Has she been placed in custody?"

The cop raised her chin to look up at Cozy, who was suited in yards of fine wool and looked quite imperial.

"Um . . . no. Not that I . . . no, she's not under arrest, but—"

"Thank you, Officer, for clarifying that. I'm so relieved I didn't overlook something so important. It would have been most embarrassing." He turned to Brenda and said, "I hope you and your daughter have a safe trip. I'll speak with you both later today."

The officer said, "I . . . um . . . need to get some instructions from my superiors."

Compassionately, Cozy said, "Why don't you do that? There's a phone right over here."

I smiled at Cozy's panache as I walked over and assisted first Merritt and then Brenda into the ambulance. Finally, I leaned in and said to Merritt, "I'll see you later today. You hang in there."

She caught me with her eyes and without touching me held me as tightly as I've ever been held in my life. She waved good-bye to me, a delicate trill of the fingers of her left hand. I could not have been more moved right then had she spoken a thousand words.

Sam Purdy emerged from some shadows across the parking lot as I made my way to my car. There was no way I would have seen him lurking there if he hadn't wanted me to. I raised my hand to wave and slowed my walk. He immediately receded again into the darkness.

I figured he had appointed himself Merritt's guardian angel, willing to risk whatever it took to make sure that the transfer to Denver occurred without incident.

I changed my direction and headed toward him. When I arrived at the place where he had been standing, he was nowhere to be found.

Fifteen

Serendipity prevailed to allow me to meet Merritt's friend Madison before Madison knew that Merritt was under investigation for murdering Dr. Edward Robilio. I rushed from my office after my ten-thirty patient to get up Broadway for my lunchtime rendezvous with Madison Monroe. Parking was sure to be a bitch on the Hill, so I grabbed a ride on the Hop.

Madison was almost a foot shorter than her friend Merritt. The color of her hair was the exact hue of coffee ice cream, but what was most striking about it was its texture, which was as fine as corn silk. It seemed to blow away from her face, moved only by the air I displaced as I approached.

On first blush, Madison seemed every bit as wary of me as her friend had been. She apparently guessed who I was by the way I hesitated and scanned the room. I kept my distance and sized her up.

She was already round and feminine in all the places where Merritt was still transforming from girl-child to woman. Madison's hips were mature, and her breasts swelled against a short sweater that exposed an inch or two of her trim abdomen. She wore a jean skirt and tall black clogs with clunky Vibram soles that caused her butt to thrust out and up.

From at least five feet away, I said my first line, which had come to me as I was riding the bus. "Hi, you must be Madison. It's a pleasure to meet a hero. I'm Alan Gregory, Dr. Gregory."

"Yeah."

It wasn't a great line, but I thought it warranted more of a reply than "yeah."

"Can I get you something, some coffee?"

"You buying?"

"Yes, of course. You're doing me a favor. I appreciate it."

"A, uh, frappucino. Grandé." She pronounced it correctly—*grand-ay*—

but without much confidence. "With whipped cream. And a chocolate chip scone, too." Madison's apparent vanity didn't include any worries about an avalanche of calories finding their way to her hips.

I waited in line and picked up her order along with an espresso for myself and joined her across the room at a high table about the size of a large pizza. We sat on metal stools.

Although I'd asked her to come to my office, she had declined. Meeting at the Starbucks at the corner of University and Broadway, close to both Boulder High School and the University of Colorado, had been her idea, but since I had expected her to refuse to see me at all, it seemed like a reasonable compromise.

I handed her the coffee and pastry.

She said, "You didn't have to call my mom, you know? To set this up. She doesn't know what I do." Her tone was at once swollen with dismissiveness and disgust.

"I'm sorry. I . . . you're not eighteen, and I felt I needed your parents' permission—"

"I don't need my mother's permission to talk to people. So you sure as hell don't need my mother's permission."

This, I suspected, was an argument I wasn't going to win. I shifted gears and hoped she would tag along. "You did something wonderful, you know that? You saved Merritt's life by what you did."

She sucked on her straw and swallowed before she replied. "Yeah, well, I don't know. I mean, I'm glad she's alive and all, but . . ."

"But what?"

"How does it go? Every coin has two sides."

I waited. When it became apparent that she wasn't planning on flipping the coin over so I could see the other side, I said, "Meaning what?"

"Meaning that Merritt's not especially thrilled about my heroics."

"She's angry?"

Madison had just bitten off a mouthful of scone. After she swallowed and chased it with a draw of frozen coffee long enough in duration to induce brain freeze in lesser beings, her voice turned sour and she said, "You tell me. You're the shrink, right? She hasn't said a damn word to me since she woke up. She won't take my calls. I even went to see her once in the hospital and all she did was glare at me. Yeah, she's grateful. No doubt about that."

I wondered about the sudden animosity but decided to be reassuring. "People sometimes feel that way initially after a suicide attempt. They believe they still want to die. So at first they treat you like you're a bad guy for saving them. That will change, believe me. I've been there before."

"With her? She did this before?" She was incredulous, I suspected, not so much that it might be true, but that it might be true and that she didn't know about it.

"No. With others. I've been doing this, being a psychologist, for a while. Unfortunately, I've been with a lot of suicidal people."

Before I finished my sentence I knew I'd lost her; Madison wasn't paying attention anymore. As I waited for a reaction to what I said, she offered a reluctant wave and a wan smile to someone across the room. She lowered her head, rolled her eyes, and under her breath said, "Dweeb."

"Excuse me?"

"That guy. He's so lame. I can't stand it when he smiles at me like that."

"Oh." Madison had just reminded me that I was sitting with someone whose age was on the shy side of seventeen.

As fascinating as a detailed probe of Madison's social life might have been in other circumstances, I felt a need to try to keep her talking about Merritt. "As I told you on the phone, Madison, I'm hoping to try to learn some things that will better help me understand why Merritt tried to kill herself. Everyone says you were closer to her than anyone else. I hope you can help."

"Who says that? Who's everyone?"

She had caught me exaggerating. With an adolescent, I should have known better. "Uh, well, her mother said that, I guess, mostly."

She looked up at me, smiled, and winked. With definite joy in her tone, she asked, "Merritt's not talking to you either, is she?"

"I can't really tell you what she's saying or not saying. I'm just not allowed to."

She intertwined her fingers around her sweating frappucino. "I knew it. She's not talking to anybody, is she? Nobody. This is rich, so rich. What about her stepdad? Is she talking to him?"

"I can't say."

"I bet she isn't. This is *sooo* cool."

"What is?"

"Nothing. You don't know anything, do you?" She scrunched up her nose and smiled, disbelieving, like I had just told her I was giving her free backstage passes for Smashing Pumpkins.

"What do you mean, Madison?"

"Nothing." The smile endured. "So, what did you want? Why did you want to talk to me?"

"Why did you mention her stepdad in particular? Why him, and not, well, her mom?"

Small head shake. "He's normal. She's a star. What did you want?"

Suddenly I was much more interested in what she thought I wanted than in sharing what I really wanted. "Well, what do you think I want?"

"She's really not talking?"

I shrugged. This adolescent was getting the best of me and I didn't like it.

"Cool."

"I'm trying to find out why Merritt might have wanted to kill herself."

With the straw of her iced coffee already touching her lips, she said, "I guess she was real upset about her sister. I guess that was it."

She said it without conviction, as if she was guessing at an answer in class, and hoping for some good fortune from the high school gods. "You may be right. It may be that she's worried about her sister. As a psychologist, though, I find sometimes that it's too easy to look at some awful event in someone's life and say that because of X a person has a good reason to kill herself. The hard question to answer, usually, is, 'Why now?' See, I don't know why Merritt did it the day she did it. Why then and not the day before? Or why then, and not two weeks from now? If she was so upset about Chaney, what was different the day she took the pills?"

Her eyes more wary than confused, Madison asked, "What's X mean? What did you mean when you said X gives somebody a reason to kill herself?"

"It's just a shorthand way of saying 'something that might be upsetting her.' You know, like moving, or changing schools, or Chaney's illness. That kind of X."

"It's like math?"

"I guess."

Madison shrugged. Mollified by my response—or my apparent ignorance about something else, I wasn't sure—she again seemed remarkably

uninterested in doing anything other than checking out the latest cus-
tomers who were walking in the door of the coffeehouse.

"She have a boyfriend?"

Madison tried on a facial expression that I interpreted as a mixture of
serious disgust and total amusement and said, "Noo. She isn't there."

"Trouble with friends?"

"I'm her friend. We're cool. Were cool before this, anyway."

"Anyone else she might have had trouble with?"

"Nope."

"School going okay for her? Problems with teachers or classes?"

"Merritt slides. The teachers like her. And everyone cuts her extra
slack now because of Chaney. It's like a get-out-of-jail-free card for her."

I thought that Madison sounded almost envious that Merritt had a
terminally ill sibling and she didn't. Before I could figure out a way to respond, someone apparently walked in the door behind me who rated a
smile from Madison that was warm enough to reheat my tepid coffee. I was
tempted to turn and check to see who had come in, but I didn't. I guessed
it was a male person.

"So, what do you think? What was it that got her to take those pills?
You know her better than anyone. You must have a theory."

"Like I said: Chaney. She hated what was happening to Chaney. The
hospitals, the publicity, the hassles, her parents' being so . . ."

"So?"

"Whatever."

I waited. She browsed the room. I wished we were in my nice, boring,
nondistracting office. "Had she talked about suicide?"

"No . . ."

"Were you going to say something else?"

"She . . . she had thought about going to live with her dad. Thought
she could travel with him, help him out, be like his assistant or something.
Oh, God, I shouldn't have told you that. Now she'll really be ticked."

"Why? Why will she be ticked?" When I ask "why" questions in
situations like this, I know I'm lost.

She appraised me as though she couldn't believe what a dullard I was.
She said, "Work on it."

"Nothing else?"

"That's all I know."

With what I hoped was a deft move, I changed direction. "The day you found her after she took the drugs, she was upstairs in her bathroom, right?"

Madison nodded as she fished around in the frappucino foam with her straw, hoping to discover a pool of untouched slush. She knew something I didn't know, and she knew that in this match she had me on points.

"See anything else, anything unusual, when you were in the house that day?"

The straw stopped in mid-swipe.

"Like what?"

It was my turn to shrug and act indifferent. I'd been paying attention to the technique, and I thought I did a pretty good job. "Like anything."

"What do you mean, 'Like anything'?"

I leaned forward, closing the space between us. "Merritt's in a lot of trouble right now, Madison. I'm wondering whether you saw anything when you were there that might explain any of it."

"Trouble? What kind of trouble?"

"What did you see?"

"Why is she in trouble?"

I sat back on my chair and drained my coffee. "She screwed up."

Her voice betrayed some anxiety. "Screwed up how? I don't know what you're talking about. All I can tell you is that it was all too weird. Finding her like that. I don't remember anything but how dead she seemed. I thought she was dead." She shivered.

I thought the shiver might be an act, but I wasn't really sure. Madison was pretty good. I asked, "You didn't wait for the ambulance to come? Is that what I heard? Do I have that right?"

"I freaked. Totally freaked."

"You freaked?"

"You see someone you think is dead, you freak, you panic, you do stuff you shouldn't do. Ever done that, just walked in on somebody and thought they were history?"

"Yes, I have. Earlier this week, as a matter of fact."

She wasn't really interested in my experience with dead people. Her question had been rhetorical, and my answer, to her, irrelevant.

"Maybe I should have stayed. I don't know what difference it would have made. Tell you what, next time it happens, next time I walk in and find a dead person, I'll try and do better. How's that?"

Few things in life are more unpleasant than an irritated adolescent. Maybe aggravated cobras and perturbed grizzly bears would offer a good approximation.

I used my confrontation voice from the office, firm but burrowing. "But you thought she was already dead when you got there?"

She was staring at the dregs of foam in her cup. She said, "Yes, I think I said that. I thought she was already dead. She was laying there all unnatural, like one of those rubber dolls you can bend any way you want. And I didn't think she was breathing. I thought I was way too late."

"But you called the ambulance anyway?"

"I called 911. The ambulance was their idea."

"Why did you call 911?"

"It's what you do when something messy happens. Don't you watch TV?" The sarcasm was inflated.

"Why did you go to the house that day? Did you and Merritt have plans to do something? Or maybe, had she told you she was going to take the pills and you went over to talk her out of it? Was that it?"

"*What?*"

"Why did you go to Merritt's house? Why that day? Why that time? Why did you go inside and walk upstairs and go into her bathroom even though no one answered the door?"

"What on earth are you talking about?"

I tried silence. It didn't faze her; she seemed to regroup before my eyes and I feared that my recent advantage was slipping away. I said, "Why did you decide to visit Merritt that afternoon?"

"We're friends. Okay?"

"Do you have a key to the house?"

"The house wasn't locked. She left it open for me."

"So she was expecting you? You had already talked to her, right?"

"No, I mean, I don't know what you're talking about. I didn't know anything about any drugs she was going to take. Nothing, all right?"

"What about a gun? Did you know anything about a gun?"

Her eyes opened wide, and I saw the light reflect off her contact lenses. So that's where that incredible blue tint came from.

"A gun? What? What gun? What . . . what do you mean, a gun?"

"Were you afraid the police were going to come when you called 911? Not just an ambulance? Is that why you didn't stick around after you found her?"

"Why would I be afraid of that?"

"I don't know. I'm not sure. Why would you be afraid of that? Why are you worried that Merritt's in trouble? Maybe it has something to do with that gun?"

She tugged at one of her earrings and sipped from her straw noisily, as though there were actually still some liquid in her glass.

I felt I was close to something, and I wanted to keep the pressure on. My voice as soft as I could make it, I said, "Madison?"

Incongruously, the warm smile I'd seen earlier again graced her face and she slid off the stool in one graceful motion. A young man in black jeans and a too-tight T-shirt appeared next to her and placed a long arm around her waist.

He was the kind of boy I was envious of in high school and college. He was as comfortable around pretty girls as Wynton Marsalis is around a horn. The fact that I was sitting with Madison didn't interfere with his advance for a second.

I said, "Hello, I'm Alan Gregory." I offered my hand.

His was firmly around Madison and he left it there. He said, "Brad."

Madison said, "Listen, lunch is over and I have a class now. I have to go. Thanks for the coffee. Say hi to Merritt for me. Bye."

She and Brad made for the door without looking back.

I watched them exit. Her smile dissolved into anger the second they were out the door. I watched her fumble for a cigarette and fail twice to get it lit with a little plastic lighter.

Finally, she got the thing ignited and started walking, inhaling, and scolding Brad simultaneously.

He seemed amused.

I guessed that Brad's arrival at Starbucks had been choreographed by Madison in advance.

And that he had been late.

I called Sam Purdy at the police department when I returned to my office to see my next patient. He answered, it seemed to me, before the phone even rang.

"I met with Merritt's friend Madison."

"Anything?"

"She's a clever kid, Sam. You know the type. Slippery."

"Does she know anything?"

"Maybe. She didn't tell me anything, but I got the feeling that she knows something. But just when I got some pressure going, she had some guy come in and rescue her. Maybe you'll get more than I did."

"I should probably keep my distance from witnesses. Officially speaking, anyway. I'll talk to Luce." Detective Lucy Tanner was Sam's partner in criminal investigation, and occasionally in crime.

"After she hears that Merritt's under investigation, I think she'll clam up and get real stupid, Sam."

"Happens all the time. You moved Merritt to Denver all right?"

"Signed, sealed, and delivered. Will she be arrested today?"

"Barring a confession by somebody else, probably. Blood on her clothing types like Dead Ed's. Gun is definitely Dead Ed's. Two rounds are missing. Get your arguments ready about why she needs to stay at Children's and not get moved to the Fort. You'll need them."

"Okay."

I hesitated now. I wanted to cover one additional piece of territory with Sam. And then again, I didn't. I finally said, "Sam, I think I've come up with a motive."

He was tapping something, the rhythm relentless. "Yes, I know. Me too."

"Chaney?"

"Chaney."

"DA has probably figured it out, too."

"I imagine. Mitchell Crest isn't stupid."

"You know, it's a good motive, but it doesn't make perfect sense."

"I know."

"What about what we talked about last night, Sam? The suicide note? On the little computer? Could Merritt have done that? Right now, they have to be assuming that she wrote that or forced him to write it."

"That's a problem. But they'll manage it, finesse it some way. Watch for something on the five o'clock news. Nobody in the department wants to take the flack they took for the JonBenet case. If they have something good that won't compromise the investigation, the public's going to know it."

S i x t e e n

Diane Estevez walked, no, *strutted,* into my office when I left my door open between patients early that afternoon. Her hands were on her hips, and her chin had that mild outward thrust that always made Raoul, her husband, so anxious. Instantly, I guessed what was coming. The story wasn't in the newspaper yet, so I didn't know how she could have found out about Merritt's latest troubles, but I would have given good odds right then that she had. I figured we were about to have an unpleasant conversation about why she didn't hear about it from me first.

She said, "Well, is it true?"

I nodded.

"This complicates things, you know that?"

Damn right it complicated things. "What do you mean?"

"You know who Edward Robilio is—was—don't you?"

I was about to impress her with my wisdom. "Yes, Diane, he was the founder and chairman of MedExcel." MedExcel, I thought, being the insurance provider who was not bending its own rules to permit cute, adorable little Chaney Trent to receive a potentially lifesaving, albeit highly experimental, and highly expensive, medical protocol.

Her eyes said, "So what?" Her mouth said, "And?"

"And what?"

"You know who his wife is?"

I hadn't had anywhere near enough sleep. I said, "Mrs. Robilio?"

She took her hands off her hips and took a stride toward me, and I felt that I might be in some physical danger. "Don't be cute."

"I'm not being cute. I don't know what you're talking about, Diane."

"Really?"

"Really."

"The custody case that John Trent is doing? With my patient who has a connected wife? Remember? Two kids; the husband's above average, the wife drinks? I told you about it at lunch at Jax?"

I was totally befuddled now. "Yes, I remember."

"I told you that his wife's sister was married to a gazillionaire?"

"Yes." I recalled the conversation. She had even said "gazillionaire."

"Well, now, it turns out, thanks to your patient, my patient's wife's sister has just been widowed from her gazillionaire."

"This is too confusing. Give me a name. Your patient is?"

"Call him Andrew. The wife he's divorcing is Abby."

"And Abby's sister is Mrs. Robilio?"

"Yes, Abby's sister is Mrs. Robilio. And now, if what I'm hearing is true, the daughter of the primary custody evaluator is charged with murdering the husband of the sister of one of the principles."

It took me about three silent repetitions of everyone's roles to completely comprehend the connections Diane was sketching. When I did I said, "So I guess that means you win."

"What do you mean, I win?"

"There's no way John Trent's custody recommendation will be accepted by the court now, given his daughter's involvement in Robilio's death. The dual relationship problem will eliminate him. You'll get a fresh eval. You win."

Her shoulders sagged. "I hadn't thought about that."

"Then what were you thinking about?"

"The connection. I was thinking it supported my theory that someone had gotten to John Trent about his recommendations in the custody case."

"What do you mean?"

"What else could it be?"

"Diane, MedExcel—Robilio's company—is the insurance carrier that's refusing to grant permission for Chaney Trent to have that procedure she needs. I'm afraid that gave my patient—remember her, my patient?—Chaney's sister, a plausible motive to kill Dead Ed."

"*Dead Ed?*"

"Dr. Robilio."

She looked at me as though we were discussing a nickname I'd devised for a potted plant. "You call Dr. Edward Robilio 'Dead Ed'?"

"It's kind of tacky, I admit. I picked it up from Sam Purdy. It's a cop thing."

She shook her head. "Figures. So, if I'm following you correctly, you say that your patient was thinking, like, okay, what if she killed the guy, then for sure his company would suddenly be more compassionate about investing a few hundred thousand dollars in helping her sister stay alive? Huh? I'm supposed to believe this makes sense? Is your patient retarded, or is she merely suffering some intermittent severe thought disorder?"

"She's an adolescent, Diane."

"Adolescents aren't stupid, Alan. They're impulsive, they're mysterious, they're at times incomprehensible, but they're not stupid."

"Who knows what happened at his house! Maybe the shooting was accidental."

She made a face. "Two . . . accidental shots from close range? The second one accidentally between the eyes?"

It wasn't actually between the eyes. I liked that she had some of it wrong. "You're right. That's hard to explain." I desperately wanted to tell her about the suicide note, but Sam would kill me if I let that news get out.

"Of course I'm right."

"Oh my God!" Involuntarily, I covered my mouth with my hand.

"What?"

"I just realized something."

"What?"

"The leverage that your patient's wife's family had with John Trent."

"Yes?"

It was one of those rare moments in life when Diane was a step behind me. I relished it for a moment, not wanting to pause too long for fear she would catch up on her own.

"It wasn't political."

"Money?"

"No."

"What?"

"Chaney."

Kachink, kachink, kachink. I watched her face as the balls tumbled down chutes into their inevitable slots.

She said, "Oh my God."

I said, "Diane, this is a consultation we're having. You can't tell anyone about this."

She said, "Of course it's a consultation, Doctor," as she felt behind her for a chair.

Seventeen

I rearranged my afternoon appointments so I could get to Denver before rush hour clogged the Boulder Turnpike and I-25. Getting Merritt's admission routine accomplished was going to require some significant time. First I had to meet with her, and then I hoped to find time to interview at least one of her parents. In addition, I had to compose an initial treatment plan and confer with the unit staff. Of course, I also had to complete the rest of the admission paperwork and deal with MedExcel's institutional reluctance to spend money on psychiatric admissions.

I figured three hours, easy.

The staff at Children's had settled Merritt into the unit without any fuss. In my initial telephone orders the night before, I had asked them not to pressure her about speaking, and they hadn't. She had been admitted on the lowest level of privileges—Level One—which permitted her only limited activities, like, say, breathing, without asking the staff for permission. She was, of course, confined to the unit, and was on suicide precautions—all routine for a new transfer after a serious suicide attempt.

On the way to Merritt's room, the nurse assigned to her prepared me for what I'd find. "Her roommate's name is Christina. She's being stabilized on lithium right now and that hole you're about to see in her cheek isn't the only one she has. She's been pierced in a few other places, too, if you know what I mean."

I didn't, but I could guess. The details weren't important. Merritt's assigned roommate turned out to be a skinny Chicana with big brown eyes full of heat and the promised large piece of metal coming out of her cheek. She was standing just outside the door listening to a CD player on headphones, but I could hear the Latin rhythm seeping out all the way from the door. I waved hello. She waved back.

The nurse paused before she left and pointed across the unit toward an empty consultation room that I could use for psychotherapy sessions. I asked Merritt to join me. She smiled a good-bye to Christina, who smiled back, exposing a metal-embedded tongue and a mouthful of braces. The kid would be hell going through security at the airport.

Merritt sat. I talked. I asked her if she was doing all right. She shrugged. I asked her if she understood the rules of the unit. She nodded yes. I asked her if she needed anything. She shook her head. I asked her if she wanted to be able to see her sister.

She did. Finally I saw some animation.

"I figured that. It's a privilege, like any other privilege that's earned by patients on the unit. The way it works is that you won't be allowed off the unit for anything, even to visit your sister, until you earn the trust of the staff. They will teach you how to accomplish that, how to earn privileges. The intent isn't to keep you from your sister; it's to keep you safe. I'm sorry. That's just the way it works."

She looked away from me then, and didn't look at me again. Permission to see Chaney was apparently all she wanted from me. I'd already decided not to do anything more than invite her to talk. That having failed, I had nothing left to say; it was apparent she hadn't changed her mind about staying mute. I led her back to her room and watched her lower herself to her bed. She curled up facing the wall.

One of the nurses on the cardiology unit helped me track down Brenda Strait and John Trent in the almost deserted hospital cafeteria. They were sitting alone in the far corner of the room, sharing a piece of apple pie, holding hands across the table.

I thought they looked old.

Before I disturbed them, I poked my head into one of the private dining rooms adjacent to the cafeteria, hoping to find a place we could meet privately. The Doctors Dining Room was empty.

Brenda saw me approaching the table and released her husband's hand. She whispered something and John, too, looked my way.

He wasn't what I'd expected. Until that moment, I hadn't realized that I had expectations about his appearance, but I did. In my mind's eye, John Trent was robust and hefty with a generous smile and abundant hair the color of autumn grasses. In the hospital cafeteria that day, though, he was thin and gaunt and somber and what hair was left on his head was crew-cut and almost black.

He stood.

I said, "No, no, please, sit down. I'm Alan Gregory; it's nice to finally meet you."

"John Trent."

I looked toward Brenda and said, "Hello, Brenda. Well, we pulled it off, the transfer. Thanks for all your help last night."

She offered a weak smile in return.

"I just checked the Doctors Dining Room over there, and it's empty. Why don't we move in there and get some privacy and I'll catch you both up with what's going on."

Trent said, "Fine. Brenda, you want any more of this pie?"

She shook her head.

We all settled at one end of a table in the private room. The room smelled of burnt toast. In the distance, some food-service workers were complaining about not getting their breaks.

I waited to see if either John or Brenda was eager to start. They weren't. I said, "How's your little one doing?"

Trent answered. "Chaney's . . . all right. She's resting now. She had a decent enough day today, wouldn't you say, Bren?"

"Decent. Yes. A decent day. The pulmonary treatments went well. That's something."

"I'm glad to hear that. I'm looking forward to meeting her. Maybe to-morrow? I just came from the psychiatric unit where I saw Merritt. You saw her earlier, too?" The nurses on the unit had informed me that Merritt's parents had stopped by.

Brenda said, "Yes. She looks fine to me. Totally recovered, I would say. Trent?"

"From the overdose, sure. She looks like herself. Still silent, though. She won't talk to us at all, not a word. You either?"

"Nothing to me or the staff. She may be talking to the other kids, but if she is, we haven't heard about it yet," I said.

John's eyes were warm as they held mine. "I think she realizes what's at stake now, though. Brenda and I told her what we could, what we've learned from the lawyers and the police. She realizes how serious things are, how bad it looks with the clothes and the blood and everything."

I assumed "everything" was a palatable euphemism for the gun.

Brenda stared at me, away, then she leaned forward, halfway across the table before words spilled from her mouth like ice from a bucket. "How could she do it? Kill that man? How could they accuse her of that? With a gun? How? She's a child, she doesn't know about guns, and, and . . ."

John took her hand across the table. "The situation is bad, Dr. Gregory. We talked to that lawyer, Mr. Maitlin, an hour ago. The evidence doesn't look good for Merritt. When you found us, we were talking, trying to come up with some way to cope with the possibility that Merritt may have actually gone and . . . killed that man."

"And what were you coming up with? Anything?"

John seemed prepared for the question. He didn't hesitate. "If she did it—and I'm not convinced she did, despite how it looks—it was stupid, stupid, stupid. An awful tragedy for his family. And now another tragedy for ours. But for Merritt, right now, I—we, Brenda and I—we have to view whatever happened, if Merritt was involved, as an act of . . . for lack of a better word . . . honor. If she did it, it was like sticking up for her sister in a schoolyard fight—don't get me wrong, this was much more serious. Twisted somehow, but honorable."

I thought I could guess where John Trent was going, but I wanted him to finish, I wanted to hear the rationalization in his own words. "Go on."

"For the sake of argument, let's assume she was involved somehow. All I can think is that, that Merritt must have viewed him, Dr. Robilio, as a bully, a bully who was hurting Chaney, picking on Chaney. Merritt went over there, to his house, to stick up for her sister, to stand up to the bully, and something went terribly wrong. The shooting . . . was an aberration, an . . . accident, I'm absolutely sure of that. Merritt's not an aggressive kid. It's her biggest liability on the basketball court. She just isn't aggressive enough, won't play to her own advantage. So I don't know what happened at his house with the gun, maybe no one does. I don't think she could have shot him; I just can't picture her . . . you know. But what drove her there in the first place was honorable, I'm sure of that. Merritt was trying to help her sister stay alive and she saw Dr. Robilio as the enemy."

Brenda had started to cry and to make those little popping noises with her lips that I'd heard for the first time in Boulder.

Therapeutically, I had a half-dozen choices about which trail to follow. I didn't take any of them.

Instead, I asked, "How did she know about Dr. Robilio's relationship to Chaney's medical care? It's not the sort of information a typical teenager would understand or have access to."

They looked at each other.

Brenda said, "We've wondered about that, too. And we're not sure. We knew, of course, about Dr. Robilio, that he founded MedExcel. We've researched everything we could about MedExcel to try and get some leverage to get them to grant an exception for Chaney's protocol and the transplant. We talked about it at home, Trent and I, openly. Our frustration, whatever. Merritt must have overheard us and remembered his name. That's the best explanation we've been able to come up with."

"You talked about it?"

Brenda answered, "You know that Dr. Robilio was a local doctor, that MedExcel was his company, that he could order them to approve the protocol Chaney needs if he wanted to. We were angry, bitter—especially after we appealed to their medical board. Half a million dollars is nothing to MedExcel. The head of the medical board," she closed her eyes and shook her head, "his response to our appeal was so cold. He ignored Chaney, he focused on the danger of the precedent. They can't go start approving risky experimental procedures, that's what he said. We're even more angry and bitter than we were at the beginning. What's risky is doing nothing. If we do nothing, barring a miracle, Chaney is going to die, Dr. Gregory. The fund-raising that's been going on is stalled. Merritt knew all that. Trent and I have been over this stuff a hundred times together. Merritt must have heard us once or twice."

My eyes were on John as Brenda spoke about knowing about Dr. Robilio. His face betrayed nothing but compassion for his wife. I wanted to ask him about the custody situation he was evaluating that just happened to involve Mrs. Robilio's sister and brother-in-law. I wanted to ask if he had received any feelers from the family about cutting a deal that would result in MedExcel granting approval for Chaney's medical needs. I wanted to know if maybe Merritt had overheard any of that. But I couldn't press him. I had no reason to know about any of those connections myself.

I asked about money instead. "Merritt knows how far short the family is of being able to pay for the protocol and transplant through fundraising?"

Brenda scoffed. "We don't have a prayer of self-funding this, barring some benefactor stepping forward. My divorce and the move to Colorado killed us financially. Our total net worth isn't even a hundred grand and most of that's in the house. The Chaney Fund that Channel 7 organized has raised, what, honey, a little over thirty thousand? Which is great, we're grateful, but most of that will go to cover expenses here in Denver. We won't come up with the money we need to pay for Seattle in time."

"There's no family money?"

"No. They've offered everything they have. But we both come from blue-collar families. There's no family wealth to tap, no rich aunts, if that's what you're wondering."

"And Merritt knows all this?"

John replied, "She asks us things. We tell her. She's mature, responsible. We try to treat her that way; she's earned it. Yes, although she may not know the details, she knows how gray things look for her sister."

"Black," corrected Brenda.

"Black," said John.

"Does this make sense, though? Think about what you're saying. Merritt heard the two of you talking about how desperate things are. And she hears you mention this local man, Dr. Robilio, who has the power to help her sister. And she felt she could influence his decision by going to his house, and what, threatening him with his own gun? Does that sound like something Merritt would do?"

Immediately, John said, "No."

Brenda opened her mouth and then closed it.

John continued. "No, it doesn't sound like Merritt at all. That part I don't get. I told her today when we visited that I didn't get it, why she went to his house on her own, what she was thinking. I said, 'Merritt, how did you think this was going to help?' "

I waited for John to tell me Merritt hadn't answered.

He didn't.

"How does it not sound like her, John?"

"She's . . . not a leader. She's not . . . she's not a kid who will even confront a teacher who she thinks has graded a paper wrong. Don't misunderstand me, she's an independent thinker, she does her own thing, but she's not a kid who fights the system."

Brenda said, "But this time it was about her sister, Trent. Not about some English paper."

He smiled ruefully. "I know, Bren. That must be it. I mean, if she was there, that must be it. If she did something, she did it for Chaney. Whatever it was that happened is horrible. But if Merritt went to Dr. Robilio's house, she did it thinking she could help Chaney."

"How did she respond when you told her you didn't understand her going to his house? What did she do?"

Trent answered. "She looked down. Shook her head a little bit. She didn't say a word."

I asked, "What about the silence? Has she done this before? Just totally stopped talking?"

Brenda said, "Like this, no."

"But something similar?"

"When she's in trouble, she clams up. I think it's my fault. I'm the cross-examining type. She always tells me that I use what she says against her. So sometimes, when I'm really going at it with her, she just won't talk to me. Says it's the only smart thing to do."

"John?"

"After a while, maybe a few minutes, maybe a couple of hours, she'll talk to me. It never lasts long. She and her mother do all right, eventually. Brenda cools off. They iron it out." He paused before asking, "Any chance this is hysterical?" His tone said he didn't believe it, but felt he had to ask.

I said, "Not in my opinion, no."

"Organic?"

"The neurologists have ruled out an organic etiology."

Brenda interjected, "There is something else. Trent, you remember right after we got to town and I was doing the plastic recycling story that was getting so much play? Remember, we had that discussion at dinner where I was incredulous that people kept answering my questions when they didn't have to, really digging themselves in deeper and deeper?"

"I remember."

"Was Merritt there?"

"Yes, she was. I'd made those ribs she likes so much. She was there at dinner that night."

"I wonder, maybe, if she's just been taking my advice. I remember saying that the best thing to do when someone sticks a microphone in your face is smile politely and walk away. Well, she can't walk away, and there's not much to smile about, but she's certainly not digging herself in any deeper by keeping her mouth shut."

"Do either of you recall how she reacted to your comment, Brenda?"

"No," she said.

"It was just another dinner conversation," John said.

"Well, it's a provocative explanation. Maybe I'll explore it with her. Did you two get a chance to meet the unit social worker? She'll schedule some time to get a detailed history and maybe meet as a family."

John said, "She introduced herself. We're going to try and get together tomorrow." He paused to see if I wanted to go somewhere else. "Can we talk treatment plan for a minute, Dr. Gregory?"

"Sure. That's easy; I don't have much of one. Right now I want to keep her safe and reduce pressure on her, let her settle in. We also need to be prepared for more bad news, from a legal point of view. The treatment planning team will meet tomorrow and we'll put something more long-term together."

I was aware of the sounds of traffic increasing in the cafeteria as the dinner hour approached.

I continued. "To change the subject for a second—we're facing two bureaucratic problems right now. If—when—Merritt is arrested, the court is going to have to approve her receiving continued care here, as opposed to at the state hospital at Fort Logan. They don't have to allow her to stay here, at Children's. Second, in the meantime, MedExcel is going to need to approve Merritt being in a psychiatric hospital. You understand that?"

John Trent did, of course. "Oh, I think they'll approve the admission, Dr. Gregory. Her suicide attempt was potentially lethal, so the inpatient stay is indicated. They won't argue that. And I think MedExcel will eat a thousand dollars a day in inpatient costs just so they don't have to take the public relations flogging they would get for turning our family down a second time. The policy allows twenty-one days of approved inpatient care. They'll give us that and they'll hope the problem goes away before then."

"I hope you're right, John."

"It's a cynical point of view. That alone makes me think I'm right."

Brenda was heading to Channel 7's studios to tape a piece about lax inspections at highway scales. John was going back upstairs to be with Chaney. We said good-bye, and as I waited for the elevator I wondered how I would cope with the latest assault that the Trent/Strait household had suffered and decided that finding honor in my teenage daughter's arrest for murder would be relatively adaptive.

I had tossed it around a lot already and could fathom no motive for what Merritt was accused of doing other than to protect Chaney's welfare.

There *was* honor there. At least in the motive.

So what was troubling me? Something didn't feel right about the meeting with Brenda and John.

The elevator arrived. I entered with a crush of employees and a couple of distraught-looking parents who were holding hands with a young boy of around seven.

The mother had a twangy voice that caused her words to bounce around the elevator. She was impossible to ignore. She said, "We're so proud of you, honey. You acted like such a big boy down there."

Her words clanged through my reverie. And suddenly I knew what had been troubling me. Brenda and John weren't just rationalizing Merritt's actions as being honorable.

They were *proud* of her. If Merritt had done this, her parents were proud of her. Maybe not of what she had done. But at least they were proud of why she had done it.

That's what was so troubling.

Eighteen

The Children's Hospital in Denver seems to remodel and renovate its facilities more often than Martha Stewart changes her sheets. I had climbed an unfamiliar staircase, nothing was the way I remembered it from previous visits, and I managed to get lost on my way to the psychiatric unit. My journey took me past a ward of glassed-in, vestibule-fronted isolation rooms that were intended to protect the world from children with contagious illness, and vice versa. Maybe half of the rooms were occupied by patients. And maybe half of those patients had their televisions turned on. In one room, the last one in the row, the familiar visage of Mitchell Crest filled the television screen and stopped me in my tracks.

From my position in the corridor, I couldn't hear what Mitchell was saying, but I guessed that it was all too likely that his appearance on the news had something to do with Merritt's plight. Knowing him and knowing the Boulder DA's office through Lauren, I guessed that Mitchell would, at least initially, be circumspect with the press and not reveal Merritt's identity. She was a minor, and early in an investigation her identity was protected by Colorado law. If he chose to charge her, and especially if he chose to charge her as an adult, Merritt's identity and photograph would become fair game.

Mitchell Crest was a wise choice for the press conference; he would leave a good impression with the public. His manner was so forthright and honest you almost wanted to trust him.

At the conclusion of the clip, Mitchell's mouth closed and his face dissolved into a commercial so fast that it actually appeared to me that a Camaro had driven out of his mouth. I walked back in the direction I had come and checked the television in the adjoining room. No Mitchell; just another commercial. This time Jake Jabs was encouraging everyone in

Denver to buy a houseful of furniture from his stores, apparently because he was already rich enough to own his own zoo. I didn't get the connection, never had.

Sam had warned me to keep my eyes on the news for updates on Merritt and Dead Ed, and he'd been right on. I was dying to know what Mitchell Crest had said during his news conference, so I renewed my quest for the adolescent psych unit in search of another TV.

The television in the psychiatric inpatient unit dayroom was turned to MTV. I was grateful for Sheryl Crow. Merritt was sitting by herself, off to the side of a group of kids. She was half on, half off a huge green bean-bag chair, looking restless. She wasn't handling the remote control, and I could only guess how badly she wanted to be watching the local news instead of MTV.

I asked one of the mental health counselors where I could find another television besides the one the kids were watching in the dayroom.

"You catching up on the soaps?" he asked.

"No, actually, I'm afraid my new patient might be on the news."

"The quiet one?"

"Yes. Merritt."

"Is it about her sister? I didn't hear anything."

"No, I think it's about her."

He led me to a room the staff used as a lounge. I flicked on a small black-and-white TV and started dancing through the local channels, hoping to catch a repeat of Mitchell Crest's performance.

After five minutes of channel-surfing, I found what I was looking for on a "Top Stories" update on Channel 9. The camera angle was wider than the one I had seen earlier; in fact, it was wide enough to show that Mitchell Crest had been flanked at the press conference by Detective Scott Malloy and the Public Information Officer for the city, a woman whose name I always forgot. I recognized the setting as the wide corridor that ran on the north side of the courtrooms inside the Justice Center on Canyon Boulevard.

Around the DA's office, Mitchell was a loose-collar, rolled-up-sleeves type of guy. For the media, he was buttoned down, Windsor-knotted, and double-breasted. I had apparently missed his opening remarks. What I heard was, ". . . pleased to announce that, as a result of a thorough investigation by the Boulder Police Department, we have identified a suspect in the recent murder of Dr. Edward Robilio. The suspect is an adolescent—a minor—whom we expect to bring into custody in the near future." He turned and whispered something to Malloy as he waved off a couple of questions shouted at him from off-camera. Again facing the camera and the microphone, he said, "The suspect is not, repeat, not a flight risk; we know her current location and we are monitoring her movements closely while we develop further evidence in the case. Flight is absolutely not a concern to us at this time."

The assembled reporters went nuts at the least bit of information. "Her?" they shouted, almost in unison. "It's a girl?"

Then, "How young? Mr. Crest, Mr. Crest, how old is she? What's her age? What's her name?"

Mitchell Crest didn't respond, and the follow-up questions peppered at him blended together on the soundtrack to sound something like a canary being attacked by a cat. Mitchell popped off screen, this time without the Camaro in his mouth.

The in-studio anchor segued to a story about farm gangs in Larimer County, and I flicked off the television. I didn't want to know what farm gangs were or what they were doing in Larimer County.

Behind me, I heard muffled sobs.

I turned to find Merritt standing at the entrance to the lounge, holding the doorjamb with both her hands, one neck-high, one at midthigh, staring at the gray-green tube, oblivious to my presence.

I said, "I'm sorry. I'm so sorry, Merritt. I didn't know you were there."

I expected her to run. She didn't. She released her grip on the doorjamb and continued to stare at the TV as though she hated it.

"Merritt, sit, please. Let's talk about this. I'm very sorry."

I meant for her to sit on a chair, inside the room, but she slithered to the floor precisely where she had been standing. Her limbs were elastic, and she curled into herself with the flexibility of a small child. Her soft hair was mostly down, but a wide clump was rubber-banded into a ponytail on top of her head. The splash of freckles down her cheeks had darkened with her tears.

"It doesn't look good, does it?" I said. "I'm sorry. I wish there was something I could do."

She looked at me as if she wanted to talk right then, that she wished she could. But she didn't say a word.

"I'm sure you've decided that not talking is somehow in your best interest, Merritt, but I'm really at a loss as to how it's doing any good. I wish you could help me understand that. Right now I don't know how things could look any worse for you than they do."

She shook her head in one long, slow swipe from side to side. Her hair didn't swing.

I wasn't certain what she meant. I guessed. "They could look worse than this? How? It sounds like you're about to be arrested for murder."

She didn't move. She shook her head again. This time her eyes were frustrated. I took it to be a "No, you don't get it" shake.

She was telling me something important and I fought a surge of anger that she couldn't just cease her stubbornness and actually speak a sentence or two. This odd dance felt to me like trying to do psychotherapy by playing charades. I also felt that I was exhibiting remarkably little skill at the game, as though I were insensitive, missing something obvious.

"The silence—you keeping quiet all this time," I said, "are you telling me it isn't something you're doing only to protect yourself? Is that it?"

Without moving her head, she looked over at me with wide eyes that weren't blinking, and she held my gaze as softly as a mother cradles a baby. She smiled a tiny smile. Her shoulders sagged.

I said, "Merritt, is this—the silence, what happened with Dr. Robilio—is this somehow about Madison? I told you I was going to meet with her today and I did."

Merritt's eyes narrowed, but her expression didn't change perceptibly. She waited a good fifteen seconds for me to expound on the meeting. When I didn't, she shrugged her shoulders as though my words hadn't mattered at all.

She stood and slowly made her way back to the dayroom.

I flicked around the channels one more time hoping to see another version of Mitchell's news appearance, but didn't. I moved back out to the nursing station to complete the required paperwork on Merritt. When my admission note was almost complete, a counselor called me to the phone.

John Trent was on the line. In a voice that sounded tinny and hollow, he said, "I'm glad I found you. Chaney's deteriorating quickly. The doctors say this could be it for her."

I didn't want what he was saying to be true, so I said something stupid. "She had a decent day, didn't she? Isn't that what you said before?"

John Trent sighed, weary of having to carry the awkward weight placed upon him by the denial of others. "That was then. Now, I'm afraid, she's crashing."

"Is Brenda there?"

"No, I just paged her at work."

He paused. I sensed he was steeling himself for whatever he wanted to say next. I steeled myself for not wanting to hear it.

Without a note of pleading in his tone, Trent said, "I want Merritt to come down here, Dr. Gregory."

"I don't—"

"I know it's against the rules. And I know that clinical judgment says you don't take her off the unit after a suicide attempt like hers. The truth is that her baby sister may be dying as we speak, only a couple of hundred feet from Merritt, and it is absolutely criminal not to make an exception to the rules. Right now. Right . . . now."

"John, I'm so sorry. Can I have a minute or two to think about this? How to go about it. Certainly, I would have to arrange for some staff to go with her."

"If I had minutes to give, I'd give Chaney and Merritt a million of them. Take the minutes you need, but the account we're using is almost empty. Do what you can. Please be humane about this. And please hurry."

I needed permission from the ward chief or the medical director—or someone with some similar clout—to authorize a radical departure from hospital policy for a patient who was on suicide precautions. But I didn't have the luxury of time to move the system to compassion.

One of the enduring lessons of my years working in hospital settings is that if you want something difficult, or impossible, accomplished, find a nurse with some courage and cunning. So that's what I did.

The head nurse of the inpatient unit was a tall woman with wispy hair and a quick smile. As far as I could tell, she was as firmly rooted as a giant redwood. During moments of crisis, only if you looked incredibly closely could you detect the slightest sway in her.

I walked to her office door and found her packing her things into a big canvas bag in preparation for heading home for the day.

"Georgia," I said, "may I speak with you for a minute?"

She pulled a *Toy Story* lunch box from inside the canvas bag, shook her head, and said, "I ended up with my eight-year-old's lunch box today. How did I do that? God knows what he ate for lunch. Do you ever suffer temporary brain death? I'm sorry. I'm rambling. What can I do for you?"

"May I close the door?"

"Uh-oh. Can it wait until tomorrow? I can give you, gosh, ten whole minutes tomorrow. Teacher's conference tonight, I have to pick up some food for the kids and their babysitter. It's bad form to either starve the children before a teacher's conference or to be late. Do you have kids, Alan?"

I shook my head. "I'm afraid it can't wait; I wish it could. And no, Georgia, no kids yet."

She looked at her wristwatch and sighed the sigh of overburdened managers everywhere. The one that said, "They don't pay me enough for this." She waved me to the empty chair by her desk and closed the door behind me.

She didn't sit. "It's your nickel."

"I just received a call from Merritt's father. He's down in ICU. Merritt's sister, Chaney, is deteriorating, may be dying. He made an impassioned plea for Merritt to visit her. He would like her to come down right now."

Georgia sat. She dropped her coat and let the canvas bag fall to the floor. "God. God. God. Don't you hate doing this some days? Listen to me, really, I'm bitching to you about having to run like hell to get to Boston Market before my kids' teacher's conferences and look at the alternatives life has to offer. Look out there, in the dayroom. Look at those poor kids. Or God forbid, look down in the ICU or over in oncology. I'm so ungrateful." She dabbed at her eyes. "I'm babbling again. What do you need from me to make this happen?"

"I need the policies regarding patients being restricted to the unit during suicide precautions to evaporate, at least temporarily."

"You can't just d/c the precautions, can you?"

"No. With what's going on right now, no. She's still mute. Her sister's in crisis. And I take it you heard about the arrest?"

She shook her head.

"The Boulder DA went public that they have an adolescent female suspect. Merritt knows about it. And now Chaney may be dying. I can't d/c precautions or increase privileges with those stressors on the table."

"Is she about to be arrested?"

"No way to tell. It could happen anytime, I imagine, based on what I saw on the news."

Georgia's tongue was between her upper and lower teeth. Her lips were parted. She said, "Don't worry about the administrative side. That crap won't jell before tomorrow. Write the order for the ICU visit. I'll get staff and security lined up to go with. We'll take her on the road and worry about policy and procedure in the morning if this thing goes south, and hopefully it won't. There's no time to discuss it with anyone, right?"

"Right."

"I'll leave a message for Joel, he should know what we're doing. And I'll have my players together up here in, like, five minutes. You get her ready, okay? Let her know what's expected of her and let her know that she'll be surrounded by sumo wrestlers."

I wanted to kiss the head of the head nurse. I said, "Thanks, Georgia, a lot."

"The karma price is too damn high for some omissions in life. Refusing this visit, I'm afraid, would be way off the negative karma scale. No thanks are necessary."

To ensure against omissions of my own, I phoned down to the ICU, identified myself, and asked to speak to Chaney's nurse. The ward clerk said she wasn't available.

I asked, "How is Chaney doing?"

Quick exhale. "Bad. Real bad."

"Thanks, I'll call back."

I felt guilty for checking on John Trent. But at least I knew that he hadn't been lying.

Nineteen

My feelings were jumbled, which is not a good posture for a clinical psychologist during a crisis. The strongest feeling I had was that I wanted to protect Merritt from the world. From death, and tragedy, and neglect, and hostility, and loss. Right then, I didn't much consider the atrocity she was accused of committing. I only wanted to shield her from the horrors that hovered nearby. I knew my feelings were paternal, and not therapeutic. But they were as big as life and I couldn't ignore them.

Paradoxically, my actual job was to protect Merritt from herself. Despite all the objective evidence—and given a near-fatal suicide attempt, I didn't require much more objective evidence—I was having trouble convincing myself that she was actually in grave danger of self-destruction. If there was any ambivalence on my part about permitting Merritt to visit with Chaney in the ICU, it wasn't about fear that she would attempt suicide while free of the safety of the adolescent psychiatry unit. Rather, it had to do with an ill-conceived sense that nothing awaited her downstairs but further pain and suffering.

I didn't want her to have to experience that anymore.

If Chaney survived this night, it was likely that a night where she didn't survive was lurking on a near horizon. The cards determining this baby's eternal life were being dealt by fate, or by some callous God I didn't want to contemplate, or by some bureaucrat at MedExcel. I felt an absolute helplessness that I could do nothing to prevent Merritt from feeling the pain of watching her sister die. All I could do was help her prepare for it.

In the meantime, though, I was charged with keeping Merritt alive during the visit to the intensive care unit.

With that I had some help. Three counselors who had volunteered to stay after shift change and two uniformed hospital security guards accompanied Merritt and me on the journey from the fourth floor to the second. One of the guards used a key to make sure we had an elevator to ourselves on our way down to the ICU.

As we made our way down, I had an eerie sense of having come full circle with Merritt. I had met her days before in an intensive care unit and now she and I were on our way back to one. The circle, I hoped, wasn't really complete. Being surrounded by benevolent guards and having a little sister near death was no way to complete it.

Merritt's poise was remarkable. She hadn't panicked when I told her that her sister was in a new medical crisis. Merritt had stood from her bed as soon as she heard my words, expecting to be taken immediately to her sister's bedside. Assuming it was her right to be there.

Which it was, of course. I wasted a minute or two telling her about suicide precautions and warning her that staff would be with her at all times.

She listened impatiently, picking at the sleeve of her T-shirt. This one was black and read CHURCH GIRL in a soft script across the front. I realized that I didn't know youth culture well enough to know whether the church girls were a rock 'n' roll band, and that I didn't know my patient well enough to know whether or not she was making some religious statement with her choice of T-shirts.

When I was done with my speech, she raised her eyebrows tenderly and mouthed the word, "Please."

I asked myself whether I trusted her. I knew I did. We left her room.

As we reached the entrance to the intensive care unit I asked the security guards to wait in the hall, one by each of the two doors to the unit. I asked the mental health counselors to wait in the nursing station and to keep their eyes open should Merritt require their help.

Merritt and I entered the ICU through a tiny vestibule where we took turns washing our hands with foul-smelling antibacterial soap. We pulled on gowns. Merritt's preparations were deliberate and measured. She washed her hands with care, lathering liberally, rinsing well. She was patient. That's what John Trent had told me about his stepdaughter. She's patient.

The intensive care unit at The Children's Hospital is a long rectangular space with a glassed-in nursing station on the center of one of the long walls. Beds and cribs are spaced regularly along the other walls. Sometimes curtains are pulled between them, sometimes not. Behind each bed were enough electronics to land a 777 in a whiteout.

Chaney's bed was in the far corner. Nurses, doctors, and assorted health techs surrounded the bed, their activity a magnet for everyone's attention. John Trent stood back from the crowd that had assembled around his young daughter's bed. A pale yellow hospital gown was tied behind his neck, but not at his waist. His arms were crossed loosely in front of him.

Merritt left my side without asking permission. I didn't know what she planned to do, but sensed it would be the right thing. Her slippered feet made hardly a sound as she crossed the unit and approached her stepfather and embraced him from behind. He turned to face her and the tears he had been damming spilled loose in a silent torrent as the two of them hugged.

Merritt cried with him. She wiped a tear from her stepfather's cheek. I'd never met Chaney and, by myself in the center of the big room, I was crying for her, too. And for John. And for Merritt.

I stood back respectfully at a distance of about ten feet. John Trent began to whisper into Merritt's hair and I couldn't tell what he was saying, didn't think I had a right to know. After about fifteen seconds, Merritt stepped back from him, gazed at him ruefully, took his hand, and began to lead him toward Chaney's bed.

She released Trent's hand, or he released hers—I couldn't tell—at the foot of her sister's bed and she weaved naturally, ducking and bending her way through the assembled health care workers and their equipment, toward the head of Chaney's bed. Merritt maneuvered the maze with ease and grace, as though she was threading through friendly classmates jammed around her locker at school. Once she was through the throng I could no longer see her.

A doctor approached Trent at the foot of the bed. Trent said something that earned him an enthusiastic reply. He added a few more words. The doctor nodded again, looked my way, and smiled warmly. I waved and watched her stride back to Chaney's bedside. I assumed it was Chaney's primary doc, temporarily thrust into a secondary role by the acute crisis. The critical care specialists would run this show for now.

Trent continued to stand back. I took a few steps forward and joined him.

After a pause, he said, "Thanks."

I remembered Georgia's karma warning. "None needed. Any change, John?"

"She's laboring badly. Rapid breathing. Respirations are up to sixty. Something new is going on with her lungs. They don't know whether it's a new disease process or a reaction to one of the meds. There's a pulmonologist in there with her and a respiratory therapist. They're trying to get it under control. So far without any luck."

"Is she awake? Will she know her sister has come down to see her?"

Trent said, "Oh, she'll know. She knows already. I can feel it."

The work around the toddler was being done in whispers and hushes. The motions of the health care workers were rehearsed and precise. Their voices conveyed their urgency and their intensity and masked their fears.

Behind me, a monitor beeped on the far side of the room. It was a warning bell, not a clarion call. Not an alarm. A nurse hustled toward the unattended bed. The body in it was so small I couldn't be certain the crib was occupied.

Behind me, near the nursing station, someone dropped an empty can of Sprite. It sounded like a bomb going off. As it rolled across the linoleum, it reminded me of a military drum roll.

A phone rang.

Two people stepped back from Chaney's bed, just one step back. A nurse stepped away, too, leaving three staff people behind. One of the remaining nurses reached up and adjusted a control on Chaney's monitor. Then she played with another dial. The last two people at Chaney's bedside were leaning over the child. They, too, stood upright. One of them, a husky man with a full beard, pulled his stethoscope from his ears and hung it casually around his neck. He shook his head and said something. I would have tried to read his lips, but I couldn't even find them underneath the shroud of his facial hair.

I wanted to scream. I didn't. But I thought, *Oh God, she's dead*. It all seemed so uneventful. The anticipation of death is all pathos. Death itself is just a baby's sigh.

Those last two docs, both in white lab coats, started walking toward John Trent, who was standing still as a monument beside me.

My eyes were fixed on the bed, on the sisters. Merritt was in Chaney's bed, on her side, resting on one elbow, with Chaney's tiny body curled against hers. Merritt's free hand caressed her little sister's face, tracing soft ellipses on the dusky cheeks that were visible above the transparent oxygen mask that was clouded with mist.

The bearded pulmonologist introduced himself to John Trent. He said, "Respirations just came down to around forty, Mr. Trent, and her oxygen saturation is up. We're not out of the woods, but it's good news. We're getting new blood gases. Hopefully, they'll be better, much better."

Merritt tucked her head in close to her sister's ear. I saw her lips move and I knew she was talking. She didn't try to hide it. She didn't care that I knew that she was talking, she didn't care that anyone else knew. She was locked tight to her sister and was whispering magical sounds into a conduit that led directly to her sister's will.

John asked the pulmonologist, "Did she start getting better before her big sister got here, or after?"

The doctor's face said he thought the question was curious. He said, "After."

I watched as the doctor examined Trent's face. "We'll keep her down here overnight, of course, just to be sure," he said, and walked away, back toward Chaney's bed.

I said, "You knew, John? How?"

He replied, "I didn't know. I guessed. I hoped. I don't have much faith left, but I felt a lot right then, when she came down, when she hugged me, and especially as they touched, Chaney and Merritt. I felt it deep inside. It was powerful, profound." He closed his fist against his chest. "What I was thinking was that I'd just located my soul."

"What did you say to her? To Merritt, when she first came down?"

"I told her that no matter what anybody else said, no matter what she'd heard from you upstairs, no matter how somber the doctors looked or how bad Chaney looked, that she wasn't down here to say good-bye to her sister."

Brenda burst through the door behind us.

Twenty

There are many permutations of hunger. I was feeling most of them by the time I left Children's after returning Merritt to the psychiatric unit. I couldn't magically transport Lauren back from Washington. And I couldn't do anything about the dual tragedies unfolding for Merritt and Chaney, but I took the opportunity of being in Denver to drive to the west side of town and treat myself to some Mexican food at Tacquería Patzcuaro. The carnitas were as good as I remembered. After dinner, I picked up some goodies at the Denver Bread Company before heading north on I-25 toward home.

Emily heard my car coming down the lane and was bouncing off the walls, and ceiling, of her dog run as I stepped out of the car. She wasn't accustomed to being in doggie jail for long hours, but with Lauren out of town my daily absences in Denver to treat Merritt were causing Emily some unfortunate incarceration problems.

She wanted to pee, she wanted food, and she wanted to chase and kill tennis balls. Deciphering which of the activities was most important to her at that moment felt a little like trying to decide precisely what Merritt had been telling me with her limited communicative repertoire of half-smiles and narrowing eyes.

Emily peed before all else, her abundant urine pooling in the dust like a miniature Lake Gatorade.

I said, "You want some dinner?"

She jumped in the air, spinning 180 degrees to starboard. That meant an enthusiastic yes, as did the identical spin to port. She had forgotten, temporarily, about throttling the evil tennis balls.

I laid out a bowl of food and some fresh ice water for her and called Lauren at her parents' house in Washington. No one answered and I left a message. I needed to talk with Lauren to try to work through some of the intensity that was buzzing in my head. I needed to feel her skin against mine. I needed to smell her hair and I needed to be seduced and to make love so slowly it lasted all night. But Lauren was a thousand miles away, and I had never believed in the asceticism of cold showers.

I stripped off my work clothes and pulled on some reflective Lycra and a windbreaker, checked the air pressure and the lights on my bike, and took off for an evening ride. I knew even thirty hard minutes would help clear my head of confusion.

My ride had taken me no more than two miles from my house when my pager went off. I had to stop the bike to read the screen on my beeper, which was flashing a number I didn't recognize. Although I was tempted to ignore the page for now and complete my ride, I didn't. There were too many crises nearing a boil in my vicinity. It didn't feel prudent to ignore one of them at random.

Emily acted, again, like I'd been gone all day. I worried sometimes about her internal clock. Her stomach full, her bladder empty, the tennis balls were her only focus in life. I threw one for her, then another. She waited for me to throw yet another as I put my bicycle away. To my amazement, she heeded my low whistle, joined me at the front door, and followed me into the living room. Still wearing my bicycle cleats, I punched in the number from my pager.

A female said, "Hello."

"This is Dr. Alan Gregory, I'm returning a page to this number."

"Oh, thank you, Dr. Gregory. This is Marie Monroe. Miggy Monroe? We talked yesterday afternoon about my daughter, Madison. Remember me?"

"Yes," I said, "of course." I'd called Madison's mother to get permission to meet with her daughter.

"Madison didn't show up at school this afternoon. They called me at work, at the library, and told me. And she hasn't come home yet, and she hasn't called, and I'm really worried and I wonder if you would have any idea where she might have gone." She was breathless but seemed to be making an effort to speak in a normal voice.

"Is this unusual for her, Ms. Monroe? Skipping classes, not coming home? Has she ever done it before?"

"No, not for this long, not that I know of. She always calls, well, most of the time, anyway. I've had trouble with her on weekends, sometimes, you know, staying out late. But not during the school week." She exhaled loudly as she recognized that I wasn't going to be of any help. "You don't know where she is, do you?" Her voice was decompressing, gliding downhill toward despair.

"I met with her just before lunchtime at the Starbucks on the Hill. You know where it is? On Broadway? I bought her a cup of coffee. We talked for fifteen, maybe twenty minutes, mostly about her friend Merritt. Afterwards, she met up with somebody and told me she had to get back to class. I watched them leave, they took off down University toward Boulder High School."

"Which friend? Was it Merritt? I think she's a good influence on Madison." Madison apparently hadn't told her mother about Merritt being in the hospital.

"No, a boy. I think he said his name was Brad.

She sighed. "I don't know anybody named Brad. Did he say his last name?"

"No, he didn't. I'm sorry."

"Is he a student?"

"I don't know him. He looked older than your daughter, if that helps. He may be old enough to be a CU student, not a high school student. But it's hard to tell with kids, you know?"

"She's not allowed to go out with college boys. She knows that. And you haven't heard from her since then? She didn't call you back or anything?"

"No. But I didn't expect her to."

"She didn't mention anything about going anywhere after school?"

"I wish I could tell you something helpful. You've checked her room, of course? Is there anything missing? Any sign she might have packed a few things to take with her?"

"Take with her where? Where was she going?"

"If she was planning on leaving—"

"Leaving, what do you mean, leaving? Where was she planning on going?"

"Running. Kids usually pack some things up when they run away."

"Why was Madison running away?"

"I don't know that she was, Ms. Monroe. I'm just trying to puzzle this out with you."

"Like what would she take?"

What? "You know, underwear, a coat, extra clothes, money. Things like that."

"I'm not sure I would know what's gone from her room. She takes care of her own things, clothes and such. And sometimes she gets money I don't know about, I guess from her father. I never know how much she has. You understand?"

She really wanted me to, I could tell. At once, I did understand, and I didn't.

I thought about the conversation with Miggy Monroe while I showered, and decided I was going to tell Sam about it. Madison's absence from her afternoon high school classes was probably meaningless, and I guessed that she would probably show up at her own home any minute. But I knew Sam well enough to know that giving him a dead-end lead was much more salutary behavior than keeping one to myself.

I paged him. My phone rang twenty seconds later.

"What's up?" he asked.

"Probably nothing, but I thought you should know about something. Merritt's friend, that kid Madison? Her mom just called me. She skipped her classes this afternoon at Boulder High, hasn't called and checked in or come home. Her mom says it's not like her."

"No history of running?"

"Mom says not."

"Lucy ran her for me this afternoon after we talked. Two petty offenses. Shoplifting, something else, um, I don't know, I don't remember. Notes the last time she was picked up say she hangs with some scummy kids."

"Sounds a little severe based on what I saw, Sam. She has boys on the brain, acts like a punk. What's curious is that she apparently skipped right after I met with her."

"And what? So what are you saying now? Is that important? Why are we having this conversation?"

"I'm wondering if I spooked her by meeting with her this morning. I pressed on her about her role in finding Merritt. Maybe it spooked her."

"Why would that spook her?"

"I left thinking she may be mixed up in this. I pressed her hard at the end about how she happened to find Merritt, and why she didn't stick around for the police. I also asked her if she knew anything about a gun. That's when she was most uncomfortable during the interview. I was thinking that maybe you were right, that she's involved with Merritt in this thing with Dead Ed. That she knew about the gun I found in Merritt's bathroom."

His voice covered the territory from curious to disdainful. "You told her about the gun? I can't believe you told her about the gun."

"I didn't tell her about the gun. I asked her if she knew anything about *a* gun. That's all."

"Now maybe that's an important distinction for a shrink. It's not much of one for a cop. Jesus, I think your interviewing techniques need some work. Maybe I could arrange a refresher course."

"Maybe, Sam. I don't have the same agenda here that you do. I'm trying to keep Merritt alive."

"That's true, I'm just trying to keep her out of prison for the rest of her life. Sorry for my insensitivity. Please forgive me."

This wasn't going the way I had hoped. "Sam, look, I apologize if I screwed up. I'm doing my best here. I thought Madison's disappearance this afternoon might be important, and I wanted you to know about it."

"You know she's probably shacked up with a boyfriend, someplace. Or she decided to run. Hard to say."

"I agree. That's what's most likely. The only help I can offer on that front is that I met a guy with her this afternoon. Name is Brad. Older than her, maybe a CU kid, I think he might've been wearing a fraternity T-shirt."

"You have a last name?"

"No."

"You remember what frat?"

"My Greek's not too good, but something Delta something. Three letters."

"We'll check on Brad, too. Anything else?"

"No. I just don't like coincidences and this feels like one."

"I suppose I need to find a way to look into this little disappearance that doesn't upset my supervisors. You saw Merritt, how is she?"

I had to think for a minute to convince myself I had the freedom to tell him what had happened that afternoon at the hospital. "There was a crisis with Chaney, Sam. Late today. I don't want to get in the middle of things between you and the Trents, but I don't want you left out, either. It was pretty serious for a while."

"What happened?" His voice was hollow. Sam's optimism had vanished; he was expecting to hear tragedy.

"She had a respiratory crisis of some kind. The doctors thought she might be dying. I was upstairs with Merritt when John called. I broke some rules, allowed Merritt to go down to the ICU to be with her sister. After she was there for a few minutes, the crisis eased. When I left, Chaney was resting comfortably."

Sam was breathing through his mouth. I could hear the hollow gale gusting in my ear.

He said, "You broke some rules?"

"Yes."

Inhale, exhale. "She's okay? Chaney?"

"Same as before, if you call that okay. She's still in intensive care. They're going to watch her overnight."

"What about Merritt? You saw her earlier? How is she doing?"

"Her condition hadn't changed when I saw her this afternoon. But earlier this evening, she saw Mitchell Crest's little news conference on TV. It scared her, shook her up."

"I bet."

"Not just for the reason you think. I think she's trying to tell me that she's protecting someone else, Sam."

"She started talking?"

"I'm not talking about anything she said. Not with words. With her eyes, with her expressions, with gestures. I think she's telling me that she's been clamming up to protect someone else. Maybe it's Madison. I don't know who else it could be."

"And you're absolutely sure you're reading these expressions correctly?" I knew Sam's skeptical voice well, and I knew I was hearing it right then.

"No, I'm not sure, Sam. But I believe what I see. I'd love some more ammunition to use with her. Did you learn anything today that will give me some leverage with Merritt, maybe encourage her to talk to me?"

He was quiet for a few seconds longer than I expected. Finally, he said, "No, I have nothing new."

I wanted to keep him talking. I didn't want to feel as alone as I suspected I would as soon as I hung up the phone. "Why are they waiting to arrest her, Sam? Do you know that? It seems odd to me."

Sam Purdy could lie to me as seamlessly as Houdini could pick my pocket. It meant something important that I could tell from his voice that his next words were untrue. "Oh, you know—PR, mostly. Don't want to pull a kid out of the hospital to put her in jail. Looks bad, especially with Chaney and all."

"It's not an evidence problem?"

"I'm out of the loop, you know that. But there may be a couple of loose ends they would like to line up before they pick her up. They're not in a rush. She's safe. They're not too worried."

"What loose ends?"

"There're always anomalies. You know that. But nobody's talking to me."

"You mean Lucy's not keeping you informed? That's hard to believe."

He was done fencing with me. "Listen, Edmonton game is tomorrow night. They're only two points back. See you around six. You'll be at your house? I'll drive."

"No, I'll already be in Denver, seeing Merritt. I'll need to meet you at McNichols. Top of the stairs on the east side, let's say ten to seven or so? I'm looking forward to it."

We hung up.

I'd been up since four o'clock that morning and the day felt as long as a bad week. I called Lauren and once again got her parents' machine.

Two minutes later I stripped and crawled into bed. It's not often I remember my dreams. And this night was no exception.

Twenty-one

I woke still missing Lauren and still worried about Madison. It was too early to call Washington, but I phoned Miggy Monroe to check on her daughter before I left for the office to see my eight-fifteen patient.

"Ms. Monroe? Miggy? It's Dr. Gregory. Did you hear anything from Madison overnight? Did she come home?"

"No, not a word. I haven't slept a wink; I'm worried sick. The police won't help me at all. Some of her clothes are gone, I'm pretty sure. I checked real carefully, like you said. Why would she run away? She and I do okay. I'm not a bad mom. Why would she leave me? Do you think it's the boy? I have to think it's him. I bet it's the boy."

I asked if there was anything I could do to help. She said there wasn't.

"Would you please call me when you hear from her? I'm concerned about her, too, and would like to know that she's okay. Would you do that?"

She said she would call.

Diane Estevez came into my office at nine-forty-five, after I had seen two morning patients and she had seen one. She said, "You want coffee? I made a fresh pot."

"That would be great, thanks."

She disappeared for a moment and returned with two mugs. Handing me one, she said, "You saw the news."

"Thanks for the coffee. Yes, I saw the news."

"They're not releasing her name to the news media. How am I supposed to get John Trent's custody eval thrown out if I can't tell the court what the hell the kid is supposed to have done?"

"It's not your problem, Diane. It's a lawyer problem. Let your pa-tient's lawyer worry about it. You know it's all going to come out in the wash eventually. You know what I think? I think you just don't like being out of the loop." I raised my mug. "Good coffee, is it something new?" The coffee tasted the same as always to me, but Diane had a predilection for trying exotic blends and was scornful of me when I didn't notice her efforts.

She nodded about the coffee being novel. I could tell she also knew I was right about what would happen with the custody eval. The question was merely one of following form. For Diane, that meant protesting.

"Why are you so sure? And what do you mean I don't like being out of the loop?"

"Being right isn't good enough for you, you know that. You always want to be sure that you can influence the universe whenever and however you see fit. You should find a red cape to wear to work."

"I have a red cape. It's cute."

"There you go, then."

She adopted a civilized tone and asked, "How's your patient?"

"Same, thanks for asking. You know anything you can tell me about Edward Robilio? Other than the basics, I mean. I'm still trying to figure out how this whole crazy situation came down the way it did."

"What happened to 'Dead Ed'? Raoul thought it was a hilarious nick-name, by the way. Said it fit dear Dr. Robilio in real life, too."

"What did he mean by that?"

"Raoul met him a few times on the hundred-dollar-a-plate muckety-muck circuit. Says he was a total boor. Tedious, always talking about his money, or his toys, or both. Big toys. He had an airplane, some big ski boat, and condos here and there and a—"

"Big freaking RV."

She laughed. "Yeah, that too. How did you know about the RV?"

"Mitchell Crest lives in the low-rent end of the same neighborhood where Dead Ed lived. Mitch said the RV is like the size of a nuclear sub-marine or something. Caused a neighborhood uproar when Ed tried to park it semipermanently in the driveway. Apparently it's bad form in Boul-der's new suburbs."

"Raoul said that Dead Ed loved the thing, had pictures of it in his wallet. Had a name for it, too, oh, oh, I can't remember. You have any idea what it cost?"

"No. No clue."

She paused for effect. "After he gilded it, three-ninety. That's what he told Raoul over cocktails. Raoul says Ed lowered his voice reverentially when he said the number."

"No way. Three hundred and ninety thousand dollars? For a Winnebago? That's more than my house. That's more than two of my houses."

"You don't have two houses; the other one belongs to Lauren. And your one house is not exactly a yardstick by which wealth is measured."

"True, but—"

"Apparently the thing has a marble bathroom and cherry cabinetry and leather everywhere and a surround-sound home theatre and gold-plated this and that. If you can believe it, it even has a satellite dish on the roof that automatically rotates to find its signal."

I thought about an RV like that and wondered aloud, "What do you do with one, Diane? I mean, sure, you can drive it around to pretty places, but at the end of the day, you have to plug it in somewhere, right? For water and power and sewer, correct? Which means, half a million or no half a million, you end up spending the night in a trailer park. Am I right?"

"Raoul would probably tell you that spending the night in a trailer park would make Dead Ed feel right at home. And that it's right where he belonged."

"Anything else you can tell me about him?"

"No. He wasn't popular, even among his peers. He apparently wasn't much of a physician when he was practicing—I think he was a dermatologist—and he didn't do much to endear himself to others in the health care industry after he founded MedExcel. Pissed off a lot of other doctors and the other insurers. He sounds ruthless, in a business sense."

"You have him diagnosed?" I knew she had. For Diane it was a hobby, like presumptive astrological forecasting for a hairdresser. The fact that she had never met Dr. Robilio wouldn't impede her musings for even a moment.

"Narcissistic personality with borderline features."

Tough assessment. You don't go through life with those diagnostic characteristics without pissing people off. Plenty. "So he had enemies?"

"Going fishing for alternative suspects, Alan? Well, not to worry, the pond is probably well stocked. Half the doctors in Colorado wanted him dead. The trouble is that none of the other fish swimming around have Dead Ed's bloody clothes stashed under their bed."

She had Merritt's dilemma a little wrong, but still I was impressed. "How do you know about the clothes? It hasn't been in the news."

"I have my ways." She pointed at the little light on my wall indicating my next patient had arrived. "Time to get back to work, Doctor."

I surfaced again at eleven-thirty. I was hungry, was concerned about Madison, and was continuing to feel some nagging curiosity as to why the DA's office was procrastinating about arresting Merritt.

Madison's mother wasn't at home and I had been stupid in not getting her work number, or even asking at which of Boulder's many libraries she worked, so I couldn't reach her. I paged Sam and waited ten minutes for him to call back. He didn't, which I found interesting. Finally I called the adolescent psychiatric unit at The Children's Hospital to get an update on Merritt's condition.

The mental health aide said Merritt was the same. And he said "Cool" when I told him I'd be in to see her close to six o'clock, depending on traffic.

I walked over to the Mall to grab some lunch.

My pager went off as I was walking back in my office door after a clear-my-head stroll to the east end of the Mall. Sam Purdy had left a voice mail message.

"Brad, the boy you told me about, didn't return to his frat last night. By the way, he's a Phi Delta Theta. That's what those little symbols stand for. Hasn't been to class this morning; his roommate doesn't have any idea where he is. Lucy ran him for me. He has a juvenile prior for car theft. Just one. I'm checking on reports of missing vehicles from last night to see if I can link anything up to these two. My guess is that they're joy-riding someplace, or that they ran. I'll keep you posted."

I arrived at McNichols Arena for the hockey game before Sam did. The evening was mild. While I waited for Sam to arrive, I stood at the top of the east stairs and turned down five offers to sell my ticket.

Sam was running late because he had stopped for dinner, which he was carrying in a brown McDonald's bag that he knew the ushers would absolutely not permit him to carry into the arena. While he ate, we stood at the railing at the top of the stairs, enjoying the lights of the Denver skyline.

His meal was one of those super-size things that come with a drink large enough to convert the emptied cup into a children's wading pool. He pulled out two fish sandwiches and then he rummaged around in the bottom of the bag as though he were trying to find the prize in a box of Cracker Jacks. He said, "Yep, there it is."

"There what is, Sam?" I was looking around; I didn't see anything worthy of my attention.

"A french fry. When you get fast food there's always a french fry in the bottom of the bag. You ever noticed that? It's reassuring to me; it's kind of the way I look at hard times."

I smiled and glanced at him. "That's like what, your philosophy of life? That's how you keep going when things look this bleak? A french fry?"

Sam raised one eyebrow and held it there. I could only see the one eye, but I had to admit it looked pretty philosophical. "Given current events, it's an optimistic point of view for me to have, don't you think?"

I had to consider it. I said, "Yeah, I guess." I was trying to find some common ground between Ronald McDonald and Heidegger.

"Anyway, that's how I keep going some days. After everything seems to be settled, after you think you're all done, that you've done all you can do, there's always something more. There's always that one last fry. You eat fast food, ever? Or do you still count fat grams?"

"I eat more fast food than I should, probably."

"Good, I'm glad to hear it. It's human of you. Then you know about the renegade fry phenomenon. The one in the bottom of the bag? The damn thing is almost always cold, and sometimes it's ugly—you know, kinda pointy and brown and dry, like this one." He held up the current suspect for my examination. "But after I finish my burgers and my pie and everything, I always look in the bottom of the bag. There's always a french fry there, and—I don't know about you—I'm always kind of glad there's a french fry there. This time, too. It was right down there where it's supposed to be."

I thought more about what Sam was saying. I was forced to admit he had a point. "You know, sometimes it's more than one fry, Sam. Sometimes it seems like they spill half of the order down there."

Sam's face softened into a private smile, as though he were recalling a special sexual experience. "I don't know if it's just me, but I sort of appreciate it when they do that. It's like a bonus. No matter what, though, there's always at least one fry in the bag. That's the rule, the one you can count on."

Wanting to believe we were really discussing more than portion control at McDonald's, I said, "So what you're saying is that you're going to keep looking for answers?"

He swallowed, looked toward the new aquarium under construction in the Platte Valley. "You mean even if Merritt doesn't start talking?"

"Yeah. But I guess I mean especially if Merritt doesn't start talking."

"Of course. Absolutely, I'll keep looking." He balanced his drink on the railing and leaned it against his abdomen. He was searching the bag, fervently hoping for another renegade fry. "Throw away the napkin, look under the ketchup packet, it's always there someplace. One more fry. Yeah, I'm going to keep looking. I'll find something."

Something found him.

His pager went off at 11:06 of the second period while the officials were assigning major penalties to four different players after a brawl. I was surprised by the number of minutes the penalties earned; it didn't really seem like the players' hearts had been in the fight at all.

Even though Sam had a portable phone with him, he went out the tunnel to the concourse to make his call. He was back in three minutes, max.

"Grab your coat. We're out of here."

"What?"

"Come, come, I'll fill you in."

I followed him down the stairs to the concourse. He led me to the men's room. "I should pee first. It's a long drive, apparently."

I unzipped, too. "What's a long drive? Where are you going?"

"Do you ever have trouble peeing in stadiums and arenas? I don't know what it is, but it's like there's a kink in the hose sometimes. Just doesn't work. Only in arenas and stadiums, though; I'm fine in theaters. I don't get it."

"Want to make an appointment to talk about it? Probably has something to do with job stress. Maybe I can get you a disability pension."

He grunted a little, trying to get his flow going.

"Or I could call my urologist friend, Adrienne, for you, arrange a consult. I'm sure she'd have some ideas about what's wrong with your dick."

He exhaled, and I heard his urine begin to splash into the trough. The thought of discussing his privates with Adrienne had apparently been therapeutic.

He said, "We're going to the mountains to see Lucy Tanner."

Lucy was Sam's partner. "Now?"

"Yep."

"I don't think so, Sam. I have patients early in the morning. I've had to shuffle half my schedule around to make time to get to Denver to see Merritt every day. I'm even seeing some people on the weekend."

"Oooh, guilt." He stabbed his chest with his free hand. "Nice touch—elegant—but it won't work. Not with me. One of the things Sherry doesn't like about me is that I'm highly resistant to guilt." He had initiated the shaking and rezipping routine. "Someone, an intruder, has apparently been camping out in Dead Ed's mountain cabin. Lucy is up there checking it out for the department. Wondered if I would like to be an unofficial observer."

"Are you sure it's wise getting involved? You should let her handle this, Sam. Stay out of it. You're too close to it. Anyway, the hockey game is tied. You don't really want to leave."

"Just like you let all of us law enforcement types handle Lauren's little problem last fall? Like that kind of staying out of it? That's what I should do?"

I zipped up and said, "Guilt works both ways. Only I'm not immune." I looked at my watch. "Can't you go up alone? Why do you need me?"

"I want you to be there. That's all. Is that sufficient?"

"Why?"

"You repeat what I'm about to tell you and I'm dead, and so's the cop who told me this. You understand?"

"Yes, I understand."

"Merritt wasn't just in the basement of Dead Ed's house."

"What?"

"That's right. She looked around. Prints on the banister going from the basement to the first floor, and a few locations in the kitchen."

"What the hell was she doing wandering around his house?"

"I don't know. The detectives don't know. The DA doesn't know. They figure they know how all this ended, but they're not sure how it began, and that makes them less sure about the wherefores and the whys. Merritt's not talking. So Dead Ed's going to have to tell us what happened. That's why we're going to the mountains."

"Okay, where's the cabin?"

"Summit County, north of Dillon someplace. Lucy called it a 'ranchette.' "

I looked at my watch. It was only eight-twenty. With luck, we could reach the accessible parts of Summit County in ninety minutes. "Whose car?"

"You kidding? You're driving. My car's getting new brakes. I took RTD to Denver. Anyway, I need to grab some sleep. I have a funny feeling it's going to be a long night. Ever get those feelings?"

"Only when I'm with you."

Dead Ed's ranchette turned out to be adjacent to Highway 9, not more than five miles north of I-70. With the new rural speed limits on the interstate and with the assurance that the sleeping hulk leaning against the door next to me in the front seat was a peace officer who would put in a generous word for me with the Colorado State Patrol, I made good time on the ride up. We reached the town of Dillon on the other side of the Continental Divide at 9:45.

I said Sam's name a couple of times to try to get him to stir. No luck. I decided to wake him by sliding the passenger door window down until his head started to fall out into the breeze.

It worked. His hair started blowing in the wind and then his whole big head just kerplunked into the night. He stiffened his neck with a jerk and pulled himself back inside.

I said, "You awake? I need directions. We're in Dillon already."

He said, "Shit, what the hell?" and looked at his watch. "What were you doing, ninety? Couldn't you have driven the speed limit? This barely qualifies as a nap. I wasn't asleep until we got to Idaho Springs."

I scoffed, "Sam, you were snoring before I turned onto Sixth Avenue." Which he knew was only three minutes from McNichols Arena. "Where's the ranchette? Which way do I go?"

He flicked on the dome light and held a little piece of crumpled paper close to it. He couldn't read it without his Kmart glasses. "Go north. Mark your odometer carefully. Lucy said the road is approximately four-point-three miles from the exit ramp."

The cold air had refreshed me; I was feeling feisty. "Isn't that incongruent, Sam? Wouldn't it be *approximately* four miles or *exactly* four-point-three?"

Sam rubbed his face, trying to get some circulation going. I could hear the stubble of his beard crackle beneath his fingers. He said, "If I knew you were going to be an asshole, I would have left you in Denver."

Four-point-three was accurate. The dirt road that led east off the highway was in good repair and after a hundred yards or so led to a gated entry below a carefully clumsy wooden sign that read, THE NOT SO LAZY 7 RANCH. From the fences that were visible, I guessed that the property comprised maybe twenty fenced acres that extended from close to the banks of the Blue River up to the borders of the Arapahoe National Forest. Maybe a quarter of the land was sparsely wooded with ponderosa pine and aspen. Dead Ed had probably been able to cross-country ski on his land much of the winter and fly-fish the Blue River all summer long. The ski and golf resorts of Keystone, Breckenridge, and Copper Mountain were only minutes away.

I found myself thinking that if I had a few extra million like Dead Ed, I might have been tempted to buy this little ranchette, too.

It was too dark to determine what animals, if any, Dead Ed had kept on his ranch, but he had strung enough barbed wire to contain quite a few head of something. We followed the dirt road up the steep slopes of the hillside, past a big red barn, through a thick stand of woods to a clearing.

Sam said, "That's Lucy's car," pointing to a red turbo Volvo parked next to a Nissan something.

I parked between Lucy's car and a four-by-four from the Summit County Sheriff's Office, pulled myself from the driver's seat, and stretched. Sam got out even more slowly than I. I watched him raise his arms above his head and suggested he might want to tuck in his shirt.

He suggested I might want to fuck myself.

Dead Ed's ranch house may have been made of logs, but it was definitely not a log cabin. The two-story V-shaped house sat on a prominent rise with exposures to the south and west. I guessed it contained in the neighborhood of four thousand square feet—larger than a cabin, smaller than a mansion.

The black sky above was speckled by a billion stars. I said, "Incredible view up here, don't you think?"

Sam said, "Yeah. Where is everybody?"

"Maybe Lucy's inside rustling you up a sandwich. You disappointed? You expected maybe she'd be waiting for you on the porch with a cocktail?"

He ignored me and lumbered up some wide front steps. He pounded on the door with a door knocker that had been constructed from an ice ax.

Lucy answered the door and smiled.

Lucy Tanner was classy, which distinguished her from her partner. Although Boulder had many law enforcement officers who did their job professionally, the city had few cops who could walk the corridors of power and be mistaken for a member. Lucy oozed confidence and grace. Although I'd never asked her, I assumed she chose to be a cop only after ruling out other options available to her, like law firm partner, investment banker, or CEO of some prominent company.

I said, "Hi, Lucy. Nice outfit." Lucy liked clothes the way Dead Ed liked diesel-powered toys. I knew Sam wouldn't notice how she was dressed and I knew Lucy felt good when people noticed.

The outfit I was admiring was a one-piece bodysuit of some soft flannel-looking fabric. The places where it might be too tight for a police officer on duty were hidden under a long mustard-colored four-button blazer.

"You really think it works? Sunny and I just went into Dillon to grab some dinner and we stopped at the Donna Karan outlet to look around. I wasn't sure about this when I first saw it, but she convinced me the colors are good for me. So I picked it up. Can't beat the price."

"It works, Lucy. You look lovely. Don't you think she looks great, Sam?"

Sam grunted.

She turned to face her partner but spoke to me. "He's hopeless, Alan. Don't bother. You guys made good time, Sam. Sunny and I just got back here a few minutes ago."

"Alan mistook I-70 for the Bonneville Salt Flats. Listen, I appreciate the call about this, Luce," Sam said. He hesitated, stuffed his hands in his pockets. "You know I can't have been here."

"I know that, Sam. Don't worry. Everybody's cool about you being here."

"Who is everybody?"

"A Summit County deputy named Larsen. He's the one who called us; he's on the ball. And the Robilios' oldest daughter, Helen. Says everybody calls her Sunny."

"And she doesn't know I'm Merritt's uncle?"

"She thinks you're a specialist in this kind of thing. You know, like a consultant."

"And exactly what is 'this kind of thing,' Luce?"

Lucy was already walking toward the back of the house. Without turning, she said, "Wing it, Sam. I'm not sure what we have yet."

"What about me?" I asked.

"You're Sam's driver. Hang around the back of the room and act bored. It should be easy for you."

Twenty-two

"Hello, I'm Sunny Hasan. This is Deputy Larsen, Craig Larsen. You must be the consultant from Boulder. Come in and have a seat. Would you like a drink? Some coffee? The snacks are nothing special, but," she pointed at bowls of nuts and chips on the plank coffee table, "it's all that was in the kitchen. Please, everybody help themselves."

A fire was smoldering in a red granite-faced fireplace that was flanked by two leather sofas of an almost identical hue. A fresh piece of green oak had just been thrown on the grate, and the sap in the wood was escaping in gaseous little bursts that were snapping like a string of tiny firecrackers.

I said hello with a weak wave, and moved to a corner of the huge room, where I settled at a game table. I grabbed a magazine from a stand that was fashioned from the racks of a pair of good-sized bucks, the whole time trying to appear both superfluous and inconspicuous. The magazine I chose was the latest edition of *MotorHome*.

I was absolutely certain that it was the first time I'd had an opportunity to read *MotorHome* magazine.

Sam introduced himself to the deputy and to Sunny without revealing his affiliation to law enforcement. Maybe I knew him too well, but I thought he wore his status like a neon-lit COP sign attached to his forehead. Sunny Hasan might be fooled by Sam's act, but I guessed that Deputy Larsen had been cajoled by Lucy to play along.

Sunny had a wedding ring on the appropriate finger of her left hand, the stone a size considerably smaller than a man of her father's station might have offered to adorn the finger of his new bride. She wore an outfit that looked every bit as fashionable and new as Lucy's. I guessed it was another Donna Karan outlet special. Wisely, I thought I would keep my compliments to myself this time.

Sunny was a surprising woman. Dead Ed, her father, had been a defiantly rotund guy with a thick neck and wiry hair in few of the desirable places and many of the undesirable ones. Sunny was a total contrast: small, blond, and cute. Her hair was tied back in a ponytail, and the curve of her hairline had an intriguing asymmetry. Her brand-new Donna Karan special was a short khaki skirt, a white v-neck T-shirt, and a black blazer. I was guessing that Sunny was in her late twenties.

Sam had removed a notepad from one of his pockets and was poised for work. In a soft, seductive voice I'd never heard him use before, he asked, "Now what exactly happened that caused you so much concern?"

Sunny smiled at Deputy Larsen and said, "Shall I begin or do you want to?"

I couldn't figure out Larsen's agenda. Was he hitting on Sunny or was he just bored enough with the alternatives in his life that this seemed like a reasonable way to spend an evening? He nodded politely to Sunny and said, "You go right ahead. Go on."

She perched herself on the arm of one of the sofas before she started. "I've been in Denver with Mom since . . . everything happened. You know, the things with my father. George—he's my husband—and I live in Grand Junction. After Dad's funeral, George had to go right back home for work. I didn't need to be back so quickly, and I decided to take a few days here at the ranch to, I don't know, consider things, reflect. Grieve, whatever. So I said good-bye to Mom this morning, took George to the airport in Denver, and drove up here.

"I got to the ranch, I would guess, about two. Is that when I phoned you, Craig?"

"It was closer to three when you called us. But later on, when we talked, you said it took you awhile to realize what was wrong."

"That's true." The fire was roaring and spitting and Sunny moved off the arm of the sofa to a seat farther from the heat. "None of you knew my father, did you?" We all shook our heads. "He was an, um, orderly man. He liked things his way. You did things the way Dad wanted or you did them behind his back and hoped he either didn't notice or didn't catch you. Those were your choices with my father. I've known all that my whole life. Okay?"

The psychologist in me was hearing Sunny rearranging the cards in her hand so she could find a palatable way to play the grief card for a father for whom she'd had a lot of negative feelings. Everyone nodded but Craig Larsen. I imagined he'd covered this territory already. Or maybe he was as taciturn as he looked.

"One of Dad's things was that no one ever came to the ranch without him. That was a rule. This was Dad's personal retreat. Even Fred and I—Frederick's my little brother—needed an invitation to come here. Mom has still never been here without my father. That's one of his things. Got it?"

Sam said, "Sure, gotcha."

"The second thing is that every time I've ever been here to visit, the place has been immaculate, clean, neat. That's another one of Dad's peculiarities. Order. Cleanliness. At home, in Boulder, Mom gets housekeeping help now. She didn't used to, even in that big house. But not up here. Dad expected her to keep this place clean all by herself. He once told me that she doesn't fish, she doesn't ski, she doesn't hunt, she doesn't ride horses, what else does she have to do? That's my dad."

She sighed. Her efforts were transparent as she struggled to balance her sorrow and anger with some more enduring feelings about her father, feelings that caused discomfort but not pain, like ill-fitting shoes. "When I arrived here this afternoon, the place was not . . . tidy. There were crumbs on the kitchen counter, and some spilled liquid that had dried on the floor. There were dirty dishes in the dishwasher. And the trash hadn't been taken out. I checked his bedroom, upstairs. The bed was made, but it wasn't made well. Not like my mom makes it. Like Dad insisted Mom make it.

"It all seemed . . . suspicious to me. Like I said, you would have to know him." Again, she sighed. "I phoned my mother and told her I'd arrived safely and asked her when she and Dad had last been here. She said they hadn't been here for weeks. 'Your father has been traveling,' is what she said. Then, in as much of a joking voice as I could—I didn't want to alarm her, she's been through an awful lot—I asked her if he still made her leave the place looking like a show home when they left. She said he did."

Sunny was done. She folded her hands in her lap and crossed her legs at the ankles.

Craig Larsen said, "When she called us she reported a possible break-in. I responded, listened to her concerns. When I heard about who her father was and what had happened to him in Boulder, I thought I should call you guys in, let you have a look. That's where we are."

Sam said, "Thanks for putting the pieces together so quickly and bringing us on board," before he rotated in his chair and faced Sunny. "And now, what you suspect, what you feel, is that someone else has been here?"

"Yes."

"Without your father's permission?"

"He wouldn't give it. His permission."

"If your father came up here alone and just didn't tell your mother, would he have cleaned up after himself?"

A laugh caught in her throat. Sunny found the thought amusing. "No, my father did not clean. He messed."

"So, it's possible he came to the ranch and just didn't inform your mother? The, uh, lack of order you see is because he had no one to clean up after him?"

"I suppose it's possible. But if he did, it would have been the first time in ten years he didn't bring someone along to clean up after him."

"Is there any sign of anyone breaking into the house? Any broken windows, forced locks?"

Deputy Larsen said, "No. No evidence of forced entry."

"Anything missing?"

Sunny shrugged. "I don't know the cabin well enough to inventory it. But I think the electronics are all here. I suppose a burglar would have taken those first. Wouldn't he take those first?"

Sam said, "Frequently, yes, that's what's taken first. Are you thinking that if it wasn't your father who was visiting the ranch without your mother, that it would have been what, squatters, then? Is that it?"

"I don't know. I suppose that's a possibility. I thought this was your specialty."

At that moment, Lucy turned in my direction, away from the conversation. She was trying to stifle a grin.

Sam was on his game. He said, "It is. It is. But sometimes vics, uh, victims, have a wonderful intuitive sense about these things. I always like to hear their point of view before I speculate."

Lucy covered her mouth to keep from laughing. I kept my nose buried in an article about the advantages of the new breed of diesel generators for class A motorhomes. The author thought it might be wise for me to upgrade now.

Sam said, "Deputy?"

"Craig."

"Craig. You looked around? What did you find? What do you think?"

"As I said, no evidence of forced entry. House was locked up from outside when Miss Hasan arrived. Whoever has been here has a key. Disturbances in the routine she described are limited to the kitchen, the playroom—it's where Mr. Robilio kept his home theater, a pinball machine, a Foosball table, some other stuff—the master bedroom, and the master bath."

Sunny said, "Oh, I forgot about that. There are used towels hanging in the master bath. No way Dad would permit that. A fresh towel every time for him. 'If it's good enough for Hilton, it's good enough for me,' is what he used to say. And even if he allowed someone else to use the cabin, there is not a chance in the world that he would permit them to use his bedroom or bathroom. No. Not a chance."

"Food? Anything atypical in the refrigerator?"

Sunny responded, "There's no beer."

"No beer!"

"Dad always kept local beer up here to impress people. Ten kinds sometimes. There's nothing, not one bottle, not even in the bar refrigerator."

"Maybe he ran out?"

"Not Dad, he didn't drink the microbrewery stuff. He's an old friend of Peter Coors and that's all Dad drank, Coors Light. Dad's loyal to those who are loyal to him. Hershey's friends don't run out of chocolate. Dad didn't run out of Coors Light. The other stuff was for guests, for show."

"Is there a caretaker? Anybody see any traffic up here that didn't belong?"

The deputy answered. "There's one old boy who lives on the ranch. Name's Horace Poster. He takes care of the horses, gets a free cabin. The horses are kept down by the river, near Poster's cabin. I interviewed him. He can't see this house from there. Says he didn't notice anything unusual the past few days. But then, Horace doesn't strike me as the type who would notice a pimple on his own nose."

"Tire marks outside?"

"It's been dry for a while. There are plenty. Now that you're here, I'd bet that there are even more."

Sam was scribbling notes. Lucy was examining titles in a tall book-case. Sunny was trying to mask her disappointment with how things were going with the consultant from the city. And Craig Larsen was acting like every bored cop I'd ever seen.

Without glancing up, Sam asked, "You get many squatter situations in these vacation homes, Deputy?"

"We get a few each year. It's not a big problem. It's usually the truly isolated places, the smaller cabins off by themselves in the woods. Some-body camps out a few days. Eats some food, takes a shower. That sort of thing."

I wrote out a note to Sam and handed it to Lucy. "Please give this to him."

She read it first, of course.

Sam took the note from his partner, glanced at it, and glared at me with narrow eyes before he nodded slightly and turned toward Dead Ed's daughter.

"Sunny? I understand your father has a motor home that he keeps up here at the ranch?"

She swallowed a smile and shook her head. "Half the people I meet who know my father know about that darn thing. Mom tell you about it?"

Sam said, "It just came up in interviews," as he glanced sideways at me.

He was daring me to say something. I knew better.

"The big red barn you passed on the other side of the woods when you were coming up the hill? Remember seeing it? That's where Haldeman lives."

"Haldeman?"

"The motor home, actually Dad preferred the term 'motor coach,' is a Holiday Rambler. Initials are H. R. Dad named it Haldeman. Get it? H. R. Haldeman—the Watergate guy. It was way before my time, but Dad's Re-publican friends all think the name is pretty funny."

"Anyone checked it since you came up this afternoon? The barn?"

Sunny said, "No, I didn't think about it. I suppose we should. I really don't even know where the keys are. I'll have to call my mother and see where Dad kept those things. You want me to do that?"

Sam said, "Please. Do you mind?"

Sunny walked into another part of the house to make the call, and Sam's voice returned to its normal timbre. "Why the hell didn't you tell me about this damn motor home before now?"

"I didn't think it meant anything. Mitchell Crest mentioned the thing to me—said that Dr. Robilio brought it up here after the homeowners association refused to let him keep it on his property in Boulder."

"Lucy, did you know about it?"

"I knew he had an RV, Sam. I didn't think there was anything special about it. And I didn't know he stored it up here. Honest."

"Anything else I don't know before I continue with this interview? Huh? Either of you?"

Larsen's boredom had been interrupted. He was grinning.

I was trying to figure some ethical way to get Trent's custody evaluation of Robilio's relatives into Sam's consciousness. I said, "Dr. Robilio may have had some family in the metro area. Maybe he gave them permission to use the ranch. Did anyone explore that?"

Sam checked with his partner. I could feel his irritation at needing to rely on others for basic information. "Lucy? Any family?"

She thought for a moment and said, "A sister—or sister-in-law maybe—I'm not sure which, in Denver."

I was also going to tell Sam what Diane had told me, that the motor home was apparently not a pedestrian Winnebago. But Sunny returned before Lucy or I could elaborate. Sam's voice once again became sweetness and light as he asked her, "Did your mother know where to find the keys?"

Sunny held up a jumble of metal and plastic and nodded. "My father liked things organized. But it was my mother who did the organizing."

Sam said, "To get back to visitors for a second, you have family close by? An aunt or an uncle or something? Do I have that right?"

Sunny raised her sandy eyebrows in a manner that everyone but Sam found comical. "Nice try, but dead end. Daddy loved his children but we didn't get to use the cabin by ourselves. He didn't even *like* Mom's sister or her husband. There is no way that the Porters would have been granted a stay at this ranch. Sorry."

"Your father and his sister-in-law didn't get along?"

"You could say that. Abby, my aunt, drinks. It's a problem. Daddy found her weak. Her husband, my Uncle Andrew, loved to tease Daddy.

My father didn't have much of a sense of humor, so Andrew's act never went over well. Anyway, my aunt and uncle are in the middle of a divorce. It's messy, a custody thing, you know?"

Craig Larsen stepped forward, his boot heels causing loud smacks on the wood floor. "Sunny, you said something about your father hunting a little while ago, didn't you? Did your father keep guns up here?"

"I suppose he did. He has some he used for hunting. He didn't keep any rifles down in Boulder. So he must have kept them here or in Aspen."

Sam turned to me and mouthed, "Aspen?"

I shrugged my shoulders.

Nonchalantly, Craig asked, "Where would you think they would be? The playroom?"

Sunny giggled and said, "Game room. Game room. I suppose that's where he would keep them. It's down this way if you'd like to look."

We followed her through the kitchen to a room similar in size to the living room. It was filled with Dead Ed's toys and games. A corner bar had stools for six serious drinkers. I was looking around for an ostentatious gun rack, while Sam, Lucy, and Craig Larsen spotted the locked gun cabinet immediately.

Deputy Larsen tried keys off the ring that Sunny had produced, hoping to find one that fit the hefty lock on the cabinet.

Offhandedly, Sam asked, "Sunny, your folks own a place in Aspen, too? Like this one?"

"No, it's a condominium, in town. My mom likes Aspen, the shops and things. It's not country like this, though, and it's much smaller."

"Anyone been up there since your father died?"

"Not that I know of. There's a management company there that looks after things. I'm sure we could have someone check it out with a phone call."

Larsen finally found a key that opened the cabinet door. He rooted around inside before facing Sunny. He said, "The cabinet is empty. There's room for half a dozen rifles or shotguns in here, and drawers for three handguns at least." He stepped back so we could see the empty case. "See, no weapons."

Sam asked, "Any ammunition?"

Larsen shook his head. "Sunny, you have any way of knowing what weapons should be in this cabinet?"

She shook her head. "Mom would know. But I'd rather not upset her."

Lucy said, "Well, it appears we may have a crime now. I don't especially like it when weapons are missing. How about we all start being a little more careful with what we touch."

Larsen used the telephone to request some backup and some forensic help. When he was done, we took two cars, mine and the deputy's, down the hill to the barn to check on the RV. On the way, I asked Sam what he thought was going on.

"It looks like Sunny might be right. Someone may indeed have been staying in the house without permission. It's not a typical B and E. They don't appear to have taken anything except the weapons, assuming the weapons were actually there in the first place. They didn't do any damage. At this point, I don't see that it's much more than a security concern. I imagine the locals can handle it just fine."

If I allowed myself the luxury of believing him, his opinion would be good news. Indulging myself, I smiled as I was driving. I had a fleeting image of lowering my head to my pillow in Boulder as the bedside clock signaled midnight.

But I didn't believe what Sam was telling me. He was being uncharacteristically optimistic.

"Would you be saying the same thing, Sam, if you weren't sure of Merritt's whereabouts for the last few days?"

"What do you mean?"

"What if our suspicions are right and her friend Madison is hooked up in this thing with Merritt somehow? What if it was Madison and her boyfriend, the frat kid, who have been camping out in Dead Ed's cabin?"

He waved me off as though he'd already run the idea through the mill and rejected it. "The place is too neat for a couple of teenagers on the run. That's what I think. If it were a couple of teenagers camping out, they would have trashed the place. You know kids."

"Maybe that's the point. Maybe they tried to make it look like they weren't there."

"Couple of kids, Alan. They'd be sloppy."

"They were sloppy. Sunny picked it up in a second."

"Still, too neat for kids."

"Don't underestimate them, Sam. Merritt's a kid, too. So far, it hasn't proved to be much of a defense for her."

With that, we arrived at the barn.

I admit that I'd barely paid any attention to the structure on the original drive up the hill. After all, the Not So Lazy Seven was a ranch, and the building was designed to look like a barn. But examining it more closely the second time, it was apparent that the barn had been built not to service the ranch or to shelter animals but, instead, for the primary or exclusive purpose of garaging the motorhome that Edward Robilio had named Haldeman.

The entry doors to the barn were huge, at least fifteen feet tall, and the double doors to the ersatz hayloft were, on closer examination, an obvious facade. On one side of the building a lower section was attached to the main structure under a long shed roof.

Sunny stood next to a steel door on the shed side and said, "This is where you go in." She waited. "Craig, I think you still have the keys."

The cops were hesitating. Sam whispered something to Craig Larsen and Craig nodded twice while he whispered a reply. Lucy walked around to the side of the structure and peered through a dusty window. Sam said, "Alan, why don't you take Sunny back to your car for a few minutes while we look around. We would like to be certain that none of those missing guns ended up down here."

I was opening my mouth to reply when I saw an automatic in Sam's right hand. I had no idea where it had come from. Lucy was almost next to him, and she was pulling a weapon from her purse. Beside her, Craig Larsen was unsnapping his holster.

All in all, it seemed like a good time to be cooperative. I said, "Of course. We'll be in the car."

Twenty-three

Once the three cops drew their guns, every solitary second seemed to linger like a summer cold.

Beside me on the passenger seat of my car, Sunny Hasan was breathing deeply through barely parted lips, her expelled air sounding like a breeze whistling through a narrow canyon. Her wide eyes were fixed on the barn door, and she hadn't said a word to me since she had perched herself primly on the seat. If I gave her a tub of popcorn and a Pepsi she would appear to be somebody's date caught up in Bruce Willis's latest extravaganza at the drive-in.

CR-ACK.

My instinct told me that the shot came from the barn, but I was so stunned by the fierceness of the explosion that I couldn't be sure.

Sunny screamed and turned toward me. Roughly, I forced her head to her knees and threw myself on top of her. I wondered if the cops were wearing bulletproof vests. I thought of Lucy's Donna Karan and I knew she wasn't. I thought of little Simon Purdy, and I hoped his daddy was.

My heart jumped as Sam's voice creased the night. "Down! Everybody down!"

I whispered, "Stay low," and felt the deep purr of a whimper roll through Sunny's body.

CR-ACK.

The second shot seemed even closer, so close it rocked the car.

Sunny said, "Oh my God, oh my God, I'm pregnant. Oh my baby, oh my God. My baby. Don't hurt my baby."

The Land Cruiser listed to starboard.

* * *

Between Sunny's sobs, I thought I heard the crunch of gravel. I raised my head at the sound of a motor whirring in the barn and saw the tops of the big white doors start to swing outward.

The side door of the shed flew open and Sam ran out in a crouch, rolled once, and came up behind a propane tank with his automatic in his hand. Although the move had been graceful and athletic, the strategy was flawed. Sam, too, recognized immediately that using a tankful of compressed gas as cover in a gunfight might not be advisable, and ducked away. I couldn't tell where he went.

Lucy covered Craig Larsen as he made a dash out the front doors of the barn and tried to camouflage himself behind a withered pine. Once they were in place, all the cops were quiet, not eager to draw attention to themselves. Their eyes scanned, trying to find a target, trying to find out if they were a target.

I knew they would all have been safer in the barn. They were risking themselves by spreading out. They were doing it for Sunny and me.

The roar of a high-revving engine fractured the silence, and in the confines of the river valley the whining of high RPMs and the melody of quick gear changes echoed as distinctively as heartbeats.

Of the three cops, Sam had the best cover. He was behind a boulder the size of a Volkswagen bug. He called out, "Anybody hurt?"

I said, "No, we're fine. Scared."

"See anything?"

"No."

"Damn."

Craig Larsen said something into his radio and waited a few long seconds for a garbled reply.

We all held our breath for the next gunshot. Sunny had lowered herself all the way into the footwell and had quieted her mantra to a hollow whisper: "Don't hurt my baby, don't hurt my baby, don't hurt my baby."

Except for the brightly lit spot where the cars were parked, the night was dark. I realized that Sunny and I were the only well-defined targets and felt, suddenly, as though I were wearing a bull's-eye on my chest.

As though someone could read my thoughts, the floodlights died on the barn and I felt the darkness as though it were a blanket made of Kevlar. In a voice loud enough to be heard by her colleagues, Lucy said, "That was me. Just wanted to level the playing field."

Sam said, "Good. Everybody stay down. Stay cool."

In the distance, the whine of the morotcycle engine cleared the river valley, and the sound evaporated like mist in the sun.

I said, "He shot out my tire. There were two shots. Maybe he did Craig's, too."

Larsen broke his silence. "Too risky to check right now. This could be an ambush. Let's wait for backup. Everybody be patient, keep your eyes open. Backup's on the way. It won't be long."

Long, I decided, is relative.

Crouched over a frantic, pregnant stranger in the crossfire of a potential shootout, the twelve minutes we waited for the Summit County sheriff to begin to arrive en masse seemed like an incredibly protracted time.

The reinforcements approached gingerly. They parked their vehicles a distance from the barn and scoured the surrounding woods and pastures carefully as they approached the two vehicles that were parked in the clearing in front of the barn.

It took a good twenty-five more minutes before someone yelled, "All clear."

I sat upright and helped Sunny back onto her seat. She was holding both hands to her womb.

"You all right, Sunny? Is the baby okay?"

She was looking straight out the windshield, nodding rapidly, like a woodpecker attacking an ash.

I said, "Good. It's over now. You're both going to be okay."

She faced me and narrowed her eyes, still nodding. Finally, she said, "Where's Haldeman?"

I stared into the dark tunnel of the barn. Just then, Lucy flashed the lights back on and revealed a huge empty cavern where the motor coach was supposed to be.

Stupidly, I said, "I don't know."

Sam was with the local cops for a good half-hour before he found me struggling to get my damaged tire back in place under the car. He said, "You want some help with that? We spooked them coming here. Damn perps got away on the motorcycle."

It wasn't a question but I said, "That's the way I worked it out, too.

Came down the hill without power, rolled away without power. Started the bike down near the gate. What do you mean, you spooked them? Hand me that thing, there."

"What thing? This thing?"

"Yeah."

"It's called a lug wrench," Sam said. "They were here, in the barn, when we came down. Think they went out a back door as we came in the front."

"How do you know?"

"Heat was on. A light was on in a tool room in back. Two cold drinks were open. One beer, one Diet Pepsi. They weren't careful, we'll get latents, lots of them. What are you guessing, they took off to the north?"

"That's the way it sounded to me. The engine noise disappeared in that direction. Though I would think that there would be more options to the south, toward I-70. That's the way I would have run."

Sam shook his head. "Backup would have been coming from the south. That's where the population is. He'd risk running right into them. Anyway, I don't think he's running. He's just returning to ground."

"What do you mean?"

"They have the RV. They have it parked somewhere to the north. That's their safe house." He paused. "Bet you that the vehicles up at the cabin have flat tires, too. They didn't want to be followed."

"If they already have the RV, why would they risk coming back here?"

"They're having generator problems. They were poring through Dead Ed's service manuals and magazines, trying to figure it out. The books are open on the workbench."

"If they're worried about the generator, it means the thing isn't hooked up to power any place, right? That means they're not at a campground."

Sam smiled at me as though I were an imbecile. "To say something that stupid, you must be really tired. A campground? Why didn't I think of that? Maybe I'll call the local KOA to see if the kids checked in. How about that? And while I do, you go home. You obviously need some sleep. I'll catch a ride with Lucy."

Although I didn't think the campground conclusion was *that* stupid, I didn't have to think twice about the offer. "Great idea. Sam, Sunny's pregnant. She's real worried about the baby."

He nodded. "Listen, you did good with her. You weren't in a pretty situation there, with the lights on and all, and you didn't panic."

It was almost midnight as I was climbing the steep incline of I-70 toward the Eisenhower Tunnel. I figured I would be in bed before one-thirty. And I figured I would wake up to find a message from Sam that it was Madison and her boyfriend, Brad, who were on the run in Dead Ed's luxury motor coach.

I decided that the time had come to put some more pressure on Merritt to tell me exactly why.

Twenty-four

My office voice mail had plenty of messages when I woke up, but none of them was from Sam.

Lauren had returned my calls and suggested I try to reach her at the hospital. She left a number. I could hear frustration in her voice on the tape.

Adrienne had called about a "personal thing." Was I free anytime soon?

Cozier Maitlin sounded quite pleased that he had cajoled the DA's office into offering to give him a tour of Dead Ed's home. He wanted me there, too. At eleven-thirty. He warned me not to be late.

Miggy Monroe had left a message that she still hadn't heard from her daughter. Hope had deserted her; her tone was as flat as the Colorado prairie.

And John Trent wanted to see me. He'd be in Boulder this morning, back at The Children's Hospital this afternoon. Would either of those work?

I wanted to go back to bed.

Lauren's mom was recovering well from her heart attack. That was the good news. The bad news was that her doctors had just discovered a lump in her breast.

"Oh, God. I'm sorry, sweets. She doesn't need this. How is everybody taking it?"

"Teresa's here, she's keeping everyone's spirits up." Teresa, Lauren's younger sister, was a stand-up comic. "Teresa's absolutely sure it's nothing. You know my mom's kind of flat-chested? Teresa said the lump would have to be benign, that the alternative is too ironic. She says that my mother having breast cancer would be like Dan Quayle having brain cancer."

I laughed. "When will they know?"

"Biopsy is today around three."

"Call me, okay?"

"Yeah. Miss you. Can you come out? I think I'll be here for a while. Dad's helpless."

"I'm going to try. This case—the adolescent I told you about?—is still acute. When I'm sure this kid's safe, I'll be out. Are you feeling all right?"

"Same."

"Is that okay?"

"No, but I can live with it."

I was going to have to guess what she meant.

Although there were a lot of things about the case I was working on that I couldn't reveal to Lauren, I had told her that Chaney was Sam's niece. I don't think she was surprised when I changed the conversation and said, "Sweets, I want to offer Sam some money. For his niece's medical fund."

"How much?"

"The remodeling money."

"How much is that?"

"Almost thirty-one thousand."

She didn't hesitate. "Go ahead, I think it's a great idea. But Sam won't take it."

"Why do you say that?"

"I've known him a long time, Alan. I don't think he'll take it."

"It's for the little girl. Not for him."

"We'll see."

We talked mindlessly for a few more minutes, trying to find some way to feel some connection across the miles of despair. I desperately wanted to jump on a plane to do what I could to comfort Lauren, and to allow her to do what she could to comfort me.

I agreed to meet with John Trent at nine-thirty at my office and told Cozier Maitlin's secretary that I would meet him at the Robilio house at eleven-thirty.

I left a return message for Miggy Monroe telling her that I didn't know anything new about Madison, and not telling her what I suspected.

Adrienne and I agreed to try and have a late dinner after I got back from seeing Merritt and after she got her son to bed that night. I said, "What, eight-thirty?"

She said, "No, closer to ten, Jonas is a night person. Will you pick up some food? I have a hell of a day ahead of me."

She hung up on me before we had a chance to compare the horrors lurking in our Day-Timers.

John Trent looked like a daddy who had been up all night wondering if his baby was going to continue to breathe.

Seeing a fellow psychologist in a therapeutic milieu is always tricky. There's a tendency to want to treat him like a colleague, not a patient. I fought the temptation.

After I asked about Chaney and he filled me on her uneventful night, and he asked me about Merritt and I told him that there was nothing new, I said, "You wanted to see me, John?"

"Yes."

I waited. He knew I was waiting, so he cut the delay short.

"There's something you should know. Two days before he died, I went to see Ed Robilio to plead for his help with Chaney."

My pulse jumped and I knew my breathing was about to change. I said, "Go on."

"I've been thinking maybe Merritt knew where I went. Maybe she heard me discussing it with Brenda, maybe she followed me somehow. I don't know. That night, I came home, and . . . and Brenda and I talked in the kitchen for the longest time. I told her all about my visit to Robilio's house. I don't remember seeing Merritt, but she could have heard the whole thing."

"What whole thing?"

He rubbed his open hand over the bald parts of his head. "I told Brenda I was so angry at his reaction to my visit that I could have killed him. And then I said . . . that . . . if I thought it would do Chaney any good, I would kill him. I was furious."

"Tell me about your visit to Dr. Robilio. The same way you told Brenda. The same way Merritt might have heard you tell Brenda."

John started by saying, "You have to understand how desperate this feels—the situation with Chaney. I'm cornered, Alan. I don't have any good choices. This was one of the bad ones."

I said, "I understand." I thought I did.

"I decided to approach him personally after all attempts to work through channels at MedExcel had failed. There's a medical board—you probably know all this—that reviews atypical medical procedures like the one we want for Chaney. They'd reviewed her case already and turned her down. Her physicians at the hospital wrote a long, eloquent appeal for a reconsideration. The head of the medical board seemed gracious enough, he invited her cardiologist in for a meeting. I attended, too, though they wouldn't let me talk. The doctor who ran the meeting, the head of the board, he seemed, I don't know, open-minded. But the next day, they turned down the appeal."

"On what grounds?"

"Same ones as before. If they approve a heart transplant, what's to keep the virus from infecting the new heart? The cardiologist argued that the drugs being used in Seattle have shown promise in two cases. The head of the medical board replied in his finding that that sounds to him like the very definition of 'experimental.'

"I called him, the head of the medical board, oh, half a dozen times after that. He wouldn't talk to me. His secretary told me the matter was closed.

"That avenue seemed like a dead end, so I learned what I could about Robilio. That he's a father. Where he lived. What he liked. He's quite a public figure; it wasn't hard to get the information, found most of it on the Internet. I tried to act professional at first. Called him at his office. He wouldn't return my calls. I asked his secretary for an appointment. She wouldn't give me one. She told me to address my concerns to the director of the medical board.

"I felt like I was going around in circles. It was absurd. I lost it with her, I admit I was a jerk. I raised my voice and asked her if she was a mother, if she had kids? And she hung up on me. Maybe I deserved it."

Trent stood then and walked to the window of my office. He gazed outside vacantly. Without turning toward me, he continued. "My good choices were used up. So I started on the bad ones. I followed Robilio home from work twice. He left early, three, four o'clock. He went inside, changed clothes, came back out wearing these ridiculous matching sweat-suits. They made him look like one of the three little pigs. Then he went for a walk. By himself. Maybe thirty minutes.

"The third day I waited for him after his walk. He has this portico over his front porch where there are a couple of wooden benches between these immense cement pineapples. The pineapples are a traditional sign of welcome. Did you know that? Anyway, I decide to act as though I was welcome. I waited on one of the benches."

I almost said, "I did, too," recalling the day Dead Ed's body had been found and I was waiting for Sam Purdy to finish up inside so we could go to the hockey game. I was also embarrassed to admit I thought the statues were artichokes.

"Robilio walked up, right on time. I said, 'Hello, I'm John Trent, I've been trying to reach you at your office about my daughter, Chaney.' What he did then was so cowardly." Trent shook his head disdainfully and returned to his chair. "He turned around to make sure his path of escape wasn't blocked. He had been carrying this bottle of water and it just slid out of his hands to the ground.

"I remember being so disappointed in his voice; it was like listening to a weasel. He said, 'I'm sorry I can't help. You shouldn't be here. Call me at work. You need to go. I'm sorry.' And then he took a step back, like he was afraid I was going to swing at him. God, that pissed me off."

Trent tugged up his shirtsleeves. "You know, I've never hit anybody in my life. And all I wanted to do was slug him. But I didn't. I picked up the water bottle and handed it back to him and—politely—I said, 'No, Dr. Robilio, you're wrong. You're the only one who can help me. And you're the only one who can help Chaney. And I'm not going to go away. I'm going to do whatever I need to do to save my daughter.'

"Then he squealed, 'Don't you dare threaten me. Our medical review process has given your family every consideration we're required to give. And *more*. The director of the board has bent over backwards to let you plead your case. He has been more than fair.'

" 'Then overrule him,' I said.

"He said, 'I can't do that. I've done everything I can.' He was a self-satisfied, rationalizing little prick. Right then, I knew he believed it. He had already convinced himself he had no moral responsibility for Chaney's well-being. He'd done exactly what the damn insurance policy said he had to do. And he'd washed his hands of her."

John pulled a four-by-six piece of paper from inside his jacket. "I held up a photo of Chaney—this one." He turned the piece of paper so I could see it. The photograph was of a vibrant, beautiful little girl on a tricycle with a sparkling Christmas tree behind her. Chaney's wide smile could have illuminated Cleveland.

"He wouldn't look at it. So I moved it where his eyes were pointing and he looked someplace else. I said, 'Dr. Robilio, you're killing my baby. This is my daughter, this is Chaney. This is who you're killing. Take a good look. You can save her.'

"He walked past me, mumbled, 'Leave me alone, don't ever come here again or I'll call the police,' and he rushed in the front door of his damn mansion and he slammed it. He never looked at Chaney's picture. Not even a damn glance.

"That's when I could've killed him. Right then. I'm glad I wasn't armed because I could have killed him."

"And Merritt may have heard you say exactly that?"

"She may have."

"Did she ever say anything to you?"

"No."

"Did you ever go back to the Robilio house?"

"No."

"Did you ever talk to him again?"

"No."

"Did Brenda?"

"No."

"Have you told the police or Mr. Maitlin any of this?"

"No."

"I'm going to see Cozy later this morning. May I have your permission to fill him in?"

John Trent nodded. "I'm afraid I armed her and pointed her in his direction. I'm afraid Merritt was my guided missile."

Twenty-five

I would have loved to spend the rest of the day riding my bike, but I'd promised to meet Cozier Maitlin at Dead Ed's house. When I arrived, the crime scene tape was down and the front door was unlocked. Cozy walked in as if he knew what he was doing. I followed.

Singing drifted from somewhere deep in the big house, arriving at the front door winded by the long halls and bruised by the hard stone of the entry. Given my mood, and the circumstances, the music sounded almost profane.

"Hey Jude, don't make it bad . . ."

The tenor's voice was lush, rather rich for the lyrics, and he hugged the tune too tightly, as though it had been grafted to him. Every Beatles fan knew that this melody absolutely needed to float.

"Who is that, Cozy?" I asked.

Cozier Maitlin, at whose invitation and insistence I was about to witness, for the second time, the precise spot where one of his clients, my patient, had allegedly murdered a man, whispered his reply. "I could make a guess. Don't you hear the edge? He sings like a prosecutor."

I knew it was a dig. I bit anyway. "My wife is a prosecutor, Cozy. She sings quite sweetly." It actually wasn't true; Lauren couldn't carry a tune in a suitcase. "Who were you expecting to meet us here? The detectives? Who?"

He shook his head, put his finger to his lips, and slid out of his loafers, which were large enough to sail refugee families from Cuba to Florida. He looked every bit of his six feet eight inches. I removed my own shoes and followed him up toward the bedroom wing of the house.

"Hey Jude, don't let me . . ."

A canary-like whistle, in perfect pitch, replaced the lyrics, and I thought I heard the shuffle of footsteps searching to find the beat.

In front of me, Cozier Maitlin looked like a giraffe on the prowl. He tiptoed up the carpeted stairs.

The bedroom hallway was wide and bright, lit by a high clerestory, but the bedroom and bathroom doors had been placed unimaginatively, lining the hall as though it were a corridor in a dormitory. At the far end, a lithe figure in a business suit, his back to us, crossed from one open doorway and disappeared into another. He held his arms out as though he were cradling an imaginary partner. His feet were lively and he hovered lightly, as though he might have really been made of meringue.

"Who's Gene Kelly?" I whispered.

With a devious smile, Cozy whispered, "You don't know your old movies—or your dancers. That's a Fred Astaire wannabe, not a Gene Kelly." He shushed me before I had a chance to respond and preceded me down the hall. He stood in the doorway where the Fred Astaire impersonator had disappeared, and seemed to puff himself up like a prizefighter at weigh-in. I could barely see around him.

After a five-second wait, Cozy barked, "What the *hell* are you doing in here?"

I started at the sound.

Mitchell Crest, the chief trial deputy of the Boulder County District Attorney's Office, started too. He came running from an adjacent bathroom, tripped over the base of a wooden valet, and fell on his face in the center of what appeared to be the master bedroom.

Cozy leaned against the doorframe and with supreme casualness said, "Oh, hello, Mitch, how are you doing? You're a little early, aren't you? I thought you said eleven-forty-five. And it didn't cross my mind for a single second that it would be you snooping around in dead people's bedrooms. Shame, shame on you."

"Maitlin," Crest said as he tried to lift himself up from the floor with some dignity, "if I didn't get to beat you in court occasionally, I swear I'd have to kill you just to retain my mental health."

"Careful, I have a witness with me, Mitch."

I poked my head around Cozy and said, "Hello, Mitchell. It's me."

"Hi, Alan. Cozy, I could take out a billboard with a death threat against you and it wouldn't make any difference. There isn't a jury in the county that would consider your murder by a prosecutor anything other than justifiable homicide. So why are we here today? Why on earth am I doing you this courtesy? What do you want to see?"

"You're taking requests? I think 'Singing in the Rain' would be a nice encore. Or, if you in insist on staying with the Beatles, how about 'I Am the Walrus?' Tough melody, though, for a dancer. Alan?"

Cozy was having more fun than Mitch was. I didn't think playing along any longer was going to accomplish much. "Whatever you have to show us, Mitch. I would just like to see what you and the police think happened here."

"Fine. This . . . is, um, the master bedroom. As you are well aware, the homicide took place downstairs, in what might be called the basement in a lesser house. Here, I prefer to think of it as the lower level. Follow me."

We did, Cozy last. He seemed to linger upstairs as long as propriety would allow. A series of two wide, open staircases led from the second floor down to the bright lowest level where I had first joined Sam to consider the demise of Dead Ed Robilio.

I took in details that had escaped my consciousness after the initial visit. A long wall of French doors faced east. The main room was set up as a home theater, complete with a wet bar, a dozen rocker seats, and a carnival-style popcorn popper. I couldn't imagine inviting ten people over to watch a video. Maybe it was just me.

Someone, either Ed or his wife, had a fondness for contemporary acrylics. Huge canvasses covered two big walls. A Remington sculpture sat on top of a bird's-eye maple table that I imagined contained the video projector for the home theater.

Mitch said, "This way."

A short hall led to a closed door that led to the room where I'd seen Dead Ed in the bag on the floor. Mitch opened the door to the room and stepped aside, so we could precede him in.

He said, "This is where she shot him."

The room was more barren than I recalled.

"Where's the furniture?"

"Evidence. You want to see pictures of how it looked, I'm happy to arrange that. We have lots of pictures. Lots and lots of pictures."

My memory said that the furniture had been mostly heavy walnut pieces chosen from some decorator's vision of the home office for the macho man.

I heard Cozy's breathing change. With every advocate's bone in his huge body, his impulse was to defend his client against this prosecutor's claim that Merritt had shot someone down here. But now wasn't the time. Cozy would get an opportunity to argue Merritt's innocence with Mitchell Crest in court soon enough.

Too soon, actually.

"Story is this: Victim's wife came home from a weekend at some Navaho spiritual cleansing thing in Taos and found him. Bloody, bloody scene, truly messy, one of the worst. I feel sorry for her, what she walked in on. Two shots had been fired resulting in two wounds, one to the upper abdomen, second one some minutes later to the head—specifically the face—right next to the nose. Coroner thinks the second one was the fatal shot, although the victim eventually would have bled out from the chest wound. As you both know," Mitchell paused for effect, "no weapon was found at this location." Mitchell allowed himself a half-smile, knowing that it was I who had inadvertently led the police to the murder weapon.

"Bloody footprints that tentatively match the type of shoe later discovered under your client's bed, Cozy, leave the scene, go out through that theater room there, and then finally out those garden-level doors, around the side of the house, and . . . gone. Dogs had the scent for quite a ways, then lost it just east of Broadway, about six blocks from what turns out to be your patient's house, Alan. That is, coincidentally, the same place we recovered the murder weapon. Based on environmental and scene circumstances, coroner estimates that the victim died sometime between Friday afternoon and Saturday morning, so he had been dead awhile when his wife got here on Monday, which was a few minutes before noon. Her alibi is solid, by the way, we talked to her spiritual guru in Taos. We found the wife's bloody footprints all over the lower level of the house, too. After she found the deceased, she ran around out there like a chicken with its head cut off. She used the phone in the wet bar to call 911."

All around the room I spied evidence of a meticulous once-over by the crime scene investigation team. Chemicals for raising fingerprints coated everything that could reveal a latent image. Sections of the wool Berber carpet had been cut out and removed. I knew that every last square centimeter of the surface had been dusted and vacuumed and photographed and videotaped. I wondered what trace evidence had been removed by the CSIs in their sweep.

"Prints?"

"In this room, the victim's—Dr. Robilio's—the suspect's—Merritt Strait's—the wife's, and the housekeeper's. That's it. Your patient's and the wife's latents are nicely fossilized in Dr. Robilio's blood, by the way. Out there—" he pointed toward the family room "—there are lots of latents that aren't yet identified. The housekeeping is not as good as you would like."

Cozy asked, "No unknowns in the office? Not even one?"

Mitchell grinned. "A few strays. That's to be expected. We're ruling out family and business associates."

"Entry was how, Mitchell? How are you imagining that a fifteen-year-old got in to do this?"

"No forced entry. Maybe she came in the same doors she left by, maybe he let her in, I mean, wouldn't you let her in if she came to your door? A cute kid in a basketball uniform? But we don't have that pinned down yet. Neither the victim nor the suspect is doing much talking to us right now."

"And the weapon?"

"His."

"How did she find his gun?"

"I don't know, counselor. Have you thought of asking her?"

Cozy ignored him. "What were you doing upstairs, Mitch? In the master bedroom? Did you find some evidence up there that I should know about?"

Mitch turned his back and took a step toward the door before he pirouetted and answered.

"Not now, Cozy."

"What do you mean, not now? I have a right to anything you find. You know that."

"It's a little early in the game to start jabbering about disclosure, isn't it, Cozy? Your client is a suspect; she hasn't been charged. And don't forget I'm doing you a huge courtesy here. Act grateful."

"In my mind, it's never too early to poke at a prosecutor. What did you find upstairs? I saw lots of dust up there, Mitch. Whose latents did you find?"

"We were being thorough. Me? I was just looking around, Cozy. That's all. You want to go back up there and jerk off, go ahead. You know the rules, though."

Maitlin was not going to be so easily deterred. "Difference between us is I don't know what to look for upstairs. What did the police find that makes upstairs important? Don't make this difficult for me, Mitch. There's no margin in it. You know I'll find out soon enough. Did you find my client's fingerprints upstairs?"

Mitchell Crest wanted to talk about something else. "*If* it turns out there is anything to discuss about evidence that was recovered upstairs, 'soon enough' is fine with me. Alan, have you seen what you wanted to see?"

"I guess. May I have a few more minutes?"

He looked at his watch to let me know what an imposition my request was. "Yeah."

I walked around looking at everything, not knowing what was important. I was cataloguing. The initial scan felt familiar; it was like the starting minutes of psychotherapy. Everything was important. Nothing at all was clear.

"What's in there?" I asked, pointing at a closed door on the opposite side of the theater.

"Exercise equipment. A home gym, treadmill, bike, stair-stepper. Dr. Robilio liked his toys."

"May I?"

"Go right ahead."

I walked into the spacious exercise room and checked out the high-end stuff while I listened to Cozy continue his maneuvers with Mitchell Crest.

"I'll file a motion to discover what you have. Is that what you want?"

"Go ahead, Cozy. I enjoy your motions. They almost always amuse me."

I rejoined them and as soon as it seemed they had concluded their jabbering, which seemed listless and pro forma to me, I asked, "What's that other door?"

"Laundry room. You want to go in there, too?"

"Should I?"

Mitchell looked at me as though I were crazy for asking. "That's up to you. They use Tide. And liquid fabric softener. No dryer sheets."

"I think I'll pass, thanks."

"Are we done, then?"

"Yes," Cozy said. He seemed satisfied. About what, I didn't know.

Mitchell locked up and left us in the driveway, where Cozy and I leaned against his BMW.

"I met with Merritt's stepfather this morning, Cozy. He signed a release for me to talk with you. He told me that he'd been here to put pressure on Dr. Robilio a couple of days before he died."

"Really?"

He didn't seem surprised.

"Trent says the meeting left him quite angry. Talked about it at home with Brenda. Merritt may have heard it."

"Did he threaten the doctor?"

"No. But he was belligerent. And he says he told his wife he'd kill Robilio if he thought it would do any good. He's afraid maybe he gave Merritt the idea."

"I already knew he'd been here. My investigator interviewed all the neighbors. One of them remembered his car from earlier in the week. I assume the police already know all this, too."

"Is that what you were pressing Mitchell about?"

"Upstairs? I was fishing, trying to get Mitchell to admit they had Trent's prints."

"And they don't?"

"They're not saying. Something is confusing them or they would have taken Merritt into custody already. There's too much evidence and this is too political a case for so much procrastination."

I thought about the delay. "You know, they may not have file prints for John, Cozy. He's new in the state. He may not even have bothered to get a Colorado driver's license."

"I hadn't thought of that. Wonder if they've thought of it. We'll keep it to ourselves for now. Where's he from? Where'd he live before?"

"Kansas, I think. Wichita."

"Okay."

"Cozy, is there something else that's important about the master bedroom? What was Mitchell doing up there? Any idea?"

"I don't know. An inconsistency of some kind. Typically, the prosecution doesn't hesitate to gloat about things that they consider to be crystal clear."

"Are Merritt's prints up there?"

"I'm guessing yes. But I don't know."

"John's?"

"Don't know that, either."

"Do Merritt's prints make burglary more likely as a motive?"

"If they are there, I suppose. More than that, it just makes it more difficult for the police to pin down a scenario. The handgun that killed him? The wife says he kept it upstairs in a little box in a drawer in his bedside table. Somebody went upstairs and retrieved the weapon. Him? Was he afraid of her? Did he think there was an intruder in the house? Her? If she was planning on killing him, she wouldn't break in hoping to find a weapon, would she? But she's a kid. Who knows what she was thinking? See, it's confusing."

He concluded, "They think she did it. They're not sure how it came down. That's why they're hesitating."

I stuffed my hands in my pockets.

Cozy said, "I like a client who knows when to keep her mouth shut. But this is over the top. I need this kid to talk to me, Alan. Do something."

Twenty-six

I stopped at Abo's for a slice of pizza after leaving Dead Ed's house and barely had time to eat it and squeeze in a return phone call from Sam Purdy before my one o'clock patient.

"Hi, Sam, you made it back down from the ranch?"

"Got back around five this morning. Lucy just woke me up. The Summit County cops haven't located Haldeman yet. And the prints on the pop cans in the barn belong to the two kids. You were right."

Having my suspicions confirmed disappointed me. I was hoping Madison and Brad were simple runaways well on their way to someplace like Sacramento or Billings. "So how do you have it? How are they mixed up in this?"

"Great question. And how the hell did they know about Ed's cabin and his damned RV? I don't know any of it. Lucy's presenting everything to Malloy and the brass at a meeting right now. Maybe they've developed something that will help make sense of it."

"Someone should call the girl's mom, Sam. She's worried sick."

"Yeah, don't worry. I'll get someone to call her. Lucy's good at that."

I was trying to finesse a way to let Sam know about John Trent's visit to Ed Robilio a couple of days before his death. But I couldn't find a detour around the confidentiality issues. Cozy figured that the cops already knew, and if Lucy knew, then Sam knew, so I decided to let it rest.

"I was just at the Robilio house with Cozy Maitlin. He talked Mitchell Crest into giving him a little tour of the crime scene. Cozy's suspicious that there's some evidence that your colleagues haven't explained, some physical evidence or some fingerprints or something, and that's why Merritt hasn't been charged. You know anything?"

He was silent.

"Okay, let me rephrase my question. You know anything you can tell me? Anything I can use with Merritt to goose her to talk? I have to get her to start talking, Sam. She's not helping Cozy at all. And I can't judge how suicidal she might still be."

When he spoke, his voice had slowed and softened. The change in tenor grabbed my attention. He asked, "You saw her the first day in the hospital, right, after her overdose?"

"Yes, I did. Not in the ER, but upstairs in the ICU. She wasn't conscious, though."

"When you were there—think back—did you notice her hands, her fingernails?"

Oh, God. "Yes, they were painted red. A bright cherry red."

He was silent again. Waiting for me to join him somewhere. Guiding me someplace significant with his formidable will.

I said, "One nail was broken. Badly. The kind of break that would really hurt. Let me think. It would have been her left hand. I was sitting on the left side of the bed. The ring finger. The ring finger of her left hand."

"Okay. Anything else?"

"The next day when I saw her upstairs, after she regained consciousness, the nail polish had been removed and the break had been filed down." I paused, trying to remember. "I think that's it."

"Remind me, what was your question before?"

What? "I asked if there was anything that you could tell me—"

"Yeah, I remember, that was it. Listen, I have to go. Brenda's agreed to have lunch with me, if you can believe it. I don't think I should be late. Good luck with Merritt later on, say hi for me. Tell her I love her."

As was becoming our routine, I greeted Merritt in the dayroom and walked beside her as we made our way across the locked unit to the walk-in-closet-size interview room. Other than the night she visited her sister, she had not been allowed off the unit.

On the aggravating drive into Denver I continued to question my therapeutic strategy with her. From the start, I had been treating her as though she were any other patient, any other *talking* patient, and would schedule and start a daily psychotherapy session, as though such a thing could exist solely in silence. And as though time were on my side and the corrosive quality of familiarity and routine would eventually sway her enough so she would trust me sufficiently to begin talking.

So far, though, my strategy hadn't worked; no words but mine had fractured the silence in the interview room.

I'd decided that today would need to be different. The eroding quality of time wasn't working well as a strategy. Two kids were in significant danger. And the police were going to be questioning John Trent about his actions soon enough.

I turned the knob and pushed the door inward. Merritt preceded me inside, as she had each time. This time, though, she walked across the room and curled herself casually in the chair that I had used the previous three days.

The room was furnished with a total of six chairs so that small groups and families could meet. I chose one of the chairs about five feet from her and sat down. I had spent much of the hour on the drive from Boulder to Denver pondering how long I would permit this session to go on in silence before I exposed my new strategy. Was ten minutes long enough? Twenty minutes too long? Or should I go right after her from the first bell. What?

Joel Franks and the treatment planning team had felt from day two of the admission that I should be putting some increased pressure on Merritt to start talking. As was common in this milieu, they were tempted to use privileges on the unit as bait. She could do *this* if she talked; she could do *that* if she talked. Or we could threaten her with a transfer to the state hospital at Fort Logan and use that as an incentive.

With another kid, I might have signed on. With Merritt, I wasn't sold.

Merritt's silence had never felt like a behavioral issue to me. In fact, other than the consideration that she hadn't spoken a word since her arrival, she was a model of decorum on the unit; this wasn't some kid zipping it up in order to be defiant. And as paradoxical as it sounded, her silence had never really felt like a control issue to me, either.

I had already decided by then that her silence was tactical. I hadn't concluded exactly what the battle was, or what the tactic was supposed to accomplish. But there was a method to the silence. And the method, I had been assuming, had to do with Dead Ed, the gun, and the bloody clothes that Merritt had stuffed under her bed. Now I was adding two additional motivations and complications: Merritt's stepfather, John Trent, and her best friend, Madison Monroe.

If I was being totally honest with myself, I would have admitted, however, that even before this day, I had grown frustrated with the lack of progress and with the fact that Merritt was more patient about our standoff than I was. I consoled myself with the reality that at least I was being more patient than just about everyone else who was involved in the case: the treatment team, Joel Franks, Cozy Maitlin, Merritt's parents, MedExcel, and the Boulder Police Department.

I said, "You chose a different chair today?"

If she wasn't going to talk, she couldn't much object to my little con-frontation, and I supposed I could be as trivial as I wanted to be. So far, I'd done serious soliloquies on Madison's reaction to our meeting at Starbucks, reasoned explanations of Merritt's incredible legal troubles, poignant pre-sentations on the sorrow surrounding her sister's illness, and provocative commentary on the state of women's basketball in America.

A petulant diatribe about what chair she sat in didn't seem too far out of line.

Her eyes were warm. Her lips formed the words, "Thank you."

It struck me that she was entirely too comfortable sitting with me in silence, day in, day out.

I said, "You're welcome. I assume you're talking about my breaking every rule in the book to allow you to go visit your sister?"

She nodded.

"It appeared that it made a remarkable difference for Chaney, your being there."

She tightened her jaw and widened her eyes. I thought she was trying not to cry.

On another day, in another mood, with another agenda, I might have exploited her vulnerability in an effort to weaken her resistance. But not this day. I was planning a more direct approach.

I said, "You're in a tough battle, aren't you?"

Instantly, her expression turned as bland as oatmeal. But I thought I detected a flash of curiosity in her eyes.

"This fight you're in, it's tough. You're alone and you don't have many weapons on your side. Silence feels like all you have going for you. But from where I sit, it doesn't look like much leverage anymore. The other side has all the big guns. You have silence. That's nothing."

Finally, after examining my words from every possible direction, looking for subtext, she nodded suspiciously.

"The other side? Your opponent? They're not playing fair anymore. Do you know that?"

She shook her head.

"They've started taking prisoners and they're spying on the good guys."

She shrugged, too quickly. I was sure her pulse was quickening. I was circling close to something.

"I don't know what you think. Maybe you think you have them out-foxed. You don't. They know about your stepfather's visit. The police know he was there."

Merritt looked away and pulled her long legs up to her chest and rested her heels on the lip of the chair. Her torso was almost totally screened from my view. Finally she peeked at me from around her right knee.

"And Madison? Your friend? She has a boyfriend named Brad some-body? A frat boy? They screwed up big time. Broke into Dr. Robilio's mountain home and stole his RV. Half the cops in the state are looking for them right now. They're armed and the cops know they're armed."

Merritt looked enraged. She stood and spun toward the door. The act was cat quick, and startled me.

In a tone that I knew was too parental the moment the words es-caped my lips, I said, "We're not done here. You're not going back to the unit just because I've succeeded in making you uncomfortable. This isn't about retreating from me anymore. Though I admit you're good at that."

She stopped. Her back puffed out and I could see the definition of her musculature as she inhaled.

I adjusted my voice. "This isn't about retreating, Merritt. It's about surrendering."

She faced me.

"Please have a seat. It's time for you to hold up the white flag. It's time for you to surrender. Let me help you do that. Let me help you surrender."

I thought she looked like a caged animal. Not like Emily in her dog run. Emily always wanted the gate to open. Merritt preferred the cage. She was a fearful animal. She was fearful that the cage would be opened. And that she would no longer be safe.

She sat. Folded her arms across her chest. I noticed that she was wearing her CHURCH GIRL T-shirt again.

"Merritt?" I said. "Look at me, please."

Petulantly, she did. In that instant, with that expression, I was reminded that there was still plenty of adolescent residing in this remarkable girl.

"One more thing you should know. The police have your fingernail. The red one. The one you broke when you were at his house."

This time she couldn't stop the tears.

A good five minutes later, her eyes were dry and she was staring at me with a mixture of indignation and surprise. I imagined it was the look she would flash at a referee who had just fouled her out of a game on a questionable call. My ambush, I was afraid, had failed. She wasn't going to talk.

Her shoulders dropped. She swallowed. Before my eyes, her resolve crumbled into pieces, and she said, "Okay, I think I'm ready to talk."

The sound of Merritt's voice should have shocked me, but it didn't. I'd imagined her voice before, of course, but I'd imagined it wrong. I'd anticipated an edge to it, a snarliness, but her voice was soft and tentative and was graced with the soft curves of a young girl's melody. I'd imagined, too, the poignancy of her first words to me, and I'd imagined that wrong as well. She was matter-of-fact about beginning to speak, almost as though talking was something she had been doing her entire life.

I said, "Great."

She said, "I guess."

"Hi," I said. It was probably clinically ill advised to smile, but I couldn't help myself.

She smiled back. My indiscretion, I decided, had been worth it.

The times I don't know what to say in psychotherapy are easily as numerous as the times I think I do. Most of the time, I think, my patient and I are better off when I admit that I'm at a loss for words. I said, "I've already talked too much, Merritt. I don't know what to say now. I think now that you've decided to speak that it's up to you to decide what happens next."

She smiled again, the rueful smile I'd already witnessed where the corners of her mouth actually turned down a little. She held up her left hand and spread her fingers. She said, "The police know I broke my nail?"

"I don't know what they suspect. I know that they recovered the broken part."

"And they know about my—about Trent?"

Brenda called her husband by his surname. Merritt had apparently adopted the name, too.

"Again, I don't know what they suspect. They know that he was there."

She retreated for almost a minute, and I feared that she had decided to once again be dumb. Finally she said, "I have some other questions."

"Okay," I said. I almost said, "Shoot." Sometimes I'm really stupid.

"Trent's a psychologist, you know that, right?"

"Yes."

"And I know all about the rules that you keep reminding me about that says he, or you, can't say anything about what happens with somebody that they're talking to. But he does, you know? Not seriously, but he'll tell my mom that my patient, George, or whoever, said this or that, or did this or that, or whatever. You know?"

"Yes, I know. Unfortunately, it happens. Are you concerned I will do that, too?"

"Can you wait before you ask your questions?"

Chastised, I said, "Of course, please continue."

"My roommate told me something last night that I didn't know. She said I have rights, even though I'm a kid, that I can talk to you and tell you things and that you can't tell anybody, even my parents, what I said. Is that true?"

Colorado law grants fifteen-year-olds many of the psychotherapy privileges and protections that are enjoyed by adults.

"Yes," I said, "that's true. With some exceptions."

She seemed surprised and troubled by my reply. "What are the exceptions?"

"Child abuse is one. Or if I think you're going to kill yourself, or if you threaten to hurt someone else. That's about it."

"That's *about* it? Or that's it?"

"That's it."

"Can I even keep you from telling Mr. Maitlin what I said?"

"Technically, yes, you can."

"Even though I'm a kid?"

"Even though you're a kid."

"I am fifteen, you know."

"I know."

"Good." She looked at her feet. "I'm including your wife. You have a wife, right?" She moved her gaze to my left hand searching for a ring.

"Yes, I'm married."

"Not her, either. You can't tell her."

"Not her, either. That's no problem."

"That's it?"

"That's it. Except for the trusting me part."

She rubbed the place on her arm where the IV catheter had been pulled. "I already trust you. I was beginning to trust you before Chaney got so bad the other night. That night aced it for me."

"I'm glad you trust me, Merritt. Consider yourself warned, though, I'm not convinced that keeping everything secret is what's best for you, especially not from your attorney and your parents."

"Well . . . maybe that's because you don't know what I have to say."

"Maybe."

"You remind me of Trent."

Dangerous ground. I didn't comment.

Merritt read my reticence and said, "Don't worry, that's a compliment."

"What about me reminds you of your stepdad?"

"You don't get caught up in stuff. Things go nuts all around you and you act like it's going to be fine. And like I said, I think I can trust you."

"Thanks. You trust him? Trent?"

"Yeah, I do. Maybe more than my mom. What do you want to know first? Why I've been silent?"

"Sure."

"Wait, what about the people here at the hospital? The nurses, and Dr. Franks? Can you tell them what I say without my permission?"

In all my years of inpatient work, I'd rarely had a patient ask for confidentiality from the treatment team. "Again, technically, you can keep me from telling anyone what you tell me. Including the treatment team. I doubt if I have to tell you that I think that's a bad idea. But it's your right to prohibit me from telling anyone."

She straightened in her chair. "Okay, let me list the rules. If you want me to tell you what's been going on, then you're going to have to consider yourself prohibited. From telling anybody anything. My parents, my lawyer, anybody here, anybody."

I thought about her offer and said, warmly, "Fine. I understand what you're asking. And with that restriction in place, our session is over."

"What? I've just started talking." She couldn't believe I would walk away from the opportunity to hear her story.

"Merritt, you have rights, and because of those rights you can set the rules. Clinically, I'll accept that you may have valid reasons for wanting confidentiality from your parents and even your lawyer. I'm not saying I agree, but I'll abide by those rules. But I disagree with your exclusion of the treatment team here at the hospital. And I do have a choice about that. I won't be manipulated by your rules. I won't conspire with you around them, and I won't let them dictate my treatment of you. If you insist that I keep our conversations secret from the treatment team, then I have to do that. What I don't have to do is be your collaborator. As long as you insist I keep secrets from the hospital staff, I won't listen to your secrets. We won't have conversations until you change your mind."

She pulled her legs back up onto the chair, again resting her heels on the lip of the seat. She lowered her head to her hands and gazed at me through the space between her knees. She eyed me, unblinking, lips parted, for what felt like an eternity of seconds.

"The reason I've decided not to talk is that I think that if I start talking, I'm afraid that I'll screw up and say something that will . . . hurt other people."

"Have you changed your mind about the treatment team?"

"No."

"Then I can't let you go on, Merritt. I'm sorry. I owe you confidentiality. So, as much as I would like to hear what you have to say, I'm forced to decline to listen."

"I'm trying to talk to you here. God, I thought that's what you wanted."

"More than you know. I just can't accept your limitations. And it appears you can't accept mine. So we're back at stalemate, I guess. We can both think about our positions and go over it again tomorrow."

"I didn't do it."

"We need to stop, Merritt. I'm sorry."

"I didn't do it."

I felt an incredible compassion for her struggle right then. I was sorely tempted to grant her anything she wanted just to keep her talking. But what I said was, "Give up, please, Merritt. Let me help you surrender. I won't leave you alone."

I stood to escort her out the door.

She stopped to look at me. I thought, for the first time in this treatment, that patient and therapist were equally exasperated.

I hoped I had made the right decision.

Twenty-seven

Before I left the hospital, I stopped by the cardiac care unit and checked on Chaney. John Trent was in the corridor outside, pacing. He said the docs were once again worried about his daughter's pulmonary function. If the trend continued, it would be a sign of the beginning of the deterioration that everyone knew was inevitable.

I used the nursing station phone to call Lauren at the hospital in Washington where she was camped out with her mother. The frozen section of her mom's breast biopsy had come back negative. Most of the family had gathered and were celebrating in the room.

I was thrilled for them. But the background joy sounded peculiar and foreign.

Dinner with Adrienne could be anything, one of life's most certain rolls of the dice. Since the day we became friends, she had maintained an elliptical orbit around my life. At any time she could be as distant as the most distant comet, or as close as a meteor on a collision course with my planet. With Lauren gone and Sam so consumed with Merritt and Chaney, I was hoping for a close encounter with Adrienne.

On the way home from the hospital in Denver, I stopped and picked up pud Thai and chicken satay and a bottle of Gewürztraminer. When I arrived at Adrienne's door with Emily by my side, it was almost ten and Adrienne had just managed to get Jonas to bed.

We ate in the kitchen. I wasn't certain her dining room had ever been soiled by food.

I filled her in on Lauren's mom's condition and on the situation with Merritt. I told her more than I should have about Madison's disappearance. She asked me about Chaney's condition.

I told her what I knew, and added, "Ren, you ever think about, you know, donating money to help a sick kid?"

She didn't look up. She smiled at her plate and used her don't-tell-me voice. "How far are you in?"

"Lauren and I? A hair over thirty thousand."

"What do they need?"

"Total? The hospital requires a deposit of about three hundred and fifty thousand."

"And what has the family raised?"

"Not much. Without us, under fifty."

"I'll think about it."

"Great, thanks."

I expected to be cross-examined more about my motives. I wasn't.

She said, "Friend time, okay? When you hear what's going on, it may sound like I want you to play shrink, but I don't. Okay? Are we clear?"

My mouth was full. After I swallowed, I said, "These days, Adrienne, I'm always grateful for the opportunity not to play shrink."

"Good. I've been dating Cozy for what, like months already, right?"

I nodded. It had been months. I was there the night they met.

"I like him."

She seemed to want me to say something. I said, "Yes? That's good, right? He's a good man, Ren."

"He is. And yes, it's been . . . it's been good. But lately I've gotten"— she smiled coyly—"confused about something. See, a couple of weeks ago he introduced me to his ex-wife. He really wanted me to meet her twin girls, whom he adores. The twins aren't his; she's been married twice. His ex-wife's name is—"

"Erin, I met her last fall. She's an investigator. She's nice. I know their situation."

"Yes, Erin's . . . nice." Adrienne coughed. At first I thought it might be the spiciness of the satay. "Real nice," she said, coughing again. "The thing is, well, the thing is that I think we've started dating."

It wasn't the satay.

"You and. . . ?"

"Erin."

"Erin. You're dating?"

"Well, we're going out. And it doesn't feel like a girlfriend thing. The going out."

My brain cramped. I asked, "Have you, um—?"

"Not yet, but I think we might be getting close to, um . . . you know."

"And you're okay with—?"

"Sure, I guess. I don't know. We'll see."

"Well," I said, "it sounds to me like you're a willing volunteer on this expedition into the wilderness. What's the trouble?"

Adrienne had scoffed at my choice of wines and poured herself a Miller Lite. She drained half a glass of beer and belched a little bit before she continued. "I'm a little confused here, can't you tell? I'm still seeing Cozy—I mean I saw him last night—and believe me, he and I, we're way past 'close,' if you know what I mean. So I don't know exactly what to do with this little sexual preference problem that I'm experiencing."

"Is this . . . attraction to women something new, Ren? I mean, have you ever—"

"No, I've *never*. Of course, it's something new. I mean, sure, I've . . . you absolutely promise you're not going to go judgmental on me here? You promise? I'll kill you, I swear I will."

I knew her threat wasn't idle. My physical well-being was at stake. I said, "I promise."

"Peter and I always used to like the same pornography. Girl-on-girl stuff. I thought that was weird. But, you know, I just ended up thinking that it was another sign of how compatible we were. That's ironic, right?"

It was also denial, but it was certainly ironic. I said, "Sure, Ren."

"Are you patronizing me?"

I stood up and walked across the counter and hugged her. "This is a little more complicated than dating two different guys, isn't it?"

"Tell me about it. How do I know what the hell I should be doing?"

"I don't know. Just pay attention to how it all feels. Sometimes the best way to get off the fence is just to get off the fence."

She almost coughed up some beer through her nose. "Jesus. People *pay* you for this? I can't even decide between AT&T and MCI and you're telling me to decide who to sleep with by jumping off a goddamn fence?"

I couldn't help but smile.

"Adrienne, I don't care who you sleep with or who you love." I pulled back and put my hands on her cheeks and looked her in the eyes. "You've stood by me through some pretty questionable romantic choices. If Erin makes you happy, I'm thrilled. If she mistreats you, don't worry, I know where she lives."

She looked at me plaintively. "What about Cozy? What do I tell him?"

"Don't be too concerned about him. He's a big boy, Ren."

"He certainly is. And believe me, given my line of work, I've seen the competition, so I know what I'm talking about."

Her phone rang.

Adrienne answered. "What?" She listened for a few agitated seconds and handed it to me. I was dumbstruck to learn I was being invited to go for a helicopter ride.

After I hung up, I explained the situation to Adrienne. She astonished me by being understanding. She said, "Thanks for the advice."

I said, "That wasn't advice. I don't give advice."

"Whatever. Thanks for making me feel like I'm not totally crazy."

"Ren, this feels like the first time in days that someone has wanted my counsel on something where someone's life wasn't in danger. It's actually refreshing." I paused. "And I didn't say you weren't crazy. I merely said that it was just fine that you felt like dating Erin."

She laughed and said, "Go, you have things to do." And before I had a chance to ask, she added, "Don't worry about Emily. She's sleeping over here tonight."

The call had been from Lucy Tanner, Sam's partner. I didn't know how she had tracked me down at Adrienne's house and wasn't sure I was eager to.

But she wanted me at the Boulder airport in twenty minutes, which gave me barely enough time to change my clothes and grab a heavy jacket and some gloves and get to my car.

She and I were, apparently, going to be crossing the Continental Divide in a helicopter in the dark, something far down on the list of things I've always wanted to do.

But the sheriff's office in Routt County thought they had found Ed Robilio's Holiday Rambler near Steamboat Springs.

* * *

Lucy was waiting for me in the parking lot at Boulder Aviation, dressed in black jeans, heavy ankle boots, a black turtleneck, and a leather bomber jacket.

"You know Sam can't go. He's not supposed to be anywhere near this case. But it was his idea that I take you along. I sold my sergeant on it and I told the locals that you were a psychological consultant to the department and that you just happened to know both of the kids and that you might help us end this peacefully. The local cops seemed grateful for the help. And Sam told me to tell you—as a matter of fact, he told me twice to tell you—that his conversation with his sister-in-law was fruitful. He actually said, 'Fruitful.' He surprises me sometimes. He surprises you, too?"

"Constantly."

She led me through a gate in a chain-link fence. The helicopter was parked on the side of the tarmac. I'd expected a police helicopter borrowed from another jurisdiction. Instead, we were about to board the news helicopter owned by Channel 7.

"What's the deal?" I asked.

"The department doesn't have a helicopter and we needed a quick trip. The TV stations provide help sometimes on searches and things. We asked Channel 7. They declined. We told them it might relate to the Brenda Strait story. They balked. We told them nobody else would have the story. They said okay."

"Just us?"

"Pilot's coming. We all thought that would be a good idea. And I expect they'll send a cameraman."

"Person."

"Whatever. I probably should have asked you this already. You don't get airsick, do you?"

"Never have before. But then I've never crossed the Divide in a helicopter before. Certainly not in the dark."

"That's okay. Neither has the pilot."

She watched my face turn ashen before she said, "Kidding. Says he does it all the time. Come on."

The pilot was walking toward us. He was a little older than me and had the easygoing been-there-done-that manner of Marty Klein, my ER doc friend. He was dressed in corduroys and a polo shirt covered with a jean jacket and a down vest.

He introduced himself and said, "We're ready. You know the rules?"

I looked at Lucy. She was impassive. I said, "No."

"Do what I tell you. If for any reason you need to quickly exit, do so toward the front. If you can see me, you're okay. Got it?"

I said, "Yes." But I was thinking, *Why might I need to quickly exit?*

"She's fueled. Let's go."

The cameraman and the pilot took the front seats and Lucy and I climbed into the back and buckled up. I asked her if she did this sort of thing often.

"I dated a guy who flew in the Air National Guard. But that was a while ago."

I discerned her last few words by lipreading. The pilot had started the engine of his Bell Jet Ranger and was pantomiming to us to put our headphone/microphone units on.

The engine noise disappeared and the Bose headphones offered the clear voice of the pilot. "Any questions?"

"How do you know where you're going?"

He laughed. "I know the way. I also have a GPS—Global Positioning Satellite—system. The thing can guide me to a specific elk during hunting season if I ask it to. The people we're meeting have a portable GPS, they're going to call in the coordinates to me. We'll hit them like a hammer hits a nail."

I wasn't fond of the analogy.

A moment later we lifted off gently, and I was immediately mesmerized by Boulder's lights as we headed northwest.

Lucy asked, "Tim, is there a way you can separate out our headphones from the ones you guys are using up front? There are some things we need to talk about privately."

"No problem." He touched a button on the control panel and raised his fingers in an okay sign.

Lucy touched me on the knee to get my attention. The lights had disappeared below, and I wondered how close we were flying to the ridge tops I was seeing so clearly.

"Yes?"

"Two new developments that I think you should know about. First, I think you should know that MedExcel contacted the Arapahoe County DA's office this morning about an extortion attempt that was phoned in to Ed Robilio's secretary late yesterday."

"What kind of extortion attempt?"

Lucy shrugged. "There's no tape of the call. But the secretary thought the voice was of a young female. She threatened to, quote, 'bring the company down' if 'their' demands weren't met. Said it was about Dr. Robilio. Something that the company wouldn't want made public."

"Do you think it's related to these kids? What are the demands?"

"Don't know. And no demands yet. A voice in the background, a young male, was screaming at the caller to hang up. The secretary thinks he sounded angry, agitated. We think maybe he was timing the call, afraid of a trace. Silly, how would MedExcel have the capacity to trace a call that they didn't know was coming?"

"Caller ID on the phone?"

"No such luck."

"You think it has to do with these kids, Lucy? Did they find something at Robilio's cabin? Or is it a bluff because they know half the cops in the state are looking for them?"

"I don't know what to think, Alan."

"What could they have found?"

She turned her palms up.

"What else?"

"What do you mean?"

"What else should I know? You said there were two things you thought I should know."

"Oh, yeah. The missing girl's mother, hell, what's her name?"

"Madison's mother? Miggy Monroe?"

"Yes, good. Miggy Monroe. She called us at five-fifteen this evening, feels certain her daughter came home while she was at work today."

"Really?"

"She says a couple of things are moved around and that some heavy boots and gloves are missing that she was sure were there before."

"That's it? Madison would risk coming home for some boots? Do you guys give much credence to this? It doesn't make sense."

"We're not sure what to think. Her daughter has a key, of course. The place wasn't a crime scene, so we didn't work the place for physical evidence before, and the mom's living there, so it's hard to tell whether or not the story has merit. She's the kid's mom, so it could just be wishful thinking on her part. On the other hand, she could be right on. Maybe Madison is still in Boulder."

"Anybody see anything?"

"Wits? Are you kidding?" She tapped the pilot on the shoulder and indicated that she wanted the communications opened again.

We listened in as Tim made radio contact with the local authorities and had the Routt County Sheriff provide wind speed and direction information for their location. He asked them to check for wires and other obstructions near the landing site.

They asked him how he wanted the site marked. He requested a fifty-foot square of highway flares.

I surmised from their conversation that we were supposed to land in a corral at the Somersby Ranch, about a mile from the location of the suspect motor home. A while later, I looked down as we were dropping from the sky toward the corral, which was lit with the requested highway flares in a square that seemed to be about the size of a king-size bed. I felt as though we were trying to land on a postage stamp in an ocean of black water. I didn't like our odds.

The touchdown was uneventful.

On the ground we were met by eight deputies of the Routt County Sheriff's Office, the entire Oak Creek Police Department, four deputies from Summit County, a firefighter from Steamboat Springs, and a few troopers from the Colorado State Patrol.

So far the authorities had surrounded the site but had made no contact with the kids and had seen no signs that they were even in the RV.

After introductions were made, Lucy said, "You probably know that they had a motorcycle yesterday. Is it there?"

"We know about the bike. We haven't seen any sign of it."

"Okay, what's the plan?"

The kids had selected a pretty good spot to stash the huge motor coach. At this time in the spring, the backcountry in Routt County, outside Steamboat Springs, was relatively untraveled.

Haldeman, the RV, was cloaked in a tight clearing in a thick grove of denuded aspen and lush ponderosa pine. A dirt road climbed straight up the hill toward the clearing. Madison and Brad had cut branches from the pines and covered the entire top and front of the vehicle with foliage.

A maintenance man for the nearby Somersby Ranch had been checking the perimeter of the property for fence problems and had spotted the camouflage. He had reported the suspicious vehicle to the Routt County Sheriff. The Routt County cops knew that the Summit County Sheriff was looking for a big, fancy RV and within minutes the Boulder Police Department had been notified, too, and was negotiating to send an observer to the scene.

The plan was organic. Surround Haldeman. Assess the situation. Rouse the kids from a distance. Negotiate their surrender.

The firefighter from Steamboat was fitting a headset and camera rig over his head. Lucy asked him what it was.

"It's called IRIS. We just got it. It's a remote infrared imaging system. Helps us see through smoke inside buildings. Thought we might be able to use it tonight to locate your suspects." He scanned us and pronounced the device operable. Then he focused the headset on the Holiday Rambler for about two minutes, scanning in narrow bands. Finally he said, "I don't think anyone is in there. I'm not picking up anything hot. Not even anything warm."

The surrounding-the-hilltop part of the plan seemed to go without a hitch. All the cops checked in from their positions with military precision.

The rousing-the-kids part was less successful. A combination of halogen lights, megaphones, and the helicopter hovering above with spotlights trained on the clearing earned no response from the RV. No lights came on in the bus, the door didn't open.

None of the police reported seeing any movement. The firefighter still reported no positives on his infrared unit.

My role during this phase seemed to be limited to staying out of the line of potential fire and trying to keep warm.

I was significantly better at the former than I was at the latter.

Twenty-eight

A motorcycle engine revved and upshifted somewhere in the adjacent canyons. The sound echoed off the stone walls, and each shift in pitch of the distant drone froze the assembled cops like the assured click of a gun cocking.

Someone said, "Shh. Quiet," and we all stilled and listened.

The canyon walls trapped and distorted the sound. At first I thought the high-pitched whine I was hearing was identical to the drone I had heard fading away from Dead Ed's ranch the night before. Then I wasn't so sure. And at first I thought the motorcycle was north of us, heading toward the west, and then I thought it was south of us, heading farther south.

By the time the engine noise finally disappeared, all I was certain of was that the motorcycle wasn't coming up the hill to rendezvous with Haldeman.

Lucy said, "False alarm."

The Routt County deputy said, "Infrared still negative?"

"Yes. It's ice cold in there."

"Let's go check out the RV."

"Everybody have vests on?"

"I don't," I said.

The Summit County deputy helped me pull one on. He told me to stay back until we found the kids.

I thought it was great advice.

The approach to the Holiday Rambler reminded me of the stealth my friends and I used to employ while capturing an unprotected treehouse when I was a kid. Everyone skulked up the hill waiting for an attack nobody really believed was forthcoming.

"Police, open up!" yelled a Routt County deputy as he tried the door on the RV. It swung open. "Police!" he called again, then once more, the barrel of his handgun pointing toward the Big Dipper.

Everyone waited. There was a moment of shared doubt. Maybe the infrared was wrong.

Maybe it was an ambush.

"Scope?"

"Just you guys bright as Martians. Nothing's glowing inside. Nothing. It's cool."

"Okay, go in."

Three deputies did, one after the other, their guns ready, their hearts, I was sure, beating like steel drums.

Lucy appeared beside me. Coolly, she said, "They're not here. Damn. Sorry about pulling you away for this."

"It's fine, Lucy. The helicopter ride was great."

I heard a radio call. "Clear."

One of the deputies poked his head out of the RV and said, "We have a crime scene here. Lot of blood inside."

"Vic?"

"No vic."

"Weapons?"

"Half a dozen of them."

Lucy said, "Shit."

The flashlights were out now, and all the cops were scanning the area around the RV for physical evidence.

The Routt County deputy was silent for a minute; then, in a loud voice, he ordered the area cleared. He wanted a perimeter set up at fifty yards.

Someone said, "Wait. Blood trail goes out the door and then down here." A Summit County deputy was pointing his flashlight at some large pine boughs that were resting against the side of the vehicle, midway between the wheel wells.

"See anything else?"

He crouched and adjusted the beam of his flashlight. "Dark stains. There are some big doors behind these branches. You know, like for luggage on a bus."

The Routt County deputy called for a camera. He took shots of the pine boughs and the blood before removing the branches. He pulled latex on his hands and tried the handle of the left-hand door. As the door raised on hydraulic lifters, he stood off to one side.

The converging beams of the flashlights showed an empty cavern.

The deputy moved to the other door, clicked it open, and again stood back as it lifted up to a horizontal stop.

This cavern wasn't empty. I thought what I was seeing inside was a pile of rags. Then I saw the wispy hair, the hair so light that it could be lifted by baby's breath.

Lucy said, "It's the girl."

All the flashlight beams focused on the body. The firefighter with the infrared helmet had his scope on her. He said, "Don't bother disturbing her. She's stone cold."

I said, "Oh, Madison."

Lucy and I stepped out of the helicopter onto the tarmac at Boulder Airport at one-thirty in the morning. We had spoken little on the ride back over the Divide. She was husbanding her energy for her next errand—heading off to tell Miggy Monroe that her daughter had been murdered.

I was going home.

My head found my pillow a few minutes after two o'clock. But I couldn't sleep. The night's events felt unreal, my subconscious rendering them into the hazy stuff of dreams. I didn't think I had slept at all when I looked up and saw the clock at four-forty-two. At five to five I crawled out of bed, took a shower, dressed, and headed to Denver before rush hour.

I had my own notifying to do.

The adolescent psychiatry unit at The Children's Hospital was still. The kids were all asleep, and the night shift was putting finishing touches on the kids' charts, looking forward to going home. My arrival surprised everyone. The nursing staff wasn't accustomed to doctors showing up before dawn for psychotherapy sessions, especially on weekends.

After I explained the circumstances, they handled my request to awaken Merritt with aplomb and informed me that Merritt had not started speaking with any staff members.

Generally, adults awaken looking like leftovers. Kids awaken looking soft and tousled and unkempt. And Merritt was still a kid. Her skin was puffy and pink and she held her hair back from her face with one hand. She examined me with a combination of vigilance and fire in her sleepy eyes. Defiantly, she said, "Is Chaney okay? Is this about my sister?"

"I'm not aware of any change in Chaney's condition, Merritt. I'm here about something else. Please sit."

She did.

"There's no easy way to tell you this, but—"

"Are my parents okay?"

"As far as I know, yes." With a cushion in my voice, I added, "Please, may I go on?"

She nodded.

"Merritt, I'm afraid your friend Madison is dead."

Merritt released so much air from her lungs that I expected her to collapse in on herself and implode, like a punctured balloon. I waited for the inhale. The delay was inexorable and when she finally breathed, she gulped at the air, swallowing hungrily.

"Are you sure? What happened?"

I searched for a euphemism. I didn't find one. "She was murdered. Sometime yesterday, probably. The police aren't sure yet."

"Was it Brad?" No hesitation.

"We need to make some decisions about the ground rules, Merritt. I need the freedom to let the treatment team know what we talk about here."

She looked injured, mumbled, "God."

"It's essential, Merritt."

"Not my parents? You won't tell them?"

"No, I don't need to tell them."

"Not the police?"

"No, certainly not the police. Not unless it's about child abuse or hurting someone."

She stretched her neck back and tried to tame her unruly hair. "I think . . . I'm about to trust you. Do you deserve it?"

"I hope so."

"Okay. You can tell the treatment team what we talk about if you also tell them not to tell anybody else. That's important. And you can tell the lawyer, Mr. Maitlin, too. Now you tell me, was it Brad?"

"It may have been. She was with him."

"Did he beat her again?"

"Has he beaten her before?"

"He's hit her before. He has a temper. Did he beat her?"

I thought about the bloody trail and Madison's pitifully crumpled body. I said, "Someone may have."

"He beat her to death?"

"No, she wasn't beaten to death."

"How did she die?"

"She was shot."

"Did you see her?"

"Yes."

"Where?"

"In the mountains. Near Steamboat Springs."

"No, no. Where was she shot? Where on her body?"

"She was shot a number of times, Merritt. Different places."

"Was it really awful? Like . . . Dr. Robilio?"

"I didn't see him. What happened with Madison wasn't pretty, Merritt. I don't think she suffered, though." I had no idea whether or not Madison had suffered. But I desperately wanted to put a Band-Aid on Merritt's hurt.

"She's so stupid. I told her not to stay with him. He's, he's trouble. He's . . ."

"What?"

"He scares me, okay? I told her not to tell him. He's such a jerk."

"Tell him what?"

She looked at me with total concentration. I knew we had reached the edge of the frontier. She had to decide whether to guide me through it.

She hesitated, hugged herself, and said, "It's about Chaney."

Twenty-nine

"It's about Chaney?"

When she answered me, Merritt's voice was low, tentative, as though she were speaking to herself. She said, "Yes. Everything is about Chaney."

With another agenda in different circumstances the therapist in me could have mined the sibling issues in those words for a mother lode. But my agenda this day insisted that I dig differently, cautiously. So I waited.

A minute or so later, Merritt said, "I hate it when Trent does that."

"Does what?"

"The silent thing. Waiting for me to talk. To say something stupid."

I said, "You think I'm waiting for you to say something stupid?"

She slapped her open hand against the knee of her sweatpants and yelled, "*Don't!* Damn it, don't! This is too important for your games. Jesus. I thought you knew that. Don't you see what's going on?" And she started to cry.

I felt as though I'd been slapped across the face. I said, "I'm sorry." And I was.

"I don't want her to die."

"I know you don't."

"Everything I did, I did because I don't want her to die. You have to believe that."

"I do. I believe that."

She looked at me. She said, "I have to pee."

I almost smiled. In the same situation, an adult would have held it in. I said, "After you do, we'll continue?"

"Yes."

"Let's go find a nurse."

* * *

Peeing took a long time. Merritt returned in her familiar leggings and T-shirt, with heavy socks on her feet. This T-shirt was inscribed HICK. Her T-shirts were like hieroglyphics to me. Her face was washed, her hair combed and down. She ran her tongue across the front of what I guessed were freshly brushed teeth.

She said, "I feel better."

I said, "Good."

"I promised I'd never tell anyone this story."

"I'm sure it's hard."

"But Madison's dead now, so . . ." Her face tightened and she fought tears.

"The promise was with her?"

She nodded. "You really won't tell?"

"No."

"What I did was Madison's idea. Don't blame her for everything. It wasn't her fault. It was my fault. Blame me for what happened. But it was her idea."

She paused for a moment as I considered why it was so important to her that I believe that Madison had been the instigator of whatever had transpired. Merritt seemed to soften as I sat with her. Intuitively, I guessed that she was trying to determine if I was planning to permit her to tell this story her way. I forced my face to remain fifty times more impassive than I felt.

"Trent knew where he lived. Dr. Robilio. I'd heard my mom and him talking about Dr. Robilio. They said that there were two people who could give Chaney the procedure she needs. One was the insurance guy, the head of the board that decides who gets what. And he had already turned us down. The other was Dr. Robilio. He could give Chaney the procedure if he wanted. If he said okay, then Chaney could go to Washington and get those drugs and get the transplant.

"I followed my dad there a couple of times. To his house, Dr. Robilio's house. Madison helped me tail him. She's older than me. She can drive. She'd get her mom's car. And we would sit and wait a block away while my dad just sat and waited outside Dr. Robilio's house.

"One day, Trent finally talked to him. I couldn't see them the whole time, but I think they went in the house. I was so excited. I couldn't imagine anyone would turn us down. Trent just had to make him see that it was a choice between money and Chaney. I thought we'd won for sure.

"That night at dinner, though, Trent was mad, as mad as I'd ever seen him. He was pi-issed off. I finished up eating as fast as I could and excused myself and went and sat on the stairs and listened to him tell my mom that he'd gone back to Robilio's house and he'd been turned down. That Dr. Robilio had said no." She closed her eyes. "And he said that he thought that . . . he could kill him."

I had the impression I was supposed to be shocked here. But I'd already heard this story from John Trent. Merritt seemed puzzled at my neutral reaction.

"I finished my homework and went over to Madison's apartment. I took the bus. Just told my mom I was leaving. I told Mad what had happened with my dad and Dr. Robilio. I said something like, 'All he cares about is his money. He doesn't care about my sister.'

"And Madison gets this funny grin on her face and she says, 'Maybe he cares about something else. Maybe there's something else he wants. We could trade it for your sister.' "

My heart was doing a drum solo in my chest.

"And you know what she does then? She can be really funny sometimes, and she can also be really gross. You know what she does?"

I said, "No, what?"

Merritt grew as nervous as I'd ever seen her. She played with her hair, she looked away from me, she folded and unfolded her arms. Finally she said, "She lifts up her top, and holds it up under her chin, and she grabs her boobs, and holds them up, too." Merritt giggled, raised her eyebrows, and said, "Boy, she has big boobs. Anyway, she has one of her tits in each hand, and she says, 'These.' "

The moment was snapped by three sharp raps on the door.

I said, "Just one second," and opened the door far enough to see who it was whose timing was so bad.

Georgia, the head nurse, stood at the door with sad eyes.

She said, "I'm so sorry to interrupt. But it's Chaney. She's crashing."

Merritt was behind me in a flash. She had both hands firmly on my shoulders. For a second, I thought she was going to throw me to the floor.

She said, each word clearly enunciated, "Take me to her, now."

I said, "Yes."

"Let's go!"

Georgia's mouth was agape. She had just heard Merritt speak for the first time.

I said, "Georgia, what privileges does she need for this? To leave the unit and go see to her sister? With staff?"

"You would need to, uh, d/c the suicide precautions and increase her level to II, at least."

"Merritt, do you promise not to try to hurt yourself?"

"I promise."

"I mean it."

"I promise."

"And you promise not to run?"

"I promise. I need to be with my sister. She needs me right now."

"Georgia, consider it done. Will you write those orders, please? I'll sign."

For Chaney, this crisis was different from the last one. But for me, watching helplessly from across the intensive care unit, it looked remarkably the same.

Brenda Strait was sitting by herself on a chair next to an empty bed, two beds down from her daughter. On the way down the stairs, Merritt had prepared me for Brenda's presence in the ICU. "Mom was here last night, not my stepdad. Trent's in Boulder. She's not going to handle this as well as he does. You need to know that. Okay?"

The "Okay?" was this fifteen-year-old's way of reminding me that I had a job to do when we arrived at the ICU.

Merritt hugged her mother, whispered something I couldn't hear, and walked confidently over to her sister's bedside. She weaved through the staff and disappeared from view. I couldn't see Chaney through the crush of equipment and the thick crowd of staff that was surrounding her.

I stood next to Brenda and said, "I'm so sorry, Brenda. How bad is it?"

She held a hand in front of her pale lips. "Bad. She's so sick. My baby is so sick."

"Her lungs again?"

She nodded.

"Anything else?"

She nodded again.

I waited for her to elucidate. She didn't. I asked, "Have you called John?"

"He's on his way."

"Anything I can do?"

"Save my baby."

Tiny popping sounds rat-a-tatted from her lips.

The crowd around Chaney didn't thin for another thirty minutes. During the half hour some docs and nurses retreated and some reinforcements arrived with new equipment. But the throng stayed thick.

I knew that Merritt was in there somewhere whispering encouragement to her sister, providing her the essential spiritual nutrition that modern medicine couldn't provide via intravenous line.

John Trent arrived at the ICU in a rush and barely said hello to his wife and me before he asked, "Is Merritt over there with her?"

I said, "Yes."

He said, "Good, thanks, Alan," and jogged over to try to corner one of Chaney's critical care docs to get an update on her condition.

Brenda said, "It's in God's hands now."

I thought, *It's been in God's hands all along and He hasn't been doing too great a job.*

We watched the gradual thinning of the armies who were helping Chaney stay alive. They departed in ones and twos. My fear, the one that had my heart bobbing against my Adam's apple, was that at some point all who remained would depart the bed together.

That didn't happen.

Finally, after two remaining respiratory techs retreated to the nursing station, I was able to see Merritt, stretched on her side like a big letter S, her upper body curled around her sister. I couldn't see Chaney's face but could hear the rhythmic hiss and pulse of a ventilator. Chaney Trent was no longer breathing on her own.

John came to his wife's side and took both of her hands and kneeled down in front of her. He said, "It's not good. Pray, Bren. Pray."

My mind wanted to escape, to be somewhere else, anywhere else, and my thoughts kept drifting back to the provocatively inane question: What on earth did Madison Lane's breasts have to do with any of this?

I looked at my watch and knew the answer was going to have to wait.

A patient I'd already rescheduled once would be expecting me to be in my Boulder office in seventy-five minutes.

Some things don't sort quickly.

My drive back to Boulder was a jumble of the last twelve hours. My mother-in-law's negative biopsy. Adrienne's sexual confusion. Merritt's revelation about trailing her father. Chaney's deterioration. Madison's murder.

Madison's breasts.

And Merritt's contention that she thought John Trent had gone inside Edward Robilio's house.

What the hell did that mean? Had Merritt seen him go in or was she assuming he went in? Why didn't John Trent tell me that himself?

I arrived in my office with seven minutes to spare. I used them to call Sam Purdy to fill him in about the latest crisis with Chaney.

He sounded beaten down by the news. He asked, "But she was alive when you left?"

"Yes. She's on a respirator now. She didn't look good, Sam. Nobody was making any optimistic noises."

"I'll call right down there. Listen, thanks for going with Lucy last night. Sorry about the way things turned out. I thought you might be able to help if the kids didn't want to come out on their own."

"I'm sorry, too. Mostly, I'm sick that Madison's dead, Sam. Any word on the boy?"

"No, it's going to be a lot harder to find a kid on a motorcycle than it is to find a fifty-foot land yacht." He paused and lowered his voice. He was at the police department, in a little cubicle surrounded by other detectives in their little cubicles. "I want to tell you something about the inside of the motorhome that you aren't supposed to know. Maybe it will help you with my niece. You understand?"

"Absolutely."

"Before she was shot, the girl, uh—"

"Madison."

"Yeah, Madison. She was beaten around the face and head with a videocassette."

"A videocassette?"

"Yeah. The cops who did the scene said it was violent, a real rage thing. The damn cassette was crushed into a hundred pieces, tape loose all over the place, the poor kid's blood was everywhere. Whoever did it almost ripped her damn ear off."

"Jesus. And it was Brad?"

"Probably, his latents are everywhere. The kid's not using his head at all anymore. That worries me."

Merritt apparently was right on the money. Madison had reason to be afraid of Brad. "What does it all mean?"

"Don't know. But it must mean something. The attack took place in the middle of the motorhome, in the kitchen area. The VCR and the tapes are in a fancy cabinet above the driver's seat. The boy had better weapons close at hand—knives, pots and pans. I don't know why he used a videocassette."

"What was the tape? Do they know what's on it?"

"No. The label's handwritten, says, 'PRETTY WOMAN.' "

"Do you think these kids had anything to do with the extortion attempt?"

He was silent.

"Lucy told me about it last night."

"I don't know any more than you do. It's unclear whether that was them. The kids. I just don't know."

"I'm still seeing Merritt every day. I hope I can learn something that helps with all this, Sam. I'm doing my best. And Sam?"

"Yeah?"

"Lauren and I have some money. We want to donate it to Chaney's fund." I thought I could hear his teeth grind. "It's almost thirty-one thousand dollars. I know it's not enough, but maybe—"

"Thanks a lot. That's generous of you. I'll see if it will help. I'll let you know. Sit on it for now."

"We want to help, Sam."

"I appreciate it. Listen, do you think it's funny that the threats against Brenda stopped shortly after Chaney got sick? Is that a coincidence, do you think?"

The change in direction unnerved me, which was probably Sam's intention. "I don't know, Sam. I haven't thought about it, but I would guess that the guy's boiler just ran out of steam. Or maybe he heard about

Chaney being sick and figured that God had answered his prayers. Biblical retribution. You know, an eye for an eye."

"Exactly. That's what I was thinking, too. But see, I asked Brenda about it when we had lunch yesterday and she said that the threats and harassment stopped a few days *before* she went public with the insurance problem. So if the asshole who was after her stopped because he figured that Brenda had gotten hers, you know, with Chaney being so sick—"

"How did they know?"

"Exactly. How did the asshole know? He cooled his heels before Chaney's story was on the news."

"You're speculating here, aren't you, Sam?"

"No, I'm theorizing. Civilians speculate."

"You working this on the side?"

"I'm talking to some people. You know, unofficially."

"Are there suspects?"

"The Denver police had some leads."

I smiled as I hung up the phone. Sam was searching the bottom of the bag for that last remaining french fry.

Thirty

My first patient was a thirty-four-year-old gay firefighter named Roland who, over the past eight months, had lost his partner of six years and his two closest friends to AIDS. Over the weekend he had discovered that another good friend was HIV-positive. We talked mostly about the promise of protease inhibitors. How Roland found the will to continue to believe that each new day would start with a fresh sunrise baffled me. But he did. Each week as we talked I permitted myself to be inspired by him.

My first scheduled break of the morning came at eleven. I called Cozier Maitlin's office to leave him a message. His sweet secretary answered, and I convinced her that my news was probably more urgent than whatever it was Cozy was doing at the moment.

"Alan? What's up?"

Well, your girlfriend is about to dump you for the chance to have a go at your ex-wife . . .

"Lots, Cozy, but I just have a minute now. Can I meet you somewhere at one-thirty? Your office? Coffee?"

"Come here. No clients on Saturday. 'Bye. I'm on the eighth floor."

If you said you were on the eighth floor in downtown Boulder, you didn't need to use an address. There was only one building that tall in the center of the city and it is such an architectural abomination that its construction resulted in an ordinance prohibiting any copycat developers from building their own brick-and-glass privacy fences between the rest of the city and the mountains.

One of Cozy's building's glass facades faced the mountains, and one faced the eastern plains. I wasn't surprised that Cozy's office had the western view.

It's easy to find views of Boulder from on high. Many hiking trails and roads leave town to the west and provide stunning views of the city and the endless plains to the east. But a view of the city from this height with the mountains as a backdrop was breathtaking and novel.

I said, "Nice office, Cozy."

Cozy barely looked up from his desk. "That's what people say. It's my turn to be running tight on time. Sit."

My back was to the view as I filled him in on the developments with Madison and Brad, my helicopter trip over the Divide, and Madison's murder.

The news I was providing caused him to sit back on his chair while he air-drummed an imaginary snare with two pencils. He said, "What's it all mean?"

"I was hoping you would tell me that."

He shrugged and raised his eyebrows.

I said, "I have a patient soon and I know you have limited time and there's more for you to consider. First, and maybe most important, Merritt started talking to me."

"What?" His voice was a sandwich of elation and alarm. The alarm part, I supposed, was his recognition that as long as Merritt wasn't opening her mouth, she couldn't very well stick her foot in it.

"Initially she insisted on total confidence. From everyone, you included, Cozy. I finally managed to get her to agree to let me fill you and the hospital staff in on what she was telling me."

He slapped the pencils on the desk. "You need to be incredibly careful what you put in the chart."

I said, "I know. No facts, Cozy."

"And? Come on, Alan, what'd she say? I'm not big on suspense. There're lawyers who are calm waiting for juries to come back; I'm not one of them."

"Nothing yet. We were interrupted before she told me much. Her little sister is critical again. All Merritt's told me so far is that she followed her stepfather when he went to Dead Ed's house and that she thinks he went in and that she and her girlfriend were cooking up a scheme to save her sister. That's it."

"A scheme? What kind of scheme?"

"I don't know yet."

"And now the girlfriend is dead?"

"Yes. Merritt says that Brad—the boyfriend—had a mean streak. She didn't seem surprised."

"If I go to Denver, will Merritt talk to me?"

"I don't know, Cozy. But I don't recommend trying. Clinically, I mean. The trust level between her and me is fragile. I think it's important to give her control of this now that she's decided to talk. If we press her, she could clam up again."

"Hell." That was as close as Cozier Maitlin ever came to cursing.

I looked at my watch. I had eight minutes to get four blocks. "I almost forgot. It seems that Merritt broke a fingernail during some part of this affair. I saw the broken nail on her hand that first day when she was in the hospital. The cops have it. The broken nail."

"You're sure the cops have it? Who told you? And where did they recover it?"

"I don't know where they recovered it. And you'll just have to accept my word that I heard it from a reliable source that . . . should remain anonymous."

"Oh." Cozy knew immediately that my source was Sam. He put down his drumsticks. It was his turn to look at his watch. He said, "I should go, too. I'm having a late lunch with Adrienne. She can get irritable when I'm late."

I smiled meekly, bit my tongue, and told him to enjoy his meal.

My afternoon was relatively uneventful. Before returning to Denver, I stopped home long enough to amuse Emily for a while and give her an early dinner. I was being a neglectful parent and still she greeted me as gleefully as a child greets Christmas morning.

The situation hadn't changed much at Children's. Chaney remained stable. Critical, but stable. Merritt was camped out two inches from her sister's bed. When I arrived, she was reading a dog-eared copy of *Catcher in the Rye*. She waved at me and smiled a greeting. Brenda was sitting in a rocking chair, keeping vigil with her daughter. John was pacing in the hall and saw me enter.

With a wave, he beckoned me over to the nursing station door. He said, "Merritt won't talk to anyone but Chaney. And when Chaney stirs she won't shut up, just puts her mouth next to Chaney's ear and whispers to her."

"How is she, John? Chaney?"

"Same. The transplant team repeated their imaging this afternoon. Her primary has been on the phone with Seattle. Chaney's eligibility for the procedure is now questionable. If her lung function deteriorates much more they won't take her even if we get the insurance approval."

"I'm so sorry."

He was looking at the floor, sliding the toe of one shoe back and forth. "I'm an old hippie, Alan. Stuff doesn't mean much to me. It just doesn't. I can honestly say that this is the only time in my life I've ever been envious of rich men. And today, I want to be a rich man, too. My baby's dying in that room, in that bed, and I can't do anything about it. A rich man could do something about it. Do you have any idea how that feels?"

I wanted to touch him, but he had wrapped himself in his grief. I said, "No, John, I don't. I can only imagine."

"Merritt's calm as can be. She seems absolutely convinced that her sister's going to be fine. I worry about what it's going to be like for her when she realizes the gravity of what's happened, what's going on." He looked up from the floor. "She's going to need you then. You know that?"

"I know, John. I'll do everything I can."

We both knew I could do precious little. Maybe put a pillow down to cushion a ten-story fall.

I waited with John and Brenda about ten minutes until the respiratory technicians arrived to do a treatment on Chaney. As she left her sister's bedside, I casually invited Merritt to join me in an empty conference room adjacent to the intensive care unit.

Without a moment's hesitation, she came along. I was surprised.

I said, "Hi. Tough day. What you're doing for your sister is wonderful. It really makes a difference."

She shook her head. Didn't speak. Instantly, I feared that we had returned to square one: Silence.

I said, "The police still haven't found Brad. I thought you would want to know."

One side of the conference room had glass windows facing the ICU. Merritt stood and adjusted the blinds so that she could clearly see her sister's bed. She ignored my comment about the fraternity boy, but asked, "How is Mrs. Monroe doing? Is she, I don't know . . . ?"

I was relieved that she was still speaking. "I haven't talked to Ms. Monroe. I'm sure it's an incredibly difficult time for her."

In a halting voice, Merritt asked, "Does she blame me? For what happened?"

My next words were crucial, I knew that. I softened my voice and narrowed my focus. I leaned forward on my chair, resting my elbows on my knees. I said, "I don't know, Merritt. Should she?"

Merritt returned to the chair opposite me and sat. Her gaze stayed aimed at the window. She said, "Probably," and she shook her head, a disbelieving kind of shake. "But I told Madison not to tell Brad. I knew he'd do something stupid. God."

My impulse was to say, "Tell him what?" I didn't. I sat back and feigned patience and allowed Merritt to find a pace for telling this story that suited her. She bit on her lower lip for a moment, then, with a thrust of her jaw, she began to bite on her upper one.

"Do you wonder why I wouldn't talk for so long?"

"Of course I do."

"Okay, here's why.

"That day, the last day, I went over to Dr. Robilio's house again. By myself this time, Madison wasn't with me. I'd been working out at school. I took the bus and then I walked the rest of the way to his house. I wanted to . . . I don't know . . . I don't know . . ."

Merritt struggled, looking for a word. The silence stretched for at least ten seconds.

"Plead with him—beg him?—to save my sister. When I got there, I saw my stepdad's car parked around the corner. Trent has this old beat-up Jetta, you can't miss it. It's an antique, at least as old as me. Anyway, I waited for him to come out. When he did, he came out of the back yard, not out of the front door, and calm as could be, he walked back to his car, started it up, and drove away."

Merritt stood and stuffed her hands into the pockets of her jeans. She was in profile to me, and she looked even taller and leaner stretched out against the window.

"I almost went home right then. Figured Trent had already done what I wanted to do."

I waited a few beats. I said, "But you didn't go home?"

"No, I didn't. I rang the doorbell. Nobody answered. I rang it again. Nothing. So I went around back the same way Trent had come out of the yard."

I reminded myself that the preamble to this story had to do with why Merritt had chosen to be silent. I was aware of her breathing being labored and wondered where she was heading.

"There's all these doors back there that go into the house. And a big patio. And a pool with a fancy fence around it. I looked inside the house, didn't see anybody. So I tried the doors. One of them opened. I went in."

I had the strangest sensation right then, as though I were watching a movie and the music was reaching a crescendo and I knew something terrible was about to happen to one of the characters. I almost blurted out a warning to Merritt not to go in, to instead turn on her heels and run home. As fast as she could.

"When I did, I realized I had walked into this *theater*. The man has his own . . . private . . . theater. I couldn't believe it. He has this big mansion and a stupid swimming pool and his own private theater and all I want is to have my sister stay alive . . ."

I desperately wanted to see Merritt's face right then, but all I could see was a distorted reflection in the glass. It told me nothing.

"I looked around. Didn't say anything at first. I was just getting madder and madder and madder about the money he has that he wouldn't spend on Chaney." She spun right then and faced me, her hands still in her pockets. "I went down this little hallway and there was this door. It was closed. I opened it and that's when I saw him."

While her left hand covered her mouth, her eyes were seeing nothing in the present. She was revisiting some horror. And it was freezing her.

I said, "Go on, Merritt."

She swallowed. "I had never seen so much blood. It was everywhere. Everywhere."

What?

"It was like he had drowned in it. And then I saw the gun, down near the edge of the desk, and I didn't know what to do. I wanted to run. Maybe I should have run."

Run! Yes, run!

"But I tried to save him. I needed him to be alive to help Chaney. He was my only hope. I didn't want him dead."

Her forehead wrinkled into a frown. "He was slumped on this chair and I pulled him onto the floor—God, I wasn't strong enough and he just plopped down and blood splashed everywhere, and I, I—I've taken Red Cross lifesaving—and I tried to resuscitate him. Mouth-to-mouth. It was awful. There was blood in his mouth and each breath I forced into him made this sick noise and I was kneeling in his blood and his body felt so awful to touch and his damn heart wouldn't start beating and between breaths I was yelling at him and yelling at him not to let my little sister die."

She slid to the floor and leaned against the window wall. "But it was stupid. He was dead."

"You didn't kill him." I forced an inflection that made the words not sound like the question that they were.

"No, I didn't kill him. Trent did."

"You've been protecting your stepfather?"

She looked at me hard. "No, no. I'm *still* protecting my stepfather. Don't forget your promise."

"I haven't forgotten."

"Good."

She gestured out the window. "They're done out there. I want to go back and be with Chaney while she's still awake."

In a firm voice, I said, "I have some questions first. About what happened."

She smiled at me coolly. "They can wait. There's no hurry anymore. The man's dead, he can't help Chaney anymore."

I tried to counter. "But what about Brad? He's in serious jeopardy. Half the police in Colorado are after him."

"Brad? Screw Brad. He doesn't care about Chaney at all. Never did. Take me back out there."

I thought about it for a long time. I was in a power struggle with a teenager who had an array of weapons I couldn't match. In addition, she had two trump cards. One, of course, was her vow to return to silence. The other was a willingness to die for her cause.

I agreed to return Merritt to her sister's bedside while I was trying to figure out some way to explain to the psychiatric unit staff what I was doing so that it resembled something like a treatment plan.

Thirty-one

I made my way out of the ICU to the elevator lobby to head upstairs to make a note in Merritt's chart. As the elevator door opened, Sam Purdy stepped out, accompanied by his wife, Sherry.

It should have been an inconsequential visit, an aunt and uncle visiting a critically ill niece. Sadly, in tertiary care hospitals like this one, such visits happen all the time. But it wasn't an inconsequential hospital visit and Sam, Sherry, and I all knew it.

I said hello to the Purdys and they replied in hushed hospital tones.

Sherry Purdy is a pleasant woman, cautious interpersonally, but not shy. Every time I had ever seen her, she had always been quick with a smile. And every time I had spoken with her on the phone looking for Sam, I'd always been grateful for the effervescence in her greeting. Not this time, though. Sherry appeared tired and worn and her eyes were heavy and dark. Her clothes seemed to hang on her.

Sam said, "Where is Chaney, Alan?"

"Intensive care unit. It's halfway down this corridor on the right. Everyone is down there. Merritt, both of her parents."

Sherry snapped, "He is *not* her father."

What was that about? "Excuse me, Sherry, I misspoke. Both Merritt's mother and her stepfather are there."

Sam jumped in to douse whatever embers were threatening to flare. "Honey, you go ahead down to see her. You still want to do this alone, right?"

She managed a throaty "Yes," but didn't sound like she meant it.

"I'll be down soon," Sam said, planting a gentle kiss on her cheek.

She tried to force a smile onto her face before she turned and headed down the hall. I didn't know her well enough to know whether her dread over her long march was generated more by her niece's illness or was residue of her ancient feud with her sister.

I said, "Sherry's lost weight, Sam."

"She's ripped up by this. Chaney. Merritt. Having Brenda in town. It's been hard." He looked down the hall at Sherry. "You said Lucy told you about the extortion attempt? The phone call?"

"Yes, she told me. Anything new on it?"

"No more calls. Let's face it, if it was the two kids, they've had a little falling out since then. Brad's a proven asshole, by the way. His last two girl-friends both say he hit them."

I wasn't surprised. "Brad may follow through on the extortion on his own."

"If he's stupid enough to do that, everybody's ready for him this time."

"Do they know what the videotape was? The one he beat Madison with?"

"They're still piecing it together. So far, it looks like it was a badly recorded copy of *Pretty Woman*, taped straight off the network, commercials and everything. All the other videos in the RV were the commercial versions. You know, store bought. And no, I don't know what that means."

"Anything else?"

"No. You leaving the hospital?"

"Not yet. I have some paperwork to take care of upstairs in the psychiatric unit."

"I'll go with you. See if I can read something over your shoulder."

I said, "Fine. You learn anything new about the threats that were being made?"

He puffed out one cheek and arched his eyebrows. I didn't know what it meant. But he didn't answer my question. I figured that he'd tell me when he had something and when he was ready. No sooner.

We had an elevator to ourselves on the way upstairs. I said, "This has to be hard for Sherry. The visit, I mean, coming here."

"Yeah, sure is. It needed to happen, though—seeing her sister and the kids. Sherry's been on the outside of this too long." He paused a moment, enough to scratch under his nose. "Listen, your empathy's real sweet and everything, but, uh, things you don't know about are getting goofy. Nothing's making much sense to me anymore about Merritt and . . ."

His voice faded as the electronic chime announced we had reached the third floor. No one entered.

Sam faced me again when the doors closed. "See, it turns out that Merritt was not only in Dead Ed's house, she was also in Dead Ed's RV."

"What?"

The doors opened at the fourth floor and I followed him out. I yanked him into an unoccupied room that had two empty cribs in it and repeated, "What? She was in the damn RV? What the hell was she doing in the RV?"

"I don't know. When we did the search of her bedroom in her house—you know, after you found the bloody clothes?—we found an earring in the trash can under her desk. Just one, a little silver cross. Didn't make much of it. Till now. Because it turns out the other one was in Dead Ed's RV."

"What?"

He examined me critically. "Great questions you're asking. You suffer some brain damage since I saw you last? I could use some thoughtfulness here."

I realized that by my stupefied reaction to his news, I had just demonstrated clearly to him that my work with Merritt hadn't covered the topic of any visits she might have made to Dead Ed's Holiday Rambler. Sam hadn't impinged on his niece's confidentiality at all and he knew exactly what he had come to find out from me.

"Fingerprints?" I asked.

"Yep. Plenty. Not matched yet, but they'll be hers. You know where they found it? The earring?"

"No, where?"

"It had fallen down between the mattress and the headboard in the bedroom. Damn Winnebago has an actual bedroom, can you believe it?"

"In the bedroom?"

Sam shook his head at me disdainfully. I sat down. I wanted to protest his news. I desperately wanted to tell him that Merritt had just told me she hadn't done it. That she had just gone over to Dead Ed's house to beg for her sister's welfare. That Dead Ed was already Dead Ed when she got there. That it was John Trent who had been there first.

That it was John Trent who had killed Dr. Edward Robilio.

But when I calculated in all the facts that Merritt wasn't telling me I also realized that my faith in what she was telling me was rapidly diminishing.

Sam recognized that I was in the midst of some kind of internal struggle. He said, "What? What aren't you telling me, Alan? Has she started talking to you?"

I said, "You know I can't say, Sam. If she has started talking, telling anyone about it would shut her up in a second. You know that."

He slapped the wall so hard I was surprised he didn't crack it. "God, I hate this crap. This is my goddamned niece we're talking about."

"I know. You're not alone, Sam. Right now, I hate this crap, too. She's downstairs with her sister. Go see for yourself if she's talking."

"This is bullshit. I'm going to go find Sherry."

"Good luck."

"Piss on that. I'd need less luck if you would just tell me what the hell you know."

With that, he headed out.

Five minutes later he had himself buzzed onto the adolescent psych unit. He found me in the nursing station struggling to write a chart note that said something without saying anything. He said, "Sherry's still with Brenda. Merritt's talking to Chaney. I don't want to interrupt them. You almost done here?"

"Couple more minutes." Sam was calm, even conciliatory. I mistrusted the change I was seeing.

He said, "Good, I want to show you something. You don't mind?"

"No." I finished up my note and renewed some orders and followed him to the elevator. I was surprised that he hit the button that would drop us off at the hospital lobby, not the second floor ICU. I didn't bother asking him where he was going.

His department car was parked in a fire zone near the main entrance. We climbed in and he drove in silence, south for a while, then east across Colorado Boulevard at Sixth Avenue and south again on Birch. The neighborhood we entered is called Hilltop and is one of Denver's finest.

He parked diagonally across the street from a huge house that had been squeezed onto its lot by a giant's shoehorn. Sam killed his engine and doused the lights.

He pointed at the big stucco house with the faux Spanish railings and said, "Why do I think I would have liked better whatever house was here before somebody scraped it off and knocked down all the trees and built that monster?"

I said, "I don't know, but you're probably right. It certainly doesn't fit in the neighborhood." Given how distrustful I was of his mood, at that moment I probably would have agreed with him even if he was contending that Darwin was full of shit.

Sam grew silent.

I was anxious. I said, "Given their meeting tonight, this might be a good time to tell me about Sherry and Brenda, Sam. I may need to know."

He made a noise with his throat before he said, "First time they've talked in, what, shit, how old is Merritt?"

"Fifteen."

"Maybe sixteen years, then. Merritt's important because Merritt's father, her biological father, the oil-rig guy? He was actually Sherry's fiancé before . . . well—"

"Oh."

"Sherry says Brenda seduced him, stole him, whatever. Brenda would probably say different. Doesn't matter now. Whatever it was, it was goofy, right?"

I digested the news. "That's it?"

"That's it. What can I say? Sherry holds a grudge. I've tried to tell her that the consolation prize wasn't so bad."

"You mean Simon, of course."

"Funny, Alan." Sam's voice shifted an octave lower. It busted into my reverie. "Homeowner's name across the way is Terence Gusman, Dr. Terence Gusman. Ring a bell?"

"Nope."

"You're sure?"

I thought about the name some more. "Yes, I'm sure. Don't know him."

Sam pondered something before he said, "He's one of the suspects that the Denver PD liked for the threats and harassment of Brenda after the recycling story."

"Ahh."

He sighed. "Don't be arrogant, Alan. You're still ignorant. You don't have a clue why I brought you here, do you?"

I knew I couldn't rely on his improved demeanor to have a half-life of more than five minutes. "No, Sam, I don't."

"Then shut up and let me educate you."

"Excuse me." I tried to keep the sarcasm from my voice. I wasn't sure how much more of his attitude I was going to put up with. He was already receiving a lot of slack from me for his family crisis, but the account he was rapidly using up wasn't infinite.

"Turns out that dear Dr. Gusman is the twin brother of that woman who had the heart attack while she watched her husband hanging himself from the rafters in their garage. Remember that story? Mayor of what—Northglenn?—I don't know, tries to kill himself after Brenda links him to the recycling scandal, his wife has a coronary when she finds him hanging from the rafters? He lives, she dies."

"I remember the story. Ugly. I suppose it certainly gives Dr. Gusman a gold-plated reason to be angry at Brenda."

"Yes, does that. Establishes motive. That's always important to me. Motive."

"You talked to him yet? Gusman?"

"No. That wouldn't be kosher. My role's a little unofficial on this."

"Are the Denver cops sure that he was the person who was threatening Brenda?"

"He looked good when they interviewed him. But they have no plans to charge him. So they're not that sure. The guy was careful. And the threats and the incidents have ended. It's back-burner time as far as they're concerned."

"What do you think?"

Sam nodded at the house and, as though Dr. Gusman was standing in the front yard, said, "I like him."

"Any reason in particular?"

"I checked out his background. Sometimes backgrounds tell you things. Knowing people's histories, you know. Kind of like your work, in a way. Anyway, know what kind of doc he is?"

"Oh, shit, Sam. He's not one of Chaney's doctors, is he?"

"Not to worry. He was a general practitioner, but he doesn't practice right now. He was disciplined by the state medical board after the *Denver Post* ran a series of articles accusing him of sexual improprieties with three female patients. Two female members of his own office staff even gave affidavits supporting parts of the women's accusations."

Now I recalled the news reports. "I remember something. This was a while ago, right?"

"June of '87. He blamed the whole thing on the media. Said the charges were groundless, that the women made it all up. Disgruntled employees. You know how the denials go, you could probably write the lyrics."

"Did he lose his license?"

"*Please.* State medical board taking away a license? Of course not, had his wrist slapped. He gave up his practice, though, decided to do other things."

"So Dr. Gusman has a predisposition to distrust media people in general, and he has a particular reason to dislike Brenda?"

" 'Dislike'?"

"How about 'hate'?"

"Better word. You could say hate."

"What does he do now?"

Sam hesitated until I looked over at him. He had a piercing, amused look on his face that reminded me of how my dog gets when she's sure she's about to corral a squirrel. The difference is that Emily never gets her squirrel, Sam rarely misses his.

"Dr. Terence Gusman's new line of work is in administration . . . what he does is he chairs the medical evaluation review board at MedExcel."

I almost chuckled at the utter simplicity of the news. "This is the french fry you've been looking for? You found it, didn't you?"

He nodded. "It's one of them. But all along, I've been working under the assumption that this meal has at least two truant french fries."

"Go on."

"In case you're having difficulty counting, I have two nieces in trouble, Alan. Finding Dr. Gusman may help me influence Chaney's situation. It's not going to do shit for Merritt's. I still feel compelled to goose that one as far as I can."

"What are you going to do about Gusman?"

"I just put the pieces together a couple of hours ago and I've been thinking about how to proceed. Time is of the essence, right? And I think things might go better for Chaney if I give MedExcel a chance to do the right thing. For the time being, leave me, and law enforcement in general, out of it, you know. So I think I'm going to need a doctor to act as a go-between with MedExcel. Perhaps encourage them to see that they have a potential public relations crisis brewing and that it may be in their best interest to make a small humanitarian gesture, if you know what I mean."

"Sam, I'd love to help, but I can't. Not while I'm treating Chaney's sister."

He seemed to find my refusal amusing. "Not *you*, asshole. I'm looking for a real doctor. I was thinking one of Chaney's doctors might help. I was going to approach them tonight when things calmed down at the hospital."

I didn't think it was wise to get them mixed up in this during an acute medical crisis. I suggested an alternative. "What about Adrienne? You know, my urologist friend? She treated Merritt. She knows the family, the whole situation. I bet she'd love to do it. And Adrienne's as Machiavellian as they come."

"She's dating Maitlin, isn't she?"

I wasn't sure what that had to do with anything, and I wasn't exactly sure how to answer that question. "Kind of," I said.

Sam was smiling. "You know, it's not a bad idea. She's relentless. She's smart. I'd like to have a ticket to that meeting. Maybe she'd record it for me, you think?"

I stared across the street at Dr. Gusman's front door and wondered whose idea it had been to paint it the color of cantaloupe flesh. "Sam, it's possible that Robilio had nothing to do with any of this, isn't it?"

"You mean that he was an innocent bystander?"

"I guess."

"That health insurance policy he's selling to the masses is like a car with a busted airbag. Works fine except in the most dire of emergencies. I wouldn't exactly call him innocent."

"But I mean, in terms of the refusal to grant the procedure for Chaney? You're thinking that Gusman engineered that, not Robilio?"

"Looks that way. But Robilio could've overruled the medical board. I checked. He's a physician, too. And he ran the company like an ayatollah. He could've approved it if he wanted to."

"This changes things. Makes me wonder about other things I haven't given much thought to."

"Yeah? Such as?"

I said, "That day, before the hockey game, at his house. How confused everybody was. You know, Scott Truscott said the scene was a puzzle, so did Mitchell Crest. You've been perplexed, too. And the note we found on the computer? I haven't thought about it much since we found the bloody clothes in Merritt's room."

"I think I hear the rustling sounds of someone digging around for that other french fry."

"Is there any way you can get me a copy of Dead Ed's suicide note? And a copy of the post?"

He laughed deeply. "Now you're thinking. You know, I was wondering when you were going to actually begin to act intelligent about all this. Maybe the time has come. I hope so."

"Well, when can I see the note? And the autopsy?"

"The autopsy report won't be done for a few weeks. But I have a copy of Malloy's notes from his meeting with the coroner. I think they're in the backseat somewhere. While I'm looking for them, why don't you see if you can track down your conspiratorial little urologist friend for me. Go ahead, use my phone."

Thirty-two

Sam parked his car in the same fire zone spot in front of the main entrance to the hospital. He was still on the phone with Adrienne.

I wasn't quite done reading the loose sheets of paper he had given me. From what I could discern from eavesdropping on their conversation, they were role-playing what Adrienne was going to say to the powers at MedExcel to blackmail them into transporting Chaney to Seattle by, let's say, tomorrow morning. Sam offered Adrienne a few juicy tidbits from his investigation that she could use as sweeteners if they were needed in her argument.

I suspected they wouldn't be needed. A few minutes earlier, when I had reached Adrienne on Sam's phone and told her what was up, she was an eager volunteer. She'd made it clear that her strategy would be to plot a devastating ambush on MedExcel, not engage them in a protracted battle. She would be attacking this surgically, as though it were a particularly aggressive bladder cancer.

The notes that I was reading had been taken by the lead detective, Scott Malloy, during an informal interview with Boulder's coroner, a forensic pathologist. I knew from experience that the findings were preliminary.

Edward Robilio had undiagnosed coronary artery disease and an enlarged prostate. He had multiple polyps in his large intestine and an ingrown toenail on his left foot that was so inflamed it must have made his last few walks around the block pretty painful.

What killed him—the cause of death—were two gunshot wounds, the first "of chest" that missed his heart and major vessels, but clipped his lung and chipped some bone in the spinal column. The wound was, according to the coroner's assessment, of "vital reaction," likely a slow but persistent bleeder. In the coroner's opinion, without competent and timely emergency care, that first wound alone would have eventually been fatal to Dr. Robilio.

The second gunshot wound was "of head," specifically, a bullet entered Ed's face just left of his nose and exited, along with a chunk of skull the size of an apricot, behind his left ear. This shot clipped major vessels, turned gray matter into jello and was fatal within minutes.

No surprises.

A copy of the death certificate was stapled to Malloy's notes. I searched for the coroner's opinion on manner of death. This category is not the "why" of dying—that's cause of death. Manner of death is about motivation or intent. Manner of death is the "how" of dying—whether by suicide, homicide, accident, or disease. And with this death certificate on Dr. Robilio, the Boulder coroner was telling his undoubtedly unhappy compatriots in the police department and district attorney's office that the manner of death on this one was still too close to call. The words were, "Pending further investigation."

The coroner could rule out accident. He could rule out disease. He could even rule out act of God. But he couldn't rule out either suicide or homicide. Those manners of death were still on the table.

Malloy's notes were comprehensive. The gunshots had both been fired from close range, estimated at one to three inches, consistent with suicide, and at angles not inconsistent with either suicide or homicide. Gunshot residue and trace metal detection tests were positive for the victim's shirt, face, torso, hair, and shoulders. But the victim's right hand—Dead Ed was right-handed—was so drenched by his own blood that the tests done on it for trace metals were inconclusive. Dr. Robilio's wounds may have been self-inflicted; there was nothing to indicate he wasn't holding the gun.

And from a forensic pathology perspective there was nothing to indicate that he *was* holding the gun.

The coroner raised two other points that Malloy labeled "subjective impressions." The first was that the deceased may have been so debilitated by the first wound that he would have been physically incapable of firing the second shot, which would indicate homicide, not suicide. And second, psychological data from coroner's assistant interviews with family and business associates provided no prodromal signs of acute depression or pre-suicidal activity other than the typed suicide note.

The second document that Sam gave me complicated everything I had just read. It was that typed suicide note, printed out from Ed Robilio's tiny computer. The note was addressed to no one and was oddly formal in tone. The structure reminded me of a business memo. The note asked that Beth be thanked for her partnership and for bearing their beautiful children. The note expressed sorrow for what Robilio had done and what he hadn't done. It left instructions on where to find some financial documents that Beth might need.

It was unsigned.

Sam held up the phone and said, "I'm done here. You need to talk to Adrienne anymore?"

"Uh, no. Would you ask her to take care of Emily for me?"

He closed up his phone and said, "She already did. After she turns you in to Dumb Friends, she's going to start making those calls to MedExcel."

"Good, Sam. You did a remarkable job in putting this together. You going to tell Brenda and John?"

"You kidding? Why?"

"You're right, they don't need to know."

He recognized my distraction. "So what's troubling you?"

I held the papers up off my lap. "What is it with Dead Ed? Suicide or homicide?"

"Heads or tails?"

"They really don't know?"

"Here's the problem with the suicide theory: Do you know what percentage of suicides use two shots to kill themselves? It's like one in googoolplux."

"Googoolplux?"

"It's Simon's word for bigger than infinity. And then there's the little problem of where the hell did the gun go afterwards? I don't think he drove it over to Merritt's house in his RV."

"But the note is good, Sam. It isn't a garden-variety forgery. No adolescent could write it."

"No, it's not. So, if it's a forgery, it's a good forgery. One written by somebody with some knowledge, you know. It's like a note that someone like you, maybe a psychologist type, might write."

Sam was leaving tracks in the sand. "You're thinking John Trent?"

"You could do it, right?"

I shrugged. I could do it. So could Sam.

"He could write it, too, then."

This wasn't making sense. "Why wouldn't Robilio have fought back? The gun was so close to him." I ruffled through the papers with the autopsy impressions on them. The coroner apparently reported no signs of struggle, no defensive wounds.

"Speculation? I'd guess he was paralyzed by the fact that there was a gun two inches from his chest. By the time the second shot was fired he was already too gorked to notice the damn gun was pointing at his face."

"Let's go back to motive, Sam. What good does it do Trent? So Robilio's dead? That isn't going to help Chaney. May even hurt her."

"I'm not arguing for a rational state of mind. Rage and retribution are good motives. That's sufficient at this stage of my thinking."

"Is that how you're putting this together? You think Trent went nuts, killed Robilio, and staged everything else?"

He turned suddenly and I tensed. His voice had the chilled hiss of compressed air. "You know something that should make me think otherwise?"

I considered what he was asking. "You won't misinterpret my answer, Sam?"

"I'll certainly try not to."

"No, I don't know anything that should make you think otherwise. But," I paused for emphasis, "I have to wonder whether you think he's ruthless enough to set his stepdaughter up to take the fall."

"Should I be thinking that he's that ruthless?"

I reminded myself to be careful. "Cold enough to trade his stepdaughter for his daughter? I think Trent would donate both his lungs to save Chaney. But—gut feeling now, okay?—I don't think Trent would sacrifice Merritt to save her."

"So how did the bloody clothes get under her bed? How did the gun end up in her bathroom?"

"Maybe she put them there, Sam."

"Merritt?"

I shrugged.

"Or . . . Brenda?" he said.

Did he know something about Brenda? I certainly didn't, so I didn't respond to his question. Merritt's revelations about her visit to Dr. Robilio's house were hovering close by. I didn't want to break that trust. "Where did they find the fingernail, Sam? Merritt's broken nail?"

From the look on his face, I harbored little hope he was going to answer, so I was surprised when he said, "I'll give you one. A freebie. Master bathroom. Second floor. Below the window."

"*Upstairs?*"

"Upstairs."

"What was she doing upstairs?"

"Funny question. It's as though you already know what she was doing in the rest of the house."

Upstairs in the ICU the girls were asleep together in the same bed. Trent was pacing outside in the corridor.

He said, "They went downstairs to talk. Sherry and Brenda. I'm really glad she came."

I asked, "How are things?"

"Same. Right now, stable feels like a gift."

Sam said, "You look like you could use a little break, John. Why don't you take one? I'll stay close to the girls until the wives get back."

"Thanks, Sam, I think I will. I could use a little time. I'll be in the building but I have my pager on. The nurse has the number."

Sam checked in with the nurse at the ICU and I followed Trent as he shuffled away toward the elevators.

"John, can I have a minute?"

"Sure."

"You, um, remember anything—I don't know—additional about your visit to Dr. Robilio's house that may help me understand things better?"

"Help you how?" His voice was edgy. I'd woken him up a little.

I felt as though I had to choose my reply as carefully as if I were adding a king of hearts to a five-story house of cards. "I'm still trying to understand what she heard, what she saw, you know, something that might have motivated her to go over there that day."

"She knew how angry I was."

"Yes?"

"That's all."

"That's all?"

I thought he hesitated, but I couldn't be sure. "If I think of anything else, I'll tell you. It's been a long day, Alan. I'm going to rest a little."

I wanted to press him, ask him if he was involved in the custody eval for Robilio's sister-in-law. I couldn't.

I woke Merritt to take her back upstairs for the night. It took two seconds to rouse her, much longer to calm the adrenaline surge she had upon awakening. She kissed her Uncle Sam on the cheek before mounting a meek protest about returning to the psychiatric unit to sleep.

When we arrived upstairs all the other kids were down for the night. The unit was quiet, surreal. Sometimes I'm surprised that adolescents actually require slumber like other homo sapiens.

A nurse checked Merritt onto the unit, made sure she had eaten.

When they were done with their routine I said to Merritt, "We need to talk some more, come with me."

She protested, her voice wary. She said, "I'm tired."

I said, "Too bad, we're all tired," and led her to the familiar consultation room.

I sat down and made certain there was an unmistakable edge in my voice as I said, "You're not being honest with me, Merritt." I wanted her to find my manner disconcerting.

She sat on the edge of her chair and chewed at her upper lip before she said, "I haven't lied to you." The tenor of her words was explanatory, not defensive.

"Well, simply not lying to me is no longer good enough."

She yawned. "How about tomorrow?"

"No, now. I actually think I'm prepared to sit here all night."

She huffed, "Screw you, then, you can sit here by yourself." She stood, reaching for the doorknob. "I'm done talking to you."

"If that's the case, you won't be going back downstairs tomorrow, Merritt."

She hissed, "You wouldn't do that."

I wouldn't do that, she was right, but she couldn't be sure. Nor could she know that I had another trump card that I was keeping pressed against my chest. I didn't respond.

Again, she said, "You wouldn't?" while she stared at my impassive face. Finally she nodded. "You would, wouldn't you? You would keep me from seeing her. God, I can't believe I trusted you."

"With any luck, your sister won't be in the ICU tomorrow, Merritt."

"What do you mean? What's happening?"

I turned my hands palms-up. "This is a two-way street. I'm not going to do all the talking."

"What is this, blackmail?"

"Technically, no. Call it leverage. That's a more pleasant word."

"I want to call downstairs and talk to my parents. They'll tell me."

"I don't think so. Unit rules don't allow middle-of-the-night phone calls. I hope your parents and your sister are resting."

"You jerk."

"Talk to me, Merritt. Tell me what happened."

"You want me to just give up, don't you?"

"Yes, I want you to give up."

"No! What good is it going to do anybody? Why should I give up?"

I said a silent prayer to the gods who controlled prescience, exhaled, and said, "Because I know about the videotape."

Ten minutes passed. She disappeared into a cocoon of confusion, or despair, or something. I considered the possibility that I had stunned her back into volitional silence. And I considered the possibility that I was so far off the mark with my speculation that she no longer considered me worth talking to.

She was looking at her feet when she said, "Have you seen it? The tape?"

"Tell me about it."

"Have you seen the damn thing? Tell me that first. God."

At that moment, it took all my professional resolve not to walk across the room and take her into my arms and rock her until all her fear and despair dissolved into the night air.

But I sat without moving. I watched without blinking. I didn't swallow and I wasn't aware of breathing.

"Do my parents know? At least tell me that."

"I haven't told them."

She blurted out, "It was all Madison's idea," and she buried her face in her hands.

I said, "Take your time, Merritt. Take your time."

She folded her arms and unfolded them. She chanced a glance at me, then away. For a moment she seemed fascinated by her hair. She wiped tear tracks from her face and tried to swallow, but her mouth was too dry.

I didn't offer her anything to drink.

"You know I didn't shoot him, right?"

Tell her you hear her, don't be too committal. "I remember where we left off earlier."

"I almost killed myself right there. In his house. With the gun. His gun. I picked it up and pointed it at my head." She extended the index finger of her right hand, cocked her thumb up, and touched her fingernail to a spot an inch above her right ear. "I put it back down once and then I picked it up again. The whole time I was kneeling in all the blood. I was covered in his blood and I could taste it in my mouth from trying to resuscitate him, and I didn't see any way out of it but to die."

Years before, in my training, as I listened to the pathos of a young woman who had survived a serious suicide attempt, I enjoyed a revelation that it was one of the only times doing therapy that I would know in advance how the story turned out. I shared my insight with my supervisor. She told me I was wrong. She said, "Don't be cocky, you don't know how the story ends. You only know how this chapter turns out."

I reminded myself of that lesson.

"The phone rang. I screamed. I needed to get out of there. I was still going to kill myself, so I picked up the gun and I ran as fast as I could." She laughed. "I got outside and I saw that I was covered in blood. And I was carrying a gun. It was all so weird, I mean, think about it. So I stopped in his backyard and took off my sweatshirt and used it to wipe some of the blood off my legs and hands and I wrapped the gun in it and I walked home. A couple of people saw me. I thought they looked at me funny. But they didn't say anything."

I sighed, saddened. I wanted to say, "No, Merritt, go back. You're forgetting to tell me about going upstairs and breaking your fingernail in the bathroom. You're forgetting to tell me about losing your earring in the Holiday Rambler."

But I didn't. Instead, I catalogued the omissions, reminding myself that they were at least as important as the inclusions.

"When I got home, nobody was there. Trent was with Chaney. Mom was at work. I called Madison and told her that he was dead, that it was all over—"

What was all over?

"And that I had his gun and I was going to kill myself with it. But I kept thinking about all the blood and I couldn't do it to myself. Shoot myself. So I went to Mom's dressing table and I took all her drugs. Everything. And then I took a shower. I didn't want his blood on me when I died.

"That's all I remember until the hospital when I had the tube down my throat."

She spoke the last line with determination, as if to say, "There, are you satisfied?"

I wasn't. "Why?"

"Why what?"

"Why did you take the pills? Why did you want to die?"

She said, "Because I couldn't save Chaney." And she managed to say those words with an almost sincere level of conviction. If I didn't know other things, I would have been likely to believe her.

But I knew other things.

"You said you told Madison 'it was all over.' What was all over?"

She was silent.

I said, "This looks like it's going to be a very long night."

She muttered, "It already is."

I closed my eyes and felt a luxurious moment of calm. When I opened them, I said, "Your missing earring?" She flicked a glance at me. "You've been wondering where you lost that, haven't you?"

Her lower lip dropped.

"The earring—the little silver cross?—it was in the Holiday Rambler, Dr. Robilio's motorhome. And the videotape? We haven't talked much about that yet, have we?"

"You know everything already."

"This isn't about what I know. It's about what you are able to tell me."

"I don't get it."

"I'm a psychologist, not a cop. I care about the facts, but not as much as I care about you."

A quick couplet of knocks cracked on the door. A nurse poked her head into the room.

"Dr. Gregory? May I have a minute? I think it's important."

I left the consultation room door open so I could keep an eye on Merritt. The nurse cupped her hand and whispered, "Detective Purdy called. He said to tell you it looks good. That it's up to the doctors now. That the docs here at Children's will talk to the docs in . . ."—she looked at a pink index card in her hand—". . . Seattle in the morning. You know what all that means?"

I nodded, smiling, and thought, *Good work, Adrienne.*

She said, "Is this about the little girl? Merritt's sister?"

"Yes. She may be getting a break. Keep it to yourself, okay?"

"Of course."

"Thanks. Could you please find us something to drink? Something with caffeine for me, something without caffeine for Merritt."

She was back with two cans of pop in less than a minute. She handed them to me and said, "Good luck in there with her. She's a tough kid." I thought I heard some admiration in her words.

I half smiled. "She is that."

Thirty-three

Merritt was curled up on the loveseat in the consultation room, asleep, her hair falling over one eye like a spill of fine lace. She looked innocent and fresh and vulnerable, a huge child right then, not a young adult.

I considered letting her sleep. I also considered tracking down an empty on-call room and sleeping myself. Tempting, but not prudent.

I said, "Merritt?" She didn't respond.

A touch to her shoulder caused her to twitch, but not to waken. I leaned my mouth close to her ear and spoke her name again. She sat up in a panic, the side of her head crashing into the side of mine just above my ear, the impact sending me tumbling across the room.

She woke dazed but with some recognition of what was going on. She touched her head with her hand and said, "God, I'm sorry."

I asked, "Are you okay?" as I pulled myself to a sitting position.

She rubbed her ear. "I think so. You?"

"I'm fine. It woke me up. I guess that's good." I nodded toward the table. "I brought you a Sprite. Thought you might be thirsty."

She popped open the can and took a tentative sip. Over the top of the can, she eyed me and said, "Thanks. What did you mean before? That you cared about me more than you cared about what happened?"

Like her uncle, she surprised me. "When I first saw you in the hospital in Boulder—remember?—your doctors weren't sure you were going to live. Your suicide attempt was that serious. I haven't forgotten that morning. Since then, it's been difficult for me to, I don't know, feel much confidence that you aren't still planning to find a way to kill yourself. I'm not going to pretend that I don't want to know what happened with you and Dr. Robilio, and what Madison had to do with it, because I do. But more than that, I need to know that you can be trusted, that you're safe, that you've found a reason not to try to kill yourself again. And it's important that I learn what I need to know tonight."

"Why tonight?"

I frowned. "It has to do with your sister, Merritt. Your Uncle Sam is a remarkable man. I know you hardly know him, but he's a special guy, believe me. Anyway, he's been busy trying to help, and he may have managed to work some magic in regard to the insurance situation. Your whole family may get some long-overdue good news in the morning. If that happens, I'd like to feel enough confidence in your mental state to consider discharging you from the hospital so you can be part of it."

"Won't they just arrest me if you let me out?"

"I don't know the answer to that. They haven't arrested you yet. Your lawyer says that's a good sign."

She sat forward. "What did Uncle Sam do? Tell me. Is it about Chaney?"

"Nothing is certain yet. Sam is still working on some things. We'll know in the morning."

"She'll get the drugs? And the new heart?"

Despite myself, I smiled. "We'll know in the morning."

"I'm going with her."

I nodded. "Now you see my dilemma. If it does turn out that Chaney is able to go to Seattle, I'd like you to be able to go with her, too. You have a remarkable relationship with her. But—"

"You need to make sure I'm not crazy."

"I know you're not crazy, Merritt. What I want to be certain of is that you're not concealing a plan to try to kill yourself as soon as I give you half a chance. You're a bright kid, you could fool me if you wanted to."

She was taken aback by my frankness. "Whoa. I didn't think you were supposed to say things like that to patients. That's not too subtle."

"What you did wasn't subtle, Merritt."

Her mouth widened and her eyes smiled sadly. "Oh, yes, it was, Dr. Gregory," she said, "oh, yes, it was. It was a very good plan."

She was waiting for me to react. I could tell. But I was too far in the dark to do much more than raise an eyebrow and shrug.

She exhaled and said, "You haven't seen the videotape, have you?"

I shook my head and said, "No, I haven't."

"Good, I'm glad. That will make it easier to tell you what happened. A lot easier. Because I really can't believe what I did."

My sense right then was that she had crossed an important threshold and my work no longer had to do with inviting her to talk, or putting enough pressure on her resistance to cause it to fracture. My work now had to do with being patient enough to let her tell her story.

I smiled, warmly I thought, and said, "You know, it was all Madison's idea."

She laughed.

"When we left off, last time, you were telling me about Madison's breasts."

She smiled again, and then I watched her face dissolve into sadness. "I haven't cried much about her yet. I think I will when everything else settles down."

"Yes."

"Madison thought we could blackmail him. Dr. Robilio. Trick him into doing something, you know, sexual, with her—Madison—and take pictures of it. Then, you know, we'd blackmail him. Make him give Chaney the treatment she needs or we'd give somebody the pictures. His wife or his boss or somebody. The newspapers, I don't know.

"At first I thought she was kidding. Then, when I realized she wasn't kidding, I told her she was crazy. Then I thought about it some more. I thought, Trent had tried to do something to help, and he couldn't do anything. My mom had gone on the news, and she had begged for help, and she couldn't do anything. I felt I had to try to do something, too. For Chaney.

"So I called Madison back and asked if she was serious. She was, she was ready to go. She'd already been thinking more about it, too. She said she was sure she could get him to come on to her. She was absolutely sure. All I had to do was get in a place to take the pictures. That was all.

"I said no, that I'd been thinking about how to do it, too. That Chaney was my sister. That I was the one who should seduce him and that she was the one who would take the pictures. She laughed. She thought I was crazy. She wondered what I knew about it. She meant," Merritt paused and looked at her lap, "what did I know about sex . . . and seducing someone and . . . what did I know about men. I don't even have a boyfriend, Dr. Gregory. Everybody thinks I'm kind of a prude."

She shrugged. "I said I could do it. She could teach me. She said, 'Fine, I dare you,' and said she'd get her mom's video camera.

"She gave me some ideas about what to do and say and the next day after school we went to his house and I waited till he came out for his walk, and after a block or two, I jogged after him. I ran up next to him and I asked him if he minded some company, that I didn't want to run by myself anymore, some kids had been bothering me. He said he didn't think he could keep up with me. I said I was just about done, it was okay with me, could I just walk with him, did he mind?

"I thought it was sort of cool. What I was doing—I mean, he didn't know who I was. He didn't know I was Chaney's sister. He didn't know I was setting him up. It felt kind of . . . I don't know, I don't know."

"Powerful?"

"Yeah, powerful, but also scary. He asked me my name. I told him it was Merritt. He said he had a daughter about my age. I asked how old she was. He said she was *twenty*, can you believe it? I didn't know if he was, you know, BS-ing me or what, but he didn't come on to me. I was sort of hoping he would, it would have made it easier, I guess.

"When we got back by his house, he pointed at it from the sidewalk, and said, 'I'm home.' I acted impressed, said what a great house it was. I wanted him to invite me in, but I didn't know if his wife was home, or if he really had kids, or even if Madison had a way to take the pictures we needed if I went inside with him.

"I got more scared then. All of a sudden, I felt like my plan sucked and I didn't know what to do. I mean, Madison and I hadn't thought this through as well as we thought. I saw the RV in his driveway. Have you seen it? It's a big thing—I mean it looks like a rock star's bus."

"Yes, I've seen it."

"I asked him if it was his. He asked if I wanted to see it. I told him I had always wanted to go inside one. He told me to wait, he would go in the house and get the keys."

"Madison was there?"

"Yeah, she was sneaking around somewhere taking her video. I didn't see her, she was good, you know, at staying hidden. Her mom's car was parked a couple houses down. When Dr. Robilio went inside the house to get the keys I pointed at the RV behind my back so Madison would know where I was going next."

I was flooded with feelings. Merritt's motives were admirable. The story I was about to hear, I felt certain, was abominable, the outcome undoubtedly catastrophic. I was breathless, and inwardly anticipation was clawing at me. Outwardly, I pretended I was listening to a problem she was having at school.

"When he came back out, he had changed his clothes, put on these awful jeans and this big sweater with CU on it over this big brown buffalo head. Not a sweatshirt, a sweater. He said, 'Come on, I'll show you my baby.' He was gross, I wanted to puke. He unlocked the door and climbed in. I followed him. He sat in the driver's seat. He said something like, 'You could live in this, live well, too. This thing has satellite TV, surround sound, full kitchen, big bathroom, king-size bed. Better than a yacht. Pretty neat, huh?'

"I can still hear him talking to me, Dr. Gregory. I was looking at this crazy, fancy bus, and I was getting so mad and I was feeling sick to my stomach, like I was gonna puke, I swear. That would have been cool, right? I asked him how much it cost. I didn't care, I mean like I wasn't impressed by it. I just had this crazy idea that maybe I could just steal the thing and trade it back to him for Chaney, that I wouldn't actually have to . . . you know."

I knew.

She was mimicking Dead Ed's voice when she resumed her story, " 'It's a ninety-six Holiday Rambler. Custom interior, totally custom. You want to know what it costs? Well, are you ready for this? After I put in a few special touches, this baby cost me four hundred and fifteen thousand dollars. And I wrote a check for it. You should have seen Manny's face when I did that. Manny was the guy who sold it to me. He couldn't believe I would just write a check for it like I was buying my wife a damn Hyundai.'

"I don't know if I should tell you this part, because I don't even know if it's true. Madison used to, she used to lie sometimes. But Madison . . . anyway, you would need to know her to understand. She was . . . I don't know. Madison says she—don't think of her this way, okay?—she says she hooked a little bit, you know—she did it for money. With some rich guys. They would buy her stuff if she slept with them. That's what she said. She showed me the stuff—jewelry, a watch, and shoes, God, she loved shoes. She says the men bought it all for her just for doing it with them. She said

I could do it, too, if I wanted. She would introduce me to this lady who sets it all up. Said it was easy."

Merritt waited for a reaction. I eased back into statue mode. There wasn't a way of knowing what a correct response might be. No response would have to do. I'd heard about middle-class girls hooking for spending money. I'd never run into it up close, though.

"Maddy told me to be shy with him, you know, like coy. She said they liked that better. She said to kind of accidentally let them see something, then not act bothered, and then wait." She shrugged, shook her head. "So that's what I did. You ever been inside this thing, this motor home of his?"

I was grateful for the non sequitur. "No."

"The bedroom's in back. The door was open; I could see in. There was this big bed with this gold bedspread on it. It looked like my mom and Trent's room, but, I don't know, tackier. I didn't want to go in there, I really didn't. Oh, I almost forgot, Maddy had given me a rubber. I had it in my sock. The night before, she made me practice putting them on a zucchini. This is all so weird." She covered her eyes with her hand and shook her head. "I didn't know how I was going to explain that to him, I mean, having a condom in my sock. I was about to seduce an old, ugly man, and I was worrying about the strangest stuff. You know how I kept going?"

I could have guessed.

"I thought about Chaney. I mean, how strange is this? I'm about to screw somebody for the first time in my life. Somebody I hate. And in order to make myself go through with it, I'm thinking about my baby sister.

"Anyway, he sits back on one of these leather sofas near the front and I start fumbling around in the kitchen. I mean, I'm so nervous and I ask if he has anything to drink. He tells me to look in the fridge. There's a Coke. I grab a can and go to take a drink and when I do, I pour some down my front, you know, like an accident, but on purpose.

"I kind of squeal and pull off my T-shirt." She closed her eyes and I felt three thumps of my pulse before she continued. "I know what I'm doing, okay. When I crossed my arms to pull up my shirt, I hooked my fingers under . . ." she lowers her head, her eyes still shut, "under . . . my bra, you know, it's a running bra, and I pull everything over my head together, all at once. The T-shirt and my bra and everything.

"And I said, 'Oops,' and I laugh. And I let him look." She opened her eyes and looked past me into someplace I would never visit and crossed her arms over her chest. "I let him look. I kept asking myself what would Madison do, and I knew she would laugh, so I just laughed some more and then I said, 'Well, do you have anything dry?' "

I had the same useless urge I'd had when Merritt was telling me about her decision to go into Dead Ed's house. I wanted to tell her not to. I wanted to tell her to run.

Thirty-four

"He didn't move. He just sat there with his hands in his lap and he, and he . . . he, um, stared at my chest, you know, at my breasts. And I . . . I, I let him. I didn't do anything to cover up. I kept saying to myself, *I'm Madison, I'm Madison*. It wasn't that hard to be there, you know, naked. I thought it would be harder than it was. I don't know how long I stood there. Time sort of disappeared, kind of like I wasn't really there at all. Finally, I put my hands on my hips and I said, '*Well?*' and he mumbled something and pulled off his stupid sweater and he gave it to me. He was really fat." She covered her mouth with her hand. "I'm sorry, I shouldn't have said that. But this is all really, really gross."

"It's okay," I said, just to say something. That she thought Ed Robilio was fat was the least vile thing I had heard since she began her monologue. The truth was that nothing about any of this was less than vile.

Her voice lowered and the speed of her words increased. "My parents can't know any of this. They just can't. You promised, right? You're not going to tell them, right?"

"I promised."

The irony stunned me like a blow to the chin. This girl was willing to let her parents think she killed a man to save her sister. But she wasn't willing to let them think she sacrificed her virtue for the same goal.

Her shoulders sagged. "Nothing else really happened. Madison drove up in her car and honked her horn and honked her horn until he got up and looked out the windshield and said, 'What the hell is that all about?' I could see her car on the street and while his back was turned, I dropped his sweater and pulled on my T-shirt and said, 'That's my friend, she must be looking for me. I have to go.'

"He stood between me and the door. The motor home or whatever it is only has one door, so I had to go past him. He says, 'Maybe you would like to go for a drive sometime? See how it handles.' I'm scared again now, my heart's pounding like crazy, and Madison's horn is honking. I don't know what to do. I say something like, 'I run every day.'

"He says, 'Good. Same time tomorrow? I'll wait for you. We'll go somewhere.'

"I say, 'Sure. Tomorrow.' And I ran out the door."

As I listened to Merritt's young voice my own heart was breaking. I wanted this terrible story to be over. But an important piece was missing; Merritt hadn't lost her earring, yet. She hadn't been in the back of the RV, in the bedroom, yet.

So I knew there was more to come.

"I jumped in Maddy's car. She said she couldn't get any pictures. There was no way she could see what was happening inside the stupid RV. That's why she was honking the horn. She didn't want me to waste it— doing it with him. Without the video it would be a waste. That's what she said. We needed a plan so that she could make sure she could get some pictures while he and I, you know . . . did it.

"She wanted to know what happened. I told her. I told her what happened on the sidewalk and inside the motor home, what I did, what I said. Pulling off my shirt and everything. She said, 'No! You didn't! No! What did he do? Did he grab you? Did he like have a heart attack?'

"I said, 'No, he just looked. He said he wants to take me for a ride tomorrow.'

"She said, 'I bet he does. What a prick. We're gonna get him, Merritt, we're gonna get him. All we need now is a little plan on how to get me inside that bus with the camera. Because none of this does any good without some video.' "

It seemed like a good place to stop. My watch told me it was ten minutes after one. My joints ached and my brain seemed starved for sleep. I asked, "Would you like to stop for tonight? Finish this up tomorrow?"

"No," she said, her voice so sweet. "I don't want to think about it all night. It's better that I finish this now, I think. Anyway," she smiled that intriguing flat smile I'd come to know, "tomorrow is reserved for good news. Tomorrow is for Chaney. We'll bury everything ugly tonight. Promise?"

"Your call," I said.

"Promise?"

"Promise."

She didn't hesitate. "That night, we made a plan, Maddy and me. A new plan. I thought it was a pretty good plan, we'd thought of more things, were more careful. We were going to use two cameras, one for some pictures, you know, photographs, and one for the video. I was more confident, I told myself I could go through with it. That time would stop again, that I would disappear again. And when I came back, that Chaney would get her procedure. That's all that mattered.

"The next day I caught up with him—Dr. Robilio—when he was on his walk. He had his keys with him this time. Went into this long thing about how he wasn't allowed to park his precious motor coach at his house and that he had to take it up to his ranch where he stored it and I could come maybe and we could stop for dinner if I wanted. Madison had told me to act kind of uninterested with him, which wasn't hard, so I did. He kept trying to convince me that it would be great—he even told me I could watch a movie on the way up if I wanted."

Don't go.

"The plan was that I would go with him. So I said okay, like I had nothing else to do. Maddy was ready. We figured he would drive the RV someplace and park it, like he said he would. We figured a campground or something, or maybe he wasn't BS-ing about the ranch. She had her mom's car and a lot of gas. Fresh battery in the camera. She was ready, figured it would be easy to follow something so big. The drive up to the mountains was fine. He wasn't gross to me or anything on the way up. Mostly wanted me to be impressed with his stupid RV and his stupid mountain ranch and his stupid cabin and all his stupid money.

"We're new here. I don't know the mountains very well. I didn't know where we were going. We were on the freeway for a while and then a smaller road and then we pulled onto a dirt road. When we turned, I could see Maddy's car a little ways back. She had pulled over.

"He got out of the RV to open a gate and then he got back in and pulled through the gate. He stopped again—I guessed he was going to go back and lock up the gate. If he did that, Maddy couldn't get through. To distract him, I touched him on his leg and said, 'We can get that later, right?' He smiled this sick smile and said, 'Sure.'

"We went up the hill. First he showed me his 'cabin,' which is huge, bigger than our house. I'm like wanting to ask how many kids died so he could build this stupid cabin, but I don't. I'm acting kind of cool and an-noyed, impatient, like. It's easy. And then we drove back down the dirt road to a barn. It's not really a barn, he built it just to hold the RV, but it looks like a barn. I was getting worried. I didn't know where Maddy was, I couldn't see her car anywhere. I didn't know whether she had made it in-side the gate. I didn't know whether to go through with it. You know."

Don't.

"He opened the doors to the barn and backed the RV in. I didn't want him to shut them, the doors—Madison had to get inside, too—so I asked him to leave them open, told him that I liked the view. I asked him if I could have a Coke. He said something really stupid, like, 'If you'll spill it like you did yesterday, you can have a whole case.'

"Right then, I hated him. Right then, everything changed for me. All my, um, my doubt was gone. And I knew I could do it. He wasn't going to screw me. I was going to screw him. In a sick way, I was even looking for-ward to it.

" 'You haven't shown me the back. Show me the back,' I said, and he grabbed my hand. God, his was even clammier than mine, and he showed me the shower and the toilet like they were so special, like maybe I'd never seen plumbing before, I don't know, and he showed me . . . the bed. He patted the mattress, like I was a dog and he wanted me to jump up on it. Everything he was doing seemed to make it easier for me, for what I was about to do.

"This is the part that Maddy and I had planned and planned because I had told her what the inside of his precious RV was like. I even drew a diagram for her. I told him I needed a minute in the bathroom and asked him to wait for me. I did something flirty with my hair, then I said some-thing, you know, stupid, and then I slid the door shut between the bed-room and the bathroom and started running some water real loud and then I ran toward the front of the bus and signaled for Maddy to come in. Thank God she was there. She came on board and she had the little cam-era and the video camera and she hid in the toilet compartment, just like we planned, and after a couple of minutes I went back into the bedroom. I closed the door behind me, leaving it open just a couple of inches so Maddy would have a way to take the pictures.

"He was more nervous than I was. His face was kind of blotchy and pink and he didn't seem like he knew what to do. That helped me, that he was nervous.

"Maddy told me what it would be like. You know, what would happen, how it would feel. Some of it she was right about, some of it she wasn't. I don't think she was, anyway, but what do I know?"

Merritt's face grew pensive, her eyes heavy. Suddenly she looked exhausted.

"I don't remember all of this, what happened next. I'm not leaving stuff out. I just don't remember."

I hoped she was being honest. I didn't want her to remember. There are times when dissociation is absolutely the best thing the psyche can muster. I said, "I know."

"She said to make it his idea. Make him ask. Be reluctant. We needed to get it on tape, his asking. He needs to be the one, not you. You need to make it be his idea. So I went and sat against the headboard. He was still at the foot of the bed. I said, 'Does that TV work?' He hit the remote, showed me it did. Then he said, 'If you're going to be on the bed, why don't you take your shoes off?'

"I took them off. I left my socks on, though, you know—the rubber? I was still wearing my running shorts—they're Lycra, like tights? He liked my legs. I could tell. He stared at them long enough.

"He asked me what I wanted to do. I shrugged. I mean, what did he expect me to say: *I want to screw your brains out, you disgusting jerk.* Hardly. I mean, huh? He asked if he could sit next to me. I shrugged again. He sort of crawled up the bed and sat so close we were touching. He was breathing through his mouth. The noise was disgusting. After a couple of minutes, he told me I had beautiful breasts and asked if he could see them again.

"I was like, *what?* I asked him why should I? He said he thought I liked him. I said I like lots of people. I don't show all of them my tits. He looked so, I don't know, devastated. I liked it, his reaction. I took the remote control from his hand and I started flicking through the channels. It was the end of *Oprah,* you know, where they're showing that hotel in Chicago where all the guests of the *Oprah* show stay? That part of *Oprah?*"

It seemed like she wanted me to say something. I didn't know anything about the end of *Oprah,* but I nodded and said, "Yes."

She shivered. The shudder moved up her body from her feet in long waves, as if a flurry of pencil-thin snakes were racing to her head.

"What he did then is he kissed my neck. And then he kissed me on my ear. With his tongue. It was really wet. It was *awful*. Awful."

Merritt leaned forward, rocked back once, and stood. She turned away from me before she spoke again. Her hands were behind her back, her long fingers laced together, exposing her tender palms.

"This is when I start to not remember. It's choppy. I remember weird things. He was like lost, he reached under my T-shirt and tried to unfasten my bra. You know, in back, but it doesn't have a clasp and I thought it was kind of funny and I had to keep from laughing and I had to tell him it didn't open, it just came over my head.

"Right at the beginning, I asked him, kind of annoyed, what he thought he was doing. I did it for Maddy, for the tape. He said he wanted me. I wondered if that was good enough and I remember thinking you won't get me, but I'll get you. Then I turned the sound up on the TV. I wanted to protect Maddy, and I didn't want to have to listen to what was happening . . . to me.

"He was in a hurry, I can tell you that. Things happened fast, much faster than I thought they would but I was watching them happen like they were in slow motion . . . my shirt came off . . . and he just pushed my bra up under my arms . . . and then he tugged and tugged at my shorts and he was touching me all over and saying stupid things about how beautiful I was and how good I smelled and he was so heavy on top of me and I told myself I wouldn't look down because I didn't want to see . . . I didn't look at his dick because I didn't want to see it and I didn't want to remember it and when I heard him open his pants I remembered about the rubber and I asked him if he had one and he said, '*What?*' like he didn't know what one was and I reached down and pulled the one I had out of my sock and said here's one and I wondered how that would sound on the tape and I heard him grunting and ripping open the packet and mumbling about something and I figured the guy had never used a condom before, I mean not even on a zucchini, Jesus."

Jesus.

"Maddy had told me to make sure I was on my back with his back to her so she could take the pictures without him seeing her and she told me to sit up once so my face was on the video and he couldn't pretend it was some grown-up he was with so I did. I sat up and saw her standing there with the camera and the red light was flashing and then he was like spreading my legs and climbing on top of me and I felt him like stabbing at me and it hurt and he said he wanted me to help and I was thinking like *help what?* and wondered what I was supposed to do and then he looked up and I thought he was looking at the mirror behind the bed and that he had seen Maddy's reflection in the mirror but then it went in and he started— and I kind of disappeared then until he was done and he was like grunting what do you do with this thing after and I was saying like is it over is it over like I'd just woken up after I was in intensive care and I remember thinking that I was so glad he didn't really take off much of his clothes and I climbed off the bed and picked up all my things and held them against me and I said I needed some time in the bathroom again and he was just laying back on the bed panting and pink and I was so mad because his dick was still out and I didn't want to see it and I closed the door behind me and Maddy hugged me and kissed me on the cheek and whispered to me that she had all the pictures and we got him now we really got him now and that it was over.

"She said I was a hero."

Thirty-five

I couldn't remember ever being so exhausted. Merritt's dark story was draining me of every bit of my vitality; I felt as though a catheter was open in my arm and I'd been donating blood the entire time she spoke.

She said, "There's more."

Oh God. "You sure you want to go on?" *I don't.*

"Absolutely. Yes."

Softly, I said, "I'm listening."

"We watched the tape that night at Maddy's apartment. It's pretty good. I mean the quality. She caught his face in the mirror a couple of times and she got my face like she said she would. Most of the time you can only see my legs. The sounds are disgusting. Gross." She shivered.

"The pictures, you know, the photographs, weren't as good. She had them developed at one of those one-hour places and they're too dark. But you can tell . . . you know, what's going on.

"I went back and surprised him the next day during his walk. He was really uncomfortable. Me? I was like, totally cool, relaxed. It was my turn now, that's the way I felt. He wouldn't even look at me. He actually told me he was too busy to *visit* with me that day, he was sorry. *Visit with me? Can you believe it?*

"I started jogging backwards in front of him, like, facing him? I asked him how old he thought I was. He said nineteen or twenty. I said guess again. He ignored me. I said I was fifteen, I can't even drive. He stopped and stared at me like I was this disgusting little thing. I stopped, too. 'Fifteen,' I said. 'Fifteen.' He said he didn't believe me and he started walking again. He tried to speed up, walk past me. I wouldn't let him. So he turned and headed the other way. I caught up with him.

"I said, 'I have a videotape, too.'

"He looks at me real quick, then he says, 'Of what?' like he doesn't really care.

" 'Our little encounter yesterday.' That was Maddy's word. 'Encounter.' I liked it.

"He didn't look at me, he just said, 'Bullshit.'

" 'And a witness. I have a videotape, and a witness, too,' I tell him. 'A friend of mine followed us up to your ranch and videotaped the whole thing. Took some pictures, too.'

" 'Bullshit,' he says again.

" 'Dr. Robilio,' I say, 'I think you're in a heck of a lot of trouble.' That gets him. He asks me how I know his name. I tell him I know everything. I know about his company. I know what stuff he does. Who his friends are. I got all that from the research Trent did, it's in the file at home. I'm ready, I've done my homework. It was sweet.

"He says I'm lying. I ask him if he wants to see the pictures.

"He does. I give him two. They're not very good, not as good as the video. But they're good enough. He knows it's him. He won't give them back to me. I say I don't care, my friend has the negatives and the videotape.

"He wants to know who my friend is and I say no way. But I say, 'You want to know who I am? I'm Chaney Trent's sister. Remember her?'

"I thought he was about to croak. He gets bright red. Turns away from me, then looks back over his shoulder.

"It takes him one more second, and he asks me how much I want. I say I want a lot and not just money. I want my sister. But later, we'll get to that later. I'd like to show him the tape first, so he can see what kind of a mess he's in. How about five o'clock, his house?

"He turned on me then. I was afraid he was going to hit me. So I stepped back and he called me 'a little flesh-peddling whore. How dare you do this to me?' I couldn't believe it.

"I said, 'To you? You're the one who lets babies die. You're the one who has sex with kids.' I almost hit him. Talk about money for flesh; he was the one who was killing my sister just to save money. I said, 'I'll be at your house at five o'clock, warm up your VCR,' and I jogged away. I felt fine. My heart wasn't even racing. His reaction told me that he knew we had him. We had him good."

She stopped as though the story was over.

Puzzled, I said, "And you went back at five, with the tape?"

"Yeah, I did. But Trent was already there. I told you I saw his Jetta, remember?"

"Yes. But what you told me before is that you had gone to plead with Dr. Robilio for your sister's life. But what you're saying now is that you had actually gone back to blackmail him with the videotape?"

She seemed stunned by the bluntness of my summation. She said, "Yes, I guess that's right." With both hands she lifted her hair off her shoulders and twisted it into a knot above her head. "Before, when I, um—"

"Lied?"

"Okay. Lied. I guess . . . I wasn't sure I was going to tell you about the videotape at all."

"And the rest of the—"

"The rest is just the way I told you. The way I look at it now is that I feel I may have done what everybody says I've done. Killed him, you know. But I didn't pull the trigger. That was . . . Trent."

"You went home with Robilio's gun? As you told me before?"

"Yeah, the same as I told you already. I really was going to shoot myself with it."

"And the videotape, you took that with you?"

"That, too."

"The police never found it in your room."

She lowered her hands and her hair spilled back down past her shoulders. She swiped a few strands from her eyes. "I, um, left it outside . . . for Maddy. When I called her I told her where it was. I didn't want anybody to know what I'd done. I figured she would get rid of it, the tape. I made her promise not to show it to anybody. Especially Brad."

"You didn't know about any scheme that they cooked up? Madison and Brad? To try to extort Robilio's company for money?"

She shook her head. Her tone was incredulous as she asked, "You think I would do this for money?"

I dropped my chin to my chest to try to stretch the tendons in my neck. They felt like they had been surgically replaced by steel cables. When I raised my head again I focused on Merritt's eyes and knew my heart was not in what I needed to do next. I didn't want to confront this kid. I wanted to comfort her. But I did what my training, and not my instincts, told me to do. I said, "You're not being totally honest with me, Merritt."

She looked surprised, then offended. "What do you mean?"

"The fingernail? Remember? The red one? The police found it."

"Oh yeah. I forgot about that."

What she meant was that she forgot I knew about that. I said, "Do you know where they discovered it?" I wanted her to tell me.

She shook her head. Her ignorance seemed genuine. But then again, picking liars out of the soup of life wasn't one of my more developed talents.

"They found it in the master bathroom. On the second floor. You were upstairs in the bedrooms?"

She looked at the door and played with her hair before she said, "Yeah."

The police had found no blood on the stairs. "That same day? Before you found his body?"

She nodded. "When I first went inside, I went looking for him. I went upstairs, all over."

"And the nail?"

"I broke it."

"How?"

It was beginning to register that Merritt was much more adept at omissions than she was at lying. She said, "I, I don't know. I guess I, um, I hit it on something."

This was painful. "What? What did you hit it on?"

"I, I don't know."

"Come on, Merritt, tell me. Let's finish this tonight."

In all my years doing this work I'd come to recognize that many patients have a need to secrete something away, to protect it from the harsh light of examination and confrontation. Early in my career, I was puzzled to learn that the secret was often not necessarily of much consequence, but instead that the motive had to do with my patients' need to retain one safe place, to underscore their independence, their separation from me.

I waited.

"Do I have to?"

I didn't answer. My lips felt rusty, my tongue uncooperative.

"This is Maddy's secret. Not mine. I don't want to tell it."

I felt heaviness above my eyes. I was done arguing.

"Okay, okay. Maddy was with me, you know, when I went back to see him, Dr. Robilio, to show him the tape. We both thought it would be better. At first, she went upstairs looking for him. I checked the first floor, the kitchen and living room, you know. Then I went upstairs and I caught her up in his bedroom stealing stuff. Jewelry, perfume. I mean she was looking through drawers, everything. We had a fight about it. That's how I broke my nail, fighting with Maddy. I made her put everything back."

Fighting? That could explain the blood in Merritt's urine in the ER. "Did she hit you in the gut?"

She narrowed her eyes and said, "I don't know. Why?"

"Never mind. Did Madison put everything back?"

"At first."

"What do you mean?"

"A few minutes later I found him, downstairs, just like I said—dead. Maddy was still prowling around on the first floor. When I screamed she came downstairs, too, and saw me with him, you know, all bloody and everything. She stood in the doorway and then she ran back upstairs. I didn't know where she went. After . . . you know, we got out of there. On the way back to my house, she was really cool, like level. Not panicking like me. She showed me she had stolen his keys. She kept saying these may come in handy. I was going nuts over what I'd just seen, I didn't care that much about his keys. I mean he was dead, right? What good were his keys? What good was he to me anymore? What good was he going to be to Chaney?"

I offered her my silence as a host might offer a guest a tray of hors d'oeuvres. She could choose anything she wished, or she could choose nothing at all.

She said, "I'd like to go to bed now."

It was almost two. I said, "Yes."

The night was cold, even for April. My car was cold. Boulder was forty minutes away. My house was empty. My dog was well cared for.

Despite the fact that I couldn't afford it, and without much second thought, I drove a few blocks downtown, turned my car over to a valet, and checked into the Brown Palace Hotel. A bemused bellman who was dressed much more nicely than me led me to an elegant corner room on the eighth floor. I called Lauren and left another message on her parents' machine. I drank all the cognac from the minibar and fell asleep to something nasty on Spectravision.

The next morning I ordered coffee and juice from room service. I signed the chit the waiter handed me without even glancing at it. I was not at all interested in knowing how much my indulgence was costing.

After begging a disposable razor and toothbrush from housekeeping, I dressed in yesterday's clothes and enjoyed an hour alone with CNN, reading the *New York Times*, and sipping the Brown Palace's good coffee.

Then I called Sam's pager.

A minute later, the phone rang by the bed. He said, "Detective Purdy returning a page."

"Hi, Sam, it's Alan."

"What is this number? Where the hell are you? Adrienne said you never came home. Nurse said you left Children's around two-thirty."

Sam is a good detective. "I'm at the Brown Palace."

"The Brown Palace?"

"The hotel."

"I know it's a hotel. What the hell are you doing at the goddamn Brown Palace?"

"Treating myself."

A pregnant pause. "You alone?"

I laughed. "Not that kind of treat, Sam. Where are you? Boulder?"

"Right down the street at the hospital. MedExcel faxed a financial approval to the Seattle hospital first thing this morning. Maybe half an hour ago. MedExcel's execs are shitting bricks over the possibility of Gusman's role in this whole thing getting public. Your friend Adrienne was marvelous, she left them thinking she was doing them some huge favor. Docs here at Children's are talking with the docs in Seattle about whether Chaney is still a candidate for the procedure. The Seattle docs want some new tests done before they accept her. That's all happening right now."

"How long will it take?"

"Midday if things go well. Air ambulance has already been ordered. They're standing by for an afternoon departure. MedExcel is paying for that, too. It's amazing how cooperative they are all of a sudden."

"Is Chaney stable?"

"I don't get this lung thing. She looks like death to me. But they say she's no worse than before."

"How are Sherry and Brenda doing?"

"So far so good. Sherry's coming back here this morning to be with Brenda. She's talking about going to Washington, too. So Simon and I may be spending some extra quality time together in Boulder." He made a noise, a little cough. "Listen, it seems like you were with Merritt a long time last night."

"Yeah. It felt like an eternity."

"She's talking about Robilio?"

"*Sam.*"

"You can't tell me anything?"

"Sorry. I wish I could."

"I can't tell you how much I hate your goddamn profession sometimes. Most of the time, even."

"I know. Sam, how do I find out what the DA plans to do if I let her out of the hospital?"

"Your wife's a DA, Alan. Start there."

"My wife is temporarily out of the loop. I'm serious; I need to know."

"Have Maitlin feel things out with Mitchell Crest. This one is a PR nightmare for everyone involved in Boulder. Everybody in the department and at the DA's office is afraid of screwing up. Right now I think the DA is happiest knowing Merritt's in the hospital. It's almost as good as having her in custody but they don't really have to arrest her, which if they're wrong and she's innocent leaves them looking impolite. You ready to let her go?"

"Sam, don't put me on the spot like that. Just read between the lines a little bit, okay?"

"Sorry, habit."

"I'm going to head over to see Merritt in a little while. You need me for anything?"

"No. We did what we could. My niece's fate now rests in the hands of a bunch of doctors I've never met."

"It beats having her fate rest in the hands of a bunch of bean counters you've never met."

"Amen."

Next, I paged John Trent. When he phoned back, I invited him to meet me at Ellyngton's in the Brown Palace lobby for breakfast. He protested that he couldn't leave the hospital.

I was impatient with him. I said, "John, this isn't social. I think you know what this is about."

He said, "Oh. What time?"

Trent slid into the booth looking like a death row inmate who just received word of a pardon from the governor and then was told that there had been an error.

"Coffee, John? It's pretty good, much better than the hospital's."

"Thanks, yes." He ran his fingers back over the top of his head in a manner that suggested he had once had a head full of long hair.

I signaled to the waiter.

"Good news today, huh? You heard? It's like a miracle. I wish I knew what changed their minds."

"Yes, Sam told me."

"I wonder why now." He shook his head a little. "You know, before you called, I had a good feeling about everything for the first time. I think it's a go today. I really do."

I allowed him to savor the change in the winds of fortune for Chaney while the waiter delivered coffee and a menu. Without opening the menu, John ordered oatmeal, wheat toast, and a fruit plate.

He sipped his coffee. "So, you know?"

I shrugged.

He narrowed his eyes. "Maybe you're guessing."

"And if I am?"

"Then I can enjoy my breakfast. You know, I don't think I've actually tasted a bite of food in a month. Maybe this morning I can."

"And if I'm not guessing?"

"This all gets quite complicated for me."

It was time for me to switch to decaf. I pushed my saucer away.

I said, "You know Robilio's daughter?"

He turned his head a little bit to the side the way my dog does when I've said something tantalizing but unintelligible.

He sipped from his cup before replying. "No. I don't."

"Her name is . . . I don't remember what her name is, but they call her Sunny. She lives in Grand Junction."

"That's nice."

"I spent some time with her, well, recently. She told me about her aunt and uncle. What are their names? Andrew and Abby, uh, Porter, I think." I paused. His eyes were on the silverware. "Anyway, she went on and on about their divorce, and their custody fight. Sticky situation for the family. The *extended* family, you know."

One long nod ensued. Matter-of-factly, he said, "Oh. So you do know." He folded his napkin neatly on the table, caught my eyes, and held them. He said, "I'm out of here right now unless this stops being breakfast and starts being an adjunct family session."

I thought about the offer for a few seconds, had half-expected it would come to this. I didn't care much about what I could legally report to the justice system right then. I said, "Fine. This is treatment, John."

He replaced his napkin on his lap and finished the coffee in his cup. "After I put the pieces together, and realized I was doing a custody eval on his sister-in-law, I approached Dr. Robilio with a trade. I'd make a custody recommendation to the court that was favorable to his wife's sister if he would get MedExcel's medical board to approve the procedure that Chaney needs. That's it, that was the deal. I'm not proud of it, but I'd do it again in a second if I thought it would help Chaney."

I tried to keep a straight face. I'd had no idea that Trent had proposed a bargain. "How did Robilio respond?" I reminded myself not to call him Dead Ed.

"Said he'd think about it."

"And?"

"I went back the next day, told him time was tight for Chaney. He said okay; he'd do it for Beth, his wife."

"And you wrote the recommendation to the court?"

"No. My report wasn't due for a week. I called the interested parties and suggested to them what was going to happen. Call it a good will ges-ture to Robilio while I awaited word of the approval for Chaney."

That was the call Diane had received from Trent. The one she was so concerned about during lunch at Jax Fish House.

"The day I told you about before? At his house. The day I got so an-gry, when Merritt may have overheard me? That was because Robilio re-neged, said he couldn't go through with it. Said his sister-in-law was a lush, didn't deserve the kids."

"But you went back one more time."

He closed his eyes. "Do the police know?"

I didn't know what they knew. "They know a lot."

"Did Andrew see me?"

Andrew? Did Andrew see him do what? "This isn't about me telling you what they know. It's about you telling me what you know."

"When I went back to Robilio's house, Andrew was there. His car was in the driveway. I didn't know it was his car, but I didn't want to go in while Robilio had a guest. So I waited. Fifteen, twenty minutes passed before Andrew came back out of the house."

"You saw Robilio's brother-in-law come out of the house?"

"Yeah." He glanced at me suspiciously. "The brother-in-law, Andrew. I immediately figured that maybe Robilio had told him about my offer to distort the custody recommendation and that Andrew was going to report me to the judge and get me yanked off the custody case and my leverage would be gone. I thought the game was up right then. I'd lose everything, including my psychology license."

"But you waited to talk with Robilio anyway?"

"Why not? I was about to lose my daughter, and likely my license to practice psychology. What else did I have to lose? But Robilio wouldn't answer the door. I figured he had seen my car, knew I was waiting and didn't want to see me again."

"You didn't leave then, did you?"

"Huh? They know that, too? I wondered if I had left any fingerprints back there. I guess I did. Yeah, I didn't leave. I went around back. If he wouldn't open the door, I'd yell at him through the window if I could find him. I don't have much pride left, Alan. But I didn't find him anywhere. I went home."

"That's it?"

"That's it."

"Do you think Andrew killed him?"

"Andrew? What? No. I got the impression he was killed much later. Why are you asking me that? Merritt killed him, didn't she?"

The circle of irony was complete. Trent thought Merritt had murdered Robilio. Merritt thought Trent had.

* * *

When I arrived at Children's, Merritt was prowling the unit like a big cat in a small cage. Pacing, she seemed to be traversing the width of the dayroom in only two strides. I was barely able to get my key out of the lock on the door before she was in my face.

I pointed at the consultation room. "Go have a seat, I'll be right in." I had to fight a smile as she stamped her left foot in frustration at having to wait for news even a few moments longer.

I checked with the nursing staff and read the chart notes that had been added since my barely legible middle-of-the-night scrawls. Routine stuff, other than the fact that Merritt's silence was a thing of the past. She was chattering now to anyone who would listen, mostly wanting to know what was going on with Chaney.

Her hands were in the pockets of her jeans. This T-shirt was black and read USA. She said, "Well?"

"It looks good. Nothing's final. The money's been approved for the procedure. The doctors are all discussing Chaney's condition. They want to be certain she's still a good candidate."

Merritt sat and anxiety drained from her. If her tension were liquid, there would have been a pond on the floor between us. "She'll go. I feel it." She touched the center of her chest with her closed fist.

"We'll know soon. Couple of hours. If it's approved, she'll fly out by air ambulance today."

"Me too?"

"Sorry. Not today. Maybe tomorrow or the next day."

She huffed. "Why not today? You still don't trust me?"

"That's part of it. Another piece is that I want some time to process with you all we talked about last night, how you feel about it now, you know?"

To my surprise, she wasn't resistant. She nodded and said, "I know."

"You've been through a lot."

She closed her eyes. Didn't disagree.

"And part of it is that we still don't know what the DA is going to do if you're no longer in the hospital. They may want to arrest you if I discharge you, Merritt. There's no way to predict that yet."

She swallowed, pulled her hair back behind her ears. "I forgot about that. The police."

"I figured. I'm not big on advice, but can I offer you some?"

She sighed.

"Call your lawyer. Tell him what you told me last night. Tell him what you're afraid of. You're going to need his help, Merritt."

"I want to be with my sister. She needs me."

"I agree. She does. And to be with her, I'm afraid you're going to need Mr. Maitlin's help."

"I can't turn on Trent. Chaney needs Trent, too."

"That's a tough call for you to make, Merritt. You need to take responsibility for the things you did to help your sister. And you need to let Trent take responsibility for the things he did to help her."

She turned her palms up and threaded her fingers together in a jumble that was at least as confused as were her choices. After a couple of minutes, she said, "Okay, I'll call him." She widened her eyes. "So, do you need to write an order for that, too?"

I thought the sarcasm was a great sign.

Thirty-six

While Merritt called Cozy, I paged her uncle. I'd been thinking about what to say and I thought I'd found an ethical crease that I could squeeze through to let Sam know about all the visitors Ed Robilio had been greeting just prior to becoming Dead Ed.

Sam was in his car, going where, I had to guess. "Sam, it's me."

"Figured. Any news yet?"

"No, everyone here is chewing their fingernails off. I'll page you when the word is out. Listen, I've been thinking—looking for french fries, so to speak."

"Hold your thought for a second. I'm still losing sleep trying to figure out why the harassment stopped against Brenda before the public knew Chaney was sick. Am I being obsessive here?"

"I don't know, Sam. Maybe the guy just gave up on his own. That happens, right? Every candle burns out eventually."

"Maybe, I don't know. I don't like loose ends where my family's concerned. What did you want?"

"Like I said, I've been thinking, too."

"Yeah?"

"Sunny Hasan, remember her, at the cabin? She told us about her uncle and aunt, Andrew and Abby. Last name Porter. You know, how they're getting a divorce, how there were a lot of bad feelings between them and Robilio?"

"Mmm-hmm. Yeah?"

"I'm just wondering whether any of his latents, you know, Andrew Porter's, were found at the Robilio house, maybe even in the home office?"

Pause. "You have a reason to think they might have been?"

I stayed quiet and hoped he knew why.

He didn't miss a beat. "But you think, maybe, it'd be worth checking? Asking Andrew about recent visits? Tension in the family? Like around this divorce thing?"

I wished he could see my face. "I would think more the custody thing than the divorce thing. But that's sort of it, yes."

Sam was silent for a couple of measures. "My own brother-in-law, Trent, does some of that, doesn't he? Custody evaluation work?"

"Yeah, I think he does."

Sam's voice lightened as he said, "You're out on a limb right now, aren't you?"

"Sam, I've been out here so much lately I'm actually beginning to like the view."

At one forty-five that afternoon, a twin-jet air ambulance lifted off from Centennial Airport for a two-and-a-half-hour flight to Sea-Tac airport in Washington. Chaney Trent was on board along with a nurse, a physician, her mother, her father, and her Aunt Sherry.

The Channel 7 news team had been on the story with three crews and a full graphics package—"Chaney's Hope," they were calling it—from the moment Brenda informed her boss she was going to need some extended family leave time. The other local stations were less than an hour behind with their own blanket coverage.

I had finished a long psychotherapy session with Merritt to begin to explore her feelings about her sister's illness and prognosis, and to give her a chance to look at what she had done with Madison and Dr. Robilio. Merritt's discharge planning meeting with the unit staff ate up an additional thirty minutes and I was in the unit dayroom as I watched the air ambulance take off—LIVE!—from the runway at Centennial Airport, courtesy of cameras mounted inside the same news helicopter that had floated Lucy Davenport and me over the Continental Divide.

As the plane banked west toward the Rockies, an off-camera reporter, remarkably breathless, read a statement from MedExcel that said that the corporate change of heart about providing approval for Chaney's procedure was due to a routine re-review of the facts of the case. On air, the reporter didn't question either the velocity or the direction of the corporate spin.

What was more important news, apparently, were the preparations being made for a local crew to follow the air ambulance to Seattle. We saw almost a minute of tape of those preparations.

As the piece on Chaney's departure segued into a commercial for Xantac 75, I found myself musing that Dr. Terence Gusman was probably one of the only people in Denver whose heart wasn't warmed by Chaney's story.

Merritt had missed the news reports of her sister's departure for Washington. After our session concluded, she moved into a different consultation room to engage in a much-delayed tête-à-tête with Cozier Maitlin. I was pretty sure she was busy making him crazy with her rules about what parts of her story he could use to help her and what parts he couldn't. Cozy, I figured, would soon come to the same conclusion I had reached overnight: If Merritt had simply admitted going to Robilio's house early on, she would have had a living witness to corroborate her story about discovering his body. But now Madison was dead, and Cozy had to find a way, without the benefit of witnesses, to convince the authorities of his client's innocence. And without enjoying the freedom to tell anyone that his client had been busy blackmailing the victim with a videotape of their scripted sexual encounter.

Although Chaney was on her way to Seattle and Merritt was on her way out of the hospital, there remained some jokers loose in the deck. The videotape, the real one—not the substitute one that Brad had bashed into Madison's head—had yet to surface. Sometime soon, I feared, Merritt would have to suffer the humiliation and legal jeopardy of the tape being played somewhere to somebody. And at some point, even if it took a grand jury, John Trent and the authorities were going to have a pointed conversation about Trent's repeated visits to Dead Ed's house.

I returned to the nursing station and grabbed Merritt's chart from the rack. After jotting down the specifics of the discharge plan I had just negotiated with the unit staff, I added, with profound understatement, that her legal situation still required clarification. With any luck from the DA or Cozy Maitlin, though, I harbored some hope she would be on her way to join her family in Seattle in a day or two.

I headed back to Boulder with some of my own fantasies—that my wife would be home soon, my practice would be mundane soon, and my life would again be my own soon.

Ha.

* * *

Adrienne had plastered a big VICTORY FOR THE MASSES banner across the front door of my house. In my life, I have never even had time to figure out how to get my computer and printer to print envelopes, so I couldn't imagine how she had been able to master the art of banner-making. Two explanations came to mind. Adrienne didn't sleep, which gave her more time to putz than me, and she was, conservatively, double-digit IQ points smarter than me, which usually was fine, although sometimes it really pissed me off.

Emily was as happy to see me as I was to see her. I played a long-distance game of kill-the-tennis-ball with her for a while and promised her a long walk at the end of the day. Unfortunately, the future tense doesn't exist in any known dog lexicon and she was visibly perplexed at being returned to her dog run without the appearance of her leash.

Cozy had left me a long voice-mail message about an unpleasant meeting he had just concluded with Mitchell Crest, the thrust of which was that if I discharged Merritt, the DA's office wasn't going to be happy, but they weren't going to arrest her before we whisked her to DIA.

Cozy added that I had better not be wrong about his client no longer being suicidal. He said, "You have one shot before the buzzer. Make it count." Cozy's use of a sports metaphor threw me off balance; I figured it was for my benefit.

I had rescheduled two patients at the end of the day. Their issues were blessedly routine. As the first session became the second, I felt the comforting return of my therapeutic rhythm. It reminded me of the moment when I find a robotic spin on a long bike ride. Once you're there, instinct is golden. You trust, you fly.

As I had been listening to my second patient describe the nearly daily argument he was having with his wife about what he was absolutely determined was the correct way to load the dishwasher, I had a revelation about Merritt and Madison and Dead Ed.

Ah-ha moments, flashes of insight, although not commonplace, aren't unexpected in the lives of psychotherapists. Most of the time, though, I apply the brakes of caution and keep the initial glint of percipience to myself. I do this because often I'm plain wrong, and also because there is usually no harm in sitting on the revelations. True insights aren't perishable;

there is no danger in storing them for long periods of time. Sometimes insights even age and improve like good wine. But false insight always in-
jects clutter and misdirection—the construction of an artificial fork in an
otherwise meandering but purposeful road.

The truth is that when doing psychotherapy, being right is usually
much less important than not being wrong.

I reminded myself of none of these things as I called Miggy Monroe,
invited myself over, and asked for directions to her apartment.

I don't know why I expected a chaotic apartment with ten cats, un-
dusted tchotchkes, and piles of magazines from the Johnson administration, but I did. It's not what I found.

Miggy Monroe lived in one of the brick midrise buildings on the west
end of Arapahoe near Ninth Street. The apartment had a wonderful view
of the Flatirons, and Miggy favored contemporary pieces in the colors of
the various incarnations of oatmeal: plain, with honey, with milk, with
milk and cinnamon.

The only colors in the apartment were the red lines in Miggy's eyes
and the dust-jacketed spines of hundreds of books.

She was surprised I was so young. I was surprised she was so young. I
offered my compassion over Madison's death and she invited me to the funeral to be held two days later. The coroner in Routt County had just released her daughter's body. Madison's father was flying in from Humboldt
State in California. She thought I would like him. It seemed apparent to
me that Miggy still did.

I told her I couldn't tell her why I needed to know, but I asked if she
had yet gone through her daughter's things.

"Sure, I was hoping for some answers."

"Find any?"

I thought she hesitated before she shook her head.

I was tempted to dance around my objectives but wasn't creative
enough to find a way to do it. I said, "Did you find any videotapes with her
stuff?"

She looked puzzled, said, "No."

"Is there a collection of tapes the family keeps?"

"There is no family. It was just me and Maddy."

She wanted me to focus with her on grief. I wanted to find the video-tape. I felt like all my compassionate muscles were cramping from overuse. I said, "I'm sorry. Do you have a video camera?"

A hesitant, "Yes. What's so important about our videos?"

"So you have some tapes, then? Things you've recorded over the years—home videos? Maybe some movies you recorded? Prerecorded tapes?"

"Sure. Of course. We used to take lots of videos when she was little. Madison. Not so much lately. Things were difficult lately. She recorded stuff off cable, too. We get HBO."

"May I see the collection?"

"Of course, I guess. Is this about Merritt? Are you looking for one with Maddy and Merritt on it? I don't think there are any." She opened a white lacquer cabinet to reveal a TV and VCR. An interior drawer held about two dozen tapes.

"Yes, it's about Merritt, but I can't say any more than that." I thought about what to do next. I didn't really want to sit in Miggy's apartment watching her TV and her VCR while I searched for the videotape of what-ever Madison had recorded happening between Merritt and Dead Ed in the rear end of Haldeman.

"May I take these with me, Miggy? Overnight? I need to go through them—I'm looking for something specific—and I don't want to intrude on you while I do. I'll return them to you tomorrow, I promise."

"Even the one you're looking for?"

"If Madison's on that one—at all—yes. I'll return that one, too."

She was obviously puzzled but too fractured by her grief to press me. She shrugged and said, "Why not? Let me get a shopping bag for you."

The bag was white, with handles.

Leaving Miggy Monroe's apartment, I backtracked across Boulder Creek to downtown and picked up a ready-to-bake pizza at Nick-N-Willy's before I went home. While the oven heated, I salved my guilt and played with Emily without even changing my clothes. I played with her some more while the pizza baked. I knew I was procrastinating. I didn't want to find the Holiday Rambler tape. I didn't want to not find the Holiday Rambler tape.

Mostly, I didn't want to see it.

*   *   *

My theory went like this: Madison's return trip home to Boulder after she had run away with Brad had been because she had told him about tap- ing Merritt and he was bullying her to retrieve the videotape of Merritt and Robilio, so he could begin his not-too-well-thought-out little extor- tion scenario with Robilio's company, MedExcel. Madison, I figured, was having second thoughts about having told him about the blackmail scheme she and Merritt had cooked up and didn't really want Brad to have the tape, so she had taken a copy of *Pretty Woman* to him instead, after making him promise not to watch it. But she told Brad it was the one.

Brad, of course, had watched the tape, and found nobody screwing on it but Richard Gere and Julia Roberts. He had beaten Madison viciously for her lie, using the copy of *Pretty Woman* as a bludgeon.

I shuddered at what might have followed between them, what slight by Madison had caused Brad to turn from batterer to murderer. I suspected that the proximity of Dead Ed's arsenal made it too convenient for Brad to vent his rage with his finger on a trigger.

To support her subterfuge with Brad, I figured that Madison would have picked a bogus tape of the same category as the real tape: that is, a movie taped off HBO or one of the networks. By my count, the shopping bag that Miggy Monroe had given me contained nine likely suspects.

With a Sunshine Wheat Beer and two slices of Nick-N-Willy's by my side, I fast-forwarded through snippets of *Emma*, *Sense and Sensibility*, and *Waiting to Exhale* before finding myself so amused and charmed by Alicia Silverstone in *Clueless* that I watched almost half of it.

On the sixth tape, three minutes into *Little Women*, I found myself looking at Edward Robilio's ass.

Never in my life have I been so grateful for a pause button.

I'm not offended by dirty movies. Although I can't always trace the line accurately, I have no problem believing that a demarcation exists somewhere between erotica and obscenity.

At that moment, with Dead Ed's butt filling the expanse of Lauren's new big-screen TV in front of me, I was looking at the most pornographic image I had ever laid eyes on. If Edward Robilio managed to play Lazarus and rose from the dead right there in my living room, I would have pulled the videotape from the machine and beaten him back to eternity with it. It would have been the shortest reincarnation on record. He would have been begging me to merely shoot him a couple of times.

I paced the room. I changed clothes. I opened my mail. I put the rest of the pizza in the refrigerator. I checked my voice mail. I finished the beer and considered vodka.

I watched the damn tape.

The interlude in the RV lasted three and one-half minutes. A little over halfway through, Merritt raised her head and looked at the camera with a face so dead it belonged in a wax museum.

Thirty-seven

I had the tape. Now what?

No scenario crossed my mind that would help me do anything productive with it. As far as I knew, only Merritt, Brad, and I knew the tape existed. I had Merritt's permission to share the *fact* of the tape with Cozy. That didn't mean I could show it to him. What good would it do for him to see it, anyway?

For some reason—I would have to indulge in unwelcome self-analysis to discover exactly why—the sight of Dead Ed's butt caused me to think about his daughter, Sunny.

She feared her father more than she respected him. She honored him much more than she loved him. What she didn't do was cross him.

Without a clue as to the nature of the character she was pursuing, Merritt had crossed him.

I scratched below the surface of my memories of my afternoon at the ranchette in Summit County with Sunny Hasan. I didn't know what I was trying to remember, but felt certain I would recognize it when I found it.

I thought long and hard about erasing the videocassette. Or burning it in the fireplace. Never had I held an object in my hand that was more worthy of destruction. But I didn't. As obscene as the tape was, it might turn out to be a key to Merritt's legal salvation. And I would do nothing to put that at risk.

Reluctantly, I switched off the VCR and tuned in to the ten o'clock news. The lead story on Channel 7 was, no surprise, "Chaney's Hope." I watched tape of the jet landing in Seattle. I watched tape of an ambulance delivering Chaney to the University of Washington Medical Center. I watched tape of Brenda Strait as she expressed gratitude to everyone for their prayers.

Chaney had been granted a seat at a medical craps table. At least she would get a chance to roll the dice.

If Mitchell Crest didn't change his mind about arresting her, my plan was to discharge Merritt the next day so she could fly to Seattle to be with her family.

I couldn't figure out why I didn't feel better about things.

I decided to blame it all on Dead Ed's butt.

I contemplated the vodka bottle while Emily whined at the front door. Leaving the spirits behind, I took her out on the lane for her late-night ablutions.

Since we live at the end of a dirt road, it's difficult to sneak up on us by car, especially at night. Emily and I both listened carefully as a vehicle climbed the winding incline toward the house. Headlight beams danced in the dry grasses on the hillsides. Emily recognized Sam's car before I did. She greeted him with joy. I was more restrained.

He climbed out, crouched down, and scratched her behind her ears. To me, he said, "Good, you're up. Doing anything?"

"Getting ready for bed. Why do I get the feeling you have other ideas?"

He smiled in a way that would have worried me if I were a suspect he was cornering. "I tracked down Andrew, like you suggested. He's waiting for us."

I was a little suspicious. "Why would Andrew be waiting for us?"

"Actually, he's just sitting and waiting for somebody to make his night interesting. He doesn't know it's going to be us."

"Should you be doing this, Sam?"

He ignored me, nodded at Emily. "Has she done her thing?"

"Yeah."

"Put her inside. Let's go, we shouldn't dawdle. Andrew might get lucky. That would really screw things up."

We took Sam's police department Ford. He steered us west, toward town, and said, "When was the last time you were at The Broker?"

"I don't know. Probably hasn't been long enough. That's where Andrew is?"

"His hangout, apparently, since he's been separated. Lucy's babysitting him for the moment."

"He's trying to hit on Lucy? This should be fun to watch."

"For his sake, boy, I hope he doesn't try. She told me she's keeping her distance."

The Broker is a restaurant and bar on the southeastern side of town that comes equipped with a conveniently attached motel. Historically, it's been an attractive gathering spot for Boulder's romantically dispossessed. Dozens of my newly separated patients have put in time warming seats in The Broker's lounge. I'd even visited once in the wake of my own divorce. The scene was not inspiring.

"Andrew doesn't expect us?"

"We didn't make an appointment, if that's what you mean."

Lucy met us in the motel lobby wearing a little black dress that renewed my faith in little black dresses. She said hello, nodded toward the lounge, and said, "He's still inside at the bar. Hasn't moved."

"Still alone?" Sam said.

"Yeah. He's watching TV, drinking Wild Turkey, neat."

Sam asked, "Why aren't you in there with him?"

She shuddered. "Let's just say it's safer out here. You ready?"

"You bet. Where do you want us?"

"Parking lot by the turnpike. You'll see my car. Give me five minutes to encourage him to go for a walk with me." She started toward the bar and stopped after two strides, facing Sam. "This is *mine*, Sam. You interfere, I swear, I'm history. We're doing this my way."

Sam held up his hands in protest, as though he were the most trustworthy man on the planet. I thought his act would have gone over better with an audience other than Lucy and me.

Lucy joined us in the parking lot in two minutes, tops. I didn't know what she said to Andrew to get him to leave the bar with her, but I supposed that a little innuendo from someone as interesting as Lucy would have gone a long way to mobilize someone as lonely as Andrew. I guessed that the little black dress was an inducement, too.

Andrew looked as terrified as near-drunk men can when Lucy pointed to us and said, "These are the friends I told you I wanted you to meet, Andrew." He paled and spun back to her. I think he was expecting to be mugged.

Lucy was holding her badge at about the level of her neckline. Andrew couldn't miss it. For a split second, I thought I saw relief on his face. His eyes softened, his shoulders dropped; he was perceiving Lucy as protector.

But more rational thoughts quickly crowded into his whiskey-fogged awareness and he said, "Oh shit," under his breath. He didn't slur.

She said, "Andrew? I'm Detective Tanner of the Boulder Police Department."

She didn't introduce us. Sam and I said nothing. Nobody had told me to shut up. I just knew.

Lucy said, "Andrew? You want to tell me about your brother-in-law? Edward Robilio?"

Andrew checked out Sam, checked out the asphalt, checked out the sky. He checked out Sam again. He said, "I think I want a lawyer. I have a right to an attorney, don't I?"

Lucy was nonplussed. She shrugged and said, "Sure, whatever. I guess we'll just have to go get you one," and guided him into the front seat of her red Volvo. Sam and I slid into the back and listened as Lucy used her portable phone to ask for instructions from somebody. My suspicion was that the call was a ruse. When she finished with the conversation, she faced Sam and said, "We're supposed to sit tight for a few minutes. He'll get back to us." To Andrew, she added, "I can't transport you in this. We need to wait for a patrol car to, you know, take us to . . . a more appropriate place for . . . interrogation."

"I have to go . . . to the police station?"

"That's where you can call your lawyer. We have a room there for you. You know, a holding, um, cell."

The word "cell" seemed to have its desired effect on Andrew. The next few minutes were bizarre. Lucy fixed her lipstick in the rearview mirror. Sam kept humming the same two bars of "You're Nobody Till Somebody Loves You." Without moving his head, Andrew tried to get a fix on what everyone was doing. But no one in the car said a word until Andrew belched an aromatic little bourbon cloud and asked, "Am I under arrest?"

Lucy didn't answer him. In a husky, patronizing tone more suited for the cocktail lounge than for interrogation, she said, "You know, you've asked for a lawyer. We really shouldn't talk."

After another minute of listening to Sam's persistent humming, Andrew said, "What if I changed my mind? I mean about the lawyer?"

Lucy smiled. "Well, you do that, then we can talk. Clear this right up."

I thought I saw Andrew check on Sam in the outside mirror before he said, "Well, what, what is it that you want to know?"

Lucy said, "How about we start with your visit to your brother-in-law's house on Friday afternoon? Start there."

Andrew seemed to be considering his next move. I watched Sam. He had stopped humming, and his muscles had tensed. I figured he was anticipating Andrew trying to bolt out of the car.

Andrew pressed hard on both of his temples. "Oh God. You know I was there, huh? Damn it. Well, it's not what you think. It isn't. I didn't do it. I didn't kill him." After a pause of about three seconds, he added, "Not really."

Not really?

Lucy said, "Just a moment, Andrew," and gave the sweetest rendition of Miranda I figured I would ever hear. She pulled out a small tape recorder, started it, and dictated an introduction. She faced Andrew and said, "Now tell me all about it."

"I've been planning to call you guys—I have, really. I mean if that girl was arrested, I would have called. I would have, really."

He was pathetic. I almost felt sorry for him.

"Here's what happened. This is the absolute truth. Okay? Okay? You believe me?"

Lucy smiled. A perfect touch with Andrew. For him, it was as though he were confessing an indiscretion to his date.

"Ed called me Friday afternoon and told me to come right over. I mean, he summoned me, the ass. I'm getting a divorce—Abby, my wife, and his wife, Beth, are sisters—and I figured he just wanted to play patriarch and put pressure on me about the divorce and the custody and everything. I was tempted not to go, but I finally decided I would drive over and listen to him and then tell the prick to butt out. Okay?"

Lucy said, "I'm with you so far."

"He said the doorbell wasn't working, that he'd leave the front door open, that I should just come in. He'd be downstairs in his office."

"The 'he' you're talking about is your brother-in-law, Edward Robilio?"

"Yes, that's right. Ed Robilio. I go in. I go downstairs. I call his name.

Nothing. I go into his office and he's sitting there in his leather chair, uh—I don't know any other way to put it—he's, well, he's . . . half dead. He has a hole in his chest, there's blood all over him, there's a gun on the floor. Immediately I think there's been a burglary, that he's been shot. But I know he's not dead. His eyes are following me and his breathing sounds like bad plumbing.

"It's like he knows what I'm thinking. He manages to say, 'No nine-one-one.' But his breathing is awful, he can barely talk. I can't understand him and I say, 'What?'"

"He says, 'I did this. No nine-one-one.'"

"I didn't get it. Finally he's able to say, 'Suicide.'"

"And he begs me to finish him off. He's too badly injured to get to the gun. Wants me to do it for him. I want to call an ambulance. He says no. I mean, he's like begging me."

Lucy goads him. She says, "Your big shot brother-in-law is *begging* you?"

"That was a first, let me tell you. I didn't know what to do. I almost left, but I was afraid the jerk would live, survive, you know, and blame it on me. I mean, the shooting. So I . . . I picked up his gun and I aimed it and I, I couldn't do it. I put the gun back down and started to walk away. Behind me, I hear this awful gurgle, then clear as a bell, he says, 'Please.'"

"I couldn't leave him like that. I went back over, and I picked up the pistol again. I held it out like this—" he stretched his arm and turned his head as though he were holding a soiled diaper "—and I closed my eyes and I counted to five and I pulled the trigger. I didn't even look at him again. I turned my back and I listened for a minute—a full minute, I counted to sixty—to make sure he wasn't gurgling anymore. I wiped the gun with my handkerchief and dropped it back down in the blood by the chair. And I left the same way I came in.

"That's the truth."

Five minutes later, Sam and I climbed out of Lucy's car and walked back over to his Ford. We watched a patrol car arrive and two officers move a handcuffed Andrew into the backseat for a ride over to Thirty-Third Street. Lucy stayed in the Volvo. I assumed that she was going to go home first, that she'd want to slip out of her little black dress before arriving at the police department to finish booking Andrew.

The cruiser pulled away.

Sam asked rhetorically, "You see this coming? I think I've seen it all and then, you know, I get bushwhacked. Who'd have thought that Ed was too vain to kill himself with a nice reliable head shot? Remember the coroner thought the bullet might have done some spinal cord damage? Well, apparently the coroner was right."

"You believe Andrew?"

"Except for the part about his concern about Merritt, I'm tempted to. You?"

"I guess. So when Robilio called Andrew to come over, it wasn't because he wanted to discuss the divorce but because he wanted Andrew to be the one to discover his body? He didn't want his wife to find him?"

"Yeah, I imagine that was it. Kind of hostile to Andrew, don't you think? I mean, the way I look at it, Andrew had three choices, right? He could have left Ed to die. Some would argue that that would have been hostile. He could have called an ambulance. Some would argue that, given the circumstances, that would have been hostile. Or Andrew could pick up the gun and shoot his brother-in-law to death while he's claiming he's really as benevolent as Saint Francis. I say, no matter what you're thinking, you shoot somebody you think is an asshole in the face, that's kind of hostile."

Thirty-eight

I woke without my alarm the next morning, feeling an unfamiliar confidence that triumph and tragedy had finally traded places and that life was about to resume its usual precarious balance. I drove to Children's early, met briefly with Merritt, dictated a discharge summary, and signed Merritt's discharge order. Although I felt more hopeful about Merritt's legal situation than I had since I'd seen the bloody clothes, I didn't tell her about Andrew's confession. The Boulder police had a lot of confirming to do. I would let Merritt's Uncle Sam be the bearer of all those good tidings.

Sam arrived at the unit right when he said he would and squirreled Merritt out of the hospital through a side exit, successfully avoiding a crush of media that, to my dismay, had somehow been alerted to her pending discharge and who were intent on chronicling her journey to join her sister in Seattle. While I rushed back to my house to prepare for my flight to see Lauren, Sam drove his niece to the Trent home in Boulder and waited while she packed some things for her trip to rejoin her family.

Reluctantly, I had agreed to drive to the Denver airport with Sam and Merritt. Transporting patients to airports was an ethical quagmire I would rather not have waded into, but the discharge team had convinced me that Merritt needed chaperoning until she was safely in Seattle and I convinced myself that it would give me a good opportunity to observe Merritt and test out the wisdom of releasing her from the hospital.

With his wife gone, Sam was playing single parent to Simon, and Lucy had either volunteered or been cajoled by Sam into spending her day off accompanying Merritt the rest of the way to Washington. While Sam was getting Merritt home from the hospital, Lucy was watching Simon. Since she would need her car to get back from DIA after she completed her round trip that evening, Lucy and Simon were going to meet us at the airport.

Merritt and Lucy's flight to Washington was scheduled to depart an hour and fifteen minutes before mine. I sat in the backseat of Sam's car on the drive to the airport. The time I observed between Sam and his niece was playful and lighthearted, as they argued the relative merits of his love, hockey, and hers, basketball. Merritt finally agreed to go to an Avalanche game with her uncle, and I felt a stab of loss that I might not be accompanying Sam to any playoff games. Sam promised not to miss a basketball game next season at Boulder High. Watching the two of them banter, I realized these were the first jovial moments I recalled experiencing from the moment days ago that Lauren had received the phone call that her mother was sick.

We arrived at the airport a good hour before Merritt and Lucy's flight.

I'd already recovered from all my initial annoyance with Denver International Airport. It *is* halfway to Kansas, there is no getting around that, but once you get there, the place works. DIA is attractive, spacious, and efficient. Every trip out there costs twenty extra minutes by car; every flight in or out saves at least that much aggravation. Every time I land at another airport I appreciate DIA more and more.

But in all my trips I had never checked a bag at DIA. My carry-on habit wasn't a protest against DIA's oft-maligned automated baggage system but was, rather, more philosophical. My feelings are this: if I can't fit it in a carry-on, I figure I don't need it. Merritt's packing philosophy was a little more liberal. She was traveling with a duffel bag the size of a pregnant sow and a suitcase that didn't have a prayer of fitting in the overhead compartment.

Sam pulled his car up to the curb of the check-in level on the United Airline's side of the huge tented terminal so we could check Merritt's bags. Lucy and Simon would meet us later in the train station down below the terminal. She figured Simon would enjoy watching the trains come and go.

A Skycap grabbed Merritt's bags from Sam's trunk and I waved Sam off to park the car. The Skycap perused Merritt's tickets to discover her destination, and quickly attached computer-generated tags to her luggage. He placed the bags, one after the other, on a nearby conveyor belt and the luggage immediately disappeared into a rubber-toothed tunnel.

The baggage system at DIA is the stuff of local and national legend. Being a carry-on devotee, I'd never examined it up close before and was fascinated watching its humble curbside beginnings. This was, I decided, like viewing one of the headwaters of the mighty Mississippi.

"Where do they go?" I asked the closest Skycap, pointing at some disappearing suitcases.

"The bags? Down a floor. Underneath the terminal, there's six big stations that collect bags from the curb, six more that collect bags inside at the ticket counters. Automated scanners read the tags to discover where the bags are supposed to be goin', then they get loaded on these tele-cars, like little railroad cars you might see in a, you know, coal mine, and then it shoots 'em, the tele-cars, right down to your gate on tracks. More tracks down there than at Gran' Central Station. The tracks go every which way for a while, then they all join in the middle of the terminal and scoot straight down a tunnel to the concourses. Those bags be in your plane before you're off the train."

"It really works?"

"You bet."

"What's that?" I pointed at a separate setup a few steps away. A large flat gray bin, maybe eight feet by four feet and a foot high, sat empty on a big stainless steel tray.

He smiled a toothy grin. "You recover your manners and get around to showing me some 'preciation for my help with the young lady's bags, I'll show you how it all works."

I gave him five bucks and he placed another customer's ski bag in the flat gray bin. "This one's already tagged. These skis are going home to Omaha." He punched a code on an adjacent keypad, a stainless steel door slid open, and a stainless steel cradle carried the gray tray in the same general direction Merritt's bags had just traveled. A moment later, another empty gray tray automatically slid into the place of the one that was schussing the skis to Omaha.

He said, "Oversized bags, skis, golf clubs, and stuff like that go in those gray trays. I punch in a code. Elevator takes 'em down and puts 'em in the system. They get loaded on double cars and go right to the concourse."

"Same system?"

"Same one. But the cars be different. They use big double tele-cars for these oversize bins. This stuff's too big for the beige bins on the single tele-cars. But the same system."

"And it really works?"

"God be my witness. It does."

I realized I'd lost track of Merritt. I looked around and spotted her thirty or forty yards down the curb talking to someone whose back was to me. I thought it was a man. I started down the sidewalk to join her so we could go inside to find Sam and get in line to retrieve our boarding passes.

With his left hand, the man was pointing at a car, a recent-model, dark blue Lincoln Continental, that was idling beside them at the curb. His right hand was on Merritt's back.

She took a step away—toward the terminal, not the car—and, with a quick move, he grabbed her arm. To me, it didn't look like a friendly gesture, but she didn't scream at first. A second later, though, she was mounting a vigorous effort to try to shake free. Failing, she looked my way. I knew what terror looked like when it was reflected in Merritt's eyes, and I decided she was terrified right then, and I started to run toward her. My first thought was that the man was a particularly aggressive reporter who had somehow tracked Merritt to DIA.

I closed about half the distance and watched Merritt try to free herself from the man's grasp with a violent shove to his chest. It didn't work. Then she lifted her left foot and pounded hard on the man's instep. He released his grip for a split second and she leapt backwards, sidestepping a large woman cradling a large child. The man recovered quickly and was no more than a yard behind her. Merritt saw him, and without hesitation dove head-first into one of the big gray four-by-eight trays that carry oversize luggage into the automated baggage system. This one was just beginning its journey to the concourses. In addition to Merritt, that particular tray's cargo was an aluminum tube almost a foot in diameter and five feet long.

Poof! In a blink, Merritt and the tube disappeared into the automated baggage system.

I wasn't even sure the Skycap saw her go.

I yelled, "Hey!" or something equally incisive. The man who had been holding Merritt was struggling to be inconspicuous, but I was pretty sure I saw something shiny and metallic in his hand. Fearful that it was a gun, I yelled again, "Get down! Everybody get down!" Everyone, of course, looked my way—assessing me for signs of mental instability and for indications that I might be dangerous—but nobody got down, and the man who was after Merritt took advantage of the diversion I provided. He edged to the back of the group at curbside and lowered himself onto the conveyor that carried individual suitcases into the system. In a blink, he disappeared through a tunnel, in pursuit of Merritt.

Impulsively, I went after him but a Skycap had me by the ankles before I could get down the conveyor. Somebody asked if they should call for security and I allowed myself a moment of hope before I realized that the most likely target of security's interest was me.

I stood up and said to the Skycap, "Okay, okay, listen. Two people just disappeared into the baggage system. A man is after a girl, a teenage girl. I think he might be armed. She's in trouble."

The Skycap had heard better stories recently. He made a sound like a pony neighing and said, "I didn't see anybody go in, George, did you?"

George, the other Skycap, said, "Not me."

A little girl, maybe six, maybe seven, stepped forward and raised her hand like a well-behaved schoolgirl. She said, "I did. I saw them. She went down that hole." She pointed at the elevator with the big gray trays, then moved her outstretched arm in the direction of the conveyor. "And he went down that hole. There."

I said, "Thank you."

The next voice I heard was Sam's. He was behind me. "Where is she, Alan?"

"Down there, Sam, the baggage system. Somebody's after her with a gun."

"Who?"

"I don't know, a man, I didn't get a good look at him. White, my size. Brown hair, bomber jacket."

Sam held out his badge and showed it to George. "Get us down there."

The Skycap named George had his own idea. He asked me, "You want we should shut it all down? We can call, do that. One call and we can shut it all down."

I had no idea what the consequences would be of shutting the automated baggage system down. Would it help Merritt get away, or would it make it easier for whoever was after her to catch her? Would the car she was in stop abruptly and throw her out of the bin she was in? I didn't know.

I shook my head. "I don't think we should do that. We don't know what would happen. It might help the guy catch her. Where will she end up? The girl that went in the bin? If she stays in the tray, where will she go?"

A Skycap said, "That case she's with was going to Dallas. Let me see, that's gate B-35. If she stays in that tray, she'll end up in the collecting station for oversize materials that's on the west side of B Concourse."

I said, "We have to go in after her, Sam."

The Skycap said, "Can't let you."

Sam said, "Then look the other way."

"Can't."

"You know who that girl is who that man is after? That's Chaney's sister. You know Chaney?"

"The sick girl? On the news?"

"Yeah. That's her sister. She's on her way to see Chaney in Washington and somebody's trying to hurt her."

George said, "Who are you?"

"I'm her uncle."

George seemed to be pondering his options. He was bigger than Sam, but I was sure Sam could overpower him physically and force his way into the system. Unless Sam actually killed him, however, George would immediately pick up the phone and shut the system down.

George said, "Chaney, huh? B-35, Dallas? I'll turn my back. You guys go down one at a time. I'm gonna deny this."

"Wait. Sam, you go after him, the man who's chasing Merritt. He's in that part of the system with the suitcases. I'll go after her, this way. This is where she went down."

He nodded, said, "Go."

I watched Sam climb onto the conveyor as I laid down in the bin. George punched some buttons on a nearby keypad and I felt a quick jerk as the tray slid into the elevator and fell rapidly about fifteen feet. When I came out of the shaft I was in a huge cavern of orange tracks mounted with dozens of individual tele-cars that were topped with beige plastic bins. The tele-cars zoomed above me and below me in a pattern that was befuddling. To my left, suitcases were being loaded automatically into the beige bins mounted on top of the tele-cars, and large arrays of laser scanners were reading the luggage tags and deciding where the tele-cars should go.

I saw Sam sitting Indian-style on a segmented conveyor, waiting his turn to be loaded into a beige bin on top of a tele-car. He was holding the luggage tag George had given him. George had already instructed the computer exactly where to send me and, with smooth acceleration, the big gray tray I was riding was loaded into a cradle that spanned across two of the tele-cars. With a rumble and a sudden swooosh, I figured I was on my way to join Merritt on Concourse B.

I flipped myself over to a prone position and looked back as Sam was being unceremoniously dumped into the awkward beige bin on top of a single tele-car. The bin was designed for a solitary suitcase and was way too small for Sam's big body. He seemed to be trying to find a way to sit in the bin, but his balance was precarious. I lost sight of him as he laid back and the tele-car zoomed around a bend.

I'd seen all the news reports of the infamous baggage system on television and still found myself totally unprepared for the scale of the installation. It was immense. Tracks ran *everywhere* in this space that was the size of at least two high school gymnasiums. I thought to myself, This is one of *six* collecting stations?

As my double tele-car crossed toward the far corner, I scanned the huge room where we had started but couldn't find any sign of Merritt or her pursuer. Or any workers. The system was totally automated; I couldn't find a single technician monitoring the system's progress.

Below me and behind me, Sam's car was accelerating into the system. I heard him yell, "Oh, shit," as his car migrated around a bend.

I laid back down and tried to clear my head. Who was after Merritt? And why?

Denver International Airport is designed with one large central terminal and three separate concourses built in parallel at great distances from the main building and at great distances from each other. Our destination, Concourse B, was over half a mile away from the terminal and could only be reached by passengers via a subway system that runs in two wide tunnels beneath the tarmac.

That is, unless you happen to be impersonating luggage.

Parallel to the train tunnels are two service tunnels. These tunnels contain roadways for the electric carts that transport whatever baggage the automated system doesn't. Above the roadways, suspended from the ceilings, are the tracks that shoot the baggage system tele-cars from the terminal to the concourses and back.

When Sam and I cleared the sorting area where we began our journey, we entered a cluttered interchange where our tele-cars slowed to merge with tele-cars carrying suitcases from the other sorting areas on the west side of the terminal. It was like entering a busy interstate at rush hour. I was about a dozen tele-cars ahead of Sam as we merged onto the main line.

Twice that far ahead of me was the man in the bomber jacket who was chasing Merritt.

He was looking forward, after Merritt. I couldn't see her. I prayed that she was prone in her gray tray and that he couldn't see her either. I was also hoping that George the Skycap had alerted Denver Police and that they would be waiting for Merritt whenever and wherever the system was planning on dumping her in Concourse B.

The man began to turn in his bin to check for pursuers. I dropped flat in my tray. Behind me, Sam didn't have the same luxury; he couldn't hide. He was overflowing the beige bin on his single tele-car like a soft-boiled egg in an egg cup.

And he was almost that vulnerable.

The man spotted him. Within seconds I knew my suspicions were correct. The man chasing Merritt did have a gun.

Shots echoed in the cement-walled chamber like an explosion in a pipe. Two blasts came from the direction of the man who was after Merritt.

One came quickly in return from Sam.

As the echoes died, the drones of the tele-cars on the tracks were the only sounds I heard.

The tracks made a sudden drop right then, going from straight and level to a thirty-degree decline, and the tele-cars picked up speed. The experience was not unlike an amusement park ride that was revving to terminal velocity. We were, I assumed, beginning our passage into the service tunnels on our way out toward the concourses. Without raising my head, I looked up behind me, silently counting the tele-cars that were appearing above and behind me on the sloping tracks.

I counted eighteen tele-cars before I stopped. I knew Sam was no longer riding in his beige bin.

My despair could have filled the terminal.

Twenty or thirty seconds later, I heard loud voices and my tele-car burst from below the terminal building. Looking down, I realized I was high above an intersection of roads. Below me were a cluster of electric carts and a group of about a dozen people on the tunnel roadway. In that instant, the tele-car I was riding crossed into the service tunnels, and I was now traveling on tracks that were suspended from the tunnel ceiling at least thirty feet above the cement roadway. I raised my head just enough to peek forward. The man in the bomber jacket was still in front of me. On a parallel track, tele-cars with empty bins zoomed past me in the opposite direction to return to the concourse to pick up fresh loads of luggage.

I guessed we were about halfway between the terminal and Concourse A when the man shouted something I couldn't understand and fired another shot.

Merritt screamed so clearly I thought she was right next to me.

She was.

I raised my head and was astonished to see her in a gray tray traveling back *toward* me on the parallel track.

He fired again. I screamed, "Get down."

Merritt shrieked again and yelled, "Help me."

"How did—"

"It's about to slow," she said.

And it did. As we approached Concourse A, the tele-cars slowed so scanners could read the tags and divert any bags that were destined for the A concourse. I waited for a double tele-car to approach from the opposite direction, tried not to think about what I was doing, tried to time my leap, and jumped.

My timing was better than my strategy. I landed solidly in the approaching gray tray, not remembering that the tray was not actually attached to the tele-cars. My momentum caused the tray to begin to slide out of its steel cradle. I rolled hard against the opposite side and the tray seemed to hesitate before sliding down and finding its natural place. It thunked back into position.

"Merritt, are you okay? I made it. I'm behind you."

"I'm okay. Who's after me?"

"I don't know."

"Alan, is that you?" The voice was Sam Purdy's and came from the roadway down below. My heart leaped.

I yelled, "Sam, we're heading back the other way, toward the terminal. Merritt and me."

"What? Where is—"

"Don't know."

He yelled something else, but the cars had carried me out of range of his voice and I couldn't understand him.

Thirty-nine

A few seconds later, I knew where the man was.

A gunshot cracked in the tunnel. The gunman had managed the same maneuver as Merritt and me and was behind us. I hoped far behind us, but I wasn't sure.

Just as I called out, "Merritt, are you hit?" I was reassured by a piercing shriek from her direction. Again, I reminded her to stay down.

I knew that the nature of the chase had changed significantly. One, my presence in the baggage system was no longer a secret to the man who was after Merritt. And two, I was no longer trailing him; I was now a wonderful target situated conveniently between him and his prey.

I also realized that since we had changed direction and were heading back toward the terminal, I had no idea where the system was taking us. Before, I was taking solace in my hope that the Denver police would be waiting for us at the termination point of the baggage system below Concourse B. They would protect Merritt and arrest whoever it was who was chasing her.

Now? I didn't know where these empty cars were going other than to return to pick up new loads of outbound luggage. And the Skycap had said that there were twelve different collection points on each side of the terminal. That meant there were a lot of possible destinations. I hoped that Sam could get some help in puzzling it out in time to meet us wherever we were headed.

I had a feeling Merritt and I were going to need a little assistance.

We were approaching the end of the tunnel, the spot where the tracks guiding the tele-cars would begin to climb into the bowels of the terminal. At the moment that Merritt's tele-car began its ascent, her pursuer's car would be below her and she would be visible to him. I was guessing she would be exposed, and vulnerable, for about three to five seconds. Shortly after that I would be exposed for target practice for about the same amount of time.

Based on the speed we were traveling, I had—maybe—thirty seconds to come up with a solution to the problem.

I crawled to the far end of the bin and raised my head so I could look back down the tunnel to see if the electric carts were keeping up with us on the roadway below. I spotted one, about a hundred yards back.

"Sam? Is that you?" I yelled. One of the most surprising things about the automated baggage system is how quiet it is. Speaking to someone next to you requires only a slight elevation in volume.

"Yeah."

"Up ahead, when we go up that incline into the terminal, he'll have a clear shot. You have to distract him before Merritt gets to the bottom of the incline."

He was gaining on us; Sam's electric cart was closer now, no more than thirty yards back.

Sam yelled, "Where is he?" and the man responded by firing a round at Sam's cart.

"He's behind me, in a gray tray like mine, maybe fifty yards. I don't know."

The gunshot helped Sam locate him. Sam said, "Got him. Merritt, stay down."

I watched Merritt's tele-car begin the climb from the tunnel into the terminal. The instant she was visible, gunshots began peppering the tunnel behind me. I couldn't tell whether they were being fired by the man chasing us or whether they were being fired by Sam and the Denver police.

When I risked another look up, Merritt's tele-car had cleared the incline. I had no idea whether she had been hit. Now, it was my turn to head up the same hill.

I felt the change in track angle and my guts seized into knots. Again, the gunfire erupted behind me. I covered my head with my hands as a slug ripped into the plastic three inches from my right hip.

The tele-car cleared the top of the incline and leveled off. I yelled, "Made it. Find us, Sam, hurry," and sat up, looking for Merritt.

I tried, "Merritt, are you okay?"

I didn't hear a reply.

At this stage of the system the baggage tracks have more switches and off ramps than an L.A. freeway interchange. I assumed the returning tele-cars were being automatically routed to whatever loading location required empty tele-cars.

My tele-car switched off almost immediately on a side track that angled right at forty-five degrees, and with disarming suddenness I was riding the rails upward again toward the top of one of the huge collection caverns like the one where Sam and I had begun our journey.

I looked everywhere and couldn't find Merritt. Nor could I locate her pursuer.

After fifteen or twenty seconds, my tele-car slowed and stopped in a line behind four or five others. The gray trays were being automatically off-loaded from their cradles by conveyors to await their elevator trips back to the curbside check-in area to pick up another pair of skis.

I jumped out of the tray and ducked behind an electrical equipment panel. Across the way, the tele-car transporting the man in the bomber jacket was just entering the same queue I had been in. As his tele-car bumped to a stop, he stepped out and scanned the huge space looking for Merritt. The room was so packed with lines of tracks that the task was like trying to find a specific fleck of basil in a bowl of spaghetti.

I saw the gun in his left hand.

Merritt?

He and I saw her at the exact same time. She had apparently crossed a maintenance bridge that traversed a few different tracks and was in the middle of the huge room crouching behind a stack of spare beige tele-car bins.

I was close enough to him to watch him smile.

To reach the middle of the room, he began to climb the steep steel ladder over the same maintenance bridge that Merritt had crossed. Newly loaded tele-cars zoomed past on the tracks below him. From the top of the bridge he scanned the space thoroughly, checking to see if anyone was closing in on him. From the look in his eyes, I could tell he didn't see any cops. And he didn't see me.

Merritt saw him approaching. Her eyes flattened. Death was coming to visit. This particular apparition had brown hair and a boxy automatic and a bomber jacket and a Lincoln Continental waiting at the curb.

The man released the clip from his weapon and checked his load. He was precise in his movements as he prepared. Satisfied, he clicked the magazine back into place and started down the other side of the bridge.

Merritt ran, jumped a track, and crouched low behind a series of track-mounted tele-cars with beige bins. The man fired. I couldn't see Merritt, but I knew she was still moving. I could hear her feet pound against the metal grid floor.

She leapt another track. I lifted a fire extinguisher from a nearby rack and threw it as far as I could in the opposite direction. The man with the gun spun and fired at the bouncing canister before he recognized the diversion.

He looked right at the electrical panel that I was hiding behind. I couldn't tell if he saw me. He then turned and refocused on Merritt.

She was gone. It was obvious he couldn't locate her. Frantically, I scanned. I couldn't locate her either.

The man in the bomber jacket jumped a track, almost getting himself clobbered by a tele-car. He checked behind him for a moment and was more careful as he crawled across the next track, to the place where he had last seen Merritt.

She wasn't there. I started scanning the tele-cars that were scooting on the tracks around the room. He did, too. Neither of us found her.

Frustrated, he started back toward the bridge. Above me, I heard a muffled squeal and saw Merritt as she was thrown from a beige bin on a tele-car as a cam forced it to tilt down to be certain it was empty and ready for its next load. Instantly, she realized her sudden vulnerability and cowered in a tight ball. She looked like a pile of laundry on a stainless steel tray.

The man reached the top of the bridge, raised his arm, and aimed his weapon at Merritt.

I screamed, "Nooo!" as two quick gunshots exploded.

Merritt lay immobile.

The man stood immobile, too, and didn't fire again. He seemed to lower his gun an inch or so.

Another shot rang out.

The man's knees buckled and he pitched forward over the rail at the top of the bridge, falling head first into a tele-car that was loaded with a car seat in a plastic bag. The tele-car immediately sped up an incline and started to exit the loading area to begin its journey to the concourse.

Six inches to the left of Merritt's buttocks I could see a bullet hole ripped in the stainless steel. I called out, "Merritt? Merritt?" and began to run toward her, dodging tele-cars and leaping tracks.

I watched as she unfolded herself and sat, hugging her knees to her chest. She wasn't looking at me, she was looking high above me, behind the bridge. I turned, too, and saw her Uncle Sam standing on a catwalk with three uniformed Denver cops. He was holding a handgun as though it were a precious baby.

"Uncle Sam, Uncle Sam. Did you get him?"

Sam lowered his weapon and said, "Yes, babe. I got him. It's over."

Forty

Merritt and Lucy missed their flight.

But United Airlines officials scrambled to take advantage of the goodwill opportunity and offered to upgrade them to first-class on the next nonstop, which happened to be my flight. Unfortunately for me, only two spare seats were available in front of the curtain, and I was left with my aisle seat in the main cabin.

Merritt and Sam and I spent the time until takeoff talking to Denver cops.

Sam stayed so close to Merritt, it was if he were handcuffed to her. I knew that when the time for boarding came, he had every intention of walking her onto the plane and buckling her seat belt around her waist.

The airport security offices where we were being interviewed were on the sixth level of the main terminal building, not more than fifty feet above the location where Sam had shot Dr. Terence Gusman to death. For almost ten minutes after the siege ended, none of us knew that the man pursuing Merritt had been Dr. Gusman, or that he was dead. It took that long for the tele-car with his body and the car seat to make its way to Concourse B, Gate 28.

Gusman had been carrying an ID and a neatly written note assailing the media for twice destroying his family. He wasn't naive about his plan; he had apparently anticipated the possibility of not surviving this last attempt at earning some vengeance on the media in general, and Brenda Strait in particular, by making one last assault on Brenda's family. While Lucy accompanied Merritt to the bathroom, Sam was quiet and showed no signs of regret over shooting Gusman. I wanted to provoke some words from him, so I said, "At least your loose end is tied up now, Sam."

He looked at me curiously. "What do you mean?"

"You've been wondering why the harassment against Brenda stopped when it did. Well, Gusman chaired the medical board; he knew about Chaney's illness through MedExcel. That's why the harassment stopped before Chaney's condition became public. He was sure he could keep the protocol from ever being approved for her and he was waiting patiently for her to die. Chaney's death would be his retribution against Brenda. There was no need to continue the harassment anymore."

He waved his arm in the direction of the baggage system. "This was what, desperation, then?"

"Don't you think? He hears that his medical board's decision to deny additional care for Chaney has been overruled and that Chaney is off to Seattle to get the protocol. He sees on the news that Merritt is going to follow her. Maybe he thought this would be his last chance to get even."

I expected he would argue with me. Instead he lamented that he'd let Gusman slip. "You know, I should've had him picked up. I didn't figure him for this. I played this too delicate. I should have plowed his head into the boards when I had him in the open. If I had done that, he would have been too timid for this kind of bullshit."

"Hindsight's great. Yeah, you probably should've had him picked up. And if you did, how long do you think he would have been in custody?"

Sam scoffed, "Eight hours. Maybe a day. Maybe not that long. That's not the point. I needed to send him a message to leave my family alone. I didn't."

"This isn't hockey, Sam."

"Hockey is life. This is life."

"So? What difference would it have made had you gotten in his face? Everyone survives, the way it turned out. Merritt's going to be okay. Chaney has a chance. No way of telling what would have happened the other way."

"Yeah," he said.

He was blowing me off. "Sam, thanks for all you did. You're a hero today."

He nodded, acknowledging something. I wasn't sure what. "You know, you two were great down there. Merritt, what a kid, the way she moved around. And you did good in there, too, you know that? He would have had her without you."

"I don't know about that, Sam. I will say it was the oddest ten minutes I've ever had in my life."

"You reach Lauren, tell her what happened?"

"No. I'll tell her when we get there. She has enough on her mind with her mom. You reach Brenda and John?"

"John. Told him there was a delay. That's all. They have enough stress too, you know; I didn't want to go into this on the phone. Chaney is still set to start those new drugs tomorrow. You'll have to fill them in about Dr. Gusman when you get there. Use your judgment."

"Fine," I said.

Lauren was standing with Lucy about thirty feet from John Trent as I exited the plane a long time after the first-class cabin was empty. I kissed her and held her and kissed her again. Over my shoulder, I watched Trent as he embraced Merritt ten yards away.

Her arms still around me, Lauren turned to Lucy as though she were continuing an earlier conversation. She said, "You said you missed the earlier flight? What happened?"

Lucy looked at me, hoping I would field the question. I grinned and glanced once toward Merritt, then back at Lucy before I said, "Oh, you know, just another problem with the baggage system at DIA."

Sam phoned me at Lauren's parents' house that evening. He had already spoken with his wife and learned that early the next morning, Chaney would indeed start receiving the experimental drugs from Japan that would, with luck, arrest the virus that was destroying her heart. A short while later she would be a prime candidate for a donor organ.

And another vigil would begin for Merritt and John and Brenda.

Sam mostly wanted to talk about Madison's boyfriend, Brad, and Dead Ed's brother-in-law, Andrew. "We have word from a state trooper in Nevada. It looks like Brad's been spotted. He's south of Vegas, camping illegally. They'll close in on him today and he'll go down, but I'm still kind of hoping he doesn't go down in flames. You know?"

"Yeah, I know. Where are things with Andrew?"

"He has a lawyer now, of course. Funny, took him a couple of tries to find one. The first one he called was Cozier Maitlin. How's that for irony?"

"Has he been charged?"

"Not yet. They've collected hair and fingerprints from him. They'll check out his story, see if it's consistent with the forensic evidence before they decide what to do. I'm not convinced the DA's going to press it. What's it going to be? The charge, I mean. Homicide? Assisted suicide? Mercy killing? Ask Lauren if she wants a piece of this one when she gets back to Boulder. Nobody else on the felony team in her office does. The guys in the detective squad are already calling Andrew 'Dr. Jack.' "

I smiled. "Merritt and John are in the clear?"

"Not quite. It's looking brighter for them. Some loose ends are hanging. Trent's prints are on a bottle of water that we collected in Dead Ed's mud room. That's a problem still to be solved. And there's a whole bunch of people, myself included, who would still like to know how those bloody clothes got under Merritt's bed and what the gun was doing in her bathroom. She still has some explaining to do about all that."

I pondered Dead Ed's butt and the vile videotape I hoped no one would ever see. I said, "I don't think you really want to know those answers, Sam."

"Sure I do."

Firmly, I said, "You don't. Trust me."

I heard him swallow once and imagined him narrowing his eyes. I hoped he would take my advice.

Acknowledgments

I have the great fortune of receiving generous assistance from virtually everyone I ask for help. Where license has been taken with reality, though, the responsibility is mine.

This time I needed medical attention, and I got it STAT from Drs. James Todd, Terry Lapid, Stan Galansky, Randy Wilkening, and Alfred Jackson. Joani Rogers Jackson, R.N., M.S.C.S., refreshed my memories of my days working on adolescent in-patient units. I'd suppressed a lot.

Steve Klodt showed me the bowels of Denver International Airport and Mike Silva of KCNC the skies along the Front Range, each in a way that granted a perspective I could never have otherwise gained. Authorities in Boulder continue to provide their expertise. Special thanks to Tom Faure of the coroner's office and Detective Melissa Hickman of the Boulder Police Department.

Critical Conditions involves teenage girls in difficult circumstances. I was fortunate to receive the counsel of a group of remarkable young women still in, or not far from, their teens. My deep gratitude to Holly Greenburg, Alexis Wilson, and Erin Graham. You helped more than you know.

Harry MacLean, Mark Graham, Tom Schantz, and Elyse Morgan are always among my first readers, and they usually find ways to critique without drawing too much blood. I thank them not only for their sharp eyes but also for their friendship. Jeffrey and Patricia Limerick have been there for me since the beginning. And I commend Jay and Miggy Monroe for their courage and thank them for their generosity and goodwill.

I think I'm running out of ways to show appreciation to my family long before they've begun to run out of ways to support and help me. Rose and Xan, you have my heart. My mother, my brothers and sister, and my extended family are, too, always there for me, and I thank them.

In New York, Jariya Wanapun and Julie Harston make every task and every day easier. I thank them for their graciousness and their patience as much as for their always smooth assistance. Lynn Nesbit, Michaela Hamilton, and Elaine Koster are true publishing professionals, and I'm fortunate to be in their care. It's no small sleight-of-hand to turn a manuscript into a book and they make the magic happen.

Finally, this book is dedicated to Al Silverman. He is a world-class editor and an even better human being. Al, thank you.